Head over Heels

Kate tucked the small book under her arm and started to climb down the library ladder. Her slippered foot was just reaching toward the rung below her when the door banged open. Surprised, Kate lost her balance. Her foot slid from beneath her and she fell backward, toward the hard wooden floor. She cried out, reaching for the ladder, but her fingers closed only on empty air.

Strong, hard arms closed tightly around her body before she could hit the floor. Breathless and terrified, Kate squeezed her eyes shut, but she knew who held her. She knew as soon as her arms clasped about linen-covered shoulders and she inhaled his clean, outdoor scent—Michael Lindley.

Michael Lindley had swooped down like his archangel namesake and saved her. And now she was in trouble, because she didn't want him to let her go. Ever.

Praise for Amanda McCabe's Novels

Lady Midnight

Amanda McCabe

A SIGNET ECLIPSE BOOK

SIGNET ECLIPSE
Published by New American Library, a division of
Penguin Group (USA) Inc., 375 Hudson Street,
New York, New York 10014, USA
Penguin Group (Canada), 10 Alcorn Avenue, Toronto,
Ontario M4V 3B2, Canada (a division of Pearson Penguin Canada Inc.)
Penguin Books Ltd., 80 Strand, London WC2R 0RL, England
Penguin Ireland, 25 St. Stephen's Green, Dublin 2,
Ireland (a division of Penguin Books Ltd.)
Penguin Group (Australia), 250 Camberwell Road, Camberwell, Victoria 3124,
Australia (a division of Pearson Australia Group Pty. Ltd.)
Penguin Books India Pvt. Ltd., 11 Community Centre, Panchsheel Park,
New Delhi - 110 017, India
Penguin Group (NZ), cnr Airborne and Rosedale Roads, Albany,
Auckland 1310, New Zealand (a division of Pearson New Zealand Ltd.)
Penguin Books (South Africa) (Pty.) Ltd., 24 Sturdee Avenue,
Rosebank, Johannesburg 2196, South Africa

Penguin Books Ltd., Registered Offices:
80 Strand, London WC2R 0RL, England

First published by Signet Eclipse, an imprint of New American Library,
a division of Penguin Group (USA) Inc.

First Printing, May 2005
10 9 8 7 6 5 4 3 2 1

In memory of Anne Backus, 1974–2004

"Fear no more the heat o'the sun,
Nor the furious winter's rages;
Thou thy worldly task hast done,
Home art gone and ta'en thy wages"

—Shakespeare, *Cymbeline*

Prologue

Italy, 1819

"*I*s she dead?"

"How can I see if she is dead, Maria, when she's all twisted up like that? Santi Giovanni. Here, take her arm and help me move her."

The voices came to Katerina faintly, as if they echoed down a long, empty corridor. She wanted to open her eyes, but they were sealed shut, and her head throbbed so intensely she couldn't bear to move it. Every time she tried, stars burst in her brain, white-hot, out of focus. She managed to open her hand flat, and felt the wet stickiness of sand. The same coarse sand clung to her lips and cheek.

Slowly, she touched the tip of her tongue to her teeth, and tasted the unmistakable coppery tang of blood.

Blood!

Where was she? What had happened?

Her mind was a scattered, whirling blank. She struggled painfully to remember, but the harder she grasped, the farther it all slipped away. She was almost certain she had been at a party of some sort. There were vague echoes of champagne, music, laughter—a handsome pair of gray eyes gazing down at her admiringly. How had she gone from *that* to lying on a strange shore, with blood in her mouth and her head about to explode?

If only she could *remember* . . .

Then strong hands reached for her, turning her onto her back.

Another sharp pain cracked through her head. Even those fragile wisps of memories retreated with the force of that agony. Katerina gasped, struggling not to slip back down into that sticky darkness.

"She's alive, Paolo!" a woman's voice cried. "See, she is breathing."

"So she is, barely. There's a lump at the back of her head, and this cut on her cheek is deep."

A rough fingertip prodded lightly at her cheek, and she jerked away from the sting.

"She must be a fine lady," the woman whispered. "Look at her jewels, and this silk gown."

"All of her jewels won't save her if we don't get her to the doctor now," the man muttered. "You wait with her, Maria, while I fetch Gianni and the others. We can't carry her to the village ourselves."

A quiet moment passed, filled only with the shrill of gulls soaring overhead, before Katerina felt a cool touch smooth the wet clumps of her hair back from her face. She smelled the distinctive odors of fish and lemon, as well as the salty tang of the sea. Somehow, those familiar, earthy scents were comforting, and calmed her.

"Can you hear me, *cara*?" the woman said.

Katerina spat out a mouthful of sand and blood. Painfully, she forced a whisper through her raw throat. "*Sì.* I hear you, signora."

"*Va bene!* You're awake. You mustn't worry about a thing. We will take you to the doctor. Just lie still here."

Using every ounce of her strength, Katerina pried open her gritty eyes and stared up at the woman. It was a gray, cold day, but even that faint light hurt. The woman, an elderly peasant with silver threaded through her black braids and a stained white apron over her faded dress, was surrounded by a halo of the dazzle.

Katerina closed her eyes against it. *"Grazie,"* she whispered hoarsely. "Thank you for your help."

"Poor little one! How you must have suffered. Do you remember what happened?"

"No." Nothing but that echo of music—and the tall, dark man that held her close as they danced. *My Beatrice,* he whispered. *You are far more lovely than Dante's beloved could ever have hoped to be.*

She shivered at that flash of memory.

"Nothing? Not even your name?"

She did remember that. It was emblazoned on her mind like a beacon. "Katerina."

"What a pretty name. Katerina. I am Maria." Katerina felt the woman shift around. "Ah, here is Paolo and the boys! You will soon be at the doctor."

Katerina heard the shuffle of booted footsteps in the sand, the rustle of rough wool cloth. "I see she is awake now, Maria!"

"For now. She can't remember much, though. We have to get her to the doctor quickly."

"Sì, sì. Here, boys, help me lift her onto the litter."

Hands reached for her again, lifting her high into the salty air as if she were a load of fish. Katerina screamed out against the fresh sword stabs of red agony. Just when she knew she could take no more, that she would die of the pain, the world went dark at the edges. The thick blackness spread until there was nothing at all.

When she woke from the suffocating darkness, it was not on cold, wet sand. She lay on soft, sunshine-scented linens. The pain had receded; it was no longer so sharp and urgent, but dull, hovering over her like a faint threat.

She sat up very slowly against a pile of fluffy pillows, her head spinning even with that small movement. Though her memory was very hazy, she was sure this was not her own room. It was too small, with a slanted, whitewashed ceiling, as if it was tucked beneath the very eaves of a house. The high, narrow windows were hung with sheer white curtains, which let the buttery yellow sunlight stream in over the furniture. There was only the narrow bed on which she lay, a small table that held a pitcher of water and a bowl, and one straight wooden chair.

Folded neatly on that chair was a water-stained gown of bright blue silk trimmed with lace, and a small cloth bundle.

Katerina glanced down at herself, and saw that she wore only a loose, faded nightdress of cheap muslin. This tiny movement set her cheek to throbbing as if tiny demons danced there. She reached up gingerly to find a thick bandage fixed to her skin.

San Marco, but where was she? What had happened to her? Why could she not remember! She searched her mind, but the answers eluded her, shimmering just beyond her pained grasp.

She sobbed with utter frustration, pounding her fists against the blankets. That did not help at all—it only made her realize how very stiff and sore she really was.

Surely you can remember something, she told herself. *Think, think.*

After she took a deep, cleansing breath, then another and another, she knew that she *could* remember some fragments. Her name was Katerina—she had known that all along. She did not live here, in this salt- and sunshine-scented house, but in Venice. And she had been on a boat, at a party of some sort.

But what had brought her here?

She pushed back the blankets and swung her weak, trembling legs over the side of the bed, reaching for the floorboards with her bare toes. Her whole body, from her eyebrows to her toenails, felt bruised and battered. It screamed in protest at the slightest movement, but she pressed on, gritting her teeth together. She had to find out what was happening.

She managed to stand, clinging to the thin bedpost.

But the instant she let go, she collapsed into a heap, crying out at the pain as she struck the hard floor. Helpless tears, dampening the bandage and dripping down her chin onto her fisted hands.

"Maledizione!" she sobbed.

The loud patter of footsteps echoed outside the room, and the door flew open to reveal a short, plump woman with black and silver braids wound about her head and a white apron over a plain black dress.

Katerina sniffled as she stared up at the woman. Surely she remembered her from the beach?

There, she thought. *You remembered something else. Things are not entirely hopeless.*

"Signorina! Why are you out of bed?" the woman—Maria?—cried. She bustled across the floor to slip her arms around Katerina's prone body and haul her upright. The woman might be short, but she proved to be strong, having Katerina tucked back into bed before she could even notice the new waves of pain. "If you needed something, you should have called for me."

Katerina sank back into the soft pillows with a grateful sigh. "I wasn't sure anyone else was here."

"I was just right down the stairs, in the kitchen. Do you remember me?"

"You are Maria," she whispered.

Maria beamed, as if she were a governess and Katerina her star pupil. *"Va bene!* Your memory is coming back, yes?" She smoothed out the rumpled blankets, tucking them warmly about Katerina's aching legs. "Now, what was it you needed? A drink of water, maybe?"

Katerina suddenly realized that she *was* burning with thirst. Her throat felt like coarse stone. "Oh, yes, Maria! *Molte grazie."*

Maria poured out a glass of water from the pitcher on the table and watched with satisfied approval as Katerina drank deeply. "You do look better today. Not so pale. You were like a ghost!"

"I felt like one," Katerina murmured. Her throat felt better after the water, but her cheek still throbbed. "How long have I been here?"

"This is the third day."

"Three days!" Katerina cried. "So long?"

"We were not sure you would live. You were so feverish, and delirious! Calling out for your mama." Maria laid her strong, callused fingers against Katerina's brow. "You feel a bit cooler. But not out of danger yet, I think."

Katerina did feel warm, yet also strangely chilled. It was a cold that came not from the sun-warmed room around her, but from deep inside herself, spreading a clammy touch outward to her skin. She sank down under the shelter of the blankets until they covered her to the chin. "It is kind of you to look after a stranger, Maria."

"Pah!" Maria protested with a laugh. "Though I'm sorry you're injured, signorina, I have truly enjoyed nursing you. All my children are grown and gone. They no longer need old Maria. But tell me, little one, how did you come to wash up on our beach?"

Katerina frowned, all of her confusion, her dizziness, rushing back to her. "I—I do not know for certain. I was on a boat, but I'm not sure what happened."

Maria *tsk*ed as she went about the room fastening the curtains shut and rearranging the bowl and pitcher on the table. "You must have been caught in the storm."

"Storm?"

"Oh, it was a big one! I was fortunate that my husband, Paolo, and our sons didn't go out that day to fish. It blew up very suddenly, when only that morning it was sunny and clear. You poor girl, to be out in it! Do you remember who was with you? What happened to them?"

Them? A vision flashed across Katerina's mind, like a jolt of silver lightning. There was a woman, with black hair like Katerina's own. A ruby necklace flashed as the woman laughed, her head thrown back in merry abandonment. A handsome, fair-haired gentleman, older but still trim and vigorous, held the woman in his arms, twirling as if in a wild dance. A swirl of color, noise, music.

Then they were gone.

"Yes," she whispered. "Did anyone else wash ashore near here? Another woman, or an older gentleman with pale hair?"

Maria shook her head sadly. "No, *cara*, I'm sorry. You were all alone. But then, we're very isolated here, and there are beaches and villages all along the shore. Someone may be looking for you there!"

Perhaps—but deep in her heart, Katerina knew it was not so. Those people, whoever they were, were gone forever.

Downstairs, a door slammed loudly, and a man called out, "Maria! Are you here?"

"That will be my Paolo, wanting his supper," Maria said, hurrying back to the door. "I will bring you some soup and bread later, *cara*. It will help you get your strength back. For now, just get some sleep."

"Yes," Katerina muttered. That tiny flash of memory had left her even weaker in its wake, her very bones aching with exhaustion. "I do want to sleep. . . ."

That night, in the deepest purple black of the witching hour, her fever returned with a vengeful force. With its renewed heat came frenzied dreams, as if her entire life replayed on the stage of her mind.

She saw the house where she lived, her mother's house, a wide, low palazzo on a canal in Venice. In her dream, she stood in a sunlit drawing room, surrounded by gilded furniture upholstered in lavender-and-cream brocade, precious paintings, and objets d'art. That black-haired woman—her mother—lounged on a violet satin chaise placed beneath a portrait of herself. The painted woman, like the living one, was draped in silks, sapphires, and amethysts. She was so very beautiful. Beautiful like a Greek statue or a faraway star, not like a real flesh and blood woman at all. Not like a mother.

Across from her in this glorious room sat two gentlemen. One of them was the blond older man, a person of distinguished features and elegant clothing. The other man was younger, and so handsome he was entirely unreal. His dark hair, rich as the night, waved back from his perfect oval face, and his gray eyes lit from within as he saw Katerina. He came toward her, reaching for her hand and lifting it to his lips for a worshipful kiss on her fingertips. *My Beatrice, my Renaissance princess,* he said.

And her mother laughed, her dangling amethyst earrings clicking and sparkling with amusement. "Katerina, darling! Edward has come to see us, you see, and he has brought his so charming friend Sir Julian Kirkwood. I see you remember how he admired you at the *principessa*'s ball last week. He has been so impatient for your arrival today. . . ."

Even as Katerina stepped closer to Sir Julian, the dream scene shifted. She was no longer in the palatial drawing room but on a gleaming white yacht. Her mother's friend Edward's white yacht. He held her mother by the hand as he led her aboard, at the head of a large procession of guests. Her mother's ruby necklace sparkled in the innocent sunlight.

She saw their merry party live again, as vivid as it had been on that glorious day. There were great quantities of such delicacies as pâté, lobster patties, crab salad, white soup. Champagne flowed in great, golden quantities as laughter grew louder and chatter brighter. The elegantly dressed women perched in the men's laps, their white bosoms like ivory against silk bodices and jeweled necklaces. Someone played naughty songs on a pianoforte, and Edward danced with Katerina's mother around the salon, waltzing faster and faster until she laughed breathlessly and cried out, "Edward, *caro mio,* slow down or I shall faint!"

And Sir Julian Kirkwood asked Katerina herself to dance. Their waltz was not as exuberant as her mother's, but he held her close, so close she could smell the light scent of his citrus cologne, could feel the fleeting brush of his lips against her hair.

He was meant to be her first lover—she knew that. And he was a fine choice: handsome, rich, generous, cultured. But there was something—something odd about him, something too intense in the way he watched her, the way he called her his "Beatrice," like she was a character in a Dante poem and not a real person at all. Her mother told her it was just girlish nerves, that she had to remember her training and look to her future.

This is what my life will always be like, she thought as they swayed through their dance. Handsome men who admired her, jewels, champagne, music, laughter, wild gaiety. Men who made her uneasy, but whom she had to charm. It all stretched before her in an endless vista of uncertainty and fear.

Then the skies, so bright and promising when they embarked on their journey, darkened ominously. The wind whipped up faster, colder, shrieking past the windows. The rain fell in slate gray sheets. Lightning sparked a poisonous yellow. Thunder cracked, louder and ever louder. The yacht tilted and pitched, tossing all the furniture that wasn't bolted down across the floor in a welter of splintered gilt and shredded satin.

The last thing Katerina remembered was a horrible explosion and the boat tilting precariously to one side. There were shouts, and a piercing, terrified scream—surely not her own?

She reached out desperately for her mother, but Lucrezia slid inexorably away from Katerina, falling down the steeply pitched deck into the roiling black water.

"Mother! Mother!" Katerina screamed, again and again, until the cold waves closed over her own head, and she reached out to grasp a large, rough piece of floating wood. . . .

She awoke, gasping for breath, as if the water still filled her lungs. The sweat-soaked bedclothes were twisted around her shaking limbs, and she was chilled to her very core. She buried her face in the pillows, trying to blot out the horrible images of watery death.

"Mother," she whispered, even though she knew all too well that there could be no answer. Her mother was gone, along with her kind English protector, Edward, the Duke of Salton. And the handsome, admiring Sir Julian Kirkwood—the man Katerina had thought would one day be her own protector.

She herself could easily have died with them, and that horrifying thought made her cry out again, a pitiful wail muffled in the linens.

Katerina turned her head to rest her tearstained cheek on the pillow—and noticed a small wispy movement in the shadows.

She raised herself up to peer closer.

It was a woman, or at least the outline of one. Katerina's first thought was that it must be Maria, but Maria was short and stout. This woman was tall and willow slender. Then the figure stepped into a pale beam of moonlight that fell from one of the high windows, and cold shock broke like one of those deadly waves over Katerina's heart.

"No," she breathed aloud.

The woman was her mother. Yet that could not be! Katerina had seen her mother swallowed by the sea, right before her very eyes. No one had come ashore besides herself—Maria had said so. But here Lucrezia was, as beautiful as ever, standing beside her daughter's bed clad in a white silken gown, like opals or stars. Her long, straight curtain of black hair, gilded by the moon, fell over her shoulders. There was a strange translucence to her fair skin, a shining quality that came from within.

This must be another fever dream, Katerina realized with a start. She held out her shaking hand to the figure, and whispered, "Mother? Is it you?"

Her mother reached out her own hand, and a coolness like a sweet spring breeze wafted over Katerina's fingertips. "It is me, my Katerina, 'the prettiest Kate in Christendom.' I *am* a dream, but one I hope you will remember when you awake."

It had to be her mother, even though it was a dream—no one else quoted her name from *The Taming of the Shrew*, teasing her about being "bonny Kate," "sometimes Kate the curst." Her head spun in confused circles. She longed to leap up, to reach for her mother, but she feared that to do so would make this precious vision vanish like so much smoke. "Why are you here?"

"*Cara mia,* you have been given a wonderful chance. A chance many people long for, beg for, but few are given. The chance to become—someone else."

Kate shook her head. She was Katerina Bruni, daughter of the glorious Lucrezia Bruni, envied by girls all over the city of Venice—no one would ever believe she could be someone else. Not even *she* ever believed it. "What do you mean? I only want to be *me.*"

"No. I know the truth of this, you see, because I always wanted this chance for myself."

This was the first time Katerina had ever heard such a wild thing. Lucrezia Bruni had always been so supremely self-confident, so beautiful and perfect, carrying her fame—fame inherited from her own mother, Giavanna Bruni—lightly on her velvet-clad shoulders. Katerina remembered her mother laughing on that final day, her entire being aglow with gaiety. "But why? You were famous—everyone adored you. You were so happy. We were *both* happy, in our lovely home."

Her mother gave her a small, sad smile, so unlike her old merry grins. "My dearest girl. I only pretended to be happy—I was a wonderful actress, learned at my mother's knee. I knew my place in life from the time I was a tiny child. I could never truly be anything different. And I thought *you* could never be, either. When I saw how beautiful you were growing, I knew only that you would be desired, sought after, that you would be rich. But you can be so much, have so much more! I know you can. Fame and jewels, my bonny Kate, can never feed a lonely heart. You were truly the only good, fine thing I ever had and I failed you."

Katerina sobbed in bewilderment. "You never failed me, Mother! You loved me, and gave me everything. A fine education, gowns, jewelry. You were teaching me all you knew, all your secrets. You gave me freedom and riches. . . ."

"Freedom?" her mother whispered, sadder than Katerina could ever have imagined her. "*Cara mia.* A courtesan is the least free of all women. Even a nun in her cloister has more freedom."

"But you always said that your career freed you from the mundane cares of married ladies! You had no household duties, no bowing and scraping to a husband, no dozens of brats clinging to your skirts. . . ." Kate repeated the words she had heard hundreds of times from her mother.

"I did not know the truth! I only knew the perimeters of my own life. It was truly full of jewels and fine things, but you do not know all that I did to earn them. A courtesan must be young and beautiful always. She must laugh and smile and be witty. She must never be tired or ill or make demands, or she would risk being accused by her men of being just like their wives. There is never true emotion, true conversation and meeting of the minds and hearts."

Katerina stared at her mother, confused and fascinated. "I know that being amusing and charming is part of the role of courtesan. You taught me that well."

"It is more than that!" Lucrezia cried sharply, causing Katerina to tremble anew. "Bonny Kate, you must listen to me carefully, for my time here is growing short. If you continue on the path you are on now, you will never have a family or a true home. I tried so hard to groom you for my own life. I even tried to convince myself that it was what *you* really wanted. But you were always so dreamy and romantic, always reading your poetry and your horrid novels. You saw only the surface of my life, not the reality of it. But now you must take this gift you have been given."

Katerina wiped at her tears with the blankets. "What gift, Mother? What could possibly come out of this horrible thing?" She held out her arm, displaying the purple-and-blue bruises imprinted there.

Her mother gave her a fond, rueful little smile. "You are not thinking clearly, my Katerina. And after those books you buried your nose in! Now—think. Everyone will believe you have drowned along with the rest of us. Katerina Bruni is dead. You must make certain that she stays that way.

"You need only go somewhere new, far away, and begin a fresh life. Your father, God rest his soul, was English—perhaps London would hold some attraction for you. But anywhere would suffice for a *different* life."

"Not go back to Venice?" Katerina remembered again her mother's palazzo. She remembered the wild, wondrous parties there during carnival, masked revelers packed to the frescoed ceilings, couples kissing furtively in the shadows, amid glimpses of naked limbs and bosoms and heated cries. She remembered how the laughter and the music and the champagne would go on and on until dawn—and how she would watch from the upstairs gallery, wondering, fearing, what it would be like to be in the midst of that party.

"It is the only life I know," she whispered.

"And that is my fault. I raised you in my own world. But there are other lives, *better* ones, more worthwhile ones, where you can find your own heart away from all the gilded rot. It is all there, just waiting for you to pick it up. Oh, *cara,* truly you are so much more lovely than I ever was, and more clever, too—clever in arts *besides* those of pleasing men. You can do anything you find that your heart desires."

Katerina took in those words, rubbing at her aching

temples. Her mind raced with a torrent of thoughts, dreams—and fears. Could her dream mother be right? Could a chance grow from this tragedy? A gift.

She imagined the sort of new life her mother spoke of, a life with a home and family of her own, with love and security. Laughter and books, her body and mind belonging only to herself. A tiny hope bloomed slowly, reluctantly, in her most secret heart, like the rosebud of summer after a long winter. But . . . "How could I afford to travel to a new place, to buy a new home? All our possessions are in Venice."

Her mother laughed again. "My Kate, did I not just say you were clever? You must use that cleverness— always use it."

Katerina glanced over at the cloth bundle. *Of course!* Her jewels. How could she forget? A pearl and sapphire necklace, along with the matching earrings, bracelet, and brooch. The set had been a gift from her mother on her twentieth birthday, and she wore them for the first time on that yacht.

"When I gave them to you, I meant for you to use them to entice a certain gentleman. To display your charms. Now they can bring you a new life," her mother said softly. "It is my last, and best, gift to you. But you must use it quickly, bonny Kate. Before it is too late."

With one last cool, caressing touch, she was gone. As if she had never been there at all.

Like a dream.

Katerina squeezed her eyes tightly shut and let the images her mother's words had conjured for her sweep across her mind. *A life of her own choosing.* One without the glittering trappings of her mother's life, trappings Katerina had always thought she had to have. It was hard to let all of that, everything she had known in all her twenty years, go.

But—in the place of jewels and silks could be other things. *Lasting* things, true emotions as she read of in her beloved poetry.

Now, with her "death," anything could be within her grasp. Anything at all.

She had only to reach out for it, and Katerina Bruni, daughter of the most famous courtesan in all of Venice, would cease to exist.

Chapter One

B *lood. So much blood.*
It stained his hands, his clothes, soaked into his very soul, as he lifted his wife's delicate, broken body in his arms. Caroline's golden hair spilled down in a rippling, sunshine wave, just as it always did, but her violet blue eyes were glazed, sightless as they stared up endlessly at the sky.

Pain wracked his own body, stabbing at his face, his side, with white-hot blades. It was as nothing to the pain in his heart. He held his wife close, even as he knew she would be forever beyond his touch. The splintered wood of his own wrecked phaeton was all around them.

"Caroline," he sobbed. "Caroline. This is my fault. I am so sorry—don't leave me! Caro, come back to me. Come back to me. . . ."

Yet even as he buried his face in the bright cloud of her hair, as she fell limply against him, she faded from his grasp forever. He tried to hold on to her, but she was gone.

Gone . . .

Michael awoke with a sharp gasp. "Caroline!" he called. There was no answer from the shadows of his bedchamber. Nothing but his own voice, echoing back to him mockingly.

It was that dream again. The same dream that always came back to haunt him over the last long five years, just when he thought it was gone forever.

But it wouldn't leave. Not until he could forget that warm springtime day when Caroline died. And that would be never.

Michael rolled to his back, staring up at the underside of the bed-curtains. He took a deep, cleansing breath, and slowly came back into the reality of this room, this present moment.

"I am no longer that reckless boy," he muttered. That careless life, that wild existence of gaming and drinking and dancing and coarse affairs, was buried with Caroline. He was no longer "Hellfire Lindley"; he was Mr. Michael Lindley, younger brother of the Earl of Darcy, respectable country landowner. He looked after his Yorkshire estate, took care of his family and his tenants and employees.

As far as he could get from the ballrooms and the stews of London.

Some days, when he was busy riding over his property, meeting with bailiffs, reviewing ledgers, he imagined—no, he *knew*—that life was left behind. But in the night, it was a very different story. The past and all his mistakes were waiting for him, waiting to grab and choke him.

Michael threw off the last hazy shackles of dream sleep and pushed himself out of bed. His nightshirt was damp with the sweat of his nightmare. He tore it off impatiently and tossed it to the floor. Naked, he strode across to the room's double windows. He opened the casements and let the chill night air flood over him, bringing calm with it.

The moon was nearly full, casting a pale, greenish glow over the gardens below. Far off in the distance, he saw the tall spire of the village's ancient Norman church. It glowed like an otherwordly scene from one of the horrid novels his wife had loved so much, as if restless, eternal spirits swirled among its tilting and moss-covered stones and angels. Yet on his own property, the gardens and fields of Thorn Hill, all was silent.

Michael leaned his palms against the wooden window ledge, not feeling the tiny sharp splinters that drove into his skin. He stared at the cross atop that distant spire, reaching up to the moonlit heavens.

Silent.

He closed his eyes, absorbing the night's peace into himself. Tomorrow was sure to be a busy day. It always was, during springtime in the country. He should be sleeping. But he knew that sleep was very far away, even as the night worked its slow, calming magic on his roiling thoughts.

Then he heard a noise, a soft thud, from the chamber next door to his. It was *so* soft, it would have been almost imperceptible. But Michael was always attuned to what happened in that room.

He spun away from the window and snatched up a dressing gown from the foot of the bed. He was striding from the chamber even as he shrugged the velvet over his nakedness.

The door to the other chamber was unlocked, and a solitary lamp burned steadily on a low, round table. It flickered in the darkness, casting back the menacing shadows, throwing a soft light over the child peacefully sleeping in the pink-and-white canopied bed.

Or rather the child who *should* be sleeping peacefully in the lacy little bed. She had rolled out of it, as she sometimes did despite the bolsters on either side of her, and she lay in a heap on the pink carpet. Still slumbering.

Michael smiled at the sight of her thumb popped into her rosebud mouth, and he knelt beside her to lift her gently into his arms. She murmured quietly, her head rolling against his chest, but she didn't wake. He laid her back against the ribbon-edged pillows and tucked the blankets around her.

Her tangled golden curls, full of a milky-sweet little-girl smell, tumbled over her brow. He smoothed that hair back, hair so much like her mother's, and lightly kissed her cheek. Just the sight of her brought back a portion of that ever so elusive peace.

When they first came to live at Thorn Hill, Amelia was frightened to be placed in an upper-floor nursery, so far from the grown-ups. Over her nursemaid's protests that he was spoiling the child, he moved her into the empty chamber next to his own. And he had never regretted it. Now he could soothe her bad dreams—and put her back into bed when she was restless in her sleep and fell.

"Sleep well, Amelia, dearest," he whispered. "Know that I will always be here to protect you."

As he could not protect her mother.

"Michael, my dear! I have such wonderful news today."

His mother was far too cheerful and animated for so early in the morning, Michael thought as he made his way to his chair at the breakfast table. Especially since *some people* had been up since before dawn, unable to sleep. But it made a change from her usual worried frowns, her complaints about their neighbors, so he didn't mind so very much.

He smiled at her as he moved toward his seat, wincing a bit at the bright light from the large windows. Once, in another life, he was able to dance and gamble all night and still go to Gentleman Jackson's for a round of boxing in the morning. Those days were gone. The leg that had been broken in the phaeton crash and then healed wrongly gave him twinges after such sleepless nights. It felt a bit stiff as he lowered himself into the chair.

But he didn't want his mother to know that, and he would not take out his temper on her. He nodded pleasantly as she passed him a cup of steaming coffee. "Have you indeed, Mother? Hm, good news. Now, what could it be? Ah, I know. The cook was able to procure lamb cutlets for dinner. Or the milliner in the village has some new ribbons from London in stock."

Jane Lindley, the Dowager Countess of Darcy (and she never let anyone forget the title!), laughed and shook an admonishing finger. "Oh, Michael, how you do love to tease! I think you are laughing at your poor mother. But this is serious. Do you not wish to know what my news is?"

Michael reached for the platter of eggs. a footman had left conveniently near. "You obviously want to tell me, Mother, and I do hate to curtail any of your pleasures. So why don't you go ahead and tell me?"

"A letter came this morning from the agency in London. They have found us a governess for Christina and Amelia. At last! I thought no one who was suitable would ever be willing to come all the way to Yorkshire. I do think that they—"

"Good morning, Mother! Michael!"

Whatever his mother was going to say was cut off by the noisy arrival of Michael's younger sister, Christina. She *burst* into the breakfast room, as she did into every room she ever entered. Obviously, she had been ambling about outdoors again. Her light brown curls, the same color as Michael's own hair, fell in an untidy tangle down her back, and the hem of her dress was inches deep with mud. She had also obviously left her dirty boots at the door, because her feet were encased only in thick lisle stockings.

She was fifteen now, a young lady, but anyone would have thought she was no older than Amelia with the wild way she behaved.

"Sorry I'm late," Christina said, plopping into her chair and reaching for the rack of toast. "I went out for a bit of a stroll and quite lost track of time."

Jane silently poured out a cup of tea and passed it to her daughter. The thin, pinched line of her lips was the only outward sign of her long-suffering exasperation. After a long moment when the silence was broken only by the sound of Christina's loud munching and a footman bringing in fresh eggs, Jane said, "Your brother and I were just speaking of a letter I received from London."

Christina took a gulp of tea. "Oh? From Charles, then? What are he and Mary up to?" Charles was their eldest brother, the Earl of Darcy, who lived an active political life with his glamorous wife, a daughter of the late Duke of Salton.

The beauteous Mary was one of the reasons their mother elected to make her home with her younger son and keep house for him. There was room for only one grande dame under each roof.

"No, indeed. Not from Charles. We always hear from him on Thursdays, and this is Monday," Jane answered, delicately buttering her toast. "The agency has at last found us a governess."

There was a sharp gasp, and then a horrible choking noise as Christina coughed on her tea. Michael obligingly reached over and pounded her on the back.

She turned wide, appalled green eyes toward him, her mouth inelegantly agape. "A *governess?*"

He gave her a wry smile—poor comfort, he knew. The subject of a governess had been a sore one at Thorn Hill for a long time, with Christina protesting at every turn. She had been at her freedom ever since her last governess left almost two years ago, and she took full advantage of it. There were great deluges of tears and shouts whenever their mother brought up the topic. Jane, of course, just used the tantrums as one of the foremost reasons there *must* be a governess.

As the weeks went on, and no governess could be found who would make her home in the wilds of Yorkshire, a tentative quiet returned to Thorn Hill. Now the storm was breaking over them again.

"Mother! No!" Christina wailed. "I told you I do not need a governess. I am too old! And she would surely make me give up my walks, my nature experiments, and tell me I should sit in the drawing room and—and *stitch* away my days!"

Jane sighed with patient resignation. "I do not see what would be wrong with that. It would be very nice if you spent more time on the art of needlework, and other ladylike pursuits, and less time bringing dirty plants into the house."

"Those dirty plants are rare botanical specimens!" Christina huffed indignantly.

Sometimes these quarrels burned themselves out quickly without Michael's interference. But he saw this time he would have to step in, or these old arguments would go on all morning. "Mother, Christina, please." Michael took his sister's hand in a firm clasp. "This lady will be more a governess for Amelia than you, Tina. You must agree it's past time for your niece to begin her education."

"Of course," Christina answered. "Amelia is nearly seven. But why must *I* take lessons?"

"Because you are behaving like a—" Jane began sternly, but subsided when Michael threw her a quick glance.

He turned back to Christina. "You need not take lessons—per se. But you *are* fifteen now. In a couple of years, you will be ready for your first Season. Perhaps this new governess could help you learn all the niceties that young ladies must know when they make their bows in Society. If we are going to be paying her anyway, we might as well get our money's worth. Eh, Tina?" He gave her a wink.

Christina smiled reluctantly. Her chin, though, still had a most mutinous set. Michael had his work cut out for him to jolly *her* out of her bad mood today. His mother, too, looked most unhappy, and he also had his work out in the fields today. He was going with the bailiff to inspect the plots being readied for spring planting, which was coming upon them quickly.

His old leg wound gave another warning twinge, and he flexed it secretly under the table. If his mother or sister had even a tiny suspicion that his leg ached, they would overwhelm him with fussing. *That* would be even worse than their bickering.

He took a deep swallow of his coffee and said, "All right, Mother, why don't you tell us about this governess the agency found?"

"She is probably a dry old stick," Christina muttered.

"On the contrary, my dear." Jane picked up the letter from beside her plate. "She is not old at all. In fact, she's rather young for such a position—just twenty-two. But she's a widow. An Italian lady who married an Englishman. She is well versed in music, languages, deportment, embroidery, the use of globes. Just what we are looking for."

Christina brightened a bit and sat up straighter in her chair. Michael doubted it was the lady's adeptness with globes she was interested in. His suspicions immediately sharpened. "She is *Italian?*" Christina said.

"Yes." A frown wrinkled Jane's brow beneath the edge of her cap. "That is unfortunate. A *foreign* governess. But, other than that, she appears quite suitable."

"What is her name?" Christina asked.

Jane glanced again at the letter. "Mrs. Kate Brown."

"That does not sound Italian at all!" Christina pouted. "I thought it would be something more—exotic."

"My dear Christina, you really must . . ." And Jane went on, talking to her daughter of suitability and proper behavior and what the neighbors might think. Michael heard her voice, but not the words, as he finished up his cooling coffee. He had heard it all before, and the twinges in his leg were growing more insistent.

As soon as his mother's voice paused, he said, "Well, then. If you fine ladies will excuse me, I have some accounts I must go over in the library before I go riding out."

"Oh, yes, of course, Michael, dear," his mother said, appropriately distracted. "I must be going up to dress. I told Lady Ross I would come into the village today to help her arrange flowers at the church." Her faded green eyes took on a calculating light. Lady Ross was her only rival for social leadership in the neighborhood, and every encounter with this nemesis took minute planning. It was like what watching Wellington at Aranjuez must have been like. "Christina, you will come with me, of course. Lady Ross's daughters will be there, and I know they would enjoy seeing you."

Before Christina could shout out a protest, Michael pushed himself up from his chair and said hastily, "Excellent! I am sure you ladies will have a jolly morning,. then." He kissed his mother's and sister's cheeks, and managed to make his way to the library with scarcely a limp.

Once there, in his inner sanctuary where the ladies seldom appeared, he dropped into one of the overstuffed chairs by the fireplace. The ache in his leg eased a bit when he stretched it out on the footstool, rubbing at the knotted muscle over the ill-healed thighbone.

After the crash, the doctors said at first that he would lose the leg. Then that he would never walk again. But he determined to prove them wrong. He was Amelia's only parent now, and he had to be strong and whole for her, even when his spirit longed to sink into black grief. So he worked hard, secretly at night in his lonely room, doing leg lifts and sit-ups and lunges until he wanted to shout out with the sweating agony of it all. Then he walked, across the bedroom, out the door, down the stairs. By the time they came to Thorn Hill, he could ride and run and even wield a scythe in the fields like a peasant farmer.

His leg never had fully healed, though, and still sometimes sent out obnoxious reminders of that fact. It had been paining him more of late, but he always managed to hide it well enough in their small family group.

But would he always be able to when Mrs. Brown came into their midst?

Mrs. Kate Brown. He sat back in his chair and closed his eyes, thinking about the Italian lady with the resolutely English name. A young widow, well versed in languages. She sounded rather—intriguing.

Not like Christina's last governess, the dry, gray-haired Miss Primm, who so admirably lived up to her name. He wondered what Mrs. Brown looked like. Dark-eyed, like the Italian signorinas he had met in Florence as a young man? Small, slim, with fire in their hearts and high, sweet bosoms that swelled from their silken bodices . . .

Michael laughed at himself and his wild fantasies. Mrs. Brown could be as plain as a mud hen or as glorious as Helen of Troy—it would make no difference. He was no longer the wild youth who drank rough red wine in Florence tavernas and made love to ebony-haired courtesans on rooftops overlooking the Arno. He was a respectable country gentleman, a father. No signorina would look twice at him now. And Mrs. Brown was not coming to Thorn Hill to be anything to him. She was coming to help his family, and for that he would be grateful to her.

Grateful—no more. No female servant had ever had to fear his advances beneath his roof, and he would not start now. Even if this Mrs. Brown turned out to hold all the languorous warmth of the Italian sun in her eyes.

A soft knock sounded at the library door, bringing him abruptly back to the present moment.

"Come in," he called, sitting up straight in his chair. He carefully swung his leg back to the floor, trying his damnedest to seem casual and relaxed.

Christina came into the room, Michael's tweed riding coat folded over her arm. Her hair was brushed and tied back neatly with a green ribbon that matched her eyes, but she still wore the gown with the muddy hem.

Michael smiled at her, thinking how very pretty she had become. And how wild and reckless, wandering the moors at all hours. Hopefully, this Mrs. Brown *could* help her. London Society would eat her alive if she kept on as she had.

She perched on the arm of his chair. "I brought your warm coat, Michael. It is a bit windy out there this morning. I also brought this." She pulled out a small, clear glass jar, filled with some murky yellow green substance. "It is an herbal salve I've been experimenting with, using herbs I dug up on the moors. Mrs. Sowerby says they do wonders. I thought you might try it on your leg, just as part of my experiment."

Michael squeezed her hand in his, grateful for this unpitying sympathy. Christina *could* be a wild, muddy hoyden, but she could also be patient and kind. She had a good heart. She went on social calls with their mother, even though she found them excruciating. She played games with Amelia by the hour and never tired of her niece's childish prattle.

She noticed when Michael's leg was bothering him, and helped him however she could. With salves and warm coats.

"Thank you, Tina," he said. "Perhaps you'll help me into my coat?"

"Of course." She tightened her hand on his as he stood, her fingers rough from all the digging she did outdoors. She held the coat for him to slip on, and smoothed the warm tweed folds over his shoulders. "There! You will be the handsomest man in the neighborhood when you go riding out."

He laughed. "More handsome than young Henry Haigh-Wood? I hear all the ladies swoon when he walks into assemblies."

Christina wrinkled her freckled nose. "You are a hundred times more handsome than Henry Haigh-Wood. Only *silly* ladies swoon over his foppish gold curls and pink waistcoats!"

"I doubt Louisa Ross would agree with you. Mother says they're betrothed."

"Then Louisa Ross is only the silliest lady in the neighborhood. All the ladies sigh over *you*, Michael. They weep that you never dance at assemblies, and they are stuck with only Henry Haigh-Wood."

Michael grinned at her. "You are a good sister indeed to flatter your old brother, Tina. Did Mother entreat you to say that? Has she enlisted you in her cause to see me marry again?" Unconsciously, his hand drifted to his left cheek, to the long scar that sliced from his temple across his cheekbone into his hair. The ridge was hard beneath his touch.

Christina caught his hand, pulling it down. "Michael. Your scar is not nearly so great as you think. It has quite faded away. And Mother did not bribe me—the ladies *do* watch you. Emmeline Ross in particular. And she is slightly less silly than her sister." Her smile turned mischievous, elfish. "Mother says you should marry Emmeline."

Michael laughed. "Oho, does she now? Even though Miss Emmeline, at the tender age of seventeen, has already broken three betrothals?"

"It is not so bad as all that. . . ." Christina gave in with a giggle. "Oh, very well, *not* Emmeline Ross. But there are many pretty ladies in the neighborhood. Not all of them are silly jilts. I know you say you will not marry again. . . ."

"Precisely. No lady would want a crusty widower, all set in his ways."

"Pah! You like to pretend you are ancient, when you are but thirty." Her words were stout, but her pretty face spoke of her fifteen-year-old conviction that thirty was surely near death. "You are handsome and rich. You have a fine house and a finer sister. And Mother says Amelia needs a mama."

Michael's grin faded. *That* was an argument it was becoming harder to dismiss. Amelia was getting older. She would soon be seven, and she needed a lady's influence—a lady with more energy than her grandmother and who was not a young aunt who would marry and leave their household. "Soon she'll have a governess. This Mrs. Brown."

"Oh, yes. Mrs. Brown." Christina's face took on that stubborn cast. She stepped away from him, fists planted on her hips. As she opened her mouth, Michael held up his hand to stop her predictable words.

"I know," he said firmly. "You don't want a governess."

Christina shook her head. "I just want to continue my own studies in botany," she said strongly. "That's all I care about. I'm making such progress!"

Michael remembered the rows of plants and dirt samples lined up in Christina's chamber, the bunches of herbs drying on racks. They covered up the dainty dressing table and escritoire their mother purchased for her, and unusual smells were always escaping beneath the door.

Much to their mother's everlasting chagrin.

"I realize that, Tina. Of course I do," he answered. "But how do you know that Mrs. Brown knows nothing of botany? She could be of a very scientific turn of mind."

Christina opened her mouth, then snapped it closed again. Obviously, this was something she hadn't thought of. "Really? Hm. Maybe she would know of Italian plants I haven't heard of."

"You'll never know if you don't give her a chance," he said cajolingly. "Come, Tina. She will be here at Thorn Hill anyway. You could just give her the *opportunity* to help you. If you don't like her—well, then we can discuss it further."

Christina considered this, worrying at her lower lip with her teeth. Finally, she nodded. "Very well. I will talk to this Mrs. Brown when she arrives and determine if she has a brain in her head."

"That is all I ask. Now you should run along and change your gown. Mother will be waiting for you to go to the church with her, and I have work to do."

Christina groaned. "The church! With Mother and Lady Ross. Oh, don't remind me!" She spun around and hurried to the door, her hair already springing free of the confining ribbon. But she turned back before leaving, her brow furrowed in sudden worry. "Michael, if your leg is truly paining you, perhaps you shouldn't ride out today."

Michael gave her a reassuring smile. "I'm fine. Don't worry, Tina. All is well here."

"I *do* try not to worry. But—well, sometimes I just cannot help it! Be careful today."

"And you. The petals of the lilies at church can be quite dangerous when threatened, I hear."

"So I understand. But not half as dangerous as the staring eyes of the curate!"

Chapter Two

You wanted to be as far from Venice as you could get. Well, here you are. The ends of the world, Katerina, now called Kate, thought, leaning forward to peer through the post chaise window.

From her chamber in her mother's palazzo, Kate had been able to see the wide space of the canal, crowded with gondolas and people, rich with laughter, shouts, chatter, and the teeming, sweet-sick smell of the water. She could see close-packed houses of pastel pinks and yellows and oranges, with window boxes planted with brilliant red geraniums. Even the view from the tiny room she had inhabited in London was full of life, street vendors hawking roasted almonds and hot cider, people arguing and shouting, children and dogs running about.

Here, at the end of the world, she saw—gray. Gray sky, a pale pearl hanging low and menacing over a gray landscape. Kate had never seen such a landscape before, never even imagined it. It rolled endlessly to either side of the road, a rough expanse of a strange greenish gray. There were very few trees, especially after the rich vegetation of the south. It appeared flat, but as Kate peered closer she saw the texture of scrubby growth. In the distance, shrouded in a fog of yet more gray, loomed menacing hills.

The moor. That was what the lady at the agency had called this place. "It's a lonely spot, no doubt about it," she had said as she studied the paper listing Kate's scant qualifications. "This has been a difficult position to fill, even though the family is willing to pay a very generous salary. If you're certain you want the place, Mrs. Brown, you must go and see what you can make of it.''

Kate's coins were few by then, and even a tiny room and a diet of bread and tea cost something. She had found no luck thus far in her search for employment—she had no letters of reference. And long afternoons of sitting alone in her meager lodgings, reading and studying, would get her nowhere.

So that was how she found herself in this jolting post chaise, barreling down a lonely, empty road. She was alone now—all the other passengers had disembarked at Leeds. Alone with the gray and her thoughts.

Thoughts of how this windswept place would be a perfect spot to hide in.

And of how she was becoming rather gray herself. Kate laughed as she peered down at her attire. Her new gown and pelisse were pale gray, much like the sky, and constructed of sturdy, unadorned lightweight wool. Her paisley shawl and plain bonnet were dark blue trimmed with gray ribbons, but her kid gloves were the prettiest of sunset pinks. She had not entirely abandoned her old self on that beach. Surely a kernel of Katerina Bruni still lurked under the gray wool, peeking out in those gloves.

Kate leaned back against the hard seat and opened her secondhand leather valise to find the agency's letter. It was tucked inside the pages of a book of poetry, and had been read so many times the edges were worn. Kate knew all the words neatly scripted there, but she still wanted to see it. The letter reassured her that she was not just adrift on this sea of a moor—she truly had a destination.

Thorn Hill, the estate of Mr. Michael Lindley, near the village of Suddley. A country gentleman, the younger brother of an earl, in need of a governess for his sister and daughter, girls of fifteen and six years of age respectively. Kate wondered what this Mr. Lindley would be like. He was a widower, just as she ostensibly was a widow. The letter didn't say his age, but he could not be *very* old, not with such a small daughter.

Kate had not known many "country gentlemen," not English ones anyway. Her late admirer, Sir Julian Kirkwood, had sometimes told her about his English estates, but she had the distinct sense he had rarely visited them, preferring London and the Continent. The same for her mother's Edward, the grand Duke of Salton, who had enjoyed the sensual joys of Venice—and Lucrezia Bruni—over English landowner duties.

It seemed this Mr. Lindley lived on his property all year around. A sudden rush of cold doubt assailed her, making her stomach queasy. How would she ever fit into such a household? She with her strange Italian ways, her, er, *colorful* past. But she had to try. Try her very hardest. This was her chance for an entirely new life, for getting to know her true self.

Her thoughts were rudely interrupted by a sharp jolt of the post chaise. The driver shouted out hoarsely, and the vehicle tilted precipitously, sending Kate slamming into its hard wall. She screamed at a sharp stab of pain in her shoulder, and her bonnet tilted over her eyes, blinding her.

For an instant, in the sudden darkness, she remembered the pitching yacht throwing her into the cold water, her mother slipping away from her. She took a deep gulp of air against the hot rush of tears. "San Marco!" she cried, pushing back her bonnet and struggling to sit up. She caught at the leather strap to pull herself against the tilt of the coach. Her shoulder throbbed, and she rubbed at it tentatively. It didn't seem to be broken or dislocated, luckily. But her valise was overturned, all her meager possessions scattered about.

As she reached down to gather up her books, her clothes and hairbrush and miraculously unbroken bottle of rose water, she heard the coachman's voice.

"Miss!" he called. "Are you all right in there?"

Kate stuffed her nightdress into the valise and snapped it shut, hugging it against her. "I'm fine! What has happened?"

The door was wrenched open, and hands reached in to lift her out. Once her shaking feet felt solid earth again, she spun around to survey the wreck. One of the coach's wheels was lodged in a ditch, dug deep in the mud.

"One of those blasted sheep ran out in the road!" The driver was practically spitting with the force of his ire. He swept his battered hat off his head and used it to point at the flock of dingy white woolly creatures grazing atop a hillock. "Spooked the horses like, and made them run off into the ditch."

Kate glanced uncertainly at the sheep. They regarded her with placid dark eyes, as if they were innocents who could never have caused such havoc in all their blameless days. She was very glad they were at a safe distance—she had never been around farm animals in Venice, and wasn't at all sure they could be trusted. "What can we do?" she asked the driver.

"Eh, well, not much we *can* do, miss. It won't be moved. I'll have to ride into the village and fetch help." Even as he spoke, he stepped up to the team of horses and began to unhitch one.

Kate watched him, confused. And, she had to admit, a little frightened. "Am I to stay here alone, then?" she cried, bitter panic welling up in her throat. *Alone.* Such a horrid word.

"Not for long, miss. Suddley is only a few miles off. I'll be back in a trice. Or you could ride one of the other horses. 'Twould have to be bareback, though." The man swept her a long, lascivious glance as if he pictured her naked legs already.

That expression was like cold water on her panic, and she stepped back, giving him her iciest glare. She worked so hard at appearing to be a respectable lady! If this rough post chaise driver could begin to see through her charade, surely everyone else could, too.

Then her new life would be over before it began.

This fear had plagued her ever since she arrived on English shores. But now she had a more practical worry, as well.

"I have never ridden a horse," she said.

The lascivious look turned immediately to one of shock. "What, never?"

She shook her head. All her life, water had carried her everywhere she needed to go. There was no need of big, smelly, *scary* horses.

"Oh. That *is* a pity. You won't get far around here without horses." The man swung himself up onto the fearsome beast's broad back and turned back onto the road. "Never fear, though, miss! I'll be back in two shakes of a lamb's tail."

Kate could hardly believe that this man, rude as he was, would actually leave her here *alone!* She watched in utter astonishment as he galloped off down the lane, waving his hat at her in farewell.

"But wait!" she cried, that freezing panic coming back over her. Her words were snatched away by the wind.

The coachman turned a corner on the road and was gone. Kate was completely alone. Alone—except for the sheep. And the horses.

Clutching her heavy valise against her like a lifeline, Kate gave the clustered sheep a wary glance. They completely ignored her, just went on chewing up the turf. Somewhat reassured, she made her way up the slope of a little hillock and sat down on a large, flat rock to wait. She placed the valise carefully at her feet.

To wait for *what* here? She was not sure. A sheep attack? A rainstorm? The earth to cave in?

Well, she decided, as long as she was waiting for catastrophe, she might as well take stock of her surroundings.

It *was* a lonely country, no doubt about that. There was no sign of life as far as the horizons stretched, and no sound save the faint tinkling of the sheep's bells and the constant whistling of the wind. Never in her life had she felt so alone, not even when she woke up on that beach to find her old life swept away. Yet there was a beauty to this land, too, which she had never known before. She had thought it all gray, but that wasn't true. There was also green, and yellow, white, pale pink, blackest black. It all undulated like a velvety patchwork counterpane in that wind, an entire world unto itself.

As she examined this mysterious landscape, breathed in the fresh, crisp air, her deep fears of being left alone melted away in her heart and she felt a measure of the great peace. All her life she had lived among noisy places where a girl could easily lose herself in the chaos—or never find herself at all.

Maybe here, in the fresh, crisp air, she could begin to find out who Kate truly was. *If* she really wanted to know. Was she the daughter of the wild Lucrezia Bruni, looking forward to following in her mother's flamboyant footsteps? Was she dependent on other people to survive, or could she depend only on *herself*? What did she truly seek?

That was why she had come here.

Kate closed her eyes and inhaled deeply of the crisp, clean breeze, with no taint of the teeming city. She listened very carefully to the quiet. The distant bleat of the sheep, the whistle of the wind, the rumble of wheels . . .

Wheels?

Kate's eyes flew open, her moment of rural transcendence abruptly finished. Surely the post chaise driver could not be back so soon? She *did* want to reach Thorn Hill, to meet the people she would be living with and working for. But this time was surprisingly fine, too, this just being alone, being silent, not having anyone look at her or expect something from her. Before, the solitude frightened her. Now she found she was loath to let it go just yet. And she wasn't terribly eager to see who was coming, either. It might be someone like that leering coachman.

She stood up and peered down the road, lifting her

hand to the edge of her bonnet to shield her eyes from the gray glare of the sky. There *was* a carriage coming toward her, but not from the direction the coachman took off in. And it was not the portly coachman. It was a man wielding the reins of a handsome little curricle.

The vehicle slowed as it reached the banked post chaise, rolling to a halt as the man tugged back on the reins. He twisted on the curricle seat to face her, his lips curved in a smile beneath the brim of his hat.

Not just an ordinary, everyday smile. A dazzling sunburst glow of a grin that lit up the gloomy day. The sheer, unexpected beauty, the welcome wonder of it, made Kate involuntarily fall back a step. She felt the roughness of the rock at the back of her knees, forcing her to halt or fall backward in a most inelegant way. She glanced behind her to see if there was someone else he might be smiling at, someone who had crept up on the moors.

There was no one. Only sheep.

Kate turned back, and gave him a hesitant smile of her own.

He climbed down from the high seat of the curricle, and Kate was absurdly shocked to see that the man with the heavenly smile moved in a distinctly earthbound manner. His left leg was stiff, unbending, as he stepped to the ground. For one second, he held on to the carriage, as if to get his balance, but when he walked it was with a vigorous strength. He swept his hat off politely, and light brown waves of glossy hair fell over his brow in glorious disarray. The wind played with it, as if with caressing fingers, and he impatiently pushed back the unruly locks.

Kate knew it was very rude of her, but she stared at him agape—she couldn't seem to help herself. He was like an avenging angel, a warrior god of ancient days, pulled out of a Renaissance fresco in Venice and deposited on this lonely English road. She recalled a Botticelli painting she had once seen, of Mars and

Venus. Mars was reclining, asleep, under Venus's watchful gaze, his head thrown back, dark curls falling away from the sculpted planes of his face.

Kate had stood there in that gallery, entranced by his beautiful face, wondering what the dreams of such a slumber could be. She wished she was that Venus, so quiet, so watchful, so—so *triumphant* that such a man was sprawled across *her* bed, all his thoughts of war melted away under *her* caress, leaving only love. Now Kate had an inkling of how Venus must have felt, since Botticelli's Mars stood before her now, dropped practically at her feet in this unlikely spot.

He had the same sharp cheekbones, the same sculpted jaw and aquiline nose. If he wore a drape of gauzy cloth and nothing else, the resemblance would be absolutely complete.

Kate almost laughed aloud at that mental image, and clapped her gloved hand to her mouth. *Of course* the man would not wear just a piece of gauze over his loins—this was Yorkshire, not Venice during Carnevale, when any sort of outlandish costume could be seen. Indeed, this man was dressed quite conventionally, even conservatively, in fawn doeskin breeches and a well-cut blue coat, his waistcoat a plain gray, his impeccable white cravat simply tied. A black greatcoat was pushed back carelessly, and the hat he held was black and low crowned, stylish enough but not ostentatious. Quietly expensive—and Kate should know, since judging a man's worth at first glance had been an important part of her education.

His eyes narrowed a bit as he peered up the slope at her, tiny lines fanning out from the edges of his eyes. Eyes that Kate could tell, even at this distance, were blue. A sharp, piercing pale blue, vivid as the Italian sky.

For one endless second, suspended out of time, Kate forgot to breathe. The moor whirled around her, dipping and swaying dizzily, until she was forced to close her eyes against it. She feared, *knew,* she would fall—until a strong hand caught her arm, steadying her.

Her eyes flew open, and she stared directly up into that sky-blue gaze.

His hand on her arm was so warm, burning, even through her sleeve and his glove. It felt safe. She had an overpowering longing to lean into him, into that heat, and she even swayed toward his broad chest before the deep flow of his voice stopped her.

"Are you ill, madam?" he asked in obvious concern. It was a lovely voice, deep and slightly rough but warm, just like a *prosecco* on a chilly night. It matched the man. But it was not an Italian voice, lilting and flowing. The vowels were clipped, sharp with upper-class accents as Edward's had been. As Julian Kirkwood's.

Somehow, that added to this man's powerful attraction, his aura of quiet strength—and made him slightly dangerous to her. She had come to England to leave old ways, old temptations and lessons, behind. She hadn't even *looked* at a man with attraction since her near drowning. She even thought those ways were buried beneath the waves.

But old temptations were not so far behind her as she wished. She would have to be careful.

"I—I am quite well, thank you," she murmured, stepping back from him. Her voice sounded weak and breathless, and she couldn't quite bring herself to look directly up into those heaven-colored eyes. So she stared at the knot in his cravat. But there was nothing she could do about his warmth, which beckoned to her like a mischievous demon.

"You're trembling," he said. "It's too cold for you to be standing about here."

Cold? No. It was not cold here. It was as hot as a Mediterranean island. The trembling came from deep inside herself.

"Obviously there was some mishap with the post chaise. It was criminal of the driver to leave you here all alone, madam!" he continued, his voice full of indignation.

"Oh, no, it was my fault. You see, I cannot ride a horse—" Her words broke off on a gasp as he suddenly pulled off his greatcoat and swept it about her shoulders.

She was completely surrounded now by that heat, by his clean scent of pine soap, starch, wool, and—and something deeper. Darker.

"That is no excuse for the driver," he said, drawing the coat closer about her. The leather of his glove brushed her throat, the tender underside of her jaw. A new shiver went right down to her very toes, making them tingle inside her thick stockings and half boots. "But this should make you warmer."

"Now *you* will be cold!" she protested, and tried to give the coat back.

His clasp tightened, holding the wool against her. "I'm used to the Yorkshire wind. You're not, madam."

"How can you tell?" she asked, chagrined. She had worked so hard to fit in with English ways!

He smiled at her, that bold, white grin she had thought an angel's smile when she first saw it. Now she knew she was wrong. It was a *pirate's* smile, one designed to draw hapless maidens across perilous oceans to his side, no matter what the danger.

But Kate was no hapless maiden. She might still be a virgin, yet she had *never* been hapless. She had seen too much, learned too much, in her mother's house. Men were to be laughed at, humored, amused, and used.

But here, at this moment, she felt very young and foolish. Hapless, *helpless,* before a pirate's smile.

Don't be a fool, she told herself sternly. Don't ruin this new life before it has even begun.

"I know most of the people in the neighborhood," the pirate angel answered, seemingly oblivious to her own inner turmoil. "I have never met *you* before, or I'm sure I would remember. Indeed I would."

Kate laughed at this little flattery, at the mischievous glint in his gaze. She had seen such glints before, and it made her feel like she was back on a surer footing.

His smile widened, as if encouraged by her laughter. "Also, madam, there is your accent. Most assuredly not of a Yorkshire bent."

"I do not have very *much* of an accent, sir," Kate protested. "I was told that I speak English very well."

"It is charming," he said assuringly. "And really hardly noticeable. It is just that I once traveled a great deal, and spent time in Italy." His smile turned wry at the edges, almost self-mocking. "In what seems like a million years ago."

"Yes," Kate murmured. "I know what it's like to remember previous lives."

One light brown brow arched inquiringly. "Do you? A previous life left behind in your homeland?"

Kate deeply hoped so. "Of course," she said, forcing a careless little laugh. "It seems Italy is another world. A faraway star. Or maybe it was just a dream."

"And speaking of Italy . . ." His voice trailed away as he paused, his smile fading. "I am ridiculously stupid."

"Sir?" Kate asked, surprised by this sudden turn in the conversation.

"Forgive me. Would you happen to be Mrs. Brown? I doubt any other Italian ladies would be running about the Yorkshire countryside." His expression turned apologetic, as if he was chagrined at what he called his stupidity. "I fear we did not expect you until tomorrow."

Expect her? Kate stepped back from him, away from his warmth. Could this man be—was he her *employer?*

Of course he was. Who else could he be? She had been faintly hoping that Mr. Lindley would prove to be old and plain, set in his ways, easy to disregard. Instead, he was an angel-god, well named for Michael the archangel.

San Marco. But this was not good.

"I—why, yes. I am Mrs. Kate Brown," she said, her throat dry and the words cracking.

"I should have introduced myself immediately. I am Mr. Michael Lindley, of course. I believe you are to be our new governess." His smile, she fancied, was now not nearly so flirtatious. It was much more careful, more polite. He stepped back a bit, to a respectable distance.

As she should be, at all times.

She nervously touched her numb lips with the tip of her tongue, and said, "You are Mr. Lindley."

His gaze flickered over her mouth, then shot away from her past her shoulder to some point in the scenery. So she was not completely alone in her strange, dizzy attraction—much good it could do her, since she was his respectable employee. Things *must* remain on a professional footing here in gray Yorkshire.

"Indeed I am," he said quietly. Regretfully?

Kate took in a deep breath, trying to find the same sweet calm she had felt earlier when she was all alone in wild nature. "Well, then. How do you do, Mr. Lindley?" She remembered all her careful lessons in proper deportment, and dropped him a small, graceful curtsy. "I daresay I *should* have arrived tomorrow, with all the obstacles I have faced today."

He glanced toward the listing post chaise, his jaw tightening. "Yes. That demmed driver. His employer will be notified of this outrage immediately. The man will never leave a defenseless lady alone on the moor again!"

"He said he would be back in 'two shakes of a lamb's tail,' however long that might be," Kate said, absurdly pleased by his protective words. "I'm not sure how long it takes a lamb to shake its tail. But really, I was only here alone for a few moments when you came along so providentially."

"It *is* a fine thing I came along, Mrs. Brown, for it looks as if it may rain later. May I escort you to Thorn Hill? I know that my mother and sister are very eager to meet you."

He offered his arm to her. The gesture, and his words and tone, were all so perfectly, painfully polite. They were meant to make things more comfortable, of course, more proper. But Kate could not quite stop the small pang deep in her most secret heart. A pang of regret for the pirate, buried now beneath the country gentleman.

Or maybe for the courtesan's daughter, beneath the gray governess?

Kate shoved those unwelcome qualms away and slid her gloved hand into the crook of his elbow. A shiver undulated over her, but she took another deep breath and stilled the movement before he could feel it. They moved down the slope to his waiting curricle, their steps well matched. There was hardly a sign of the slight limp she had noticed earlier.

She studied him surreptitiously from the corner of her eye. With a start, she noticed something she had missed in her bizarre, overwhelming enthrallment. His cheek was scarred with a long, thick, pale pink line slicing from temple to mouth, with a few smaller flecks surrounding it. The shocking sight made her own scarred cheek itch and burn in memory, until she had to rub hard at it with her fingers.

What could have happened to this man, to mar his angel's beauty? Had it scarred his heart, as well? Had it changed his very world—as Kate's own injuries had?

She found she ached to know these things, to know everything about him. An overwhelming temptation came over her as he lifted her up onto the high carriage seat. A temptation to lean down and press a hundred kisses, a thousand caresses, on those scars, until they both forgot all the pain of the past.

Kate sighed deeply as she settled onto the seat, arranging her respectable gray skirts around her. Oh, she was *truly* in trouble now.

Chapter Three

He was in so much trouble. Michael knew this as surely as he knew his own name. It had been a long time, a veritable lifetime, since he had felt this hot rush of immediate attraction toward a woman. This imperative urge to hold, to kiss, to breathe in her rosy perfume, her very essence, and absorb her into himself.

Why did it have to be with the new *governess?* A lady he would have to see every single day? A lady who was completely forbidden, thanks to his own iron resolve never to take advantage of any female under his roof. A lady who was, *damn it all,* a *lady.*

Mrs. Brown's waist was slim and supple beneath his hands as he lifted her into the curricle, her weight as light as a snowflake. She wore no stays beneath her plain garments—she obviously needed none. For one second, his cheek brushed the soft wool of her skirt. She smelled of rose water and her own sweet female fragrance. It made him ache and stir deep inside, where he thought surely his soul was frozen forever.

Once she was seated, her hand, gloved in butter-soft pink kid, lingered gently on his shoulder. *"Grazie,"* she whispered.

He glanced up at her, drawn by the husky Italian accent. Her dark brown eyes were wide, her rose-pink lips parted on an indrawn breath. She was not unaffected by their nearness, either. Knowing that, seeing it, sent a rush of powerful, primitive masculine satisfaction jolting through him. It took all his strength to keep from pulling her pretty face down to his, kissing those lush, parted lips until they tumbled together to the ground, sighs and breaths mingling in the cool air. . . .

No, Michael thought regretfully, shoving those enticing images away. He was no longer the reckless, wild youth he had once been, who grabbed what he wanted no matter who might be hurt. He had learned his hard lesson with his sweet Caroline, and he couldn't afford to be like that anymore. He had responsibilities, and his family's reputation to uphold.

Kate Brown was lovely—there was no doubt about that. The loveliest woman he had seen since coming to Yorkshire. Her skin was milky white, but her hair and eyes were dark as night. Those eyes, with their coffee color, tilted up faintly at the corners, giving her an alluring, almost Eastern aspect. When those eyes turned in his direction they beckoned to him, drawing him closer, teasing him with glimpses of her inner self. They told him she was not merely a beautiful doll, as many ladies fluttering around the ballrooms of London seemed. She had an indefinable elegance, a sensuality as subtle as her rose perfume, that could be the undoing of any man.

Michael stepped back from the curricle, turning his face to the chill moor wind. It seemed to shake him back to reality, and he laughed at the thought of what Lady Ross or old Mrs. Sowerby might say if she came upon Mr. Lindley kissing his new governess in the middle of the road.

Mrs. Brown gave him a frowning glance, as if puzzled by his sudden laughter. Well, he couldn't explain it to her. He couldn't even explain this sudden madness to himself.

She reached up to push back a lock of black satin hair the wind teased from beneath her bonnet. As she smoothed it away from her face, he saw with a sudden shock that she was *not* perfect. A thin scar sliced beneath her high cheekbone, thinner and lighter than his own.

She was marked—just as he was.

He almost reached out to touch that scar, but caught himself just in time. She turned away from him, as if she sensed his urge, and broke the slender thread binding them.

"I left my valise beside that rock," she said softly, with no inflection at all in her voice.

"I'll fetch it, then, and we can be off." Michael turned and hurried back up to where she had been standing when he first saw her. The valise was old and worn, of cracked, stained brown leather. It was too homely for such a woman, he thought with rare whimsy. She should have satin pouches and silk-covered trunks.

The old case also didn't latch securely. It came open as he lifted it, spilling some of its contents onto the ground. He knelt to gather them up, hoping she couldn't see his blasted clumsiness, the way he fumbled with her night rail.

The garment was a serviceable white muslin, unadorned by any ribbons or lace—not something designed to set a man's senses reeling. But somehow his breath quickened at the sight of its softness, its femininity, by the waves of rose scent that wafted from its folds. He envisioned Kate Brown asleep in this gown, loose-limbed and warm with dreams, the muslin sliding back from a slim leg. . . .

Blast! You've been without a woman for too long, he mocked himself as he pushed the night rail back into the valise. It couldn't be healthy. He should visit Becky at the Tudor Arms again soon.

The books he gathered up were easier on his equilibrium, conjuring no erotic images. They *were* interesting, though—Dante and Petrarch in Italian, Byron, Shelley, a novel called *Pride and Prejudice,* which he remembered his mother and sister reading and rhapsodizing over. He tucked them in next to the night rail, and only then did he notice a small object half hidden in the shadows. It was small and lumpy, wrapped in a scrap of stained bright blue silk.

Michael picked it up, rubbing his thumb over rough edges. Curious, he folded back a corner of the silk—and frowned at what he saw. A sapphire, big as his thumb and blue as his daughter's eyes, surrounded by a ring of ivory pearls in a brooch that could feed a farm family for a winter.

Well, well, he thought sharply, looking over his shoulder to where Mrs. Brown sat in the curricle, hands demurely folded in her lap, his greatcoat still over her shoulders. It seemed everyone had secrets in this world. The brooch could be anything—a family heirloom, a gift from the late Mr. Brown, whoever *he* had been. Or it could be something more sinister.

It was not worth sending her away over now, or even interrogating her about. But he *would* have to watch her. He had his family to think about.

"Mr. Lindley?" she called. "Is everything all right?"

Michael folded the brooch back up into its silk and placed the jewel back into the valise before standing again. "I'm afraid your case fell open, Mrs. Brown."

She gave a little laugh. "I fear it is a temperamental old thing! Just pinch the clasp together until it clicks."

He hoisted the valise beneath his arm and made his way back down to the waiting curricle—and the waiting Mrs. Brown. He noticed that his leg was stiffening a bit, and cursed that he hadn't thought to bring his walking stick. Without its support, he had to move more slowly and carefully, trying not to limp at all.

Mrs. Brown didn't seem to notice his slightly awkward gait. She watched his approach with a cool, serene smile, and nodded her thanks when he handed her the recalcitrant valise. She turned away, fussing with the clasp as he pulled himself up onto the seat beside her. She couldn't even look at him as they moved onto the road, turning the corner that led into Suddley village.

"Tell me about my pupils, Mr. Lindley," she said. "Your sister and daughter. What are their interests? What do they hope to learn?"

"My daughter, Miss Amelia Lindley, is nearly

seven," he answered, and couldn't help but smile. He *always* smiled when he thought of his little Amelia. "She hasn't had very many opportunities for education yet, but she's very bright and curious. My mother has been teaching her her letters and some embroidery. She is very fond of music, and can already play some songs at the pianoforte." He tossed her a rueful smile. "I suppose I sound like a boastful papa, going on about how my daughter is so smart and talented and pretty beyond all other girls."

She smiled, too, but hers was suddenly sunny, delighted. It transformed her already beautiful face to something beyond loveliness. "You sound like a justly proud papa. I can't wait to meet Miss Amelia. She sounds like a delightful child."

Her smile remained, but it turned wistful at the edges, as if she remembered something bittersweet. She turned her face away.

Michael wanted that brief sunny glow back. He would do anything to make her smile and laugh again. Stand on his head, make ridiculous jokes—anything. When she smiled, she made him feel younger somehow. Lighter. Whole.

But of course, he couldn't do *any* of those clownish things. Not while he was driving.

"She must miss her mother a great deal," Mrs. Brown said wistfully. "It is hard for a girl to lose her mother."

At the thought of Caroline, golden-girl Caroline, Michael turned somber, too. It shook him completely from his haze of lust toward Mrs. Brown as nothing else could. "Amelia was very young when my wife died," he answered tightly. "She hardly remembers her."

"I am sorry to bring it up," she said. "It must have been very hard for you, as well, Mr. Lindley. To lose someone is never easy."

"Yes. You are a widow yourself, are you not, Mrs. Brown?"

She turned away again, the narrow brim of her dark

blue bonnet hiding her expression from his view. All he saw was the clean, white line of her long neck rising from her high collar, the neat coil of shining black hair at her nape. "Yes," she whispered. There was a world of hurt in that one word. A hurt he knew he could not erase for her, as much as he longed to.

They drove along in silence for several long moments, until she looked back at him, her face smooth and serene. "And your sister, Mr. Lindley? She is fifteen, correct? She will be making her grand debut in only a year or two, surely."

"She will. Or rather, so we hope," Michael answered, unreasonably grateful for the change of subject. They had skirted perilously close to the edge of the personal—the painful. "Lady Christina is quite an intelligent young lady, very interested in botany."

"Botany?" Mrs. Brown said, faint dismay in her voice. "You mean, plants and such? I fear I know little of such things."

"That is quite all right, Mrs. Brown," he assured her. "Christina knows enough of that for all of us. I doubt Linnaeus himself could teach her anything. What she really needs is to learn to comport herself gracefully in Society and at Court. Conversation, dancing, fashion—that sort of thing. My mother will be able to tell you more."

She gave a distinctly relieved laugh. "Conversation, dancing, and fashion are things I *can* help her with. I promise you, Mr. Lindley, after a few months with me Lady Christina will be a veritable Diamond."

"A Diamond, eh? We would be happy if she would just cease getting mud all over her gowns!" They came up over the crest of a hill into the edges of the village. "And this is Suddley, Mrs. Brown."

"Indeed?" He watched her as she gazed around thoughtfully as they drove down the main street, taking in the buildings lining the cobblestone road. There was the inn, the Tudor Arms, where no doubt the soon-to-be unemployed post chaise driver was enjoying a pint and the buxom Becky worked as barmaid. Mr. and Mrs. Elliott's store, where any number of goods could be obtained, from London cloth to scented soaps to plowshares. The bookshop, the apothecary. The assembly rooms, where Lady Ross and her daughters vied with his mother for social supremacy. The old Norman church of St. Anne's, with its time-darkened stones and tall, square spire and ancient churchyard.

He hoped that Mrs. Brown liked it, for in Suddley was all the society that could be expected in the neighborhood. If she thought it primitive or unattractive, she would surely dash back to London, leaving him with a new, long search for another governess.

And depriving him of Mrs. Brown's rose-scented presence. Somehow, that thought was deeply disappointing.

But Mrs. Brown betrayed her thoughts not at all, remaining as serene and polite as anyone could possibly be. She nodded as he pointed out the various establishments, the modiste and the bookstore and a tea shop, and asked a few questions. Yet she didn't seem to want to jump out of the curricle and run away, which was surely a good sign.

They soon left Suddley behind and turned onto a winding, narrowing lane. The sign pointing the way to Ross Lodge drifted past, and they encountered farmers in their fields who called out greetings and doffed their hats. Mrs. Brown smiled and nodded to all of them, as gracious as a princess with her subjects.

All too soon, they moved through the open gates of Thorn Hill, passing the ivy-covered gatehouse and jolting along the treelined drive. He slowed the horse so she could get a good view of her new home. "And this is Thorn Hill, Mrs. Brown. I hope you will like it."

Thorn Hill was not like the grand country mansions of many of Michael's old friends, or like Darcy Hall, the seat of his brother's earldom. It was a working manor house, added on to as necessity dictated until the original Tudor house became a hopeless jumble of architectural styles and building materials. It could not be called elegant. But to Michael, Thorn Hill had been a refuge in the terrible time after Caroline's death. A comfortable haven where his family could heal and build a new life. He loved its strong walls, its livable rooms and overgrown gardens. It was his home.

But through the eyes of someone fresh from London, it must seem a mess. And very small and dark.

Mrs. Brown took in the house with her large, lustrous eyes. Her face remained cool and expressionless. Michael found himself almost holding his breath waiting for her reaction, as if her words would decide the fate of the world.

Finally, she looked from the house to him, a wide smile tugging at her lips. "Oh, Mr. Lindley. It is lovely! Just what I hoped for."

He felt a rush of absurd pleasure that she admired Thorn Hill, as if he had built the place with his own hands especially for her. Before he could answer, the door flew open. Christina dashed down the front steps, her long brown hair streaming behind her. Her skirts weren't muddy for once, but she did wear a stained apron over her sprigged muslin gown.

"Michael!" she called out. Belatedly, she realized she still wore the apron, and ripped it off to shove it behind a shrub. "Here you are at last! You've been gone an age. Is this Mrs. Brown? Mother heard from one of the tenants that the post chaise driver was at the Tudor Arms talking about how his carriage crashed or something."

"Indeed, this *is* Mrs. Brown, Christina," he answered. He gave the reins to a footman and jumped down, going around to help Mrs. Brown alight. She leaned against his arm for a second to steady herself, and as it had before, her scent surrounded his senses, drew him in, beckoned to him like a siren song. He longed to draw her closer, to taste the soft skin just below her ear. . . .

But Christina was watching, and the servants. And nothing about their situation had changed—or ever would.

Mrs. Brown stepped away from him, and he reached up to retrieve her valise. He remembered then the mysterious sapphire brooch, the secrets in Mrs. Brown's eyes.

No. Their careful situation was never likely to change.

"Mrs. Brown," he said, "this hoyden who is so obviously in need of your tutelage is my sister, Lady Christina Lindley."

"Michael!" Christina cried in protest. "How dare you call me a *hoyden?* Mrs. Brown will get the wrong impression of me right off. Perhaps *you* could do with some lessons in manners." She turned to the new governess with a polite nod. "How do you do, Mrs. Brown?"

"How do *you* do, Lady Christina?" Mrs. Brown answered, and moved away from him entirely to greet his sister. Her warmth and rose perfume were gone.

And he would have to go to work in the fields all afternoon to forget them.

Chapter Four

"*A*nd this will be your room." Thorn Hill's house-keeper, a tall, gray-haired, formidable woman in rustling black taffeta, opened a door and stepped aside. "Mrs. Brown," she added, the unspoken words "if that is indeed your true name" hovering in the air. She had been behaving in a suspicious manner ever since Kate arrived, though Kate could not see why. Perhaps the woman saw a governess as a threat to her housekeeperly authority.

Kate gave the annoying woman a cool smile, stepped past her into the room—and stopped in her tracks. "I—are you *sure* this is my room, Mrs. Jenkins?" She hated to betray any hint of uncertainty, but she just had to be sure. It would be so embarrassing if she settled in and then was told to move.

Kate had very little experience with governesses, especially English ones. Her own childhood lessons were overseen by a series of tutors and experts, and her one personal servant was more lady's maid than nursemaid. But Kate read a great deal before she embarked on this course, and she knew that governesses were not usually given accommodations like these.

For one thing, the chamber was not up in the attics, but along the same wide, carpeted corridor as the family's rooms. It was large and sunny, with tall windows, and window draperies and bed-curtains of yellow silk. A cheerful seascape hung over the polished fireplace, and a flowering plant bloomed on a windowsill, a yellow ribbon tied around its clay pot.

It was not as sumptuous as her blue satin bedroom in Venice, carefully decorated in colors meant to flatter her complexion and hair. But it was very pretty and inviting, and a veritable palace compared to her dusty little room in London.

She glanced toward the impassive housekeeper. "*Is* it meant to be my room, Mrs. Jenkins?" she asked again.

Mrs. Jenkins looked very much as if she wondered that exact same question. Her face was pinched, as if she had just bit into a lemon. "Of course. My instructions came directly from Lady Darcy. Miss Amelia's room is right next door, and you're meant to stay close to her. Through that door there is a sitting room which will be set up as your schoolroom."

"Oh," Kate said. For once in her life she was at a loss as to what the correct words might be. So the child had no proper nursery, either? Even Kate's mother's friends, with their highly unconventional lifestyles, had set up tidy little rooms far away from the lives of the grown-ups for their children. Here, the child was situated directly in the main part of the house.

Not that Kate *minded*. Oh, no. This cozy space suited her far better than some drafty garret. It just seemed too good to be true.

And usually, when something seemed that way, it was.

"I see," she murmured.

"The Lindleys are fine people," Mrs. Jenkins said tightly, doling out her words as if they were gold coins. "The finest people in the neighborhood to work for. But they are rather unusual in some respects."

Really? Now, *that* sounded intriguing. "Indeed?" she said brightly, turning toward Mrs. Jenkins in hope of more information.

But the housekeeper obviously felt she had said quite enough. She shook her head sternly, the lace lappets of her cap quivering. "Is the room to your satisfaction, Mrs. Brown?"

"Oh, yes. It's quite lovely."

Mrs. Jenkins gave Kate's shabby valise a sour stare. "Will you be needing any assistance in unpacking?"

Oh, yes, Kate thought wryly. *Just as soon as the wagon arrives with my twenty trunks and thirty bandboxes.* "No, thank you, Mrs. Jenkins, I'm sure I can manage. But some water for washing would be most welcome."

"I will send up one of the *under*housemaids," the housekeeper answered. With a nod, she backed quickly out of the room, her skirts rustling again with sharp disapproval.

The door clicked, and Kate was alone.

She drifted over to the small, yellow-draped dressing table and took off her bonnet, dropping it onto the table's bare surface. At home in Venice, her dressing table was littered with scent bottles, powder boxes, jewel cases, and silver-backed brushes. Here there was not a single object.

And her hair was a windblown mess, she saw as she glimpsed herself in the oval mirror. The dark strands escaped every which way from their pins, looking like nothing so much as a bird's nest on her head.

Her mother would be appalled, Kate thought with a grin. She reached for her valise and dug out the plain new hairbrush and pin box.

So the Lindleys were *unusual,* she mused as she set about tidying her coiffure. She could well believe that. Of course, she had not yet met the Dowager Lady Darcy or little Miss Amelia, but she rather doubted many titled young English ladies dashed about wearing stained aprons and sporting dirt under their fingernails. Kate had her work cut out making a lady of *her!* But she did rather like Lady Christina. The girl had an open curiosity and intelligence that was rare in English society—and even rarer in the Venetian demimonde.

And as for Mr. Michael Lindley—well, he was not at all what she had expected.

Her hands paused in twisting her hair up in a neat

knot. She was not really sure what she had been expecting. Someone older, almost fatherly, as her mother's Edward had been? A bluff, hearty country gentleman, with a red face and hunting hounds tussling at his feet? Someone pale and scholarly?

Perhaps a combination of all of those. They were sorts she had met before, and knew how to handle. Working for one of them would have been comparatively easy, expected.

She had *not* expected to find a handsome young man living out here in the wild north. A man tall and strong, with eyes like the sky, and not a hint of red bluster or pale chinlessness about him. He was the younger brother of an earl, and had the easy manners, the light flirtatiousness, of someone accustomed to living in Society. Just like her admirer Sir Julian Kirkwood.

Kate felt a sharp twist as she thought of Sir Julian— Julian, who was lost to the cold waters just as her mother was. He had also been handsome, even more handsome than Mr. Lindley, and had a similar way of joking politely, of giving admiring glances. Julian's glances, though, had a way of unpleasantly piercing through her, an air of possessiveness and need.

Mr. Lindley had something Sir Julian had not possessed. He had hidden depths of kindness in his sky-blue eyes, eyes that could look at her and see her very soul if she let him. Julian compared her always to Beatrice and Renaissance princesses, as if he did not see *her* at all. Mr. Lindley seemed like a man well acquainted with secrets and dark depths.

How she would love to know what those secrets of his were! But only if she didn't have to give up hers in return.

No, she was not expecting this when she agreed to come to Yorkshire. She was expecting something peaceful, easy, respectable.

But when had life *ever* been peaceful for Katerina Bruni? It wouldn't be for Kate Brown, either.

She would have to watch herself around Mr. Lind-

ley, that was all. No hints of attraction, or flirtatiousness, or—

Her thoughts were interrupted by a knock at the
door. For one instant, she hoped—*feared*—it was him,
summoned by her thoughts. Her hairbrush fell from
her suddenly numb fingers, clattering onto the dressing table.

Don't be silly! she told herself sternly. *Of course he
would not be so improper as to come to the governess's chamber.*

Unless it was to denounce her, to say he knew every
sordid detail of her past and she had to leave
immediately.

That was silly, too. Despite the depths of his gaze,
there was no way he could know the truth, unless Kate
herself told him. Which she never, ever would. The
past was dead. She just had to remember that.

"Come in," she called.

But of course, it was not Mr. Lindley at the door.
It was not a maid sent by Mrs. Jenkins, either, but
Lady Christina herself, with a large pitcher of water
in her hands. She gave Kate a shy smile, so at odds
with her earlier bold demeanor.

Kate well remembered what it felt like to be Christina's age. To never be sure of oneself, or one's right
place in the world. She gave the girl a welcoming smile
in return. "Lady Christina! Such a surprise."

"I hope I'm not interrupting, Mrs. Brown. I just saw
one of the maids coming to bring you this water, and
I told her I would do it."

Kate took the heavy pitcher from her hands.
"Thank you. I feel like I have all the dust of the road
to wash off!" She poured the steaming liquid into a
basin and splashed it over her face, scrubbing away
all the dirt of her voyage. It wasn't quite a rose-
scented bath in a marble tub, but it still felt heavenly.

Kate patted her face with a towel placed neatly next
to the basin, and turned back to Lady Christina. The
girl stood watching her expectantly, hands clasped behind her back.

"Perhaps I could help you unpack, Mrs. Brown?" she said.

Kate opened her mouth to say she hardly had anything *to* unpack, but Christina looked so hopefully helpful that she couldn't refuse. "Oh, yes, thank you. I don't have much, but I could use some advice on where things should go."

She opened up the sad old valise and emptied its jumbled contents onto the bed. They looked so very meager all together like that, and so shabby next to the brightness of the yellow counterpane. Yet Christina leaned forward so eagerly to inspect them, as if unearthing hidden treasures.

Just in time, Kate saw the little silk-wrapped bundle before the girl did. She snatched it up and tucked it safely into her pelisse pocket. It had been foolish of her to save the brooch—no governess should possess such a thing, and she had needed the money it could have brought to live on in London. She had given her bracelet to Maria and Paolo in thanks, and the proceeds from the necklace and earrings had paid for her journey and lodgings. Somehow, she just needed one small piece of her mother to hold on to. She had to be careful no one ever saw it.

It was yet another secret to hide away.

Christina didn't seem to notice anything amiss, though. She was looking over the titles of Kate's precious books. "*Pride and Prejudice*!" Christina cried. "Such a splendid novel. Have you read the author's *Persuasion*?"

"No, I fear I have not yet had the chance," Kate answered, shaking out her rumpled white muslin nightdress and extra chemise and petticoat. Her gowns, three muslin day dresses of pale blue, lilac, and gray, and one plain dark blue silk for evening, were also in poor shape. She would have to ask the formidable Mrs. Jenkins if she could borrow a flatiron.

"Oh, you absolutely *must* read it!" Christina enthused. "I think it is even finer than *Pride and Prejudice*. I don't often read novels, but these are special."

"Yes, they are. Perhaps we could read *Persuasion* together, then. As part of your lessons."

Christina nodded absently, still poring over the books. "Do you have any volumes on plant life, Mrs. Brown?"

Oh, yes. Now Kate remembered—Christina was a budding botanist. And she, Kate, was a complete bacon brain when it came to plants. Except for arranging blossoms in pleasing configurations. That she could do perfectly. "I fear not. Your brother tells me you are quite a fine botanist."

Christina shrugged carelessly, but a pleased pink blush stained her sun-browned cheeks. "I'm interested in botany, but I don't know as much as I would like. I have to teach myself."

Oh, this could be tricky, Kate realized. *She* was meant to be the governess, the one with wisdom to impart. Yet it was clear that, intellectually, Christina was far ahead of her. "I haven't had many opportunities to learn about botany myself, Lady Christina. Perhaps you could tell me more about it?"

Christina glanced up, her grass green eyes shining. "Oh, yes, indeed, Mrs. Brown! I can tell you about *Polypodium,* which grows near here. . . ."

"Wonderful. And *I* can tell *you* about subjects I know a great deal of."

The enthusiasm dimmed into suspicion. "What sort of subjects?"

"Dancing," Kate said firmly. "Deportment. Music."

"French?"

"And Italian. If you like. I believe there are many volumes on botany written in French and Italian which have not yet been translated into English." Kate really had no idea if that was true or not, but it sounded good.

The suspicion in Christina's eyes faded a bit, yet still lurked there. She would not be easy to win over— or fool. "I might find *that* useful," she said, clearly implying that dancing and deportment were decidedly *unuseful.*

Kate would just have to address that later. She was too tired—and too overwhelmed—right now. "Excellent! We will get started tomorrow, then. Perhaps you could also help me devise a curriculum for your niece?"

Christina nodded, and went to put the books away on a little shelf by the dressing table. "Amelia needs to learn *everything*, I'm afraid. You'll see when you meet her this evening."

"This evening?"

"Yes. That was my other errand in coming here, but I nearly forgot! I'm meant to ask if you'll have dinner in the dining room with us at seven. We keep country hours here at Thorn Hill. Michael says in London people don't have dinner until ten, or even later!"

Dinner with the family? Mrs. Jenkins had said the Lindleys were unusual, but even Kate knew this was very strange. Governesses took their meals in their room, or perhaps with their younger charges in the nursery. Never in the dining room.

"I—dine with you? At seven?" she asked, deeply puzzled. "Are you certain, Lady Christina?"

Christina didn't seem to think anything amiss. She was focused on arranging Kate's one good pair of slippers on the floor of the wardrobe and folding her blue wool shawl into a drawer. "Oh, yes. My brother told me to be sure and ask you. It will be a good time for you to meet my mother and Amelia. Amelia doesn't eat with us, of course, but her nursemaid does bring her into the drawing room before to say good night. If you feel tired after your journey, though, I'm sure it's fine for you to stay in here, Mrs. Brown."

"That's quite all right, Lady Christina. I will be happy to dine with your family. Thank you."

Christina nodded happily and hurried away, her errand complete. Kate sank down onto the edge of the bed, her wrinkled petticoat folded in her hands. What a strange household she found herself in! Disapproving housekeepers, wild young women, handsome employers, and a gray, windy moor outside her unexpectedly luxurious room.

Whatever could happen next?

"Tell me, then—what is she like? Our new governess."

Kate, her hand just extended to push open the drawing room door, paused as she heard a woman's voice speak this question. It was rude to eavesdrop—she knew that very well—but how else could she learn things in this strange new land? This household? Besides, she simply didn't have the fortitude to turn away when someone was talking about her!

She glanced back over her shoulder to make sure the footman who had pointed the way to the drawing room was not still there, and then leaned closer to see if anything else was said.

"Mrs. Jenkins took her straight to her room when you brought her in, Michael, and I didn't catch so much as a glimpse of her." The woman's voice was slightly querulous, tinged at the edges with a curiosity much like Kate's own.

"Well, you will see her very soon, Mother," Michael Lindley answered. Kate knew his dark chocolate voice *very* well now—it was imprinted on her mind, her very skin. She shivered at the sound of it, and drew her shawl closer about her shoulders. "She will be joining us shortly for dinner. If she hasn't become lost in Thorn Hill's rabbit warren of corridors!"

There was a long silence, filled with a shocked tension. So the curious lady was the mother of Lady Christina and Mr. Lindley—and she had not known Kate was asked to sit down with the family. Kate frowned. She certainly did *not* want to make a wrong step on this, her first day in her new position. This house was so very different from her mother's. Was she supposed to refuse the dinner invitation, even though it was offered, then?

There was a small click from inside the room, like

a china cup being set smartly on a table, and Lady Darcy said, "Oh?" in a toneless voice.

"We are quite informal here at Thorn Hill, are we not?" Michael Lindley said unconcernedly. "It seemed absurd to have Mrs. Brown take a tray in her room when we all want to know her better."

"Michael is quite right, Mother," Lady Christina said briskly. "I met Mrs. Brown, and she is quite lovely. Absolutely a lady. I am sure we need have no fear of her wiping her mouth on the tablecloth or spilling wine on the floor!"

Kate felt a pleased flush spreading warmly across her cheeks at their words. She had so feared that Christina, a girl not many years younger than herself but already so much more intellectual, would have nothing but scorn for a creature like Kate herself, taught only to be ornamental and inclined to read novels and poetry. Kate had never had a female friend before, or even what might be called a friendly acquaintance. In her mother's world, other women were to be suspected as rivals. The fact that a lady, that *Christina*, would be willing to give her a chance was strange and—and, yes, even pleasing.

And the fact that *Michael Lindley* had been the one to invite her to dinner, to make her feel welcome— well, the feelings *that* evoked did not bear examining. Not now. Probably not ever. For if her relationship to other women now needed to be reexamined and revised, her attitude toward men must be doubly so. Men—Mr. Lindley in particular—were no longer potential admirers. She was respectable now, or at least trying to be, and men were employers in a respectable sense. And one day, perhaps one of them—a nice village attorney, perhaps, or merchant or gentleman farmer—would be a possible husband. A source of that comfortable family life her dream mother spoke of, and which still seemed like an impossible, improbable fantasy to Kate.

One thing she did know—that man would never be Mr. Lindley. He was a nobleman, the younger brother of an earl, and noblemen did not marry governesses. That knowledge gave her a sour pang, and the pleased glow of her flush faded from her cheeks.

"I am glad you like Mrs. Brown, Christina," Lady Darcy said, breaking her long silence at last. "I hope that she can help you. But for her to dine with us . . ."

Kate did not want to hear any more. If she did, her fragile courage would surely shred altogether and she would flee back up to her room—and then out to the moors and all the way back to London and Venice. She took a deep breath, straightened herself to her full if rather inconsiderable height, and knocked at the door.

She stepped back quickly, so as not to seem close enough to eavesdrop. She just came to a halt, her hands folded at her waist, when the door was opened by Mr. Lindley himself.

"Mrs. Brown!" he said, a warm smile of welcome spreading across his sensual lips. "I'm very glad you could join us."

Kate had to take another breath before she could answer. Even then, when she spoke it sounded as if she had run a mile. "Thank you for inviting me, Mr. Lindley. I hope I am not late."

"Not at all. Please, come in and let me introduce you to my mother."

He actually offered her his arm, as if she were a fine lady at a Carlton House ball, and led her into the drawing room. She slid her fingers over the soft superfine of his sleeve. Even under the lightness of her touch, she could tell that his arm was hard, firm with corded muscles. It confirmed the easy strength she had felt earlier when he had lifted her down from the carriage. He was no idle gentleman, playing at farmer, then—he actually did some sort of real work.

Odd. And also thrilling.

She was also whimsically glad that she had chosen to wear her dark blue silk with the fitted elbow-length sleeves and not one of the muslins, for his wine red coat was beautifully and stylishly cut, his waistcoat of a fine cream brocade. And his light brown hair, all windblown waves when they met on the moor, was tamed to a shining cap, glinting almost autumn-colored in the candlelight.

Working farmer, fine man of fashion—what other guises did he hide beneath those blue eyes?

But she had no time to ponder such fanciful notions now. Christina rose from her chair to give a shy smile, her long fingers toying with the pale green satin ribbons trimming her white muslin dress as if she was nervous, or just overcome with a ceaseless energy. Her attire sported no mud stains this evening, but her wild curls still flowed free, rebelling against a confining bandeau.

"Mrs. Brown!" she called out. "Please, sit down over here."

"*After* she meets Mother, Christina," her brother told her, with an indulgent smile. Christina sank back down onto her chair, and Mr. Lindley led Kate to where a lady sat next to the crackling fire.

It was obvious that she must be their mother. She had the same light brown hair, now partially silver, falling in short, fashionable curls from beneath her lace cap, the same aristocratic nose and blade-sharp cheekbones. Her eyes were green like Christina's, but they lacked her daughter's eyes' brightness and quality of darting enthusiasm. They were solemn, filled with a watchfulness, a serious intelligence.

She was *nothing* like Kate's mother's friends, women who had always made up Kate's world. Women who laughed and flirted merrily, waving their silk scarves and ostrich plumes, declaring how they *adored* everything—while their eyes were hard, and they just waited to gossip about their "dear friends" behind those friends' backs.

The Dowager Lady Darcy had a quiet propriety, a close watchfulness. Kate was doubly grateful now for her somber blue silk, her new, simple way of dressing her hair in a low knot at the nape of her neck. Surely it would take all the subterfuge of her respectable trappings to hide from this woman.

"Mother, this is Mrs. Kate Brown," Mr. Lindley said. "Mrs. Brown, my mother, the Dowager Lady Darcy."

Kate dropped into a neat curtsy, just the right depth to pay homage to Lady Darcy's station. All the infinite varieties of curtsies had been a very valuable part of her education. "How do you do, Lady Darcy?" she said quietly.

Lady Darcy inclined her head regally. "I am glad you are here, Mrs. Brown. I have great hopes that you can help my poor daughter." Christina gave a most inelegant snort and slumped down in her chair. "As you can see, you have your work cut out for you."

"I'm sure Mrs. Brown is more than up to the challenge, Mother," Mr. Lindley said. He gave Kate a surreptitious wink, a teasing gesture that made her long to break into laughter amid the heavy solemnity of this room. "She declared earlier that she could make our Christina into a Diamond."

"Indeed? A Diamond?" Lady Darcy arched one dark, delicately winged brow. "That I should be very grateful to see, Mrs. Brown."

Kate was saved from making a reply—and from ruing her earlier arrogant words!—when the drawing room door opened and a nursemaid in starched white cap and apron appeared. By the hand she held a tiny fairy-child, surely fresh from the depths of some enchanted forest.

It had to be little Miss Amelia, Michael Lindley's daughter. She didn't look a great deal like her father— her hair was sun gold where his was dark, and fell over her shoulders in a riot of ringlets. She was very small, even for her young age, and thin in her pale pink muslin dress. But her eyes were the same clear sky blue as his, large and luminous in her rounded, sweet face.

Kate smiled at her, hoping she seemed welcoming and

friendly. Miss Amelia hung back, one little hand tangled in her nurse's skirts. One long curl was twisted around her finger. Those blue eyes were wide and wary.

Kate had never been a woman who cooed over children. For one thing, she had not been much in their company. The few friends of her mother who *were* parents kept their offspring firmly out of sight. For another, children were simply not the most adept at conversation. They knew nothing of art or poetry, and usually had sticky little paws that stained silk skirts and broke jeweled necklaces. And the children usually sensed this awkwardness in her. Even the tiniest infants howled when placed near her.

Governess was perhaps not the best choice of vocation for her—Kate knew that very well. But she could do nothing else. She would not, *could* not, go back to the profession she was raised for. And she knew even less about cooking or cleaning than she did about children. And no position as lady's companion came open at the agency while she was in London. So governess it had to be, despite any qualms.

Yet right now, as she stared down at this quiet little girl, Kate wanted so very much for Amelia to like her.

"Amelia, dearest," Mr. Lindley said, his voice full of tenderness and care. He swept past Kate and knelt down beside the girl. Amelia smiled at him from behind her twisted hair.

"Now, rosebud," her father said gently but firmly as he reached up to take her hand in his and thus remove her hand from her hair. "You know you're not supposed to twist your hair anymore."

The girl nodded, her bright curls bouncing like happy little sunbeams.

"There is someone here for you to meet. Mrs. Brown, who has come all the way from London to be your governess. Remember?" Another nod. Mr. Lindley took her by the hand and led her over to where Kate stood, feeling as stiff and frozen as a Roman statue. "Mrs. Brown, may I present my daughter, Miss Amelia Lindley?"

"How do you do, Mrs. Brown?" the child spoke at last. Her voice was as delicate and otherwordly as the rest of her, gentle and quiet, touched with a slight lisp. She wouldn't look up, though; her gaze was firmly fastened to Kate's hem.

San Marco. This was really even more nerve-racking than meeting a prince or an archbishop. At least then Kate knew what to do. "How do you do, Miss Amelia?" she answered. She decided to learn from Mr. Lindley's example, and knelt down next to the girl, bringing their eyes on a level. "I understand that you like music."

That coaxed a spark of interest. Miss Amelia looked up at last, shyly meeting Kate's gaze. "Yes, Mrs. Brown. I'm learning to play the pianoforte."

"That is excellent, for I also love music very much. I see there is a pianoforte right over there. Perhaps you would be so kind as to play a song for me? I would enjoy that very much."

Amelia glanced up uncertainly at her father, who gave her a reassuring nod. "Of course, Mrs. Brown," she whispered. "I've just learned a new piece."

Kate followed the child over to the instrument, trying not to sigh aloud in relief. If she was concentrating on Miss Amelia's music, she wouldn't have to decide what to say just yet.

Especially to Mr. Lindley himself. Or *Michael,* as she couldn't help but think of him. He was indeed well named for the archangel.

As she helped the child arrange her sheet music, Kate took a surreptitious peek at the people still grouped by the fireplace. Lady Darcy had at last turned her cool scrutiny away, and was working on a piece of embroidery. Christina appeared to be thinking of something far away. Daydreaming about her plants, no doubt.

But Michael—ah, he still watched her, his eyes slightly narrowed, arms folded across his chest.

Their encounter on the moor had discomposed her, more than she liked to admit even to herself. All her life, she had been taught to read men's thoughts and

desires without revealing any of her own. But Michael
Lindley was unreadable. He looked like the veriest
Renaissance god, a man every woman would swoon
over, a man to whom all the pleasures of the world
were freely available. Yet he chose to be a gentleman
farmer, to live with his family in isolated Yorkshire.
He was not like the men who had flocked to her in
her old life. He was not like anyone she had ever
met before.

He was kind to her, and charming even, with an
easy manner. But there was something behind all that,
something buried in the depths of his eyes, shadowed
and hidden. Michael Lindley was a mystery. And Kate
hated mysteries, except for her own.

She also hated the way she felt when he watched
her. No—*hated* was the wrong word. She felt flustered,
flushed, unsure, and very young. She felt like all her
careful, practical poise was slipping out of her control,
leaving her awkward, unprotected.

He saw too much. Could he see through her
flimsy disguise?

Kate just couldn't let that happen. She *wouldn't*.
She already liked this strange, cold, ancient house. She
liked Lady Christina, and this golden little elf-child
next to her. She didn't want to leave them yet.

She settled beside Amelia on the bench, listening
to the child's surprisingly competent rendition of "Für
Elise." She focused entirely on the music, but was still
fully aware of the instant when Michael turned his
regard away from her. The warm, sunny tingle at the
nape of her neck faded, leaving only the marble chill
of the air.

Kate took a breath in relief. But nothing could quell
the strange, brief pang of disappointment.

This was Michael's favorite time of day.

Dinner was over, the ladies were retired to their
chambers, and Amelia was safely tucked up in bed.
The house was quiet, like a fire banked down to slumber again until the morning. His work was done for

the day; there were no servants or tenants needing to meet with him, no fields to be inspected or quarrels between Christina and their mother to be settled.

He liked to come out to the terrace off of the back of the house, even on cool nights like this one. He could look out over the gardens, all sculpted shadows beneath the moon, and just breathe in the silence. It reminded him of just why he had come to this land— so far from his old wild London life—in the first place. Why he stayed here, watching the years wax and wane. It was the peace.

Sometimes, it felt almost as if Caroline were next to him in the darkness, a ghostly wisp of golden hair and gentle smiles. He would talk to her in his mind, telling her of how beautiful their daughter was. Of how sorry his heart remained for all he had put her through in their too-short marriage—always sorry.

Tonight, though, his wife's pale spirit was nowhere to be found. His mind was filled with the dark, rose-scented presence of Mrs. Kate Brown.

Michael reached for the snifter of brandy resting on the stone balustrade and took a deep, bracing swallow of the amber liquid. It was smooth and warm, with a sharp bite underneath, but it did nothing to erase the images in his mind. Mrs. Brown, solemn and attentive as she listened to Amelia at the pianoforte and asked his daughter questions about her music. Mrs. Brown laughing, her too-serious face momentarily young and radiant as she chuckled at one of Christina's jests. The way Mrs. Brown gave a quick, trembling start, like a wary, exotic bird when his hand accidentally brushed her arm at the dinner table. Mrs. Brown's dark eyes gone suddenly sad and very faraway as she stared into the fire during after-dinner tea.

She was a very intriguing woman—there was no doubt about *that*. And it wasn't just her beauty, which she tried to hide with plain gowns and severe coiffures, or her lilting, musical accent. Her clear eyes and smooth, fair skin said she was very young, perhaps not even as old as the twenty-two she claimed with the agency. But she seemed far too unhappy, almost melancholy, for a young lady whose life lay before her in all its possibilities. It was almost as if she was afraid to smile, to laugh—afraid to be close to him.

Michael took another swallow of his brandy, turning the crystal snifter in his hand as he considered the enigma of Mrs. Brown. Perhaps she was simply afraid of him because of his scars and limp. Some young ladies were—he was resigned to that by now. But that didn't seem to be the problem with Mrs. Brown. She *would* look at him directly, just not very often, and there was the mark on her own face. No, she seemed leery of all the world, on edge somehow. And sad. So sad.

Was it the loss of her husband, Mr. Brown—whoever *he* had been? Had she loved him and relied on him so very much that his death made her suspicious of all the world and everyone in it?

Somehow the thought of her deep love for the mysterious Mr. Brown stirred the embers of a forgotten temper deep inside Michael. His fingers curled tightly about the snifter, until the thick crystal creaked. Mr. Brown was surely *not* a good husband. He left his young wife alone in the world with nothing, forcing her to make her living as a governess.

Not that *he* should throw any stones about being a bad husband, Michael reflected bitterly. He had been the worst of the lot, marrying a lady of Caroline's sweetness and then leading her a merry dance into doom.

But whatever it was that etched such melancholy over Mrs. Brown's beautiful face, he wanted to erase it. To somehow make things better, as once he had made them so much worse. He wanted to make Mrs. Brown's sadness vanish, to show her how much life could still offer her.

Once, he could have. He could have showered her with jewels far finer than her mysterious, hidden brooch, diamonds and satin gowns, roses and houses and carriages. Not now. Now he was a most respectable gentleman, with an estate and a family and a position in the neighborhood. And she was his governess. His *respectable* governess.

The governess who flinched with surprise when his hand brushed her arm. His enigma of a governess, who hid a sapphire brooch among her plain garments.

Michael drank down the last of his brandy. A shadow drifted over the moon, reminding him of how late it was. He should be thinking of retiring. It promised to be a busy day tomorrow, as every day was at Thorn Hill, especially in the spring.

But as the shadow moved away from the silvery greenish moonlight, his attention was caught by a movement in the garden below. Someone strolled along the narrow paths between the flower beds, drifting ghostlike in the night.

Christina? It would be just like her to slip out of her chamber in the middle of the night to muck about in the gardens. This figure wasn't digging, though, just walking. And on the breeze, he heard a snatch of an Italian song.

"Tra le braccia, lo serra e lungamente, lo bacia in bocca."

The mezzo-soprano tones were soft and sweet, plaintive, as alluring as a sea siren's call. *Kate Brown.* It had to be. Wandering all alone in the night, singing as if to summon the spirits.

He really should just go inside the house, Michael mused. Leave her to whatever thoughts she nursed in her nocturnal perambulations. It wasn't his place, or his nature, to intrude on her, despite his urges to erase all her sadness. He knew all too well that some sorrows should be left between one person and the moon. Some hurts were too deep to share.

But Caroline's ghost felt very far away tonight, and his own heart was lonely. And he had never been good at resisting the siren's song. He abandoned his empty snifter on the balustrade and strode down the steps into the garden.

Chapter Five

*K*ate hummed a soft tune as she made her way along the twists and turns of the garden path. It was a song she had heard so many times, soaring to the frescoed ceiling of La Fenice, a lament on lost love, tragic longing, physical desire.

She *had* no lost love, of course. Yet somehow the song echoed to something in her heart this night—some longing, some emptiness she couldn't explain. She didn't want her old life, her old ways back. That was finished. But what would replace those familiar plans? She was adrift here in this strange place. She was neither Katerina Bruni nor Kate Brown.

She paused at the turning of the pathway, next to a stone goddess, and gave a deep sigh as she looked around her. It *was* a lovely place to be lost, though, a beautiful, clear night with a shimmering moon. And she liked this garden at Thorn Hill. The gardens in Italy were beautiful but so very different, carefully manicured, not a stone or a blade of grass out of place. Here, flowers tumbled together, clustered around statues and sundials and spilling over their borders onto the paths. They smelled sweet in the night air, like fresh-turned earth and rainy new greenery. Real and honest and true.

As *she* wanted so much to be herself. "Nothing about me is honest or true," she whispered, running her fingertips over a tangled shrub.

She turned around to stare up at the darkened house. It was not a pretty place. Like the garden, it had a comfortable wildness, a welcoming laziness, that was so unlike anything she had seen before. But Kate liked it, more than she could say. She liked the comfort of the rambling old dwelling, the reality of it. There was no artifice there. And she liked pretty little Miss Amelia and forthright Lady Christina. She liked their sense of family.

No, she didn't just *like* the people or their house. She *lusted* for them, for what they represented. Her whole life had been built on artifice, on deceit. On a glittering glamour that was as deceptive as the pylons Venice was built on.

Thorn Hill was real. It was a place where she could be herself—if only she knew what that was.

And only if they *never* found out about Katerina Bruni. Especially Michael Lindley himself.

Kate frowned as she thought of him, her fingers closing on the shrub leaves until the sharp edges pricked at her tender skin. He had smiled at her so often during that dinner, treated her with politeness and respect, asking her questions about her journey from London, her plans for the schoolroom and lessons. He deftly kept his mother from grilling her. His glances *were* admiring as he looked at her—as hers probably were to him. But they were not lascivious or speculative. He didn't grab at her when she walked by or grope at her beneath the table.

It was the first time since she was thirteen years old that a man had looked at her without obviously gauging her price, and she treasured that. Her heart soaked it in like a rosy balm.

That didn't negate the fact that when she studied him so secretly over the dinner table she longed to know what his sensual lips tasted like. Or what the waves of his light brown hair would feel like beneath her searching fingers. Would he be passionate and fiery as a lover, or gentle and tender?

Kate laughed aloud now as she thought of it. *That* was the Katerina Bruni part of her, but here at Thorn Hill even that section of her soul was different. She fantasized these things because Michael was handsome and charming and she rather liked him, not because he was rich and could "help" her obtain silks and emeralds. Her thoughts were secret, all for her.

A schoolgirl infatuation, for a woman who never could be an innocent schoolgirl.

It was unexpectedly sweet, and made her laugh again. "Please," she prayed in a whisper. "Please let me stay here at Thorn Hill. Just for a while."

Then, because her heart was suddenly full of the giddiness of her new life, she spun about in a circle, her somber blue skirts sweeping the flowers. *"Tra le braccia lo serra,"* she sang out, the song now shed of its sadness and leaving only the love.

Her little aria ended on an ungraceful squawk as applause suddenly filled the moonlit air. She lurched to a halt, staring appalled at Michael Lindley.

He had appeared seemingly out of nowhere, materializing from the garden shadows into a patch of starlight. He clapped on, a smile spreading across those lips she sang about. That grin brought out a small, enticing dimple set deep in his unscarred cheek.

"Oh!" Kate gasped, falling back a step. Her heart skipped a beat in shock, and even a quick jolt of fright. She was here all alone in the nighttime, and she had been cornered in dark corridors by gentlemen more than once. A jaunty word and a quick shove had gotten her out of those situations in the past, but it was not a circumstance she cared to repeat.

Especially not with a man she had just been so innocently giggling about.

Kate backed up until she felt the sharp marble edge of the sundial against her hips. She reached behind her to feel the cold security of the stone under her grip.

But Michael made no move to grab her or even touch her. "That is a beautiful song, Mrs. Brown," he said softly. "What are the words?"

Kate felt her cheeks prickle with a blush at the question. "Er—*tra le braccia, lo serra e lungamente, lo bacia in bocca.*"

"And what does it mean? My Italian is so sketchy."

It truly meant "Thereat she takes him by the chin and slowly kisses him on the mouth." But Kate would not say that aloud. "It means a kiss for the loved one—or something like that."

He nodded, seemingly satisfied, yet he still watched her closely. Did her silly blush show? Surely not—it was too dark. Perhaps she was doing something improper in being out here alone so late.

She tugged her shawl closer about her shoulders. "I am sorry to be wandering around your garden at such a late hour, Mr. Lindley. I just could not sleep, and needed some air. . . ."

He waved away her halting apology. "Please, Mrs. Brown, you may walk in the gardens anytime you feel the inclination. I hope you come to consider Thorn Hill your home."

Her *home*? Kate glanced at the quiet house. If only she could. But homes could so swiftly be snatched away, in the crash of a wave.

"Thank you, Mr. Lindley," she answered. "I am glad to be here. Your daughter is a joy, and I enjoy talking with your sister. They will be very easy to teach, I'm sure."

He gave a wry laugh, deepening that dimple. "I hope you won't live to rue those words, Mrs. Brown. Christina has a mind of her own, and Amelia may *look* like a tiny cherub, but I fear she inherited a measure of her father's stubbornness along with her mother's sweetness and beauty."

Her mother? It was strange, Kate thought, how she had never considered the reality of his late wife before. As if Miss Amelia sprang from the sea, a tiny Aphrodite born of waves and foam. But his wife *had* been a real woman, a flesh and blood creature who shared this man's life and bed, bore him a perfect fairy-child.

She must have been beautiful indeed. Beautiful and—what had he said?—*sweet*. A strange jealousy twisted at Kate's heart.

It was so absurd to envy a dead woman.

"I am sure Lady Christina, Miss Amelia, and I will rub along well, Mr. Lindley," she answered.

"I very much hope so. I wouldn't relish another governess search." He shifted on his feet, casting a long, rippling shadow on the gravel. "May I join you on the rest of your walk, Mrs. Brown? I, too, appreciate a turn in the fresh air before I retire."

"Of course," Kate said readily, though in truth she wanted to flee. Only in solitude was there true safety.

She turned back onto the path, and only as he came up to her side did she notice he used a walking stick tonight. The large piece of amber set in its head glinted in the moonlight.

She stifled a start of surprise, but he must have noticed it anyway, for his smile faded and his gaze shifted away from her. "I was in a carriage accident many years ago," he said briefly.

"Oh!" Kate cried, a crest of quick sympathy rising in her. "Does it still pain you?"

"Not at all, Mrs. Brown. I just have some small aches once in a while, especially in the evenings."

She nodded. "I was also in an accident, a boating accident. In Italy."

They fell into a heavy silence as they walked, the only sound the light crunch of their footsteps on the gravel, the tap of his stick. Kate wasn't sure what to say. She could never reveal the sordid details of that terrible day, and she sensed that he did not wish to talk of his own troubles. But still she ached for him, and for herself. Such memories could never be entirely in the past.

Only as they turned onto a new path, toward the house, did he speak.

"Has it been many years since you left Italy?" he asked, his tone very casual.

Kate tore herself away from the painful musings on loss and injury, and tried to recall the story she had so carefully concocted in her London room. "Yes, a long time. Mr. Brown was a soldier. I met him when he came to Italy after the war. When we married, I came to England with him." She was amazed at how easily the tale fell from her lips now. Amazed, and a bit scared.

"And when he died you did not care to go back to Italy?"

"No. I have no family there now. I would rather make my life here."

"Where did you live in Italy? Your accent is not of the countryside there."

Her accent? Kate glanced at him sharply, but he just gave her a bland smile. Obviously, he was not as ignorant of foreign lands as most of his countrymen. No doubt he even knew perfectly well what the words of her song had meant. She would have to increase her guard with him, not be beguiled by dark hair and dimples. "I am from Venice."

"Indeed? I have a friend who owns a house in Venice. His wife is an artist and prefers the light of Italy to the gloom of England. Sir Nicholas Hollingsworth is his name."

"Hollingsworth? Elizabeth Hollingsworth?" Kate said, startled into indiscretion after she had just resolved to be careful.

"Why, yes. Do you know them?"

Know them? Their palazzo was not far from her mother's; Elizabeth Hollingsworth had painted the portrait of Lucrezia Bruni. Kate's hands shook where they clutched at her shawl. "I—no, not personally. I have heard of her. I enjoy art, and she is quite well-known."

"Indeed she is," he agreed. "You must meet her one day, Mrs. Brown."

"Meet? Do they come often to Thorn Hill, Mr. Lindley?"

"I don't think they have *ever* been here," he said, and Kate's nerves abated just a tiny bit. "But perhaps I could lure them with the news that an appreciator of art is now in residence."

"Oh, no, Mr. Lindley," Kate said quickly. "Please

do not trouble them on my account. I'm sure their lives must be very busy."

"I'm sure you're right. Yorkshire would be too quiet for Nick and Lizzie," he answered. They had reached the house, the foot of the stone steps leading up to the terrace. "But not, I hope, for you, Mrs. Brown."

"No. I love the quiet." Kate studied him, his face half in shadows. A little half smile lingered, but his expression was unreadable. "Thank you for our walk, Mr. Lindley. Good night."

"Thank *you,* Mrs. Brown. I enjoyed our discussion." Had he believed all her answers during that "discussion"? She couldn't tell—his tone was all politeness. "My mother will help you set up your schoolroom tomorrow. Just let her know if there is anything you need."

"I will. Thank you."

"Then good night, Mrs. Brown."

Kate hurried up the steps and through the partially open glass doors into the house. She tried her hardest not to run, even though her feet told her to do so. Only when she was in the corridor leading to her chamber did she give them free flight.

Please, she thought, repeating her earlier plea. *Please let me stay here.*

She was hiding something.

Michael watched Kate Brown as she hurried along the terrace until her slim figure slipped through the doors and disappeared from view. Only the faintest hint of her rose perfume still hung in the crisp air, proving that she had been there at all.

Her words, her demeanor, were all that was proper. Her poise was admirable, something he was sure his mother hoped could be passed to Christina. But Mrs. Brown obviously did not care to answer questions about herself, her own life, her past.

It could just be modesty, of course. Yet in Michael's London life, where he had wide acquaintance with the fairer sex, he seldom met a female who did not care to speak of herself at great length.

Michael enjoyed mysteries, puzzles, especially when they were connected with a beautiful lady. But his old life, where he could indulge such intrigues, was long gone. He had his family's well-being to think of now.

He would just have to keep a close watch on Mrs. Brown, he thought as he slowly climbed the terrace steps to find the house and his rest. And *that* was a task he could look forward to with a great deal of anticipation.

He grinned at that thought. Life at Thorn Hill had not held such intrigue in a very long time indeed.

Chapter Six

"*Sancta Maria Mater Dei, ora pro nobis . . .*"
He heard the soft voice, floating from somewhere above him, softly, as if in yet another fever
dream. The click of rosary beads, the gentle rustle of
cloth. He sucked in a breath, and the scent of lavender
overlaying some medicinal tang seared his lungs. It
hurt just to breathe, to move at all.

How long had he been like this? An eternity? Was
this the afterlife, then?

It was nothing like he had expected. He had not
often contemplated Providence in his earthly life, but
he did have some vague thoughts that the Vikings had
the right of it. A mead hall, with endless streams of
alcohol and beautiful Rhine maidens to fulfill his
every wish.

Beautiful, raven-haired maidens, with skin like Dev-
onshire cream and swanlike necks. With soft laughter,
and a voice like a Renaissance princess. *That* would
be paradise. Not this aura of medicine, this feel of
cold bed linens under his hands.

He could see the woman in his mind, see her so
very clearly. She was very young, but her dark eyes
held such depths of wisdom, such pools of knowingness and delicate humor. She leaned toward him
with her willowy grace, and said . . .

"*Et in hora mortis nostrae.* Amen."

No! Not that. She would never say that to him. His
princess was all poetry and beauty, not chill prayers.

Katerina, he thought frantically. Yes, that was her

name. Katerina. Like the Renaissance princess he knew her to be, full of mystery and culture and serenity as she glided along the corridors of her palazzo, velvet skirts trailing. She would speak of art and music and the riches of ancient kings, not cold prayers.

He had to see her, to restore her to her place as his princess, his Beatrice, his Laura. His alone.

"Katerina," he gasped aloud. His eyes flew open, and he glanced around frantically. If this was indeed heaven, it was a poor excuse for a paradise. Only bare, whitewashed walls and a sloping ceiling, a floor of pale ocher tiles. An elaborate crucifix hung on the wall just opposite. There were white screens set up on either side of the narrow bed he lay on, and a table next to him held a pottery pitcher and cup, a cluster of glass bottles.

On his other side sat a woman, but not his black-haired princess. This was a nun, her round, plump face framed by a starched black-and-white veil. Her short figure was swathed in black wool, and a rosary of glistening amber and topaz beads threaded through her fingers.

She stared at him with wide brown eyes, her mouth a round *o* of surprise. The clicking and the soft monotony of her words were still.

"Signore!" she whispered. "You are awake. Our Lady be praised!"

He turned his head on the pillow, and tried to move himself into a sitting position. His bones and muscles ached, and seemed turned to useless porridgelike mush. It was impossible agony even to shift. He cried out in raw agony, frustration.

The nun leaped up from her seat and slid her hands beneath him, helping him to sit up against the pillows with practiced efficiency. She smelled of clean lavender and fresh water, and her habit was rough on his skin. Not like the rose-scented silken softness of his dream princess.

"Is this heaven, then?" he whispered hoarsely. "Am I dead?"

The sister chuckled as she smoothed the sheets over him. "Not quite, signore. But this *is* the Convent of the Queen of Heaven. And it was a very close thing. Fra Fillipo administered the last rites to you twice. I'm very glad to see you awake at long last."

She poured out a cup of water and held it to his lips. Only then did he realize how deeply parched he was. He drained the cup, the liquid like a healing miracle to his shriveled throat.

"More," he croaked when it was gone, but she shook her head.

"Slowly at first," she said, replacing the cup on the table and returning to her chair. She took up her abandoned beads and tucked them neatly into her rope belt.

He forced down a sudden rush of hot anger that she dared refuse him. She was a *nun*—he shouldn't strike her. Besides, he was so weak he couldn't kick a kitten. He had to regain his strength, to save it for what was truly important. Finding his princess, wherever she was.

"How long have I been here?" he asked tightly.

"Oh, a very long time. Several months."

"Months!"

She nodded serenely. "You washed ashore on a beach not far from here, after a great and sudden storm. The men who found you brought you here to us, for we are a nursing order. Do you remember any of this, signore?"

He squeezed his eyes tightly shut, struggling to find images that would bring her words to life, that would tell him how he came to be here in this damnably weak position. But there was nothing. No memory of the ocean, of coming here to this place of cold prayer and piety. He could only remember *her*, her soft touch on his hand, her dark eyes, whose gaze told him that they belonged together, that they had loved in many lifetimes before and would again.

"No," he muttered. "I don't remember."

"Oh," the sister clucked sympathetically. "That is

hard, I know, but it often happens that way with such dire injuries. The memories will return soon. In the meantime, you must rest." She reached out to smooth the bedclothes again, drawing a woolen blanket over his shoulders. "I am Sister Maria Clare, by the way. Do you even remember your own name, signore?"

He *did* remember that, he found. It was balanced on the tip of his tongue. "Julian," he answered. "I am Sir Julian Kirkwood."

Chapter Seven

*T*he schoolroom was not large, but it was very pleasant, Kate thought as she studied the space. It was no cramped attic, lightless and chilly. Several tall windows, draped in pale green, let in the daylight, and a fire burned cheerfully in the polished grate, chasing a lingering morning draft from the corners. The room had obviously once been a sitting room, attached to Kate's chamber, but now settees and armchairs were moved out and neat desks, stools, and cushioned wooden seats were brought in. Bookshelves lined the walls, and a comfortable chair was placed next to the fire with an embroidery frame and a small worktable within easy reach.

Yes, it *was* a nice space. Cozy, clean, and, best of all, quiet. Kate let the blessed silence soak into her conscience. This was a room that could be her own—hers and the girls she was to teach. The past, the future, they were both far away in here. Only the present mattered.

She sank down onto the soft seat by the fire, running her fingertips over the plush green velvet upholstery as she remembered the morning just past. When she first awoke in her new bed, she couldn't shake off a sense of confusion, disorientation. Her sleep was so full of dreams, strange visions of the sea, of gardens, of crazed sheep chasing her across gray landscapes. They cast their sticky-cobweb spell over her even when she opened her eyes, and for an instant she imagined she was back in Venice.

Where is Bianca with my chocolate? she had thought irritably, pulling the bedclothes up over her head.

But the sheets were not her own blue, mono-grammed silk, and there were no gondolier songs or slapping of water outside her window. And she re-membered. Venice was gone. She was in Yorkshire, at a house called Thorn Hill. The home of the archan-gel Michael.

As she burrowed deeper under the bedclothes, she recalled everything—especially their walk in the gar-den, all alone in the moonlight. The way he watched her, as if he could discover all her secrets just by studying her face. The way he smiled, with those be-guiling, unexpected dimples. How warm and strong his touch was when his hand lightly brushed her arm as they walked.

It was dizzying, almost like another dream. Yet it was real; *he* was real—not like the insane sheep she fled in her sleep.

Sheep might actually be preferable.

Kate heard a click at the latch of her bedroom door then, and pulled the bedclothes away from her face to see a young, freckle-faced maid coming into the chamber bearing a tray of rolls and tea. All she could think was praise be to San Marco that she wouldn't have to face the Lindley family over the breakfast table! She would have a few more hours to compose herself.

"Good morning, miss," the maid greeted cheerfully when she saw that Kate was awake. She put the tray down on the bedside table and hurried over to open up the window draperies. The light that poured in was weak and pale, but not gray as it was yesterday. "My name is Sarah, and Mrs. Jenkins said I was to bring you breakfast, and see if you need any help this morning."

"Mrs. Jenkins?" Kate said stupidly. The rigid old housekeeper had actually sent someone up to help *her,* the governess?

Odd. Someone, probably Lady Darcy, must have ordered her to do it.

"Yes, Mrs. Jenkins, the housekeeper," Sarah said. She poured out a steaming cup of brown, bracing-looking tea and passed it to Kate. "You met her yesterday, miss." Sarah suddenly giggled, and clapped her hand to her mouth. "Oh, no! You're *not* a miss, are you? You're a missus. Mrs. Brown. I beg your pardon."

"That's quite all right," Kate answered, bemused. She had never met a young housemaid quite so giggly before. Or so fidgety. Sarah twitched at her apron, staring around at the room.

"Here, Mrs. Brown, have a roll," Sarah said, plopping the warm, yeasty bread onto a plate. "Cook just made them—they're piping hot."

"Thank you," Kate murmured. She took a nibble of the proffered roll, and it was indeed delicious, studded with currants and almond slivers. So far, every detail of this house was perfect. It was so much more than she surely deserved. A lovely room, welcoming people, a perfect currant roll—and all the time she was lying to them. Selfishly grasping at all they offered when she had nothing to give in return.

The thought made the delicious bread turn to cold ash on her tongue. She put it back on the plate and took a long gulp of tea.

"Hot water for washing is on the way," Sarah said, oblivious to Kate's sudden fit of conscience. "Can I do anything else for you, Mrs. Brown? I'm very good with hair. I dress Lady Christina's."

Kate remembered Christina's wild mane of tangled curls and had to smile. That wasn't much of a boast. "Thank you, Sarah, but my hair is fairly easy for me to dress myself."

Sarah obviously didn't want to leave, though. She kept on plucking at her apron, her gaze darting around the room. Perhaps she had an unpleasant task waiting for her, or maybe she was just curious about a newcomer to the household. Either way, Kate took pity

on her. She pushed back the blankets, and as she
swung her legs out of bed and reached for her dressing
gown she said, "Perhaps you would be so kind as to
help me brush it, though, Sarah. As you can see, I
forgot to braid it last night before I retired, and now
it is quite a mess."

Sarah's eyes lit up. "Oh, yes! Of course, Mrs.
Brown."

Kate settled at the dressing table and handed the
maid her brush. As Sarah dragged the bristles rhyth-
mically through the black strands, surprisingly gentle
as she detangled the knots, Kate's eyes slowly drifted
shut. She had forgotten how soothing and delicious
such a simple thing as hair brushing could be. It felt
sinfully luxurious.

"So, you are from Italy, Mrs. Brown?" Sarah said,
smoothing Kate's hair over her shoulders. She pronounced it *Eye-taly*.

Kate gave a half smile without opening her eyes.
The maid had fidgeted from curiosity, then. "Yes.
From Venice."

"Mr. Lindley has been to Italy. His library is ever
so full of strange things he got there."

"Strange things?"

"Paintings of funny-looking people, and statues with
no clothes on," Sarah said in a shocked whisper. "And
glass that's ever so pretty. Blue and red—all colors."

"Murano glass," Kate whispered. She could see it
behind her closed eyes, shimmering glass in deep jewel
colors, sapphire, ruby, amethyst. In fanciful shapes of
flowers and birds and medieval unicorns. In her mind,
she walked in the bright sun of that island of glass,
the light warm on her hair, casting sparks from the
colored facets around her.

A hand appeared in front of her imagined gaze,
long, brown, strong fingers holding a red glass rose.
Kate reached out for the treasure, turning to see who
offered it. . . .

". . . do they have those everywhere in Eye-taly,
Mrs. Brown?"

And the vision was gone, burst like an iridescent bubble at the sound of the maid's voice. Murano—and the man with the rose—utterly vanished.

Kate's eyes flew open. "I beg your pardon, Sarah. I fear I was woolgathering."

Sarah giggled again. "I just asked if Eye-taly was full of strange paintings, like the ones Mr. Lindley has. Ladies in the woods wearing almost nothing, or people in funny hats."

"There is much art everywhere in Italy, to be sure. I would have to see those paintings to know if there were ones like them to be seen where I lived."

"All of Mr. Lindley's Eye-talian things are in the library, Mrs. Brown. I get to dust in there sometimes. It's like a fairyland, it is." Sarah gave a last pat to Kate's hair and stood back with a satisfied smile. "There, now! What do you think?"

Kate stared into the mirror and saw distractedly that Sarah had braided and twisted her hair into a neat crown atop her head. It was quite nice, but still her mind was far away, locked into speculation over the "fairyland" of Michael Lindley's library.

She positively ached to see it, yet knew there was no possibility. She could hardly sneak in there and pretend to be dusting, like Sarah.

"It looks lovely," Kate said automatically. "Thank you, Sarah."

Sarah beamed, and twitched at her apron again. "You have lovely hair, Mrs. Brown. Not like Lady Christina's! So curly, hers is. It tangles up again as soon as it's brushed."

Kate opened her mouth with intentions of asking Sarah more about the Italian treasures in the library, but she had no chance. The door opened again, to admit two maids bearing steaming pitchers of water and neatly folded towels. Behind them marched the stern Mrs. Jenkins, her black dress rustling sharply and her gimlet eyes taking in every detail in the room. Sarah fled before the housekeeper's stare, and Mrs.

Jenkins gave Kate her orders for the day—to set the schoolroom in order.

That put an end to any idle moments. Kate quickly dressed, and spent the rest of the morning arranging this cozy space, unpacking crates of books and inventorying supplies of paper, ink, and slates. She hadn't thought at all about Murano glass, Italian paintings, and walks with attractive men in the moonlight.

Almost.

She opened her eyes now, and stared out at the schoolroom. It was her domain, all neat and tidy and orderly. The green draperies and cushions gave it a fresh, springtime feeling. But a painting would be so nice over the fireplace. An *Italian* painting, perhaps?

A knock echoed at the door, and Kate sighed. Why were her reveries always interrupted by knocks in this house? But then, she reminded herself, this wasn't *her* house. She was only here on sufferance.

"Come in," she called, and sat up straight in her chair, smoothing down her gray muslin skirts.

Lady Christina came into the room, smiling shyly. She held a pile of books in her arms, and Kate noticed that though Christina wasn't wearing a grubby apron, there was a strange blue green stain on her white sleeve. Her hair fell in a thick, somewhat tidy braid down her back.

"Good morning, Mrs. Brown," she said, depositing the books on one of the desks.

"Good morning, Lady Christina," Kate answered brightly. She was unreasonably relieved to see the girl, and *not* Lady Darcy or Mrs. Jenkins. "You are looking very well this morning."

"So are you. And so is this room!" Christina turned in a wide circle, taking in all the arrangements. "It was just being used for storage. Michael brought back so much rubbish from the Continent when he was younger that there was no place to put it all. I thought all the trunks and cases could never be cleared out, but now look how neat it is."

"I think it will be a very comfortable space for our lessons," said Kate. "There is even some room over there for dancing."

Some of Christina's coltish enthusiasm dimmed. "Indeed," she answered. "Speaking of lessons, Mother sent these books up. She thought they might be useful. She planned to bring them herself, but then Lady Ross and one of her daughters unexpectedly came to call. Amelia is down there with them."

Kate got up from her chair and went to inspect the volumes. No wonder Christina wasn't enthusiastic about them—*A Lady's Rules for Proper Behavior, Etiquette for Every Occasion,* tomes on housekeeping, flower arranging, French verbs. "Is that usual in this neighborhood for ladies to pay unexpected calls?"

"Not at all," Christina said. She drifted over to one of the windows and pushed open the casement to let the breeze pull at her braid. "But Lady Ross said there was a situation at the Ladies' Society that she absolutely *must* speak to Mother about immediately. If you ask me, she just wanted to bring her daughter Emmeline here to parade her in front of Michael yet again."

Parade her in front of Michael? An image sprang up in Kate's mind, of a line of young blond misses in white cantering up and down before Michael Lindley's sky-blue gaze. The book she held slipped from her hands, crashing to the desk.

Christina glanced back with a puzzled frown. "Are you all right, Mrs. Brown?"

Kate gave a little laugh. "Oh, yes. I dropped the book. How very clumsy of me."

Christina nodded, and turned her attention back to the scenery outside the window.

Kate took the volumes and busied herself with arranging them on the shelves. She ought to let the matter drop, of course, but some imp of mischief wouldn't let her. She just *had* to know more—only because Mr. Lindley was her employer, of course, and his personal situation could affect her position at Thorn Hill. That was all. "Is this Miss Ross your brother's betrothed, then, Lady Christina?"

Christina gave a very unladylike snort. "She wishes she was! Emmeline Ross is here at Thorn Hill every chance she gets, tossing her curls around and giggling like a bedlamite. She nearly took his eye out with her fan at the last assembly, the way she was waving it around and crying, 'Oh, la, sir!' I'm sure she thought she was Marie Antoinette, flirting with all the gallants at Versailles."

Christina did such a marvelous job of batting her eyelashes and pursing her lips that Kate had to laugh, despite her strange jealous pangs. So Emmeline Ross liked to *flirt* with Mr. Lindley, did she? Well, it sounded as if she did it very ill indeed.

"So, no, Mrs. Brown," Christina continued, giving her a curious glance. She probably wondered at Kate's question. "My brother would never wed such a silly cabbagehead as Emmeline Ross, as much as she would like that. All the single ladies of the neighborhood have their caps set for Michael."

Well, Kate thought, she could hardly blame them. "And does he favor any of them in particular?" she said, her voice carefully pitched to reveal only careless interest, mild gossip.

"Not Michael. He has scarce looked at another lady since Caroline, my sister-in-law, died. Though there *are* rumors about Becky—" Christina broke off with a laugh. "Oh, but that's not important. I'm not supposed to listen to the gossip of the farmworkers, you know."

Kate stared at her, but Christina wouldn't meet her gaze now. *Rumors? Who is Becky?* her mind screamed impatiently. *Tell me!*

It was obvious that Christina had said all she was going to on the subject. "It's such a beautiful day, Mrs. Brown," she said. "We shouldn't spend it indoors, prattling away about nonsense. Let's go for a walk. I can show you some of the estate."

A walk would be very nice. Maybe the fresh air

would bring Kate to her senses. "That sounds very pleasant, Lady Christina. I'll just fetch my bonnet, then."

The next time Lady Christina suggested a walk, Kate thought as they clambered up the side of yet another steep hill, she would just sit down and refuse. The girl must be part mountain goat, with the way she scrambled nimbly over rocks and ditches. Her hair streamed in the wind as they navigated narrow, almost imperceptible pathways, and her brown woolen cloak billowed around her. She seemed a part of this land, as if she belonged there, as if she had sprung full-grown from the patches of heather and immediately begun to name all the plants around her.

Kate, on the other hand, had never so obviously been a creature of warmer skies and watery climes. She panted ungracefully as she stumbled in Christina's wake up another hill. Rough gorse caught at the hem of her pelisse, and the wind threatened to snatch away her bonnet. A stitch pierced at her side, and she rued the fact that she was in such ill shape. *Ladies* weren't meant to take exercise, of course; a calm stroll through a park or a lively quadrille was thought to be sufficient. But Yorkshire was *not* Venice, as was more than apparent, and the same rules could not apply.

Pampered princesses would not last long on the moors. Obviously, if she wanted to keep up with her new pupil, she would have to grow a tougher skin.

She laughed aloud to imagine what her mother might say about *that*.

Christina glanced back over her shoulder. "Did you see something funny, Mrs. Brown?"

"Oh, no," Kate answered, her voice labored and husky as her breath rasped in her lungs. "I just—just thought of something my mother once told me."

"Oh." Christina turned away, obviously unimpressed by anything a *mother* might say. But then her head whipped back around in Kate's direction, and her determined expression melted into one of concern.

"Are you quite well, Mrs. Brown? Your cheeks are very red. I'm walking too fast again—I always do that. Here, let's sit down for a bit."

"What a fine idea," Kate said, with a silent prayer of thanks to whoever might be the patron saint of poorly conditioned governesses. She perched on a low stone wall next to Christina, breathing slowly and carefully until the stitch subsided.

"I walk these hills every day," Christina said after a moment. Her voice was uncharacteristically subdued. "I'm so used to the pathways and hillsides that I forget not everyone is accustomed to them."

"It is very different from walking in the city," Kate agreed. "I see I shall have to buy new, sturdier boots soon." She held out one foot and ruefully examined her dainty half boot. The pale gray kid with ivory buttons had seemed so elegant in London; now it was scuffed and worn.

"You can borrow some of mine until then, though your foot is much smaller than mine," Christina offered. She pulled out two apples from the pockets of her cloak and held one out to Kate. "Tell me about London, Mrs. Brown. I mean, if you please. It must be a fascinating place."

"Have you never been there, Lady Christina?" Kate said. She bit into the apple, the taste of it crisp and sharp on her tongue. She hadn't realized how famished the walk had made her.

"Not since I was a child, and I saw little of it then. Just my nursery, and the park. Once, my father took me to the Tower, but that's all." Christina munched on her own apple, her sun-browned face wistful and very young-looking. "My father died when I was just eight, and we stayed in London for just a while longer, until Charles married Mary. Charles is my older brother, the earl."

Kate was oddly fascinated by this peek into another family's history. "Then what happened? Did the earl not want you living with him any longer?"

Christina shrugged. "Charles didn't mind. He's a

good enough sort, in his own way. But Mary is very grand, you see, and cutting a dash through Town would be difficult with a bossy mother-in-law and a little child dogging her steps. Mother and I would have moved to the dower house at Darcy Hall, but then Caroline died in that accident."

Caroline. The sweet beauty who bore Amelia. Michael Lindley's wife. The apple suddenly tasted a bit more sour than before. Kate tossed its remains away from her. "Your other sister-in-law?"

"Yes, and Michael was in a bad way then. He wanted to go away somewhere quiet, and he needed Mother to help him with Amelia. She was just a tiny baby then. So, then we came here."

A bad way. Wracked with grief for a lost love. Kate thought of scenes from operas, men half mad with anguish, clutching their lovers' bodies to them as they wailed out their sorrow to the heavens.

Such an informative day it had been, she thought. First the maid's confidences, now Christina's.

"And you have never been back to London?" Kate asked.

Christina shook her head. "Charles and Mary's life wouldn't suit me. I would never fit in there. But I think London itself must be marvelous!"

Kate smiled at her. "I thought you hated the idea of balls and routs."

"Oh, I certainly do!" Christina pulled a horrified face. "That's exactly why I wouldn't want to stay with Charles and Mary. Society is their whole existence. But London has bookshops and lending libraries. And museums, and lectures! I have heard that botanists come from all over Europe, even the Indies and America, to present their work." She gave an utterly rapturous sigh, one an ordinary girl might have given over receiving vouchers to Almack's.

"Yes. There are museums," Kate murmured.

"It must be so absolutely splendid. Can you tell me about it, Mrs. Brown?"

Kate shook her head. "I fear I had no time to see

any museums or hear any lectures while I was there." In truth, she had seen only her room, the route she would walk to the agency, and the secondhand bookshop. "I heard that the British Museum is quite splendid, though. I'm sure you will see it when you go to Town for your Season, Lady Christina. The Elgin Marbles are all the rage."

Christina turned her face away, folding her arms across her stomach. All Kate could see was her wild banner of hair, the stiff set of her shoulders. "Mother says that when I make my bow I will have no time for foolishness such as lectures and botanical societies. She says that once I see how grand fine gowns and balls can be, I will forget my 'distractions.' "

Christina's voice was low and bitter, and Kate wasn't quite sure what to say in response. She wanted so much to reassure Christina, but then again she was hired to perpetuate just such ideas, was she not? To teach Christina poise and manners and grace, to lead her to forget her 'strange' pastimes.

She didn't have to say anything, though. Christina leaped abruptly to her feet and turned back to the path. "Shall we go on, Mrs. Brown? We can take a smoother way back home, if you like."

Kate could only follow. It seemed that their brief moment of incipient confidence was gone. "That would be nice."

They walked along, slower this time but in silence, until they came to a wider lane in a less wild-looking space. Cultivated fields spread on either side, enclosed by more of those low, dark gray stone walls. Neat fields of wheat, barley, and oilseed rape gave way to more flocks of those unnerving sheep, woolly groups that meandered together in placid formations. Kate watched them warily, in case they decided to rush at them en masse, but Christina didn't even seem to notice. She just strode along, deep in her own thoughts.

They crossed over a twisting river, climbing up the slope of a rounded wooden bridge. Kate paused to lean over and peer at the dancing water, so clear that she could almost see the rocky bed. The hazy sunlight cast glasslike shards on the eddying currents.

Christina leaned over, too, staring down as if to glimpse what Kate was so fascinated by. "This is the River Bain. It flows into the lake called Semerwater close by."

"It seems so peaceful," Kate murmured. "As calm as a Venice canal in winter."

Christina laughed. "Right now, it is! But I have seen it in storms, when it overflows its banks and even the hill sheep cower from it."

"Truly?" Kate murmured. "More like a canal during *acqua alta,* then."

"I can show you the lake one day," Christina offered. "It's a lovely walk up there. And there's even a legend associated with it."

"A legend?" Kate asked, intrigued. She always did enjoy a big romantic, operatic story, and this land obviously had the potential to be full of them. Perhaps it was not an accident she had landed here, after all. "Can you tell me?"

Christina nodded, and turned to continue their walk. As Kate followed, she listened to Christina's tale. "The old story tells of a city that lies beneath Semerwater. Long ago, there was a rich city, and a poor man with great spiritual powers came there. He searched in vain for food and shelter among all the grand mansions, but only a poor laborer took him in. The man stood by the laborer's tiny cottage high up on a hill, and cursed the city by saying, 'Semerwater rise, Semerwater sink, and swallow all the city save this little house.' And a great flood swallowed the city whole."

"An engulfed city? Like Atlantis?"

Christina shrugged. "I suppose so. Some of our tenants say they have seen things beneath the waters of the lake. But I have been there many times and all I've seen is mud."

Kate laughed. "Mud, eh? Well, I should like to see it nevertheless."

They climbed up to the top of yet another hill. Below them stretched another twisting pattern of low walls, a darker gray against the greenish gray of the landscape. But the low hum of the wind was broken by the rich rise and fall of masculine voices, the scrape of tools against stone. A group of farm laborers were mending a section of wall, calling to each other as they mortared and piled the dark stones taken from a big pile in a wagon.

Kate shielded her eyes against the pale glare of the sun to watch them. She certainly had a fresh respect for honest labor after her long odyssey over the hills today!

Then her breath sucked in on a harsh, shocked note as she realized that one of the men was *not* a common laborer. It was Mr. Lindley himself, hauling a stone into place. He had obviously been at the task for a long while, for he was stripped to his shirtsleeves. The soft muslin sleeves were pushed back over his forearms, the light glinting on the pale brown hair on the bronzed skin. The cloth clung damply to his back and shoulders, and there was the fine sheen of sweat on his brow. He lowered the stone into place and stepped back to wipe his sleeve over his forehead. His hair waved back onto his neck, a darker brown than usual with his sweat. There was no sign of his walking stick from the night before.

One of the men made some sort of jest, and Michael laughed heartily. His grin flashed white, like the pirate god she had first imagined him. He threw his head back, showing his strong, sun-browned throat, the barest hint of curling brown hair at the vee where the lacings of his shirt were loosened.

Kate stared at him, fascinated. The scene was quite unreal—she had never heard of a nobleman working in the fields before, laboring at mending fences. The elegant Sir Julian Kirkwood *never* would. Yet somehow Michael Lindley belonged here, in the cool, fresh air, the muscles of his strong shoulders straining at his thin shirt. Her fingers tingled to run through his disordered hair, to trail over those shoulders and that long back, feeling the muscles bunch and flex beneath her caress. . . .

She couldn't breathe. She had thought her attraction to him last night was a mere product of the enchantment of moonlit gardens, of having not been around attractive young men for many months. Still, she could not help but imagine what those strong hands would feel like against her own skin.

She was a fool. For here, in full daylight, his enchantment was even stronger.

Kate shook her head hard and looked away, back over her shoulder at the way they had come. Maybe she should go dunk her head in the obviously chilly waters of the Bain. Anything to insert some sense into her foolish, schoolgirl thoughts. "Maybe we should turn back," she said.

But Christina had already seen the men and was waving her hand over her head. "Michael!" she shouted. "Hello!"

Christina dashed off down the hill, giving Kate no choice but to follow.

"San Marco, give me strength," she muttered, trailing along in Christina's wake.

Michael lifted the heavy stone into place on the wall, his muscles burning and shifting with the effort. How he loved this! The honest sweat of real labor, the feel of the sun on his bare head, the talk and laughter of the men around him. Most gentlemen would never lower themselves to mending fences—he knew that very well; his old friends and his brother would fall down with shock if they could see him now. But Michael could not care one whit. It was at moments like this that he felt truly alive. Could truly forget.

After the accident, he had been so damnably weak, unable even to stand up from his bed and walk across the floor. Now he reveled in the feel of muscles and sinews that worked, that obeyed his commands and could actually lift stones and wield a scythe. The sweat that trickled in long rivulets down his spine was real and honestly come by.

And the hard labor drove away thoughts of Kate Brown. Almost.

Michael pushed the damp hair back from his brow and turned away to reach for a new stone. Last night, when they parted in the garden, he had gone up to his chamber as usual but could not sleep for hours. She was intriguing, a beautiful puzzle, a rose-scented conundrum. He wanted to talk to her, to coax the story of her life from her, to learn why her dark eyes held such sadness.

And he wanted to kiss her pink, lush mouth, to taste her, to feel her slim body under his hands, her satin hair clinging to his fingers. Would she sigh and melt into him, pulling him against her? Would she whisper enticing Italian love words?

Michael laughed at his own ridiculous fantasies, and lifted the stone high before crashing it into place. It was past time he made a visit to Becky at the Tudor Arms. She enjoyed an energetic romp, was always laughing and joking. She was buxom and red-haired, not slim and dark, but she held no secrets in her twinkling blue eyes. She was as uncomplicated as a summer stream. He liked Becky—yet somehow the thought of visiting her again left him strangely disappointed.

"Michael!" he heard someone shout. "Hello!"

He peered up, squinting against the light, and saw Christina dashing down the hill toward him. She wore no hat, of course, and her brown cloak billowed around her like a swallow's wings. He smiled at her, and waved.

Then he saw the woman who followed sedately behind his sister. *Mrs. Brown.*

She wore her gray pelisse again, and her blue bonnet. She kept glancing back over her shoulder, almost as if she wanted to flee. And he could hardly blame her. She had probably never expected to see her employer, an earl's son, working like a common laborer. She was a *lady*.

And he was a sweaty mess. Michael looked around for his coat, but it was draped over the side of the cart along with his neckcloth. Too far away to grab quickly—Christina and Mrs. Brown were nearer every second. He ran his fingers through his hair, pushing the damp waves back, and pulled the laces of his shirt together.

The man next to him, one of his tenants, Mr. Herrick, gave a low, admiring whistle. "Who is the beauty with Lady Christina?"

Michael shot him an irritated glance. He had the flashing, irrational thought that the man was lecherously gaping at Mrs. Brown. But Mr. Herrick's gaze held no disrespect, only admiration—which was only natural when a man beheld beauty like Kate Brown's.

And he had no right to be jealous of anything connected to her. No right at all.

"She is the new governess at Thorn Hill," he said. "Mrs. Brown is her name."

"Governess, eh?" Mr. Herrick said with a chuckle. "You are a fortunate man, Mr. Lindley, sir."

Christina reached his side then, and leaned against the wall to survey their work. "You had better hope Mother doesn't see you, Michael. Laboring like a common farmer!" She gave a mocking *tsk*.

Michael laughed and reached out to pull at one of her loose curls. "She won't. She's closeted in the drawing room with Lady Ross, is she not?"

"She was when I left."

"And why are you not doing your duty to her guests, Tina?"

Christina tossed her hair back unconcernedly. "I had a most dreadful headache."

"Excruciating, I see," he teased.

"Mrs. Brown was longing for a walk. I had to oblige her."

Mrs. Brown, whose steps were much slower than Christina's, came up to them just in time to hear this.

Her lips, those lips he had so recently fantasized about, curved in a wry smile. "And very obliging Lady Christina is, too. Good day to you, Mr. Lindley."

"And good day to you, Mrs. Brown. You mustn't let my wild sister bully you. She would walk to York Minster and back again if she could."

Mrs. Brown laughed, and for one instant the serious, sad set of her lovely face melted away to reveal her true youth and the sparkle of her dark eyes. "Oh, never fear, sir! I am not easily bullied. And we did not walk nearly that far, only over the river and up a prodigious number of hills." She paused to gaze back behind her, to the looming, heather-covered slopes. "I could hardly complain. It is such beautiful country."

"There, Michael!" Christina crowed. "She enjoyed our walk. And I find my headache is quite vanished in the fresh air." With that, she whirled around and strolled off to chat with some of the farmers, who had taken the opportunity of a short respite from their labors. They laughed with Christina, whom most of them had known since she was a child, and they watched Mrs. Brown with shy admiration.

Michael was hardly aware of all this, though. He could see only Mrs. Brown. She stared out at the rough, strange landscape as if mesmerized. Her lips were slightly parted, her pale cheeks flushed with the exercise and the crisp air.

"Yes," Michael answered quietly. "It *is* a lovely place. Most people can't see that, though. They just think it is desolate, too windy and rough. Too gray."

"I thought it was gray, too, when I first arrived," she said, in her faraway voice. "But now I see that's not true. There is green, and white, and purple. And the river is silver—a dancing silver." She turned back to him. The smile was vanished from her lips, but it still lingered in her eyes. "Do you believe in spirits, Mr. Lindley?"

Michael was taken aback by the sudden question. Spirits? Did he? He sometimes fancied he sensed Caroline close to him, watching him with her golden sweetness. And when he was a lad, he had loved listening to tales of haunts in the night, restless, ancient ghosts dragging chains down palace corridors. But now, honestly . . . "No. I don't."

One of Mrs. Brown's dark brows arched in question, like a raven's wing. "Do you not? I once thought I didn't, either. I was too educated for that, too sophisticated. There is something here, though, something we cannot see, but it's all around us." She looked away again, to the fields, and it was as if she weren't there at all, but in her own realm. "There were strange things in Venice, too, to be sure. They were different from this. This is even older. And not—not . . ." Her voice trailed off into nothingness.

Michael was mesmerized. It was as if she were a sorceress of some kind, as if she could hold up her hands and raise spirits from the very earth and water. And she took him with her into her strange world, the world she summoned with her voice and her hair, her perfume, with the very essence of whoever she was. If she touched him, surely he would follow her anywhere.

He remembered an old play then, lines from Shakespeare he had thought long forgotten. They echoed in his mind, like a whisper from a vanished life.

> *For you are called plain Kate,*
> *And bonny Kate, and sometimes Kate the curst;*
> *But, Kate, the prettiest Kate in Christendom;*
> *Kate of Kate-Hall, my superdainty Kate*
> *. . .*
> *Kate of my consolation*

Kate of my consolation.

She turned her head to stare at him, her face suddenly closed with a fresh wariness, the sorceress gone, vanished into the moor mists. He feared for a second that he had said the poetic words aloud, and she would fly from him like a startled bird.

But that was not it. The words were still only in his

head, his heart. "You must think me mad, Mr. Lindley," she said, with a nervous little laugh. Her hands folded at her waist, the gloved fingers twisted together. "I promise you I am not usually so fanciful. I will not be teaching about leprechauns and water nymphs in the schoolroom."

Michael longed to put his hand on her arm, to settle her and reassure her that he did *not* think her mad. Or if she was, then he was, too, for his wild imaginings of sorceresses and Shakespeare. But his sister and the men were nearby, so he gave her only a smile and not the touch, the embrace, he longed for. "It is this land, Mrs. Brown. You are right—there are things here we cannot see. It makes even the most sensible among us fanciful at times."

Her stiff shoulders eased a tiny bit, but she did not smile again. "You are very kind, Mr. Lindley. And understanding."

Michael shrugged. "I have lived in Yorkshire for many years now, Mrs. Brown. It is an—unusual place. A healing one."

"Healing?" Her forehead puckered in a small frown. "Have you found it so?"

"Indeed I have. I was greatly in need of healing when we came here, and the moors gave that to me. I hope that they will to you, as well."

She looked as if she wanted to say something else, to question his presumptuous words, but Christina called out to them.

"It is nearly teatime, Michael," his sister said, skipping back to his side. "We should be getting back to Thorn Hill."

Mrs. Brown turned to Christina and smiled at her. The smile for his sister was free of any reserve or caution; it was open and friendly. He wished she would smile at him so. "It will surely take us hours to walk back, Lady Christina!" she said lightly. "I am not sure my poor boots could stand it."

"I will drive you both back to Thorn Hill in the cart," Michael said. He moved away from Mrs. Brown, striding to the vehicle to catch up his coat and neck-cloth. "I fear it will be a rather rough ride, Mrs. Brown, but it will be faster than walking and easier on your lovely boots."

She glanced uncertainly at the wall. "Oh, Mr. Lindley, but your work . . ."

"It is very nearly done, and I'm sure the others need to get home to their own tea. Is that not so, Mr. Herrick?"

"Aye, indeed, Mr. Lindley," Mr. Herrick answered affably. "Mrs. Herrick will have my skin if I miss her fresh seedcake again."

"In that case, I accept the ride gratefully, Mr. Lindley," Mrs. Brown said.

"I would rather walk!" Christina protested. "I saw a new growth of strange ferns back there I should examine closely."

"Later, my sister naturalist," Michael told her. "Mother will have a fit if you miss tea, especially after fleeing from Lady Ross's visit. Besides, Mrs. Brown and I need a chaperone." He winked at Mrs. Brown, and earned a small smile and a soft laugh for his teasing.

They were more precious than rubies. Or sapphires as big as a thumbnail.

Christina gave a snort of disappointment, but she let him lift her up onto the wagon seat. Once she was settled, Mrs. Brown reached her hand out to him and he helped her up next to Christina. She still smelled of roses, but also of the clean moor wind and fresh heather. Her boots were scuffed and the hem of her pelisse was snagged, but there was no denying the happy pink color of her cheeks.

"Ah, Mrs. Brown," he said. "We shall make a countrywoman of you yet."

Her laughter sounded surprised, pleased. "Do you really think so, Mr. Lindley? I pray you are right. I have a great deal of work to do to catch up to your prodigious walker of a sister."

"You kept up with me very well, Mrs. Brown,"

Christina said. "Next time, I will show you some of the herbs that grow wild here in Yorkshire."

"I will look forward to it," answered Mrs. Brown.

Michael pulled himself up onto the seat next to Christina and gathered the reins, turning the sturdy farm horses toward home. "What have I told you about bullying Mrs. Brown, Christina?"

"Indeed, I am not bullying anyone, Michael!" Christina protested, leaning against his arm. "She *wants* to know about the plants—she just said so. Did you not, Mrs. Brown?"

"I did," Mrs. Brown agreed serenely.

"You see?" Christina said. "And she has been telling me today about London. Mother always makes it sound like such a dull place, full of nothing but modistes and fripperies. Yet I am sure the museums must be splendid! Mrs. Brown said . . ."

Christina went on chatting about London, while Mrs. Brown watched the landscape jolt past with that same quiet half smile on her lips. She was a sensible, calm governess once again, all thoughts of ancient spirits apparently abandoned.

But Michael could not help but long for the sorceress.

Chapter Eight

" *Je pars, nous partons, tu pars, vous partez, il part, ils partent. Partir* is 'to leave.' "

"Very good, Amelia. *C'est bon,*" Kate said as the child's soft voice paused hesitantly on the unfamiliar words. "Your accent is quite Parisian. Go on—tell me *sortir.*"

Amelia gave her a shy, quick smile, then bent her little golden head back over her books. "*Sortir* is 'to go out'. . . ."

Kate turned back to staring out the schoolroom window, tapping her fingers to the wooden sill in time to the murmured words. In truth, she had nearly dozed off for a moment. It was warm in the room, with the sunlight from the windows and a small fire in the grate, and her stomach was pleasantly full of an excellent luncheon of venison pie. Amelia's sweet voice was a quiet, rhythmic murmur as she practiced her French verbs.

Christina sat in the corner, silent for the moment, reading a book on Court etiquette. They had spent that morning, before luncheon and the arrival of Amelia, practicing proper curtsies.

"Oh, blast!" Christina had cursed in a most unladylike fashion when she wobbled and fell on her bottom for the third time. "Why must I curtsy so low anyway? It's ridiculous!"

Kate held out a hand to help Christina up, trying not to laugh. She had to remain the stern taskmaster. "Because whoever is presiding over the royal Drawing

Room when you come out will expect it. And remember—you will be wearing a train and a head-dress with heavy plumes, so it will be even more diffi-cult than it is now. So come, try again. Hold your back leg still, like this. And don't say *blast*."

And so the curtsying went on, along with graceful hand movements and head gestures, until they both collapsed in famished gratitude at the luncheon table. Kate smiled now to think of the farce of it all, though really it was no laughing matter. Lady Christina was the daughter of an important family, and her behavior during her debut Season reflected on that family as well as on herself. Christina had an independent, stub-born spirit, but surely even she could see that. And she *did* try—Kate knew that. Her curtsies were be-coming smoother, and didn't always lead to falls. Christina would just have to learn to erase those fierce expressions on her face as she lowered herself to the ground.

Just as Kate had to learn to mind her words. Her fingers curled into a fist on the windowsill. She had been a fool to voice her fancies to Mr. Lindley yester-day, her musings on the unseen spirits of Yorkshire. Her dreaminess always got her into trouble—it must be all the poetry she read. Once, as a child, she told her nursemaid she believed water nymphs lived in the canals, flitting about causing mischief. The nurse, a sensible Neapolitan woman, just pulled at Kate's hair as she brushed it, and clucked disapprovingly.

"Now, how could a nymph live in such dirty, smelly water?" she said reasonably, quashing Kate's fancies.

But they never went away entirely, and here in Yorkshire she felt them stronger than ever. She should *never* so forget herself as to voice those airy, poetic notions to Mr. Lindley, though! He would think a woman given to notions of moor spirits and water nymphs unfit to teach his sister and daughter, to lead them through a complex society, full of pitfalls for unwary ladies.

She sensed that he was a kind man, not one to be

rigid and unforgiving with his family or servants. He joked with the farmers, was tactful with his mother and sister and affectionate with his daughter, and always treated Kate with nothing less than respect. Yet she knew that he was a man with responsibilities, and he took them very seriously. He could never want a *flighty* governess, one who dwelled on spirits and legends of drowned lake cities.

As for a daughter of a whore, an almost whore herself—if he found out the sordid truth of her past, she would find herself out of Thorn Hill on the hour. Unemployed, disgraced. Never to see Michael Lindley again, to bask, even for brief moments, in the light of his smile, the rich, dark sound of his voice. She would be out in the chilly darkness again, when she had only just found a warm, safe nest.

Kate turned away from the window into the schoolroom scene laid before her. Christina was still bent over her book of etiquette, her face set in stubborn consternation. Court manners were obviously far more complex to grasp than the Latin nomenclature of her beloved plants. Amelia murmured her French verbs. The dusty sunlight cast a glow over the child's bright curls, making them shimmer as if alive. Her white pinafore was smudged with ink, but her pink muslin frock was immaculate. The smell of ink and parchment, and sugar from their luncheon pudding, hung richly in the warm air. It was a quiet, cozy scene, replete with domesticity and safety. Kate had never known anything like it before, and its sheer ordinariness was precious beyond price.

Surely she could hold her secrets a little longer. She would never again speak of spirits with Mr. Lindley, or anyone else. It would be just between her and the moors.

"Is this right, Mrs. Brown?" Amelia asked, her soft voice full of concern. *"Je sors, nous sortons, tu sors, vous sortez, il sort, ils sortent."*

"Très bien, mademoiselle," Kate answered, re-

turning to sit beside the child and examine her copy-
book. "You catch on very quickly indeed."

"The language is almost like music, Mrs. Brown,"
Amelia answered. "I can see it in my head, like
notes."

Kate waited a moment to see if Amelia would go
on with this intriguing line of reason, but it was obvious Amelia had said all she wanted to. Amelia
smoothed the pages of her book, her small fingers
careful. "Your father will be so proud."

Amelia glanced up with a hopeful smile. "Do you
think so, Mrs. Brown?"

"Of course."

Christina was distracted from her own studies, and
examined them over the top of her book. "Your papa
is always proud of you, Amelia, no matter what you do."

"But I want to speak French to him," Amelia said
decidedly. "Tonight!"

Kate laughed. "It may be a bit early for *that*, Amelia! But these verbs are an excellent start. Tomorrow,
we will learn some useful nouns, and you will be able
to make some simple sentences."

Amelia nodded, seemingly satisfied, and went back
to murmuring over her verbs. Kate glanced over at
Christina. "And how are you progressing, Lady
Christina?"

Christina shook her head. "It's all so ridiculous! I
will never be able to remember all the topics of conversation I *can* speak of and all I *can't*. Why only the
weather and fashion? Any fool can see if it's raining
outside. They don't need me to tell them."

"No. It is just to make social discourse easy for
everyone, a way to avoid embarrassment. Not everyone is as clever as you, you know. You would not
want to make someone feel stupid for not knowing
the Latin names for the parts of a flower, would you?"

A shadow of doubt flickered over Christina's face.
"I—well, no. Of course I wouldn't, even though the
parts of a flower *are* very easy to remember."

"Then before you know more of a person's interests and intelligence, it is best to simply speak of the weather. Or the fact that pink slippers are very à la mode this Season. But it needn't be completely dull." Kate stood up and marched to the middle of the floor, wielding an imaginary fan in her hand and turning so an imaginary train swirled around her feet. "Oh, la, Sir Everyman! It has been so beastly hot of late, do you not agree? I vow one cannot even breathe in this ballroom, and every flower in the park was quite wilted today. So very sad—I do enjoy a lovely *raddianum*, don't you? It was named after Giuseppe Raddi, you know." She tossed her head, and gave a sly, sidewise smile.

Christina clapped her hands enthusiastically. "Oh, Mrs. Brown! How do you know about *raddianum*?"

"You told me, of course, Lady Christina. You said it is a variety of fern."

"Well, I vow Sir Everyman would follow you anywhere if you smiled at him like *that* while discussing the weather."

"And you, too, Christina. You will have handsome suitors trailing you all around London, tossing *raddianum* at your feet." Kate abandoned her flirtation with Sir Everyman and sat down in the green velvet armchair next to the fire.

Christina shook her head, her gaze dropping back to her book. "I doubt I shall have *any* handsome suitors. Society gentlemen are all useless fribbles, anyway. I haven't time for them."

"How do you know they are all useless fribbles if you do not give them a chance? There are many gentlemen in London. Surely there will be at least a few who share your interests. Clever, good-hearted men." *Men such as Michael Lindley.*

As if Christina heard her thoughts, the girl's smile turned a bit knowing at the edges, and she said, "Men like my brother, perhaps?"

Kate felt her cheeks grow warm, and not from the heat of the fire. Of course, that had been *exactly* what she was thinking, but she could never admit it to Christina—or even to herself. "Perhaps," she said noncommittally, turning her face toward the window.

"You like my brother, do you not, Mrs. Brown?" Christina persisted.

Kate glanced toward Amelia, but the child was still intent on her studies and paid them no heed. "Your brother seems very gentlemanly, Lady Christina."

"And handsome? All the ladies in the neighborhood think he is handsome."

"He is—not unpleasant to look at," Kate admitted carefully.

"Indeed. But perhaps Mr. Brown was more handsome?"

Kate turned back to Christina and gave her what she hoped was a stern, governess-like glare. She had never had much chance to be "stern" before. "I believe this conversation is inappropriate, Lady Christina. My—my late husband is of no concern to you. And I am not sure what you want me to say about your brother, except that he is a gentleman and a good employer."

A sudden expression of surprise and hurt washed over Christina's face at Kate's words, and Kate had a quick yearning to snatch them back. She should not have been so abrupt. She *liked* Christina—she had no desire to wound her in any way. But the talk of Michael Lindley had to cease immediately. Or surely the discretion she had had to urge on herself yet again would dissolve.

The book Christina held slipped from her hands to the floor. As she bent down to pick it up, she muttered, "He was not *always* such a great gentleman. Even I have heard the tales."

Not always a gentleman? Kate opened her mouth to question Christina about her most intriguing words, but she was saved from her own folly by the schoolroom doors swinging open.

Lady Darcy stood there, poised in the doorway to examine the scene before her, as if she were a dowager queen observing her kingdom. The yellow silk and white lace cap on her head was a crown, the paisley shawl over her shoulders a royal mantle. Her sharp green gaze swept from Amelia, so intent on her work, to Christina and Kate seated next to each other near the fire.

Lady Darcy gave a tight, satisfied little smile. "Well," she said, "it appears everything is well in hand here." Her tone clearly said that she thought *herself* responsible for the satisfactory circumstances, even though this was her very first appearance in the schoolroom.

But Kate had to be grateful for her interruption. Obviously, the Lord protected fools, after all. Kate rose from her chair and gave a small curtsy.

"Grandmama!" Amelia cried happily. She hurried from her little desk to catch her grandmother's hand in hers. "I am learning to speak French."

Lady Darcy's stern face softened as she smiled down at her granddaughter. Her elegant, beringed fingers curled around Amelia's small, soft ones. "Are you, my dear? That is a very fine thing to know. All the fashionable people in London speak French. And you, Christina? What are you learning today?"

Christina stood up beside Kate. Her sun-browned face, which Kate had seen so open and merry as they walked over the moors, and laughing with abandon as she fell on her bottom after a botched curtsy, was closed and pinched. She held her book tightly against her stomach, like a shield. "Court etiquette, Mother, and the art of polite conversation."

"Indeed?" Lady Darcy's gaze flickered from her daughter to Kate and back again.

"Yes," Christina said. "I am learning to curtsy properly when I go to Court."

"I am glad to hear it," her mother replied. "I am sure your sister-in-law, Mary, will be glad of it, too, when she sponsors your come-out." She looked around the schoolroom once more, and gave a little nod. "I shall not keep you from your lessons, Mrs.

Brown. I just wanted to be sure you have everything you need."

"Yes, thank you, Lady Darcy," Kate said.

"Christina, dear, don't forget we're dining with the Haigh-Wood family tonight. We must depart by seven, and please wear your new pink gown. It is very becoming."

"Of course, Mother," Christina answered shortly, and watched stoically as her mother gave one more nod and departed.

Kate didn't think pink would suit Christina's complexion at all, but it didn't seem an auspicious moment to mention that. She settled Amelia back at her desk with a simple little French fairy tale she could study, then went back to Christina. The girl was quietly perusing her book again.

Kate felt a bit awkward with Christina, after her earlier short words and Lady Darcy's interruption. But the silence in the room was too heavy, and she *needed* to feel comfortable with Christina again. She needed to talk to her.

But not about the one thing she was longing to ask—what had Christina meant when she said her brother had not always been a gentleman?

"So, your sister-in-law is to be your sponsor?" she asked casually. "Not your mother?"

"Mother says she is too old for the social whirl, though I'm sure she will be there at least for my ball at Lindley House," Christina answered. Her voice was quiet, but did not hold any of her earlier sulkiness. "As I told you, Mary is very grand. She absolutely *lives* for Society. And she is a duke's daughter, you know. She never lets anyone forget *that*."

"Oh, la, a duke's daughter!" Kate teased. "How grand indeed."

Christina gave her a precious smile. "Indeed. Her father died last year, though, leaving her an even greater fortune than she had before. I suppose she must be called a duke's *sister* now, since her brother is the new Duke of Salton."

Salton? The fingers Kate had just reached toward the fireplace poker turned suddenly numb, and the heavy iron clanged to the floor. Kate clutched at her pained wrist. Her ears rang shrilly. *"Maledizione!"*

"Mrs. Brown!" Christina cried. She knelt down next to Kate's chair, reaching for her hand. "Are you all right? Did you hurt your hand?"

Even little Amelia's attention was caught. She dashed over to their little tableau, her sky-blue eyes huge as she bent over Kate's hand. "Mrs. Brown, are you hurt? Are you going to *die*?"

Kate was dragged back from her shock at hearing that Christina's sister-in-law's father was her own mother's Edward. It still sat like a cold lump in her stomach, but right now these two girls were far more important.

She laughed, and put her arm around Amelia. "Of course I am not going to die, *bambina*. I was just clumsy and dropped the poker. I have cut myself, see, but it is not bad."

"I will be right back," Christina said, and dashed off, the schoolroom door slamming behind her.

Amelia cradled Kate's hand in both of hers, her little face suddenly snow-white. "Everyone dies," she whispered.

Kate realized then that there was more going on in Amelia's busy mind than concern over a simple cut. She drew the child up onto her lap, holding her small, trembling figure close. Amelia's bright curls smelled of ink and sunshine, and a sweet little-girl powderiness. But the large eyes she turned up to Kate were full of very grown-up fears.

Kate took in a deep, steadying breath. "Yes, Amelia *mia*. Everyone does die. We must all one day go back to heaven, where we came from. But I am young, and this is a trifling injury. I will not die today."

Amelia was still skeptical. "My mama was young."

Ah. So that was the trouble. The little one still missed her mother, and carried the wound of her loss in her heart. And her father said she was too young to remember.

But Kate knew that some hurts and fears lingered. And no matter how young—or old—a daughter was, it ached to lose a mother. "I am sorry, *cara*. Your mama was in a terrible accident, I understand. But that does not happen every day, and you have many people looking after you to be certain it doesn't happen to you. Your father, your grandmother, your aunt Christina . . ."

"And you, Mrs. Brown?"

Kate stared down at the child, shocked that she would feel safe with her governess after only a few days. Shocked and—pleased. It felt strangely wonderful that *she* could take care of someone for a change, instead of always needing to be taken care of. Always looking for someone to take care of her. "And me, Amelia. You need never fear when you're with me. Your mama still watches over you, too, I'm sure."

Amelia's eyes widened with amazement. "Does she?" she murmured.

"Oh, yes. She is your angel now."

"Does *your* mama watch you, too, Mrs. Brown? Is she an angel, too?"

"Oh, *bambina*. I pray so." Kate drew Amelia close to her and kissed her soft brow. She remembered the dream mother she saw, the figure in glowing white who had led her to this new life. "I pray so every day."

Christina ran back into the schoolroom, a small glass jar and some linen bandages in her hands. "Here, Mrs. Brown," she said, a bit breathless from her dash. "Some salve for your hand. I made it up myself."

"Thank you, Christina," Kate answered, surprised to find her own voice thick with tears she dared not shed. Not until she was alone. She shifted Amelia to her side and reached out for the jar.

"Are you both quite all right?" Christina asked, peering closely at the two of them. "Such a lot of fuss for a cut!"

"Oh, Aunt Christina!" Amelia cried, holding her hands out to her auntie. "My mama is an *angel*. My own special angel."

"Of course she is, poppet." Christina caught her niece up in her arms, twirling her around. "No one who ever met Caroline could doubt it. Now—do you think she will watch over me at the Haigh-Woods' dinner, and not allow me to say something embarrassing about Henry Haigh-Wood's dreadful waistcoats?"

Chapter Nine

That night, Kate couldn't fall asleep, even though she had felt so tired after her schoolroom dinner with Amelia that she retired early. Her chamber was silent, her yellow-draped bed warm and cozy, but still she lay awake, watching the black sliver of sky through the parted window curtains. It had been a very long, strange day, roiling with emotions beneath its quiet, conventional surface.

In her mother's house, there had been a Chinese puzzle box, brought to Lucrezia Bruni by one of her many admirers after his voyage to the mysterious Orient. It sat on a side table in the drawing room amid a myriad of other bibelots, jeweled snuffboxes and pearl-framed miniatures, alabaster fragments from ancient Greece and broken faience from Egypt. The Chinese box stood out not for rich ornament or bright colors, but for its striking simplicity among all the flash and dazzle. It was carved of a glossy dark wood, inlaid with only a few mother-of-pearl flowers on its surface. It appeared to be only a smooth block of wood, yet in reality it was a box—a box that would open only when pressed or turned a certain way.

When Kate was a child, she adored that box. She would hide beneath the violet satin-draped table for hours at a time, listening to the soft murmurs and laughter of her mother's guests and trying to decipher the box's secret. She turned it this way and that, shaking it, prodding at it with her little childish fingers.

One day, it finally did open, the panel gliding out

smoothly, soundlessly, to reveal a tiny parchment scroll. The scroll was covered with small, indecipherable figures, which Kate never could translate. She had been so sure that if she only *could* read it, she would surely learn all the secrets of the universe.

The family she now found herself in the midst of was a great deal like that box.

The Lindleys hid their secrets well behind a smooth, country-gentry surface. Turn them and shake them as she would, she could only discover them in intriguing bits and pieces. A maidservant's quickly interrupted gossip. Christina's muttered comments about how her brother had not *always* been a gentleman. A pretty child's deeply held fear that everyone she loved would die, just as her mother had. A matriarch's cool regalness that just barely hid her love and concern for her family. A young lady pulling ineffectually against her proper place in Society. An angelically handsome man with scars, both on his body and in his heart. Nothing earth-shattering, perhaps—no kidnapped maidens in the attic, or bodies buried in the garden. But intriguing and disquieting all the same.

And most disquieting of all was the knowledge that the Lindleys' grand London sister-in-law was the daughter of Kate's mother's own protector. The one who bought her jewels and a country villa, who had her portrait painted by the finest artist in Venice. The one she died with, in that stormy sea.

Kate turned over in her bed, staring at the shadowed wall. She had the most irrational urge to pull the bedclothes over her head, as if that would shut out the wide world. As if she could thus escape.

She came all the way to Yorkshire secure in the knowledge that she *could* escape. No one in this remote corner would know her! Yet her old life had long tentacles, and they stretched even to Thorn Hill in the insubstantial forms of Mary Lindley and Michael's artist friend Elizabeth Hollingsworth.

"They will never come here," Kate whispered to the night. Christina had said her sister-in-law rarely left London, and there was nothing here for a famous artist. Even if they did, they would not know Kate. She had never met Mary Lindley, and only fleetingly seen Elizabeth Hollingsworth when she worked on Lucrezia's portrait in their drawing room. Surely Mary would know nothing of her father's love affairs in Italy!

These were very reasonable arguments, and surely would have reassured Kate in the sensible light of day. But in the darkness, they preyed on her already guilty heart. She knew sleep was a long way away; the night encroached on her bed, creeping in like cold hands to grab at her with fears and accusations. She pushed back the blankets and sat up, reaching for her dressing gown.

It would do her no good to lie here concocting wild doomsday scenarios, she thought. She might as well go down to the library and find something to read. Something *besides* the French grammars and etiquette guides of the schoolroom. Truth be told, Kate was also lured by Sarah the maid's descriptions of the Italian treasures housed in the library.

Kate lit a candle and slipped from her room into the cold silence of the corridor. Everyone was obviously tucked up asleep, as all respectable people should be at such an hour. Lady Darcy's door was firmly shut, and Christina's chamber emanated a strange, earthy scent, but it was quiet in there, too. Michael's—well, the less thought about *his* bedroom the better! Kate scurried past his door on fleet, slippered feet, as if the stout wood could suddenly sprout arms and snatch her into the tempting sins that awaited there.

But she paused at Amelia's room, thinking she heard a small noise. She worried about the child after their brief disturbing conversation that afternoon. All seemed well after Christina came back and jollied Amelia into laughing, as if a storm cloud had passed, leaving only sunshine in its wake. During dinner, they practiced French vocabulary and talked about music.

Amelia seemed an ordinary, if very intelligent, little
girl. Kate still worried, though. She knew more than
anyone that appearances could be most deceiving.

She slowly opened Amelia's door a crack and
peeked inside, holding up her candle to cast away
some of the shadows. Amelia rested in a fairy-tale
confection of a bed, all swoops of white lace and pink
silk bows. She had kicked away the pink satin counterpane and lay with arms and legs flung out. The fire in
the white marble grate had burned down to embers
and the room was chilly.

Kate hurried over to the bedside, her footfalls muffled in a thick pink carpet. She knelt down and drew
the blankets up to tuck them securely around the
child's tiny limbs. Amelia muttered in her sleep, her
head tossing on the embroidered pillow. Kate
smoothed back the tangled golden curls, and bent her
head to press a gentle kiss to Amelia's petal-soft
cheek.

The fierce wave of protectiveness that washed over
her as she stared down at the little cherub astonished
her. In only a very few days, she had gone from a
woman who didn't care for children to a lioness guard-
ing her tiny cub. But Amelia was a special child, and
Kate rather liked these new, warm feelings, even as
they frightened her. Her heart hadn't been frozen in
that cold water, after all.

"I meant what I said, Amelia, *bambina*," she whispered. "You need never fear anything as long as I'm
near. I will take care of you."

Kate saw a small, china-headed doll peeping from
under the pillows. She tucked it beneath the bedclothes next to Amelia, and gave the little girl one last
kiss before creeping from the room as soundlessly as
she had arrived.

It was an easy voyage to the library, the rest of
Thorn Hill being as quiet as the upstairs corridors. All
the servants had long found their beds, and only the
great, winding staircase stood between her and her
destination. If there were any ghosts at Thorn Hill, as

surely there must be after its long history, they were benign, invisible ones.

The library was smaller than Lady Darcy's domain of the drawing room, and more inviting. The walls were paneled in an elegant dark linenfold, no doubt a relic of Thorn Hill's days as an Elizabethan manor, and shelves stretched from floor to ceiling on two walls, filled with enticing books. The third wall faced the outside of the house, with three deep window seats cushioned and curtained in burgundy velvet. And the fourth held a vast fireplace, flanked by armchairs and footstools. A massive, carved desk lurked in the shadows like a desert lion waiting to pounce—a lion covered with papers and ledgers.

Kate remembered the maid's words about Michael Lindley's Italian collection housed in here, and indeed it appeared there *were* many paintings on the walls, framed in flashing gilt. And low, glass-topped cases crouched between the windows, holding the inviting gleam of Murano glass and Etruscan gold.

Kate longed to explore these lures, but it was too dark to see them properly and she had no time. She hurried on, intent on her errand to find a book, and promised herself she would examine them all one day soon.

The entire space of the library emanated an enticing scent, a combination of woodsmoke, paper and ink, leather, tobacco, and a hint of Michael's own scent, sandalwood soap mixed with fresh air. Kate inhaled it all with a shiver. *This* was a room where she could surely spend many happy hours, even all alone in the witching hour of the night.

She used her candle to light the heavy candelabra at either side of the fireplace, casting away all gloom, forcing the darkness into the corners. Then she approached a most pleasurable task indeed—finding something to read.

The lower shelves held no enticements—only dry, well-thumbed treatises on farming techniques and livestock cultivation. There were no novels or vol-

umes of poetry, even though Christina had said she
and her mother enjoyed *Pride and Prejudice*. No
doubt such novels were kept tucked away, separate
from serious works on soil enrichment and animal
husbandry.

Kate climbed higher on the sturdy library ladder
and found a complete set of Shakespeare, bound in
handsome red leather and stamped with gold. She laid
a fond touch on *The Taming of the Shrew,* her mother's favorite play and the source of Kate's own name.
Bonny Kate, and sometimes Kate the curst . . .

But she had come here to chase memories away on
this night, not court them. She climbed higher on the
ladder, leaving the Bard of Avon and his shrew behind. On almost the top shelf she found what she
wanted—a volume of local folklore and legends. She
was intrigued by Christina's tale of the drowned city
beneath Semerwater, and she longed to know more
about it. Water, after all, could change anything, could
make all things clean again.

She tucked the small book under her arm and
started to climb down. Her slippered foot just reached
toward the rung below her when the library door
banged open, letting in a flood of new light.

Deeply surprised, Kate lost her balance. Her foot
slid from beneath her and she fell backward, toward
the hard wooden floor. She cried out, her hand flailing
in a panic for the ladder, the shelf, *something* to break
her fall. But her fingers closed only on empty air.

Strong, hard arms closed tightly around her body
before she could hit the floor. Breathless and terrified,
Kate squeezed her eyes shut, but she knew who held
her. She knew as soon as her arms clasped about
linen-covered shoulders and she inhaled that clean,
outdoor scent.

Michael Lindley. Michael Lindley had swooped
down like his archangel namesake and saved her. And
now she was in such trouble, because she didn't want
him to let her go. Ever.

*   *   *

Michael had not thought he could possibly move that fast. He saw Mrs. Brown—Kate—slipping from the ladder, and in only an instant he dropped his walking stick and dived forward to catch her, sick at the thought of so much as a dark hair on her head being harmed.

She landed in his arms as light as a marsh bird—or almost. She was a small woman, short and slim, but she hit his arms at a great speed, and his bad leg nearly buckled beneath him. He tightened his clasp around her until they both were steady. Her arms wound about his neck, and her breath was cool and hurried against his bare skin. The loose braid of her hair fell over her shoulder against his arm.

For a long moment, they were caught in a silken web woven of silence, darkness, breath, touch. She lay in his arms, entwined against him, like a fairy creature of the night flown through the library window into his embrace. Surely in an instant she would fly away again, and he would find that this was only a dream.

But a dream he yearned to cling to, for as long as it lasted. She was soft in his arms, his fairy creature, and she smelled of summer roses and the powdery scent of old books and firelight. He could feel the length of her legs across his forearms, the slender shape of them beneath her thin night rail and dressing gown. There was the impression, the merest fleeting sensation of her breasts pressed against his chest. They were small and high, and conjured inside him sensations he thought long buried in his callow youth, when the merest glimpse of a woman's décolletage aroused all manner of erotic dreams and longings. She felt so very *right* in his arms, as if made to fit just there and no place else. His arms molded to her legs and her back, her head nestled on his shoulder just at the turning of his neck, as if they had embraced just so for a hundred years.

Yet, inevitably, cold reality intruded on this heated fantasy. A branch outside the window cracked against the glass, blown by the night wind, and Kate stirred against him. She lifted her head and stared at him with wide, chocolate-dark eyes, lips parted, as if she, too, was waking from a dream world.

For a moment, they just gazed at each other, bemused, dazed. Then she gasped, as a person would if suddenly pushed into icy water. She leaned back, straining against his embrace as her own hands slipped from around his neck to push at his shoulders. Her gaze shifted, moving past him to the window.

"You startled me," she murmured, her Italian accent more pronounced than usual. It added a richness and mystery to the moment, contributing to the dreamlike sense that this lady was *not* the governess, but a strange, unearthly creature.

He had had the same sense out on the moor that day, when she spoke of the spirits.

The tall clock in the corner chimed the half hour, and Michael was suddenly starkly aware that time, which had seemed to stretch on eternally as he held Kate, had really only been a short second. An instant of heat and intimacy that was now fled like so much candle smoke.

"I am sorry, K—Mrs. Brown," he said. His voice was hoarse, catching in his throat as if he had run a great distance across the moors. He lowered her carefully to her feet, feeling the lithe length of her body against his. She swayed a bit, like she stood in a great wind, and he held her arm until she stood strong on her own feet. Only then did he release her entirely.

His arms felt strangely bereft as they fell to his side, his skin cold.

She took a small step back but then stood still, her arms wrapped about her waist, her gaze still focused on the window. What was she thinking? What did she see there? She gave no clues in her perfect stillness.

More and more, Michael felt that Kate Brown was a book written in some mysterious ancient language, one he desperately wanted to know the contents of but that he could never hope to read. He had lost the code to that language in the midst of hard work and respectability. The puzzles of young, sad ladies were beyond him.

He ran his shaking hands through his hair, and tightened the sash of his dressing gown. He was suddenly quite acutely aware that he wore nothing beneath the velvet robe, and that his body had responded insistently to the allure of hers.

"I am sorry I startled you, Mrs. Brown," he said again, his tone now marginally more steady. "I thought no one would be down here, and when I saw the light I wondered if it was a servant snooping about after hours. I never meant to make you fall."

She turned back to him, and gave him a small half smile. Her cheeks were faintly dusted with pink, but her eyes were clear and direct as they met his. "It is quite all right, Mr. Lindley. There is no harm done, as you see. Your quick action saved the day—or rather, the night. And I also apologize. I did not mean to—snoop. I just could not sleep and thought I would try to find a new book to read."

Michael frowned at her interpretation of his words. "Oh, no, Mrs. Brown, I did not mean to imply that *you* are a servant. Some of the footmen and maids like to use this room for a moment of stolen flirtation, despite Mrs. Jenkins's best efforts. I think they are quite harmless, myself, but it would never do for her to catch them. You are perfectly welcome to borrow any books you like."

Her smile widened, her eyes sparkling with an alluring hint of mischief. "Am I *not* a servant, Mr. Lindley?"

"Of course not. You are more of a—companion to Amelia and Christina."

"I hope I am their companion, too, as well as a potential friend. But fifty pounds per annum says differently." This last was spoken so quietly as she turned away that he almost thought he did not hear her right.

He had to laugh aloud, and he fancied he heard an answering chuckle from her. He glimpsed a volume on the floor where she must have dropped it when she fell. Its pages were splayed open. Michael bent down and picked it up, turning it over to examine the cover.

"Legends of Yorkshire?" he asked.

"Oh, yes." She hurried forward and took the book from him, her cool fingers just barely brushing his hand enticingly before sliding away. "Your sister told me a most intriguing tale on our walk this afternoon, and I wanted to read more of it."

"Which tale is that, Mrs. Brown?" Michael's leg was beginning to ache a bit, along with other, more sensitive parts of his anatomy. He sat down in one of the upholstered chairs by the fireplace and gestured for her to sit across from him. She eyed the seat uncertainly, as if it might suddenly turn into a dragon and bite her delectable backside if she tried to lower herself onto the cushions. He smiled to try to put her at some ease. "Is it the trolls that hide beneath the bridges? The barghest, with glowing red eyes? Peg o'the Well, who drags unsuspecting children down to join her at the bottoms of wells?"

She laughed at last, and sat down in the chair, holding her book on her lap. "Nothing so unromantic, though I do think now I shall never cross another bridge for thinking of trolls. She told me there is a city under the waves of Semerwater, drowned by a curse."

"Ah, yes. I have heard that, too, though I can't say I believe it. The waters there are usually quite calm, but sometimes a storm blows up almost out of nowhere, whipping up the waves and swelling the rivers that feed into the Semerwater until they overflow their banks. But no bits of any city have ever washed up."

She turned her face to the side, her smile fading, and Michael suddenly felt like the greatest heel alive. "I am sorry, Mrs. Brown. You were once in a boating accident, were you not?"

She nodded. "I was. And I was fortunate to survive, as my poor mother did not."

"I am sorry," he repeated. It seemed to be all he could say tonight. Once, he had possessed the glib gift of charming ladies. Now it seemed he could only make them sad. "It is a hard thing to lose a parent. My father died several years ago, but Charles, Christina, and I still miss him very much. He was a good man."

"And my mother was a good woman. Or at least she tried to be." Kate gave a strangely wistful, bittersweet laugh. "She would be happy to see me making a new life here, though it seems I cannot escape from cities made of water."

"But Yorkshire is hardly Venice. Almost no one wears a mask, for one thing."

Her laughter turned lighter, and she seemed to settle back in her chair a bit.

"Perhaps we could take a picnic to the Semerwater one day soon, so you can see it for yourself," Michael said. Then he really heard himself, and hastily added, "With Christina and Amelia, of course."

"Of course," she answered quietly. She seemed to think about it for a moment, then finally nodded, as if having concluded that a picnic might be relatively harmless. "Thank you, Mr. Lindley. I should like that very much. I do love this country, at least what I have seen of it. It is strange, but beautiful. Almost enchanting."

Michael thought those very words could perfectly describe Kate Brown herself. Strange. Beautiful. Enchanting. "Then we shall go on the next fine day, if you can make space in your lesson plans."

"I can make it *part* of the lessons," she answered. "I'm sure Lady Christina would appreciate a day outdoors, away from deportment and curtsies."

Michael chuckled. "No doubt of that. Poor Tina. Mother is determined to make a fine lady of her."

"She is fine enough as she is. Perhaps I can give her a bit of polish, though. A way to make her feel more comfortable when she must go out in Society."

"If anyone can, Mrs. Brown, I am sure it is you. Tell me, how are your lessons progressing?"

She settled back into the cushions and told him of Christina's mishaps with curtsies, Amelia's progress with French verbs. He laughed at the image of Christina clumping her way through deep Court curtsies, and feared he beamed proudly at the news of Amelia's quick language skills.

"She is a very intelligent young lady," Kate concluded. "Wise beyond her years, I suppose. She feels things very deeply."

Michael nodded, thinking of his daughter's solemn blue eyes, always watching everything around her. "I fear she still misses her mother. Another lost parent, you see. I try my best to help her, as do Mother and Tina. That was why I came down here tonight. I thought I heard a noise from her chamber, and I went to look in on her. She sometimes falls out of bed at night."

Kate gave him a rueful smile. "That noise was probably me. I checked on her before I came to the library. She was fine—she had just kicked off the bedclothes, so I tucked her back in."

Michael laughed. Something strange and warm sparked in his heart at the thought of Kate bending tenderly over little, sleeping Amelia. "Thank you for that, Mrs. Brown."

"Of course. She is truly a lovely child."

They fell into a silent moment, punctuated only by the click of the branch against the window. Michael knew he should retire, leave this improper situation of sitting around with Kate while they were both clad only in their nightclothes. He had more work to do tomorrow, the wall to finish repairing. But he was loath to leave her enticing presence.

"I do have a confession to make," she said softly, gently breaking into the quiet.

A confession? Michael glanced at her sharply. Midnight confidences were not what he expected from the mysterious, self-contained Mrs. Brown. But he was willing—eager—to hear anything she wanted to say. "A confession?"

"Yes. The maid who dressed my hair this morning said you have Italian *objets* in here."

"And you would like to see them? Of course you would—being Italian."

She nodded, almost shy. "I *would* like that very much. But it is too dark now, yes? And too late."

He noticed then that her eyes were shadowed in purple, her shoulders drooping. It was late, and he was ungentlemanly for keeping her awake just to talk to him, to keep him from his nightmares.

But he still did not want to let her go.

"I can show them to you tomorrow, then, or the day after," he said. "Whenever you like. I always enjoy showing off my Italian treasures."

"Thank you, Mr. Lindley." She stood up, the folds of her dressing gown falling around her. Michael followed her, reaching down to the floor for his abandoned walking stick. "I will walk with you back to your chamber, Mrs. Brown. The corridors can be quite dark."

She shook her head. "No, that is quite all right, Mr. Lindley. Thank you. I found my way down here just fine. I'm sure I can make my way back."

He knew that she was quite right. What if someone saw them together, slipping through the house so late at night? His mother, Amelia, or Mrs. Jenkins, patrolling the corridors for errant maids. What a scandal! But he still did not like to think of her alone in the dark corridors. He reached for a single candle in a silver holder and lit it from the candelabra. He handed it to her, and said, "Then I bid you good night, Mrs. Brown. Thank you for our conversation."

"Good night, Mr. Lindley." She turned, her candle held high, and walked slowly away down the length of the library. She moved like the perfect lady, back straight, head held high, her hair glossy in the amber candlelight. He watched her hungrily, longingly, until the door clicked shut behind her.

Michael leaned on his stick, his head bowed, and took in a deep breath. And another.

Once he thought he could walk in a straight line again, he followed her path along the floor, his stick thumping hollowly against the polished floor. Hanging above one of the low, glass-topped cases of Italian treasures was a portrait, small and square in a silver-edged frame.

Caroline, young and lovely in a white gown sashed in cherry red, her shining curtain of guinea gold hair falling over her shoulders. She held a branch of spring cherry blossoms between her fingers, and she seemed to smile down at him. Sweetly, knowingly. As if she sensed his intrigue toward Mrs. Brown—and approved.

Or was it his imagination?

"And good night to you, too, Caro," he murmured. Then he left the room, in search of his own bed. Sadly enough, alone.

Chapter Ten

*T*he schoolroom was quiet in the gray midmorning, full of the efficient air of scholarly industry. Kate had set Amelia to tracing a map of England and marking the various counties with different colored pencils. The child murmured inaudibly to herself as she bent her golden head over the task, obviously absorbed in the dilemma of whether Kent should be green or blue. Christina studied Italian today, copying out vocabulary. All the words she chose from the Italian grammar book had to do with plants and trees, of course.

Kate sat beside her, occasionally offering assistance with pronunciation but otherwise occupied with her own ostensible task of mending her stockings.

Her needle moved in and out of the finely knit cloth, but her thoughts were far away from the routine chore. Far away even from the cozy schoolroom. She could not forget her moments in the library with Michael Lindley last night. The few precious moments that seemed more like a dream now than anything in the real world.

She loved sitting there with him in the dim candlelight, surrounded by books and the shadowed, unseen artifacts of her homeland. Loved talking with him, hearing his voice. She knew very well she should not have stayed there—for a governess to sit about in her dressing gown with her employer was impropriety of the first order, and could have led to all manner of trouble. Yet, somehow, Kate had never felt safer, warmer, more secure in her life.

She *was* attracted to Michael—that was undeniable. He was handsome, young, strong, with the most enticing smile she had ever seen. And she knew he found *her* attractive, too. If she had ever had any doubts on that subject, they were erased by the stirring of his body when he held her against him. But that instant in his arms, when she clung to his neck and felt the rough silk of his hair on her cheek, had been sweet beyond all measure.

She had seen many good-looking men in her life. Venice was filled with them: dark-eyed Italians, English officers in their red coats, tall Prussians, passionate artists. And most of them flowed through her mother's drawing room, ballroom, and boudoir, courting the famous Lucrezia Bruni and flirting with her young daughter. Julian Kirkwood, Kate's own lost, almost lover, had been as glorious as a young Mycenaean from a fresco, black-haired, intense.

Michael Lindley was a man who was more than handsome. He was a man who had obviously been through great pain and hardships—his injuries, the loss of his wife, the removal from some ungentlemanlike past into a quiet life on a Yorkshire manor.

He was a man to be trusted—she sensed that. A man who obviously took care of the people around him, faced his responsibilities, and was not even afraid of some hard, honest work. Most of the men she met in Venice were running *away* from their lives, their families, preferring to exist in the hedonistic unreality of La Serenissima rather than face their wives and estates in England, Austria, Padua, wherever. Perhaps Michael had once been like those men, as his sister implied, but no more.

Yes. A man to be trusted. So why could Kate not tell him the truth about her mother last night when she had the chance? Why could she not unlock that tiny secret part of her soul she had vowed to hide away forever? She wanted to—oh, San Marco, but she wanted to tell him! She wanted to unburden herself of the past, to be free of it, to rest at last in the arms of a man she could trust.

Yet she knew she never could, precisely because of that honor Michael Lindley possessed. He loved his family, his daughter, and Kate sensed, *knew,* that he would always protect them and their place in this insular English aristocracy. A woman like Katerina Bruni, even if she called herself any other name, could never truly belong here. Could never be worthy of this fine, honest life. This clean country existence, free from the rank corruption of Venice.

If she was *truly* good now, truly self-sacrificing and worthy, she would leave Thorn Hill this very day, would seek another position. Before things went any further here, before her heart grew any more entangled with this house and its inhabitants.

She looked up from her needle to watch Amelia. The little girl was absorbed in her map, her face creased in fierce concentration. One perfect fat blond ringlet drooped over her brow, and she tugged at it, letting it spring back into place. Kate's heart ached at the adorable picture. And she knew she was a selfish, weak creature, but she could not leave. Could not turn her back on this haven she had discovered.

Not yet.

"Mrs. Brown," Christina said, her bemused voice breaking into Kate's wistful, longing thoughts.

Kate blinked up at Christina, somewhat amazed to find herself still in the prosaic environs of the schoolroom. "Yes, Christina?"

"Did you know you sewed the sides of your stocking together?"

Kate glanced back down to see that she had indeed sewn the edges of the black stocking together, blocking the opening so that her foot would never fit through. She laughed helplessly and dropped the mess into her workbox. "Oh, dear! What a bumble broth I am today," she said. "I cannot seem to concentrate."

Christina laughed, too, and shook her head sympathetically. "Me, neither. Though, I must say, Italian vocabulary is far more interesting than curtsies and titles. It's an unseasonably warm day outside. Perhaps that has us distracted, Mrs. Brown."

"Perhaps so." Kate gazed out the window and saw that the grayness of the morning was burning off into pale sunshine. "I have an idea. Let us go for a walk."

"A walk!" Christina cried eagerly, slamming shut her book. Amelia looked up from her map with wide, interested eyes. "To the river again? I need to collect some fresh samples."

Kate remembered too well the last time they ventured to the river, and encountered Michael laboring at his wall on the way home. She firmly shook her head. "No. To the village, I think. Suddley, is it called? It seems to be not too far away, and I obviously need new stockings."

Christina seemed disappointed to be deprived of her river plants, but she nodded anyway, obviously happy for any excuse to be outdoors. "No, it is not far. Even Amelia can walk it. May we visit the bookshop while we're there, Mrs. Brown?"

"Of course," Kate agreed. Perhaps she could buy herself some new volumes of poetry, or maybe a novel or two. Then she would never have to pay a dangerous midnight visit to the library again.

Suddley wasn't terribly crowded in the middle of the afternoon, so Kate was able to more closely examine the place than she had the day she arrived. It seemed a typical country village, with structures of Tudor half-timbering and mullioned windows jostling next to newer buildings of red brick. The streets were wide and tidy, with plenty of room for carriages, carts, and horses to pass without splashing pedestrians on the narrow walkways. The shops boasted spacious windows displaying all manner of enticing goods— bonnets and gloves, swaths of delicately colored fabrics, shawls, fans, slippers, books, boxes of sweets.

Amelia clung to Kate's hand, tugging in excitement,

as they strolled along. Her feet in their tiny half boots fairly danced over the cobblestones, and she exclaimed over everything they saw.

"Look, Mrs. Brown!" she cried, gesturing toward a passing horse. *"Le cheval."*

"Oui, très bien," Kate agreed. She stopped next to an overflowing window box and said, "And this?"

Amelia's little face crinkled in concentration. *"La fleur. La fleur est rouge."*

"C'est bon!" Kate squeezed Amelia's hand, and paused as they came level with a sweetshop. A box of glistening lemon drops shone like bits of sunshine in the window, next to candied ginger and cones of sugared almonds. "Such scholarship deserves a sweet, I think. Do you like lemon drops?"

Amelia gasped, and if it was at all possible, her blue eyes opened even wider. "Truly, Mrs. Brown? A sweet in the middle of the day? And we may go into the shop to choose?"

Kate laughed at her wonder. How utterly delightful to find such joy in the prospect of a lemon drop, to see each moment as some new, fresh, never-before-encountered adventure. It made her own heart feel light. "Of course!"

As Amelia tugged her toward the door, Kate glanced back at Christina and whispered, "Has Amelia never been to Suddley before?"

"Oh, yes," Christina answered. "Of course she has. We go to church at St. Anne's every Sunday, and we buy all our goods here. But she usually passes through in the carriage with my mother, and the shopkeepers bring items out to show them. And Mrs. Jenkins takes care of the marketing, of course. I don't think Amelia has ever been *in* a shop before."

"I see." Kate watched, bemused, as Amelia shyly approached a display case, standing up on tiptoe to peer at rows of toffees. Then it *was* all new to her.

Just as it was to Kate.

"May I go to the bookshop now, Mrs. Brown?" Christina asked. "It is just three doors down."

"Yes, certainly. We will meet you there in a few moments."

After Amelia finished selecting her treats, Kate walked with her along the street. She could see Christina through the bookshop's window, and she seemed so absorbed in the volume she perused that Kate was loath to disturb her. So they continued on, Amelia holding tightly to Kate's fingers with one hand and consuming her sweets with the other. Kate stopped at what was obviously a milliner and peered inside at the enticing display. The window was draped with creamy moiré silk, and tall stands held bonnets of pearly pink satin and forest green taffeta trimmed with striped ribbons and silk rosettes. A wide straw hat with white and red streamers promised summertime still to come, and a plaid tam-o'-shanter warned that winter's chill was not entirely banished.

Kate sighed as she examined these riches, and reached up to touch the narrow brim of her plain, dark blue bonnet. How would she appear in that pink creation? Would it make her hair seem darker, bring out a becoming blush in her cheeks? Cheeks that had been so pale of late, drained of color by all the tragedy of her world.

Would Michael Lindley look at her twice then, his sky-colored eyes kindling with that fire of admiration she so secretly enjoyed?

She had a vision of the two of them strolling through a flower-dotted meadow, hand in hand. She wore the pink bonnet in this daydream, and a gauzy white gown. They laughed as he twirled her about, all troubles, all the past, forgotten. . . .

"I like that one, Mrs. Brown," Amelia's little voice piped up, pulling Kate back down to earth from her romantic fancies. "The pink one."

She smiled down at the child and saw that Amelia's chin was sticky from her lemon drops. "Do you, *ma petite mademoiselle*? I am sure you will have one just like it when you are older." She drew a handkerchief from her reticule and bent down to wipe at Amelia's chin.

Amelia stood still for the ministrations, but clutched tightly at her bag of sweets as if she feared they might be taken away. "No," she said decisively. "I think it would be pretty on *you*, Mrs. Brown."

"Do you, *bambina*?"

"Yes. You're so pretty, Mrs. Brown, but your clothes are so plain. Not like my mama's were."

Kate almost laughed aloud at Amelia's solemn pronouncement. "All governesses dress plainly, Amelia. I'm sure it must be written in a governess rule book someplace."

"That doesn't matter. All ladies should look pretty. My mama wore *beautiful* clothes. All floaty, with lace and ribbons. And jewels, too."

Kate peered solemnly into Amelia's eyes, searching for any hint of the sudden burst of fear and sorrow she displayed when Kate cut her hand. But there was only certainty there, a certain matter-of-factness. "As you will one day, Amelia. And everyone will say you are every bit as beautiful as your mother was."

Kate straightened and was tucking the handkerchief away when she felt a strange, prickling tingle at the nape of her neck. She stiffened, reaching up to touch that spot with her fingertips.

Someone was watching her.

She knew that sensation well, though it had not come upon her since she had left Venice. On one of her last days there, before the accident, she had been shopping on the Rialto with her maid when she felt that strange tingle. When she turned then, she saw Julian Kirkwood watching her from a distance, his gaze burning with a disconcerting, intense light. He said nothing to her, did not even approach her. He just kept staring, watching her until she hurried away.

She turned now toward the street, half expecting to

see Julian's ghost hovering there. But there were no specters—just an open carriage containing three ladies. A merchant stood beside the vehicle, holding up bolts of cloth for their inspection. The ladies did not look at the wares, though. They stared directly at Kate.

Kate examined them in return, with a dawning fear that perhaps she had once met them in her old life. But they were unfamiliar. An older woman, in a stylish bronze-colored pelisse and a tall-crowned bonnet trimmed in gold and green feathers that complimented her faded red hair, and two younger ladies, obviously her daughters to judge by their matching ruddy curls. They were also fashionably dressed, in pale green and bright blue.

They did not smile or acknowledge Kate, yet they continued to stare.

"That is Lady Ross and her daughters," Amelia commented, lifting her hand to point at them with her bag of sweets.

"A lady must never point, Amelia," Kate murmured automatically. So *this* was Lady Darcy's rival for social supremacy in the neighborhood. Lady Ross and two of her daughters, pretty, perfectly turned-out girls as unlike Christina as chalk was to cheese.

Kate far preferred Christina—she knew that already. Christina never stared so rudely.

"Lady Ross is Grandmama's friend," Amelia said. "And Louisa, in the green dress, is engaged to Mr. Haigh-Wood. And Emmeline is in love with Papa. Grandmama says he should marry her, but he says she's a silly goose who never reads a book except for *The Curse of the Haunted Castle.*"

Kate laughed aloud at this frank appraisal of the situation. It was no more than what the maid Sarah had hinted at, so it should not have surprised Kate in the least. But it *did* give her a twinge, and she peered closer at Emmeline Ross. She was pretty enough, small and dainty with a kittenish face and clouds of that tawny hair.

But she was obviously ill brought-up to stare so.

Kate nodded at the Ross trio and turned to walk off down the street, drawing Amelia with her.

"Amelia, dear," she whispered, "a lady shouldn't spread gossip about."

"Was that gossip?" Amelia asked, her tone deeply shocked.

"I fear it was." Kate glanced down to see the child frowning in perplexity.

"Oh, Mrs. Brown," she said sadly. "It is so hard to tell what is gossip and what is polite conversation!"

Kate laughed again, and paused to bend down and kiss the child's soft cheek. "Don't worry, *bambina*. I will help you decipher it all. Now I must find some new stockings and stop at the apothecary. You just finish your sweets."

Kate hoped that by the time she completed her errands, the Ross ladies would be gone. But no such good fortune occurred. In fact, when she stepped out of the apothecary's shop, Christina was standing by their carriage chatting with them.

Or rather, *they* were chatting to *her,* the three of them twittering like magpies in a hedgerow, while Christina seemed frozen into a block of marble. Only her eyes moved, darting desperately from side to side as if she was about to fall down in a fit. Her arms were folded tightly around a book-shaped parcel, which she clutched against her stomach.

Kate nearly ducked back into the shop, dragging Amelia with her, but she could not abandon Christina. After all, she was trained to always be pleasant in every social situation. She took in a deep breath, straightened her shoulders, and marched right up to the carriage.

"Lady Christina, there you are," she said cheerfully. "Is it not time we started back to Thorn Hill?"

Christina nearly sagged with relief, and her frozen

figure thawed enough to allow her to turn toward Kate. "Oh, yes, indeed! It will be almost time for tea. Mother is so strict about that." She looked as if she would love nothing more than to flee immediately, but even a girl who wandered the moors alone in search of plants to dig up could not be so rude. "Lady Ross, Miss Ross, Miss Emmeline Ross, this is our new governess, Mrs. Brown. Mrs. Brown, our neighbors, Lady Ross and her daughters."

Kate gave them a small curtsy. "How do you do?"

Lady Ross lifted up a quizzing glass on a silk ribbon and examined Kate minutely before saying briefly, "How do you do?"

The two daughters just giggled.

Michael was absolutely right to reject matrimony with such a silly, kitten-faced girl, Kate thought severely. Anyone who could *giggle* on a public street was obviously not a fit mother for Amelia.

"Don't forget, Lady Christina," the one in green— Louisa—said. "The assembly is on Saturday. It will be such fun. You mustn't miss it as you did the last one!"

"Yes, dear Lady Christina," Lady Ross said. "And do bring your *dear* brother. We haven't seen him in an age."

"He is very busy, Lady Ross," Christina answered. "But thank you for the reminder about the assembly. Good day."

"Good day!" the Rosses chorused as Christina clutched at Kate's arm and hurried off down the walkway.

Kate waited until they were out of sight of the carriage full of kittens before she said, "Christina, please, slow down! Amelia can't keep up."

Christina threw her a rueful, apologetic smile. "I'm sorry, Mrs. Brown. And I'm sorry to you, too, poppet!" She picked up her niece, holding Amelia on her hip as they left the village. "I didn't mean to leave you behind. I just detest talking to Lady Ross and her daughters. They haven't one sensible thing to say between them."

"Mrs. Brown says one mustn't gossip," Amelia said severely. "Especially not about the Rosses," she went on, embellishing Kate's words.

Christina laughed. "Quite right Mrs. Brown is."

"What is this assembly they spoke of?" Kate asked.

Christina pulled a face. "Oh, it is to be at the assembly rooms here in Suddley. I got out of the last one— one of my experiments was at a sensitive stage, and I could not leave it. But I'm sure Mother will make me attend this one."

"*Make* you attend? Do you not enjoy these assemblies at all?" Kate asked as they scrambled over a stile and onto the footpath toward Thorn Hill. Amelia clamored to be set on her feet again, and took Kate's hand for help over the rocks and roots.

Christina shook her head. "The refreshments are always terrible—watery lemonade and stale sandwiches and cakes. The Ross girls dance every dance, taking all the suitable partners, and even if they did not, I'm a terrible dancer, anyway. So there's never anyone to talk to, and I feel like a fool standing about there."

Kate saw the exaggerated chagrin on Christina's face and gave her a gentle smile, even though she sort of wanted to laugh. Laughter would never encourage Christina to feel better about herself, and that was all Kate wanted. Kate might be no help at all when it came to plants and such, but she *did* know how to comport herself at parties. "That doesn't sound much fun, Christina," she said. "Yet assemblies *can* be survivable, I promise. They can even sometimes be enjoyable. I'll help you."

Christina shot her a suspicious glance. "How, Mrs. Brown?"

"Well, we can start by practicing dancing. We'll begin as soon as we get back to Thorn Hill. Gavottes, schottisches, reels—even a waltz, if you like."

"Can I dance, too, Mrs. Brown? Please?" Amelia pleaded, tightening her clasp on Kate's hand.

Kate laughed and twirled the giggling child around

in a wide circle. "Of course, Mademoiselle Amelia! You will have to make your debut in a few years, too. Though the styles in dancing will probably have changed by then. Or you can play the music for us."

Even Christina smiled at their antics as she watched Kate and Amelia swirl over the pathway. "Mother says I'm an utterly hopeless dancer."

"Well, we shall just have to prove her wrong, won't we?" Kate said merrily.

Amelia gaped up at her. "Grandmama is *never* wrong!"

Kate kissed the child's cheek again as they started up the long drive at Thorn Hill. "Everyone is wrong sometimes, Amelia, dearest. That is why we are humans and not angels."

"*I* am wrong sometimes," Amelia admitted. "Like when I called a cow a *fromage,* but that was actually a cheese. But *not* Grandmama. Or Papa."

Kate envied Amelia her certainty of mind. She wasn't sure she herself had ever had a time when she did not see that the world was made of folly and avarice. Yet there was no more time for talk, as they came closer to the house and saw that Lady Darcy herself stood under the front portico.

There was a large, unused fountain set on a round pedestal near the portico, and three farmworkers were busy cleaning it of its gathered winter detritus of leaves and twigs. Lady Darcy supervised, wrapped in a yellow cashmere shawl against the afternoon breeze.

"Be very careful to clean under the cupid," she instructed. "The water cannot flow properly if—" She broke off when she glimpsed their little party trudging up to the door. "So you are back from Suddley, Christina? I trust that all was well there."

"Of course, Mother," Christina answered, her smile entirely vanished. "I didn't cause a riot at the apothecary, or spit in the street, or anything of that sort."

"Of course you did not, dear," Lady Darcy said. "You had Mrs. Brown there to keep an eye on you."

"Lady Christina was a perfect lady, Lady Darcy,"

Kate said, hoping her words could have *some* weight. Christina *had* been polite, even if under duress with the Ross clan.

Lady Darcy nodded doubtfully. "And did you meet anyone there?"

"Lady Ross, with Louisa and Emmeline. Rose and Letitia were still at Ross Lodge," Christina answered, fidgeting with her book parcel. "They sent you their greetings, and said they hoped to see you at the assembly on Saturday."

Lady Darcy's eyes lit up, and the small frown creasing her forehead cleared. It was easy to see that she, unlike her daughter, enjoyed the dubious pleasures of the assembly rooms. "Oh, yes, of course! I have been so looking forward to it. I have not seen Lady Ross in an age."

"She called just a few days ago," Christina muttered.

Kate surreptitiously poked Christina in the side with her elbow, but Lady Darcy appeared not to have heard her. "You can wear that new yellow muslin gown, Christina—it is very becoming. And I know that Michael will accompany us. He will want to see Emmeline Ross, of course. But go upstairs now, Christina dear, and change your dress for tea. I can't wait to hear your new song at the pianoforte, Amelia, darling."

Christina nodded, and disappeared into the house as quickly as her feet could carry her. Kate followed at a more sedate pace with Amelia.

Well, she thought smugly, she knew one thing— Michael Lindley could *never* be interested in a giggling red-haired kitten like Emmeline Ross. He was much too sensible. She and her sister reminded Kate of some girls she had known in Venice, the Donizetti sisters, who pursued every man in the city with little success. Why that knowledge should give her such a frisson of pleasure, she did not dare to say, but the truth was that it *did*.

Oh, how she wished she could be a little fly on the

wall in those assembly rooms! Just to watch the dancing and hear the conversation, see the machinations
of the Ross girls and know that they would never
work, would be such fun. It had been much too long
since she was at a party.

Chapter Eleven

*K*ate was having a remarkably fine time.

She sat in a quiet, half-shadowed corner of the assembly room, watching the many young—and not so young—dancers skip happily through a reel. She tapped her slippered toes, sipped at a glass of warmish lemonade, and thought how fortunate it was that Lady Darcy's headache had kept her at Thorn Hill tonight. Well, *not* fortunate that Lady Darcy was ill, of course, but fortunate that Kate's services as chaperone were now required.

She had never been to a party in England before, and it was most interesting. There were far more people in the environs of Suddley than she would have supposed. Young ladies in pale muslins and silks mingled with young gentlemen, local squires and attorneys and curates in starched neckcloths and dark coats. They danced, and laughed, and chatted under the watchful eyes of mothers, while fathers and husbands drifted away to the card room or the refreshment tables. The musicians, local men set up on a dais with their instruments, made up for a certain lack of talent with great enthusiasm. Their joyous notes echoed to the plaster rosettes on the ceiling.

Kate had watched as Michael was adroitly cornered by Lady Ross and her pack of kittens the moment they entered the room. She and Christina had barely divested themselves of their wraps when they were neatly cut off from their escort, and he was borne away to dance first with Louisa and then with Emmeline. The glance he threw back over his shoulder, above the sea of pink ruffles and satin ribbons, was an almost comical picture of dismay. One would have thought he was being dragged down to damnation by pastel-muslin-clad handmaids of the devil. But there was nothing either Kate or Christina could do to extricate him, and it would appear unfortunately rude if he was to extricate himself.

So Kate followed Christina to what was obviously her favorite corner of the room, and they seated themselves to observe the swirl of merriment. Or at least *Kate* observed it. Christina wore a thoughtful frown on her face, as if her mind were a million miles away, and the hard, sharp lump in her reticule appeared suspiciously like a book.

At least Christina looked well, Kate thought with a certain proud satisfaction as she stole a sidelong glance at her charge. Christina had accepted Kate's gift of a jar of rose lotion, procured from the apothecary on their earlier voyage into Suddley, and her skin now appeared a bit smoother and less sun browned. She had also submitted to the coiffure experiments of Kate and the maid Sarah, sitting still while they examined the latest copy of *La Belle Assemblée* and tried various arrangements of curls and ribbons. The smile Christina gave them as they moved pins this way and that was filled with patience and condescension, but Kate was having so much fun she just didn't care.

And the results were worth it. Christina's light brown hair, streaked with pale gold from her time outdoors, was turned into smooth ringlets and caught into artful disarray with blue and white ribbons and mother-of-pearl combs. She wore a pale yellow muslin gown trimmed with small white bows, and a single strand of creamy pearls circled her throat.

She looked like a most respectable, and very pretty, young lady, Kate thought smugly as she surveyed her handiwork. Aside from the book in her reticule, its hard edges stretching out the beaded silk, Christina was perfect. Now if she would only dance. As her brother was doing.

Kate turned her attention back to the crowded dance floor. Michael had extricated himself at last from the Ross daughters and was now partnered with a surprisingly dashing lady in a stylish gown of Turkey-red silk and a demiturban of gold satin pinned with a diamond sunburst. The lady was quite tall and used her height to great advantage to stare intently into Michael's eyes as they clasped hands and turned in allemande.

Kate frowned to see that stare, the soft smile the woman gave him. A smile that was returned. The line of dancers shifted, and the pair was lost to sight.

Kate glanced down at her own dark blue silk gown. She had enlivened it as best she could, with her pale pink gloves and a silver ribbon woven through the sleek twist of her hair. But it was still a very plain, matronly gown.

A bit of the sparkle twinkled out of the evening. She sipped at her lemonade and turned her attention back to the dance.

Michael and his partner briefly reappeared, marching down the line. "That is a very dashing gown," Kate commented.

"Hm?" Christina murmured, obviously dragging herself back from her daydreams of plants and soil. "Which one, Mrs. Brown?"

"The Turkey-red one your brother's partner is wearing."

Christina's gaze searched the floor. "Oh, yes. That is Mrs. Ruston. She is the vicar's new wife. Mother and Lady Ross say she will only wear gowns from London, never from the local modiste, and that she has far too many airs for a clergyman's wife." Christina took a thoughtful drink of her own lemonade. "I think I would not mind assemblies half so much if I could wear a gown like *that,* and not these insipid pastels."

"You can wear any gown you like after you're married," Kate answered, her heart lightening. *The vicar's wife!* Surely there could be no unseemly flirtation going on *there*. "In the meantime, you look lovely in yellow. And I am sure others have noticed, too."

Christina laughed. "Others, Mrs. Brown? Such as my mother, you mean?"

"No." Kate's gaze scanned the room in search of the young man she had seen noticing Christina earlier, when they first took their seats. He was very tall, and not bad-looking despite the spectacles that perched on his nose and the extreme slimness of his figure. He had rich, blond white hair, and the bronze of his complexion suggested he spent as much time outdoors as Christina did herself.

Ah, there he was. Standing in the corner across the room from theirs. Still watching Christina, with what he obviously thought was great secrecy.

"There is that young gentleman there," Kate said. "He has been looking at you since we arrived, even though he tries to hide it."

Christina's brows arched in amazement. "What gentleman?"

Kate gestured surreptitiously with her empty glass.

"Oh. Yes," Christina said dismissively. "That is Mr. Price. Andrew Price. His family owns an estate a few miles away, Keppleston Abbey . He is rather interested in botany, too, and sometimes loans me books on the subject he buys in London. We have also shared one or two interesting specimens we've discovered."

"Well, he obviously admires you," Kate said. "Do you not think he would like to dance with you?"

"Andrew Price?" Christina exclaimed. "Of course not. He is just a friend, far too much a *boy* for me to dance with."

But Mr. Price had obviously noticed their attention. He swallowed hard, placed his glass down on a nearby table, straightened his cravat, and made his way across the room toward them. Christina had already gone back to her daydreams, but Kate watched him. He seemed rather sweetly nervous, tugging at his gloves and the sleeves of his dark green coat as he dodged knots of people, and tables and chairs, on his journey across the assembly room.

Finally, he stood before them. Kate saw that his eyes were very green, handsome and glowing behind his spectacles, but their edges twitched with anxiety as he bowed to them.

"G-good evening, Lady Christina," he said. "What a grand surprise to see you here this evening."

Christina gave him a smile, pleasant and polite enough, but rather like the smile one would give an overfriendly puppy. "Good evening, Mr. Price. May I present my governess, Mrs. Brown? Mrs. Brown, Mr. Andrew Price."

"How do you do, Mr. Price?" Kate said.

"How do you do, Mrs. Brown?" he answered. "I'm sure you must find yourself very fortunate to have such a brilliant pupil as Lady Christina!"

Kate gave a small, secret smile at his eager enthusiasm. "Indeed, I am. Lady Christina and I get along very well. I understand, Mr. Price, that you and she share an enthusiasm for botany."

"Oh, yes, of course, Mrs. Brown! Though Lady Christina is far more advanced in her studies than I am." He turned back to Christina, obviously steeling his courage to talk to her again. "I have been in Brighton these last few weeks, Lady Christina, and I managed to procure many new volumes while I was there. Thomas Nuttall's latest work is particularly fascinating. I would so enjoy discussing his theories of the genera of North American plants with you."

Christina brightened. She eagerly sat up straighter, the lemonade jostling in her glass. Kate rescued the vessel before it could spill on Christina's pretty gown, and put both their glasses down on the nearest table.

"Oh, yes, Mr. Price, I would enjoy that very much!" Christina answered. "I read his book last year, and was most impressed."

The dancers were just finishing up the set, bowing and curtsying before dispersing from the dance floor. Soon, a new set would form. Quickly, Kate said, as tactfully as possible, "Perhaps the two of you could discuss the work of Mr. Nuttall during the next dance?"

"Oh, of course!" Mr. Price declared eagerly. "I do enjoy a dance. Lady Christina, would you do me the honor?"

Christina glanced uncertainly at the milling crowd, then down at the reticule on her lap. Kate gave her a discreet nudge, and at last Christina nodded. "Thank you, Mr. Price. That would be very enjoyable."

Kate watched them walk away, arm in arm, a warm, satisfied glow growing in her heart. She had a small inkling now of how her mother must have felt when men admired her daughter—satisfied, proud, sorry, anxious. But of course, Kate was only sending Christina out to dance with a respectable young man with whom she shared an interest in botany. *Not* launching her into a life of rich, artificial debauchery, where the tilt of her head, the sound of her laugh, and the shrewdness of her sensuality meant the difference between wealth and degraded poverty.

Kate suddenly wondered, as she observed Christina taking her place in the dance with the sweet, shy Mr. Price, how her own mother could have even contemplated sending her child into such a life. Could have groomed her for the arms of men such as Julian Kirkwood, knowing the falseness, the baseness of it all. The loss of all morality and self-respect. Lucrezia Bruni had known no other life, of course. She would not have known how to help her daughter find a new way, not until after she, Lucrezia, died and could reappear as a ghost or a dream to help steer Kate's life into better channels.

But what could she have felt on the morning she arrayed her child in jewels and clinging silks, piled her hair high atop her head, and led her onto that yacht? For Kate found that she would kill any man who looked at Christina with anything less than the utmost respect, who treated her as anything less than the respectable, innocent, intelligent lady that she was. No man would ever gaze at Christina and assess her fleshly worth as if she were a mare at Tattersalls. Kate would protect her with her own life if she had to, and little Amelia, too. And her own daughters, if she was ever so blessed. None of them would ever have cause to doubt their own worth, as Kate had. None of them would ever have to submit to the touch of a man they found frightening or repellent. *Ever.*

Kate suddenly felt greatly in need of some fresh air. The room was warm and crowded, and her fierce new thoughts only added to the closeness. Her gaze sought out Christina and saw that she was dancing happily enough with Mr. Price, and the set was likely to last for a long while. Mr. Lindley was nowhere to be seen—perhaps he had escaped the Ross girls into the card room. She would not be missed for a few moments.

She stood up and crept out of her corner, slipping silently around the edges of the crowd until she found the door and emerged gratefully into the cool night. She had no shawl or wrap, and the breeze raised bumps on her bare arms and neck, but its chill felt good after the heated room. The deep drafts of clean air cleared her head.

Kate moved down the short stone flight of steps and around the corner of the building into a small garden. There was no one else about, and the pathways were very dim under the meager light of the moon and the few stars. Kate welcomed the precious privacy, and she moved between the neat flower beds in search of a quiet place to sit. The only sounds were the echo of music and laughter from the assembly room windows and the crunch of her slippers on the gravel path.

The past is dead, she reminded herself for what felt like the hundredth time. *Gone.*

Would she ever truly believe it?

She rounded a corner where a tall tree held court,

and nearly screamed aloud when she collided with firm, warm, living flesh. Her memories of the past, of Julian Kirkwood touching her, calling her his Beatrice in his eerie, intense voice, were too fresh, and bitter panic welled up in her throat. She took a swift, involuntary step back, and her flat slipper caught on a loose stone.

A strong hand caught her arm before she could fall, and the warm clasp pulled her upright. She reached out instinctively to claw the man's face, to gain her release however she could, when the sound of a whiskey-dark voice stopped her.

"Mrs. Brown?" Michael Lindley said, his words rushed with surprise and concern.

"M-Mr. Lindley?" Her hand curled around his arm to steady herself. She stared up at him in the meager light, her gaze frantically searching his visage to assure herself that it was really, truly him.

That she was safe.

"Of course it is me," he answered reassuringly. "I didn't mean to startle you. Again."

"I—it is quite all right. I'm fine now." Her breath was steadier, its frightened rush in her lungs slowing. Her skin didn't prickle anymore, but she longed to throw her arms around his neck and cling closely, losing herself in his warm strength.

But instead she stepped away, clasping her hands tightly together at her waist. "I just needed a breath of fresh air. Lady Christina is dancing a set with Mr. Price."

"Ah, yes. Young Price. He and Christina have been friends since they were children." Michael gave her a rueful glance, then held up his other hand to display a smoldering, half-smoked thin cheroot. "I escaped out here to indulge in the vile habit of smoking."

Kate had to laugh. He looked too much like a boy caught out in some mischief. "Vile, indeed."

"I will put it out." He bent down to extinguish the cheroot against the gravel, but Kate stopped him.

"No, please, don't let me interrupt you. Please finish it," she urged. "I am intruding on your indulgence."

"Not at all, Mrs. Brown. I would far rather talk with you than smoke alone."

Kate felt a sweet tinge of pleasure at his words, which quite eclipsed her earlier cold fear. He *liked* to talk to her. It was far from the most effusive compliment she had ever received, but it was much more precious than any ode to her eyes and hair and toes could ever be. "Then I will stay and talk while you finish your cigar," she said, and leaned back against the stout tree trunk.

Here, in this chilly little garden, surrounded by the sounds of dance music and the sweet-acrid scent of cigar smoke, she felt happier than ever before. The past was indeed gone—when she was with him.

Here was a man whose touch and kiss she would welcome, even revel in. But he stood apart from her, as surely he always would. At least right now she was with him, watching him, listening to his voice.

"So, what do you think of our local soiree?" he asked, exhaling a wreath of silvery smoke.

"I have been enjoying it very much. The dancing is quite lively."

"And the music?" he said, a hint of laughter in his voice.

Kate chuckled. "That, too. The musicians are so enthusiastic."

"I fear they don't get the chance to practice very much."

"Yes. Yet everyone appears to be enjoying themselves. You yourself danced several times, did you not, Mr. Lindley?" She gave him a sly glance. "You seem particularly popular with the lovely Misses Ross."

Michael laughed wryly. "You noticed that, did you? You could be very useful to me, I think, Mrs. Brown."

Indeed, I could, Kate thought. "Useful, Mr. Lindley?"

"Yes. You can report to my mother that I did my

duty to her friends. But by no means must you say that I was particularly enthusiastic in dancing with Miss Emmeline."

"Miss Emmeline?"

"Hm. Mother is convinced she would make me a most suitable bride. She and Lady Ross have been trying to set a parson's mousetrap for months."

Kate was beginning to rather enjoy their conversation. "And you think differently?"

"Indeed I do. Miss Emmeline is nice enough, to be sure, but she giggles far too much."

Kate pressed her lips together to prevent even a hint of a giggle from emerging. "Does she?"

"And I doubt she has ever read a book in her life."

"Not even *The Haunted Castle*? Books are very important."

"Indeed they are."

Kate waited to see if he would say anything further of Miss Emmeline Ross, but it appeared the topic was closed. So she decided to be very bold and ask the question that balanced eagerly on the tip of her tongue. "Do you have no thoughts of remarrying, Mr. Lindley?"

Michael studied the glowing tip of his cheroot in silence for a long moment. When he looked up at her, his gaze was solemn, no laughter lurking in the depths of his eyes, as there so often was. "No, Mrs. Brown. I don't."

Kate turned away, utterly ashamed she had said such a thing. His matrimonial goals were none of her business, after all. None at all. "I'm sorry. I shouldn't have . . ."

"Don't be sorry, Mrs. Brown," he answered, his tone still serious and distant, but not quite as dark. "You take care of my daughter—you are right to ask such things that concern her. But if you knew the truth of my marriage, you would know why I will never take another wife."

Kate was utterly bewildered. The truth of his marriage appeared to be that his wife had been a beautiful lady who died tragically young. Surely he would want another such proper, comfortable union?

Or perhaps he was still lost in grief. Perhaps no other lady could compare with his lost wife, and he would rather live with her ghost than with any flesh and blood woman. That thought was just too inexpressibly sad.

But there was no time for further questions or conversation. The music from the assembly room was ending, and Kate would not have known what to say, anyway. She watched as he extinguished the cigar and offered his arm to escort her back to the building.

She knew what she wanted to *do*. She longed to hold him close to her, to kiss him until he forgot his sorrow and his lost wife. She wanted to feel the soft saltiness of his lips beneath hers, his skin under her hands, until all the past, his *and* her own, vanished forever.

But they had reached the steps and were climbing up them into the light and reality of the assembly. Her sharp longings disappeared, leaving behind only a certain sad wistfulness, a deep ache.

They paused together in the small doorway, her hand falling away from his arm as they watched the new set forming, partners seeking each other out in the crowd. Christina and Mr. Price stood in the corner, speaking together earnestly. No doubt they were going over the finer points of the properties of Linnaeus's taxonomy, all very proper, but Kate needed to join them and fulfill her chaperone duties.

"There is Lady Christina," she said, pointing the girl out to Michael.

"Yes. I suppose we should go over there, see what she and young Price thought of the dance." Michael paused, and for an instant Kate thought he might take her arm again. Might draw her close to his side. It felt like a natural, if unorthodox, thing to do, but finally he just stepped back and said, "Would you not like to dance, Mrs. Brown?"

"Dance?" *Only if it is with you,* she longed to shout.

The thought of gliding across the floor in Michael's arms, twirling and laughing—it would be utter bliss.

Yet it could not be. Not tonight. Kate shot one wistful glance at the dancers and said, "Oh, no. I must do my duty to your sister."

"Of course," he answered quietly. "We must both do our duties, of course."

Kate nodded, and turned to make her way toward Christina—and lonely safety.

Michael watched Kate Brown walk away from him. She was like an exotic peacock in her dark blue gown, her black hair gleaming in the candlelight, entwined with silvery ribbons—a peacock among chattering pastel sparrows. Many people watched her as she crossed the room, the men admiring, longing even, and the women uncertain, curious, suspicious. But she did not appear to notice anything. She just kept walking, her posture princess-perfect, head high, not looking to the left or right, until she reached Christina and Mr. Price in the corner.

To them, she gave a sunny smile, full of open friendliness. The pale perfection lit up with that smile, turning the remoteness of her beauty into something truly glorious. Like a sunburst on a summer's day, or the end of a winter rainstorm when the light peeked forth from behind heavy gray clouds.

What he would not give to have her smile at *him* like that, to be welcomed into her mysterious heart just for a moment.

"Mr. Lindley?" a woman's voice said at his side, suddenly making him realize that he was staring at Kate Brown like a love-starved calf. Just as almost every other man in the room was doing. And people would surely notice, if they had not already. He would be an utter cad if he exposed her to gossip after only such a short time in the neighborhood.

He tore his gaze away from Kate's smiling lips and turned to see Lady Ross next to him. His mother's social rival was a small woman, not even coming up to his shoulder, and her round face possessed the echoes of a sweet beauty. The curls that peeped from beneath her purple silk turban had once been as red as her daughters', but were now a pale dusty rose. She looked to be everything that was soft and genteel.

But her cat-green eyes were sharp.

"Lady Ross," he said, giving her a small bow. "I hope you are enjoying the assembly?"

"Oh, I am really too old for such frivolity now, I fear," she answered with a laugh. "I would rather stay home at Ross Lodge next to a good fire. But my girls do so enjoy dancing, I could not deprive them. Emmeline especially." She gestured with a folded fan, sending Michael's attention toward her daughter. Emmeline was twirling happily in the dance, her cheeks pink and her tawny curls bouncing. "Such a lively girl she is!"

Lively indeed, Michael thought. But not the lady for him, if only his mother and Lady Ross could be brought to see that.

His glance slid from Emmeline Ross to Kate Brown. Her sleek, dark head was tilted to the side as she listened to Christina, a small smile on her lips—the very picture of dignity, serenity, and mystery.

"All of your daughters are very pretty, Lady Ross," he said noncommittally.

"And they always enjoy meeting with your family. Emmeline tells me that your daughter grows prettier all the time, and so accomplished. Emmeline is vastly fond of children."

"Thank you, Lady Ross. Amelia *is* very pretty, though I do say so myself."

Lady Ross nodded, then obviously decided she had made her point and changed topics. "I was sorry your mother could not be here."

"So was she, Lady Ross. But I am sure her headache will be better tomorrow."

"I shall call on her in the afternoon, with a bottle of my cherry cordial." Lady Ross's catlike green eyes slid across the crowd to narrow on Mrs. Brown. "In the meantime, your—governess, is she?—appears to be doing an adequate job as chaperone."

Michael watched as Kate said something quietly to Christina, who burst into giggles, covering her mouth with her gloved hand. *Adequate, indeed.* He had not seen Christina laugh so much in a very long time.

"Yes, Lady Ross," he answered. "Mrs. Brown has not been with us very long, but she is doing wonders for my sister."

"I am glad *someone* is able to," Lady Ross murmured. "My own daughters were never allowed to wander so freely about the moors. There are so many dangers lurking out there for young ladies. But Lady Christina is in very fine looks tonight."

"Thank you, Lady Ross," Michael said again, trying not to laugh aloud at her not well-veiled hints.

"Mrs. Brown is quite—exotic-looking," she went on. "She is not from some heathen place like Turkey or Persia, is she?"

"Mrs. Brown is from Venice. The widow of an English soldier."

"Hmph." Lady Ross's tone said that surely Venice was only a tiny step up from the stews of Constantinople. But then she dropped the subject of Mrs. Brown altogether and gave Michael her most charming smile. "I think the evening must be almost over, Mr. Lindley. Would you not care for one more dance? I am sure Louisa or Emmeline would be vastly happy to oblige you."

Michael pasted on an expression he hoped was politely rueful. "That would be a great delight, Lady Ross, but I fear my leg will not permit more than a dance or two in one evening."

"Oh, of course!" Lady Ross cried, all solicitude. "You always seem so very hale and hearty, Mr. Lindley, that one quite forgets—well, never mind. Perhaps a quick hand of cards? I have not had a good game of piquet all evening."

"Of course, Lady Ross. I would enjoy a game myself." He offered his arm to her, and she adroitly steered him toward the card room, chattering about some other sterling quality her Emmeline possessed.

Perhaps she thought that in the card room he would be shut away from Kate Brown's siren song. Little did Lady Ross know that not a wall, or a door, or a field, or even the cocoon of sleep, could make him cease to think of her. She had haunted his thoughts ever since he saw her standing alone on the moor, and surely she would continue to until he discovered all the truth about her.

Chapter Twelve

"That wasn't so dreadfully terrible, after all," Christina commented as she and Kate made their way up the staircase at Thorn Hill to their chambers. She sounded comically surprised.

Kate laughed. "No, it was very pleasant. And Mr. Price seems like a nice young man."

Christina shrugged carelessly. "He's nice enough. Better than Mr. Haigh-Wood or Lord Carrollton. At least Mr. Price is interested in scientific matters."

They had reached the door to Kate's room. "Speaking of scientific matters, Lady Christina—wait here. I have something for you."

Christina's sleepy eyes brightened. "Something for *me,* Mrs. Brown? Oh, no, you've already given me the rose lotion."

"This is different. Just wait a moment." Kate slipped into her chamber and, by the light of the fire already laid in her small grate, found the package she had tucked in the bottom of her wardrobe. She felt almost giddy as she pulled it out, its light weight balanced in her hands.

So seldom in her life had she had the chance to *give.* It was an odd, warm feeling, so different from the cold gratitude, the obligation of *taking.* It was a sensation she could get dangerously used to.

Christina stood patiently in the corridor when Kate reappeared, Christina's expression curious and excited as she took the package.

"Oh, what is it?" she asked, turning the gift over

and over in her hands. "Is it—oh." Her eyes narrowed. "It isn't another copy of *La Belle Assemblée,* is it?"

Kate laughed. "No, no! Just open it and see. I hope you don't already have it. The bookseller in Suddley said it is a new edition."

Christina tore away the wrapping. *"Species Plantarum!"* she cried. "Oh, Mrs. Brown, this is the finest gift ever. It is a classic of botanical theory." With no warning at all, she lunged across the corridor to throw her arms around Kate. "Thank you so very much."

Kate wasn't sure what she should feel, or how she should react. Her mother had always taught her that the happiness of other people was a commodity, something a woman must create and build on until she could turn it to her advantage and gain what she wanted.

But right now, at this instant, Christina's happiness was its own reward. It made Kate happy, too. It made her forget all the curious stares at the assembly, the petty snobbery and hidden whispers about her "foreignness."

The only thing *nothing* could make her forget was the sharp disappointment at not being able to dance with Michael.

She returned Christina's exuberant hug, and even kissed her cheek before the girl stepped away. "I thought you deserved a small treat after your beautiful behavior at the assembly."

Christina stared down at the book in wonder, as if it were a casket of rubies. "You do understand, Mrs. Brown."

"Understand?"

"About my interests. Botany isn't just something that's a pastime, a hobby until I get married. It's . . ." She paused, frowning as she searched for words. "It's important. When I study how nature works, I feel as if I'm catching a glimpse of the mind of God. Do you see?"

Kate watched the girl with a strange mix of awe

and envy in her heart. Christina was so young to be so learned, to know what she loved and what she wanted in life. Would Kate ever have that for herself? Or was she damned to wander forever, never knowing her place or purpose?

Impatiently, Kate shook away these pangs of self-pity. They were quite unwarranted, she thought—she was already learning about herself, here at Thorn Hill. She was learning that she could care about other people, about Christina and little Amelia. About the handsome, charming Michael Lindley, who carried such sadness in his celestial blue eyes.

If she could, she would hold them all to herself forever. But that was impossible. They didn't belong to her. They never could. It was enough that she could love them secretly in her heart, and know they would be a part of her forever.

"Yes, Christina," she said, knowing that her silence had gone on too long. "I do understand."

"When you first came here, Mrs. Brown, I told Michael and Mother that I had no need of a governess."

"And you don't. I could never teach you more of the things you love. I know nothing of science or plants—except how to arrange flowers, of course." She knew nothing of the mind of God—except that it worked in very strange ways indeed.

"But you *can* help me!" Christina cried. "You can show me how to move about in Society, how I can stop feeling so strange and awkward every time I go to a party. You can help me . . ." Her voice faltered.

"I can help you what, Christina?" Kate encouraged.

Christina stared down at her book, a red blush spreading its stain over her cheeks. "You could help me to find a proper suitor, someone I could like and who would understand me."

Kate smiled gently. Yes. That she *could* help her with. She thought of the young man she had met tonight, Mr. Price, and how he watched Christina with such admiration. "Of course. I will do my very best."

At that moment, a door opened farther down the

corridor, spilling firelight in golden squares onto the carpet runner. Lady Darcy appeared there, a large shawl draped over her nightdress, her hair covered in a ruffled muslin cap.

"Christina?" she called. "Is that you, my dear?"

"Yes, Mother," Christina answered dutifully. She slipped the new book into her reticule with the volume she had smuggled into the assembly. "Mrs. Brown and I were just retiring."

Lady Darcy pressed her hand to her brow and said, "Well, come in here and tell me all about the assembly. I'm desolate that I had to miss it!"

Christina leaned forward and whispered in Kate's ear, "Desolate that she had to leave Lady Ross as sole queen of the assembly rooms!" Louder, she said, "Of course, Mother. Good night, Mrs. Brown."

"Good night, Lady Christina." Kate waited until the door shut behind Christina before she returned to her own room. The silence felt thick after the music and chatter of the assembly, the shadows lurking in the corners deep. Kate went to open the draperies at her window, perching on the windowsill to stare down at the quiet gardens. It was all so peaceful and perfect. She could become accustomed to it.

Too accustomed to it.

Kate laughed at herself, longing after things she could never have. Her mother would have said it was all the fanciful poetry she consumed, giving her romantic notions. She lacked the pragmatism to be a true courtesan. Even if the accident had never happened, even if she had gone on in her mother's Venetian footsteps, she would never have been as glorious and famous as Lucrezia was. Her soul would have always longed for something other than what she had. For freedom.

She saw that so clearly now. In Venice, she had tried to tell herself that she wanted parties and jewels, admiration and fame, lust, renown. But it was not true. Here, stripped of those luxurious trappings, she was happy.

Kate the curst. Cursed to seek and wander, and never possess.

Kate reached up to pull the pins and ribbons from her hair, letting the heavy black mass tumble over her shoulders. Her reflection in the window glass stared back at her, and for one shocked moment she thought she saw her mother there.

People had always remarked on her resemblance to Lucrezia, the same pale oval face and glossy hair, the same winged brows and slightly too long nose.

Kate reached out to touch that face, but all her fingertips encountered was cold glass. She closed her eyes tightly.

She had hoped—feared—that her mother's ghost came back to advise her. Kate had not seen her, even in her dreams, since that night in Maria's cottage. But no. Kate was all alone.

Alone, with a sudden sharp urge to see those Italian objects displayed in the library.

Kate grabbed a shawl and left her chamber, not bothering to put her hair back up. Just as on the other night she had slipped down to the library, the house was silent. Christina either was still talking with her mother or had gone to bed, and it was quiet behind Amelia's door. Kate peeked in there, but the child was tucked in safe and warm, her arm around her doll.

She knew her routine in the library now. She lit the tall candelabras by the fireplace, and also a smaller branch of candles to carry over to the glass cases. As she held the flickering light high, she almost gasped aloud at the glittering beauty she found there.

One case held the Murano glass she fantasized about, a myriad of tiny animals and flowers in shades of red, green, blue, amber, and diamond-bright clearness. There was even a small gondola, perfect in every detail, down to the plump cushions and the flat hat on the gondolier's head. Another case held more ancient treasures: Roman coins, a gold Etruscan vase, fragments of colorful mosaics, a chipped marble head of Athena almost ethereal in its beauty.

On the wall above the cases were paintings, a Giorgione of a nude Aphrodite, slumbering on velvet blankets in the midst of an Italian landscape. A Titian of a bright-haired Madonna ascending into heaven. A darker Caravaggio, of a Gypsy woman reading the palm of a richly dressed gentleman while a small, ragged urchin stole his purse.

"Well, Mr. Lindley," Kate murmured aloud as she examined these exquisite canvases. "You have quite the eye."

"Thank you," a man's voice answered.

A scream of cold fear strangled in Kate's throat. *A ghost!* A thief! She whirled around, holding her candelabra high as a weapon—only to find Michael Lindley himself sitting in a dark corner far from the Italian display. He still wore his evening clothes but had discarded his coat and cravat. His brocade waistcoat and fine linen shirt hung open, revealing a deep vee of strong, bronzed chest, a sprinkling of crisp light brown hair.

Suddenly, something far different from fright caused Kate's breath to quicken.

Michael grinned at her, and she noticed that on a table beside him were a decanter of brandy and a half-empty glass. He was drinking, which would explain the careless way he lounged in his chair, his long legs stretched out, and that happy grin. He hadn't had very much time to imbibe, of course, and he wasn't in the least bit sloppy, as many of her mother's friends became when they drank. He just seemed casual and—happy.

Happy, but with a strange, dark edge. His smile was a bit *too* careless. And Michael was not a careless man.

Kate lowered her candelabra, and stepped back until she felt the edge of the case against the small of her back.

"I didn't know anyone was in here," she said. "I'm sorry to intrude, Mr. Lindley."

"You are not intruding at all, Mrs. Brown," he answered. His words were steady, not at all slurred, but there was an undercurrent to his tone she could not understand. "You are welcome in here anytime you like."

"Thank you. I could not sleep, and I thought I would catch a glimpse of your Italian collection."

"Ah, yes. Feeling homesick tonight?"

Kate gave a vague smile as she remembered her thoughts and memories while she was alone in her room, her fright when she thought her own reflection was the ghost of her mother. "Perhaps a bit."

"And who could blame you? Who would *not* long for Italy after an evening at the Suddley assembly rooms?" He held up the decanter invitingly. "Care for some brandy?"

Suddenly, brandy was *just* what Kate cared for. The feeling of the warm, rich liquid sliding down her throat, bringing heavy oblivion. "Thank you, Mr. Lindley. I *would* like a brandy."

He drew another chair up beside his and gestured for Kate to be seated before he poured out another glass of the amber-colored liquor. "Please, Mrs. Brown, it seems ridiculous for you to call me Mr. Lindley in here. This library is beginning to feel like our own sanctum, is it not? You must call me Michael."

Kate sipped at her drink, as it was as smooth and warm as she had hoped. It made her toes tingle most pleasantly inside her new stockings. She had thought of him as Michael, her own archangel, so many times. But to say it aloud . . . "I'm not sure I can."

"Oh, come now," he coaxed, with a smile that could persuade a woman to do anything at all—even call him by his given name. "It is a simple name, really. Very easy. Mi-chael. And my mother is not in here to catch us being improper."

Kate laughed, and took another drink of brandy. It was really quite fine. "Very well, then. Michael it is." The name felt so dark and sweet on her tongue, so perfect. "Michael."

"*Va bene.* And what of you?"

"Me?"

"What is your first name? I am sure it cannot be just *Kate*. You are as Italian as that Giorgione over there, and Kate is a most prosaic English name."

Kate glanced over at the Venus, sleeping so incongruously in the countryside. She remembered, quite irrelevantly, how she had thought Michael to be Botticelli's Mars when she first saw him. "My full name is Katerina." And it was the first time she had said it— even thought it—in months. It didn't seem like her name anymore.

Michael smiled into his glass. " 'They call me Katherina that do talk of me.' "

"How clever of you, Michael!" His name came more easily to her now, as if she had been saying it for years and years. "My mother so admired that play, I was named for it. But now I am not Katerina. 'You lie, in faith; for you are called plain Kate.' "

" 'And bonny Kate, and sometimes Kate the curst; / But, Kate, the prettiest Kate in Christendom,' " Michael said, finishing the quote. He watched her as he spoke, with his fathomless blue eyes. "But was your mother not Venetian? How did she come to be a devotee of Shakespeare?"

He refilled their glasses, and Kate took another smooth swallow. "My father was English," she said, the alcohol giving her the bravery to tell a truth she had never spoken of before. "A scholar. He came to Italy to study literature, Boccaccio, Dante, Petrarch, and he met my mother on an excursion to Venice. They were very young, my mother barely sixteen, and apparently quite giddy with love and the joys of art, books, and the theater. He introduced her to Shakespeare."

"And what happened?"

"He died before I was born." Kate took a deeper drink of her brandy. "Of one of the fevers that sweep through Venice from time to time. All my mother had left of him was Shakespeare—and me." And a life Lucrezia had only so briefly broken away from, the life of her own mother—a courtesan.

"She raised you all by herself?" He seemed so very interested in her mundane, sordid tale.

"Yes." By herself—and the *comte,* the baron, the archbishop, the general, the prince, and Edward the duke. Kate's scholar father had been Lucrezia's first lover, but not her last.

Yet he *was* her only love. Lucrezia declared that to Kate until her dying day.

"She sounds like a very courageous woman," Michael said.

"Indeed she was."

"What became of her? You said she died in a boating accident?"

"Yes. Shortly before I—before I married and came to England. It was the accident where I got this scar of mine."

"I am very sorry, Kate. I never meant to bring up memories for you that must be painful. I would never want to make you sad." He slid his hand over hers where it lay on the arm of her chair, his fingers strong and rough, but very warm. Kate turned her hand over to entwine those fingers with her own, holding them tightly. Somehow, she felt safe with that touch, anchored into a reality that was free from ghosts.

"I'm not sad," she answered. "Not now. My mother gave me much—particularly in her death. I think of a different Shakespeare work now when I remember her—'Full fathom five thy father lies; / Those are pearls that were his eyes.'"

They sat in silence for a long moment, bound by the touch of their hands, the glow of brandy and candlelight, the bittersweet ache of loss and memories.

Kate stared back at the paintings, at the way they evoked her home with only a few brilliant brushstrokes. They were glorious in their beauty—and they said much of the man who had collected them. "I do love your paintings, Michael. Especially the Caravaggio. He does not get the appreciation he deserves."

Michael laughed. "Indeed not, which is why I was able to procure that canvas so cheaply. I like the mischief on the pickpocket's face, the light of the woman's dark eyes. And the vacuous smile of the man— he is getting just what he deserves. It is so sly, so true to life."

"Yes." Kate's eyes drifted sideways from Caravaggio's pickpocket to another painting she had not noticed before. It was a portrait, not in the Italian style and not old. Indeed, she would have guessed the artist was Elizabeth Hollingsworth, for it had a similar style to that lady's portrait of Kate's own mother.

This painted lady was not dark like Lucrezia Bruni, but fair as a spring day. Long golden curls fell loose over the shoulders of the white gown, and her laughing eyes were as blue as the painted sky above her. A red satin sash encircled her waist, the color echoed in the flower she held in one hand. The other hand rested on her lap, displaying a gold wedding ring. She looked so sweet and girlish, so perfect and guileless.

In fifteen years or so, this is what Amelia would look like. It had to be her mother, Michael's wife.

Kate sat up straight, her fingers trailing away from Michael's.

He followed her gaze, his half smile fading. "Ah. I see you have met my wife. Mrs. Caroline Lindley."

"She was very beautiful," Kate whispered.

"Yes, she was. The Diamond of the Season when I met her." Michael drained his glass and reached for the decanter to pour out more. "Everyone sought her out. But she made the dreadful mistake of marrying me."

Kate had never heard that bitter note in his voice before, and she did not like it. She reached over and clasped his wrist before he could take another drink. "A mistake? But did you not love each other?"

"Oh, yes. We loved each other. But you see, bonny

Kate, I was not then the man you see before you now. I did not yet see the value of family and respectability. I cared only for the London life—gaming, drinking. Having a good time."

Kate relaxed a bit, but she still held his wrist. It was warm and smooth under her touch. "Everyone is young once, and everyone does foolish things then. There is no sin in that."

"No sin in murder?"

Kate felt her skin turn cold under the lash of those words. Surely she could not have heard him right! Her hand flinched away from him. "M-murder? Did you kill someone? In a duel, or something like that?"

Michael shook his head. "I did not run anyone through with a sword or shoot them with a pistol. But I *was* responsible for my wife's death."

Kate felt caught in a strange, hazy nightmare. The brandy made her mind slow, her thoughts sluggish. She glanced over at the portrait, but Caroline Lindley just went on smiling her serene, eternal smile. "What happened?"

"It was not very long after Amelia was born. I know Caroline—and my mother—hoped that fatherhood would help settle me, would separate me from the wild friends of my youth. But I felt so happy when I saw that tiny girl, so exuberant. I agreed that I would go to the country with Caroline and the baby, but first I wanted one more adventure. A celebration of sorts. I was going to race some friends to Brighton in my phaeton, and Caroline insisted on going along, even though it was not the sort of thing she fancied."

Kate did not want to hear any more. She was sure she knew all too well what was coming—merriment turned to tragedy in the blink of an eye. Lifelong scars. Hadn't Christina said her sister-in-law died in an accident? "Your leg . . ."

"Yes. We crashed. Something darted into the road, and I swerved to avoid it, but we were going too fast. I broke my leg, crushed it, along with my collarbone. But Caroline—she died instantly. Her neck broken."

He, too, looked to the portrait, the beautiful image that held no essence of his lost wife. "Now you know my deep, dark secret, Kate. I give it into your hands."

Yet she still held on to her secrets—and would forever. She took his hand again in both of hers, as if she would literally hold his secrets safe for him. "It was certainly a tragedy. But never a murder, Michael. An accident."

"It was my carelessness that killed her. If I had listened to her pleas . . ."

"Perhaps. We humans are prone to careless mistakes. It is one of our terrible flaws. I have watched you since I came to Thorn Hill—there is no evil in your soul, no will to hurt others or possess them against their wills, as some people have. You love your family, your home, the life you have made here. I am sure you loved your wife. You were young and foolish. You made a dreadful mistake. You were never a bad person. You never *murdered* her, and she knows that. Did she not choose you out of all her suitors? I'm sure she could see what I see."

Michael stared at her, his gaze unreadable. Yet she thought perhaps she saw the beginnings, the flickerings, of hope there, buried under the old guilt, struggling to shine through.

"Where did you learn such things, Kate?" he asked quietly. "From Shakespeare?"

She smiled at him. "Of course. And from my own mistakes, of which there are many."

"I think you are too wise for that. Too kind to make such mistakes."

"Ah, no. You see, I, too, am young and foolish. But I am trying to be better. I try every day. It is all any of us can do. We can't erase the past, but we can build a finer future." She reached up, compelled to touch Michael's face, to ease the tense lines on his brow with her fingertips. His skin was smooth under her touch, taut satin over high cheekbones, rough along his jaw. He was close, so close she could drown in the blue of his eyes. *Full fathom five . . .*

He, too, seemed enchanted by this moment out of time, woven of confidences and brandy. He caught her hand and kissed the tips of her fingers. His lips were soft and firm, so gentle where they touched her skin and left stardust behind. "I am a foolish man still, Katerina," he murmured, his hoarse voice echoing against her fingers. "Because I must do this . . ."

His other hand reached behind her head, weaving through the loose strands of her hair, drawing her closer. Ever closer.

He was going to kiss her! Kate knew she should pull back, that this should not be happening. But she could no more draw away from him than she could cease to breathe. She craved that kiss—she *needed* it. It was unlike any other kiss she had ever received.

His movements were slow, easy, giving her time to draw back if she wanted. As her eyes drifted closed, she felt the brandy coolness of his breath on her cheeks, the heat of his skin, the clean scent of him. She reached up to twine her arms about his neck, to bring him even closer. The silk of his hair tumbled over her hands, clinging to her fingers, linking them together.

Their lips met softly, gently, once, twice, slowly finding their way to each other. Then the temptation, the heat, was too great to be resisted one more second. Their kisses melded, his tongue seeking hers, parting the soft seam of her lips.

"Mmm," Kate murmured at the taste of him, so dark and rich and perfect, the smoothness of brandy overlaying something more enticing, more dangerous. Tentatively, unsure of what he might like (for different men preferred different actions), she touched the tip of her own tongue to his.

Obviously, that was the right movement to make. Michael groaned, and his arms tightened around her. He pulled her across the chair onto his lap, until they were as close as their layers of silk and wool and linen allowed them to be.

Yet Kate wanted to be closer, ever closer. She slid

one hand down his throat, along the bare skin of his chest where his shirt parted. It was hot satin under her touch, alive and vital, roughened by the crisp curls that lowered along his torso in an enticing arrow. His heart leaped beneath her palm, and she reveled in the feel of its rhythm, in the way it responded to her own heartbeat, her own desire.

Then everything around her went soft and blurry, and she was utterly lost. Their kiss, their embrace, was the beginning and ending of her whole world, and she wanted nothing else.

His lips left hers, trailing along her cheekbone, her jaw, the tender spot behind her ear. She shivered at the close sound of his breath. *"Dolce, dolce amore,"* she whispered, clinging to him as if he was her only shelter in a shifting world.

"Say that again," he muttered, his hand softly caressing the underside of her breast. "Again."

"*Caro*—" she began.

But her whispers were cut off by the sound of a door slamming somewhere in the house, the rush of footsteps in the foyer.

No doubt it was only servants, a footman locking the doors for the night, but the sensual haze she floated in was coldly ripped apart. Kate opened her eyes, and was strangely shocked to see that the library around them was entirely unchanged. They had *not* been transported to some sunny, sensual island of their own making, to some red-curtained bed surrounded by flickering candles. They were still here, at Thorn Hill, with the lights sputtering low and reality rushing in on them.

Bitter disappointment flooded coldly through her veins, drowning out all the heated delight, the joy of discovery.

Michael's head dropped against her shoulder, his breathing as ragged as her own. His hand fell away from her breast to clasp the arm of the chair until his knuckles turned chalky white.

The loss of his touch left a hollow coldness in her

heart. Kate reached up to smooth his tousled hair. Hair she had only just mussed herself, with her seeking fingers. "Michael," she whispered tentatively.

"Sh," he growled. "Kate, my bonny Kate, please. Just—be—still. For a moment."

Kate let her head fall back against the chair cushions, and concentrated on breathing carefully in and out until her wild heartbeat had slowed, and the hazy edges of her vision cleared. She felt Michael's breathing slow against her shoulder.

Perhaps she was still tipsy on the brandy. Perhaps she would have bitter regrets in the light of morning. No—she was *sure* she would have bitter regrets! Daylight made all things dangerously clear—it ripped away the masks of night. Tomorrow, she would still be the governess—he would still be her employer. The past would still be with them.

But tonight—ah, tonight was so very sweet. She had been kissed before, yet never like that. Never until all the world faded away and the only important thing was the next mingled breath, the next press of skin against skin. She had trusted Michael as she had never before trusted a man, and he had led her into such delight.

Delight she wanted more of. That could not be denied, not with her mind reeling and her flesh tingling. Yet even if they never came together like this again— and they could not—she would always have this one precious gift.

Slowly, carefully, on legs that felt turned to water, she eased herself up off his lap. As she gazed down at him, she saw just how achingly handsome he was, all rumpled hair and sharp edges. His eyes, those glorious eyes, stared up at her, full of all the things she feared—regret, sorrow, loss. But there was also a gratifying amount of sheer desire.

"Kate," he said roughly. "I don't know what came over me; I must have been foxed, yet that is no excuse. I am sorry—"

"Hush." Kate cut him off, pressing her fingers to his lips. Those delicious lips she had just tasted, and which felt damp and enticing under her touch. "There is nothing to be sorry about, Michael, *caro*. Tonight was only a dream. Yes? A sweet dream which will vanish in the morning."

He appeared very much as if he wanted to say something more, to argue, to apologize again. Kate would have none of it. She knew her heart would surely break if he was sorry for their lovely kiss. Their time together. The kiss had been meant to help heal his soul just a tiny bit, to show him that he could not be the monster he thought himself if a woman could so desire him, so care about him.

She wanted only that to linger, the pleasure and healing, and nothing else.

"Just a dream," she repeated. With a farewell smile, she slid her finger from his lips and hurried from the library as quickly as her unsteady legs could carry her. She did not look back, and she didn't stop until she shut the door of her chamber behind her. Alone again—alone with the past.

Just a dream. Kate's words echoed in Michael's head, sweet and alluring. Indeed, it felt like a dream now that he was all alone again in the flickering shadows of the library. It was like any other night, when the household was all asleep yet he could not find his own slumber. When he was left with brandy, moonlight, and memories.

Yet it was like no other night had ever been. Kate's rose perfume lingered in the air; her touch glowed on his flesh. And he could taste the sweetness of her lips, her soft skin, could feel the glory of her hair as it flowed through his fingers.

Yes—she had been very real. And unlike anything he had felt before. Her sorcery was complete, and her kiss wove a wondrous spell around him until he never wanted to be free. Never wanted to let her go. But then she vanished, slipping away from him like an elusive curl of silvery incense, a morning mist that disappeared in the light.

Just a dream.

Michael threw his head back against the cushions of the chair and closed his eyes, trying to hold on to the vestiges of her magic.

He had not thought he was overimbibing the fine brandy. Just one glass, perhaps two—certainly not a drop to the great quantities he could consume in his youth. He had been feeling only a pleasant mellowness, a slow unwinding after the crowds of the assembly, and was beginning to think he should retire. Then the library door opened.

At first he thought he *was* dreaming, for she was such a vision. Her glossy black hair was loose, falling over her shoulders in a shining river of waves. A paisley shawl was thrown over her evening gown, surrounding her in shimmering silvers, grays, and blues. She didn't seem to be of the modern age, more like a medieval lady surveying her keep, a dark witch in search of midnight spells.

He watched in enraptured silence as she crossed the room, a candle in her hand casting a halo glow over her hair. She obviously did not see him there in his darkened corner, and she crossed the room to his Italian cases. Slowly, her light moved over the glass, the jumble of antiquities, the paintings.

His mother often told him he should move his Giorgione Venus out of the library and hide it in his own chamber, away from the eyes of "impressionable ladies." But he saw no reason to exile her. Amelia never came into the library, nor did his mother, except to quibble over the artwork and the arrangement of the furniture. And Christina didn't care two straws about paintings— she wanted only the books. So there Venus stayed. She would be lonely without her Italian companions.

Kate Brown did not gasp in shock at the nudity, or at Caravaggio's pickpocket. She simply gazed at them with her dark eyes, the light moving over them as her head tilted in examination. Finally, she smiled with admiration.

And he revealed his presence to her. At first they merely spoke of the art, of Italy, then somehow—well, somehow he lost his head. Perhaps it was the brandy, the nighttime, the intoxicating scent of her perfume. Or perhaps it was his own damnable loneliness. Whatever it was, he told her everything, all the secret guilt in his heart.

He confessed the truth of Caroline's death, and he would not have blamed Kate if she had run away in horror. If she left Thorn Hill immediately. Yet she did not. She held his hand in hers, her dark gaze never wavering from his face as he spoke. Her expression held only sympathy, sadness—and a deep understanding. As if she saw the truth of his words, his actions. As if she *knew*.

When she spoke, her soft words were like balm to a raw and aching soul. There was no condemnation, no false cries of moral outrage. Only what she herself thought and saw—and she thought he was a good man, and had atoned for his youthful mistakes. Mistakes, not crimes.

He wished he could believe her, but those old mistakes—those sins—were not so easily vanquished. He had carried them around for so long now. But for the moment, it was enough that *she* believed her words. That she thought him a good man, worthy of the precious gift of her kiss, her touch.

Her magical touch.

Michael knew that Kate could not be his forever. She was too fine for a rustic life such as this one at Thorn Hill, for a man scarred in mind and body. She was obviously here to soothe some wound of her own—the death of her husband or her mother—to rest in the quiet of Yorkshire; then she would fly away. Yet for now, for as long as he could, he would revel in the joy of *her*.

And that gave him more hope, more happiness, than he had known in years. Or perhaps ever.

Michael lifted his head and met the steady, violet blue gaze of Caroline's portrait. She seemed to smile at him gently, but also to be receding away from him. Fading. He pushed himself out of the chair and crossed the library to unhook the chain that held the painting to the picture rail.

As he lowered the canvas gently to the carpet, he thought that perhaps Amelia might like to have it in her own chamber. Then he extinguished the dying candles and left the room to seek his own bed—and dream of having Kate Brown in it.

It was very nearly the dawning of a new day.

Chapter Thirteen

The morning light peeking from between the curtains pierced Kate's eyelids like hundreds of tiny pokers. Her head felt tight, as if a band were being steadily tightened around it. Surely it wasn't morning already? She had only just fallen asleep.

Kate rolled onto her side, away from the demonic bar of light, and buried her face in the pillow. She groaned, reaching out to try to pull delicious sleep back to her. She should be able to rest a little while longer. And where was Bianca with her morning chocolate, anyway? That maid was always late. . . .

Suddenly, reality crashed down on her like a collapsing ceiling made of dreams and memories. She didn't *have* a maid anymore, and hadn't for a long time. Venice was far away. She was in Yorkshire, at Thorn Hill.

And she had spent last night drinking brandy in the library with Michael—her employer. Drinking, talking—kissing.

Oh, yes. Now she *especially* remembered the kissing. A soft smile tugged at her lips, and she could feel a giddy laugh bubbling up in her throat at the memory. His kiss had been just as she imagined it might. No, it was better. Sweet, heady, it answered a longing deep in her heart she had not even known was there. His embrace made her forget everything but that one moment, the feel of his hands against her body, the taste of his mouth, the hot rush of desire like a storm breaking over the earth.

It had been glorious. Just the way she always
thought a kiss should be. Not the suffocating feelings
of dread when Julian Kirkwood's lips met hers, or
the opera buffa comedy that ensued when a fat *comte*
cornered her at one of her mother's parties so long
ago. Michael's kiss had been a dream—just as she had
told him before she slipped away. There was no fear
in it, only delight.

A sweet dream.

Kate's head gave another painful twinge as she
moved against the pillow, reminding her that the
dream was decidedly over. It was daylight, and she
had to come fully awake. There was church today, and
watching over Amelia and Christina. She was Mrs.
Brown the governess again, and she had to remember
that from now on. Playing the wanton in night-dark
libraries could lead only to trouble.

If it hadn't already.

Kate pushed back the bedclothes and swung herself
out of the cozy bed, holding her aching head between
her hands. The fire had died out long ago and the air
was chilly, but Kate welcomed its bracing effect. It
cleared her thoughts, and hurried her footsteps across
the floor to the pitcher of cold water.

Once her face was washed and her hair brushed and
pinned up in a simple knot, she felt a bit more like
her sensible self. When she glanced into the mirror,
she halfway expected her features to be transformed,
twisted into something dissipated to reflect her fast
behavior, her wild desire for Michael Lindley. But no,
she was utterly the same. The oval face she had always
thought too thin, the nose too long. She was paler
than usual, and dark purple smudges marred the delicate skin under her eyes. Hopefully, though, if anyone
noticed, they would attribute it to her late night at
the assembly.

She dressed quickly in her lavender muslin gown,
wrapped her shawl around her shoulders, and hurried
out of her chamber en route to the schoolroom. A

light breakfast waited for her there, rolls and a pot of tea, but she barely had time to eat it before Christina came rushing in, Amelia trailing behind her. The elegant young lady of the evening before was nowhere to be seen. Her *La Belle Assemblée* coiffure had turned back into a tangled riot of curls, tied back carelessly with a ribbon, and she wore her dress with the blue green stain on her sleeve. She looked happy, though, as she snatched up one of Kate's rolls and sat down with a book in hand.

"The assembly last night wasn't all bad, was it, Mrs. Brown?" Christina asked.

Kate had to laugh. "Such a ringing endorsement, Christina! But no, it wasn't bad. The music was very lively."

"I wish I could have gone," Amelia said wistfully. "I would like to hear the music. Sometimes it seems to take so *long* to grow up!"

"I know, *bambina,* " Kate said, sitting down next to the child and straightening her pink hair ribbons. "But time goes so very fast. When you are a busy, grown-up lady, you will wish you had these days back again."

Amelia looked most doubtful. "Do *you* wish you were a child again, Mrs. Brown?"

Kate remembered her long voyage to England, her first days in London. She had been so overwhelmed by loneliness and uncertainty, so deeply unsure of the step she had just taken toward a new, strange life. In those weeks, she *had* thought longingly of her old home in Venice, a place filled with luxury and noise and people. But . . . "Not since I came to Thorn Hill. Here, I have just been happy to be myself."

She was startled to find how true those words were. In her short time here at Thorn Hill, so many things had changed in her heart. The old turmoil and strain fell away, leaving her with a newfound peace. A new, bright way of looking at life.

It was all so fragile, so precious. Like one of those

tiny Murano glass flowers. She had to hold it to her very tightly, and guard it closely, for fear it could shatter.

"What was your childhood in Italy like, Mrs. Brown?" Christina asked, brushing the crumbs of her roll from her bodice. "Your home must have been very different from here."

"Indeed it was. Shall we find Venice on the globe, my dears? I think we have time before church."

They spent the next hour in a happily improvised lesson, finding different Italian cities on the globe while Kate told them of how everyone in her home traveled by water. How the whole city seemed to float above the lagoon like a shimmering golden jewel box. She told them of the glorious churches, the galleries filled with the art treasures of centuries, the shops on the Rialto, the cafés. Christina and Amelia listened with fascinated gazes, enthralled as she tried to paint word visions of a place so very different from their own home here in Yorkshire.

"Oh, Mrs. Brown," Amelia breathed. "Why did you leave it all?"

Kate gave her a gentle smile. She could hardly tell the child the true reason—that she had fled a life of rich degradation for an uncertain, but free, future. She could never tell anyone that. "I got married, and my husband was English. I came here to live with him." The story, rather than growing easier with each telling, grew ever harder. The lie felt dry and choking in her mouth.

Amelia gave a puzzled frown. "Then where is your husband?"

"He died," Kate answered quietly. "And I came here to be your governess."

"He died!" Amelia cried. "Like my mama. Do you miss him a lot, Mrs. Brown?"

Before Kate could answer, there was a knock at the schoolroom door. Probably the maid Sarah with their luncheon. "Come in," Kate called, with some measure of relief.

But it was not Sarah. It was Michael himself who

appeared there in their doorway, handsome as the devil in a fine blue morning coat and buckskin breeches. His sun-touched brown hair was still damp from a recent washing, brushed back from his brow in shining waves. He would not have been out of place strolling down Bond Street.

And she looked like a ragpicker, Kate thought wryly, with her plain dress and sleep-deprived eyes. She had wanted so much to appear at her best when she saw him again, to show him that surely his desire for her was not born merely of brandy and moonlight. Before she could fall asleep last night, enveloped in her own haze of drink and heady desire, there had been a vague fantasy of candlelight and red silk, rubies in her perfectly dressed hair, a witty remark and throaty laugh.

The schoolroom, surrounded by books and the smell of ink, was a far cry from all that. Yet Kate found that when she gazed at him, she couldn't care less about the surroundings or her clothes. His smile made *her* want to smile, made her want to run into his arms and kiss him hello, to draw him by the hand to the settee and ask him how he felt this morning. Ask him if he felt as giddy as she was to see him, or if he felt only regret. He *had* tried to apologize to her last night, after all.

She searched his face carefully as she stood up, Amelia's hand still held in hers like a tiny lifeline. She saw nothing there, though, except that smile, a genial glow in his blue eyes. He seemed—happy.

Oh, please, Kate prayed silently. *Let him be happy!*

"Papa!" Amelia cried. She broke from Kate's clasp and dashed across the room to hug her father. He caught her up in his arms and kissed her cheek.

"Michael!" Christina said. "What are *you* doing here? Aren't you supposed to getting ready for church today?"

Michael laughed, the most glorious sound Kate had ever heard. "I rode out very early, and have just returned. I hope I'm not interrupting?"

"We were just having a geography lesson, Mr. Lindley," Kate answered. She looked away from his smiling face, as one had to turn from the sun after too long, and gazed down at the globe. She laid her hand gently over Italy.

"Mrs. Brown was telling what it's like to live in Venus," Amelia said.

"*Venice,* Amelia," Christina gently corrected.

"Yes. Venice," Amelia replied. "That's what I said."

"Indeed?" said Michael. "And what is it like to live in Venice?"

"Watery," Kate murmured without thinking. "Very watery."

Michael chuckled, a low rumble muffled against his daughter's curls.

Amelia tugged at his coat. "They ride everywhere in boats, Papa! Like when we go rowing sometimes, only they do it *all* the time. Even to the shops."

"Do they? Well, that *is* funny, since water plays a part in what I came here to ask the three of you."

Kate glanced back at him, puzzled. "Water, Mr. Lindley?"

"If you can take a pause in your lessons, Mrs. Brown, perhaps you and Christina and Amelia would care to accompany me on a picnic this afternoon after church. We could go look at the Semerwater, search for hints of the drowned city." He gave her a stare over Amelia's head, one filled with questions and heated desire, and an emotion she could not name.

For an instant, she forgot to breathe. Her hand tightened on the globe.

"Oh, yes, Michael, that sounds like such fun!" Christina said happily, saving Kate from having to answer when her throat was so tight. "I wanted to examine more closely a clump of valerian I saw growing there last month. May we, Mrs. Brown? It will be a kind of lesson."

Kate gave her a small smile. "Oh, yes. I think a nature walk would be just the thing for this afternoon. We can have a music lesson when we return, Amelia."

"Excellent," Michael said, giving her a secret grin over his daughter's head. "Then I will meet you ladies downstairs in half an hour. Cook will have a picnic ready for us by then."

Kate paused in laying out the picnic items to stare out over the Semerwater, her eyes shaded from the diffused sunlight by her new broad-brimmed straw hat. It was not a particularly grand or striking sight—it lacked the drama of paintings of Scottish lochs or the sensual allure of Lake Lugano. But it was pretty, a cool, flat expanse of pale blue gray water ringed by dark green trees. Stone farmhouses dotted the nearby slopes, with the ever-present stone walls tracing snake-like patterns on the ground.

The water lay still as a millpond today, placid and serene. Michael strolled along its edge with Amelia holding on to his hand, tugging him along. Her childish chatter floated like birdsong to Kate's ears. Her bonnet had fallen from her golden head and dangled down her back by its ribbons, leaving her curls springing free, gilded like guinea coins. Michael's own hat was held in his free hand, and the light breeze tousled his brown hair like a lover's fingers would, making it fall over his brow. He casually pushed it back, laughing down at his daughter.

Kate watched them with a strange proprietary pride, a smiling satisfaction. They made such a pretty portrait, the tall, handsome man and the sweet little child. They turned and waved back at her, identical merry smiles flashing warmer than the sun.

Kate waved back, and her heart gave an aching spasm. How she cared about these people! More than she had ever cared for anything, or even thought she *could* care. A life like her mother's demanded a certain callous detachment, a cool calculation. True emotion led to mistakes, to heartache.

As surely Kate would face heartache one day when she had to leave Thorn Hill and its family, never to kiss Michael again, or smile at his daughter or laugh with his sister. But for now she thought she could cry with the happiness that washed over her, the utter contentment with this perfect moment she had been unexpectedly gifted with. If she could only freeze time, keep this forever . . .

"Mother would say she will get freckles," Christina said.

Kate dabbed at her damp eyes before turning to Christina, who was examining some plants at the water's edge close to the picnic blanket. The apron she wore over her muslin day dress was covered with brown and green streaks. An open notebook and a pencil lay on a nearby rock.

"I beg your pardon, Christina? I was woolgathering," Kate said.

"Amelia and her bonnet. Mother would say she will get freckles from letting it dangle like that." Christina chuckled. "Freckles such as the ones I have."

"I don't think freckles will suddenly appear on her nose from one hour in the sun. But your mother is right—she shouldn't make a habit of it. And I see you wore your hat today, Christina. Thank you."

Christina touched the brim of her yellow straw bonnet as if she had forgotten it was there. "It keeps the light out of my eyes while I examine these specimens," she said quietly. "But I *did* use more of that rose lotion this morning. It smells so lovely."

"And it will make your skin very smooth by the time you go to Town, I promise. Now, do you have a moment to help me lay out the food for our picnic? I vow your cook sent enough for twelve people!"

Christina laughed, and left her plants to remove containers from the large basket. There were platters of cold chicken and ham, vegetables, a pork pie, a loaf of fresh bread, jellies, and cakes. There was a flagon of tea and one of lemonade. All spread out over their blanket, it *did* rather look like a meal for a flock of hungry laborers.

Once it was all settled, Kate walked with Christina down to the lake's shore to fetch Michael and Amelia.

Amelia ran over to her, catching at her skirts. "Oh, Mrs. Brown, look at what I found!" She held up a chunk of blue glass, worn perfectly smooth by the unceasing movement of the water. It shimmered like Kate's mother's sapphire brooch in the light.

Kate took it in her hand, carefully examining it for any rough edges that might cut tiny hands. Not finding any, she handed it back. "It's absolutely beautiful, Amelia, dear. You found a jewel from the sea."

Amelia giggled. "Semerwater isn't a *sea*, Mrs. Brown! It's a lake."

"Well, a jewel from a lake is even more precious," Kate answered.

"Come with me, Amelia," Christina called, holding her hand out to her niece. "You can show me your jewel. And I think cook sent some of those lemon cakes you like."

Amelia and Christina scampered away, their young steps nimble over the uneven ground. Kate felt a sudden wave of shyness as she found herself alone with Michael. Her cheeks were hot despite the cool breeze, and she couldn't meet his gaze as he watched her. And he *was* gazing at her. She could feel the touch of his regard, like soft petals drifting over her skin.

She peeked up at him from beneath her hat, and found his glance steady, a ghost of a smile drifting over his lips. She gave him a little smile of her own, and slid her fingers lightly over his sleeve when he offered her arm.

Never had she thought the day would come when she would have no idea what to say to a man, but here it was. All her light chatter, her store of inconsequential comments, had vanished. Her boldness in the library last night must have belonged to another woman. Only the hot rush of memories, the sensation of scent and need, still belonged to today's timid Kate.

What did a *respectable* lady say to a man the morning after she drank too much brandy and ended up sitting on his lap, kissing him passionately? She had no idea. But she did have suspicion that such ladies remained respectable because they never did find themselves in such situations.

Michael slowed his steps beneath the spreading branches of a tree, drawing Kate up at his side. "Kate—Mrs. Brown—" he began, then broke off with a rueful laugh. "I am not sure even what to tell you today. I feel like such a fumbling schoolboy."

Kate sighed in relief. At least she was not alone in her awkwardness. But it seemed to her that Michael should *never* feel unsure with any lady. Surely they all flocked to him, as starving masses to a luscious banquet. As the Ross girls did at the assembly. "You can call me Kate."

"I just wanted to say—about last night," he said, then paused.

Don't say you are sorry again, Kate silently pleaded. She didn't think she could bear it.

"I wanted to say thank you," he finished.

"Th-thank you?" Kate whispered in surprise.

"Yes. Oh, I'm not saying this well at all, Kate. But you don't know, *can't* know, how much your being here at Thorn Hill means to me. To all of us. I've been frozen so long. Or perhaps *drowned* is a better word. Just like your kingdom under this lake. Things were gray. Always gray. But now . . ." His words drifted away on the breeze.

"Now?" Kate prompted. She wasn't entirely sure what Michael was trying to tell her. Yet she *did* know it was something fine and good, something to cherish.

Just as the man himself was.

He smiled down at her. "I think Christina and Amelia are expecting us. I never meant to talk your ear off, Kate. I just wanted to tell you how much our time together last night, indeed every moment we have spent together, means to me. I never meant to disrespect you in any way with my—attentions." He gave her a boyish, apologetic grin. "I'm sure you can tell how long I've been a country widower. I'm more accustomed now to working in the fields than conversing with beautiful ladies."

He thought her *beautiful*? Kate's hand strayed up to pat at her hair, a warm glow of pleasure radiating out from her heart. Other people had told her that, of course, had paid her compliments that were far more florid or poetic. But she had never believed them, until this moment, under Michael's steady gaze.

"You have never treated me with disrespect, Michael," she answered, with a little smile. "And I, too, enjoy our time together."

"What are you both whispering about?" Christina called teasingly, shattering their tiny, fragile world of two. "You will miss the lemon cakes!"

"We are coming, Christina," Michael called back.

They turned their steps back toward the girls, but in her daydreams Kate still stayed beneath that tree with Michael, going up on tiptoe to press her lips to his.

Michael watched Kate as she talked with Christina and poured out a cup of lemonade for Amelia. Her slender hand smoothed Amelia's windblown curls, and their feminine laughter floated to him on the breeze, as light and perfect and sparkling as champagne.

He couldn't help but grin like a fool at hearing that sound, at seeing his daughter's face glow as she gazed up at Kate. Kate leaned back on the blanket, balancing herself on the palms of her hands as Amelia snuggled against her. Christina held up one of her precious plant specimens, pointing out aspects of the leaves and roots. His sister looked as young as Amelia then, content in her outdoor element.

How long had it been since he had seen them looking so very happy? Weeks? Months? It was true that life had been good for all of them since they came to Thorn Hill. His mother was relieved that he had given up his old ways, and that she had a household to oversee. Christina liked being close to nature, to her plants, though he thought she would enjoy being near people who shared her interests: scientific societies, museums, and such. Amelia—Amelia was his sweet cherub, his pride and joy. But she was growing up; she was not a baby any longer. She needed a lady to look after her.

And he, Michael? What did *he* need? All these years, since Caroline died, he thought he needed only work. Hard work, and looking after his family, putting their needs first always, was the only way he knew to atone for his old sins, to begin to forget them. Building walls under the warm sun, feeling the ache of his muscles, the honest sweat, brought forgetfulness. If he labored hard enough, stayed up late enough with the ledgers, he could even sleep at night, free from dreams and ghosts.

He enjoyed his time with his family, listening to their conversation, watching the intense concentration on Amelia's little face as she played a new piece of music. He liked his occasional visits to the buxom Becky at the Tudor Arms. It was a good life, one he had cobbled together piece by piece all on his own.

But lately—ah, lately he had felt differently. A strange discontent would come over him at the oddest moments, a longing for something else. Something *more,* something grander and deeper.

He could date these longings to one particular moment. The moment he saw a lady in gray standing alone on the moors near a broken-down post chaise, gazing steadily at him with unreadable dark eyes. Every encounter with Kate Brown had only deepened his need to know more about her, to know *everything.* Yet she remained so elusive, even when she was in his arms. Whenever he thought she was in his grasp, she danced lightly away, as a sprite made of air and water.

Those brief moments when he had kissed her, felt her body against his, were perfect. She fitted there as if they had always been together, and the taste of her was sweet, like the richness of an Italian summer, the headiness of new wine.

But then he was left alone again in the darkness, and it was as if she had been a dream in truth. Until they met again this afternoon, and he felt her magic anew. He became a tongue-tied lad again.

Kate, though, appeared as cool and tranquil as a Raphael Madonna. As if she had never wound her arms about him, moaning softly under his kisses. Perhaps she had brought a twin sister with her into Thorn Hill, he thought whimsically, and it was the twin who gave him brandy-scented caresses in the library.

Whatever her sorcery was, he was becoming uncomfortably aware of one thing—he did not want to be without her. Ever. When he knew he would see her, his heart felt light and merry as it had not in a very long time. Anytime he gazed on her, as he did now, watching her laugh with his daughter, he felt—could it be? He felt *happy*.

"Michael!" Christina called, waving at him with her muddy hand. "Are you going to stand there daydreaming all afternoon, or are you going to eat with us?"

He laughed. He *had* been standing there for an inordinately long time, staring at them as if they were a dream vision. Perhaps he had gotten too much sun today, and that was what caused these roiling emotions.

But he knew in his heart that was not so. It was Kate—his bonny Kate. His curst Kate.

"I'm going to eat, definitely," he answered, striding toward them. Kate and Amelia slid over, making room for him on the blanket. Kate smiled up at him from beneath her straw hat. Red satin ribbons fluttered in the breeze, tangling with strands of her black hair fallen from their pins.

She impatiently pushed that hair back and said, "Would you care for tea or lemonade, Mr. Lindley? And Christina, please do wash your hands before you eat that sandwich. There might be some poisonous residues from those plants."

"Oh, no, Mrs. Brown!" Christina protested, but she *did* pour water over her hands and wipe them with a cloth from the basket. "Rosemary has no poisonous properties at all. In fact, it is used in salves and lotions and in cooking."

Kate poured out a cup of tea and passed it to Michael, her soft fingers barely brushing his along the smooth porcelain. She trembled, and her gaze turned away. Christina, oblivious to all but her plants, chattered on as Kate arrayed delicacies onto plates and handed them around neatly, as if she were presiding over a grand tea party. She wiped sticky lemonade from Amelia's chin and spread a napkin over the child's dress. All the while, Michael was achingly aware of how near she was, of the pink blush of her skin, the wind-tossed strands of her glossy hair, the sharp turn of her cheekbones, and the softness of her parted lips.

He had to look away from her, to jerk his gaze out over the water before he exploded with the wild need to catch her in his arms and press kisses to those lips.

She seemed to sense his desire, because she edged imperceptibly away, concentrating carefully on her food and on making sure Amelia did not completely stuff herself with cake. Eventually, the warmth of the spring day and the fullness of their stomachs brought a slow lassitude down onto their little party. Even Christina fell silent, leafing through a book, and Amelia drowsed across Kate's lap, her little limbs heavy and her hand clasped on a fold of Kate's skirt.

Michael's powerful desire grew softer at the edges, mellowing into a golden contentment, a quiet joy just in having this time with them. It was enough for now to have Kate near him.

Her hand drifted lazily over Amelia's hair, smoothing it back from the sleeping child's brow. "The lake does not look as if it could possibly have a city drowned beneath it, does it?" she said softly, her Italian accent more pronounced than usual. "It is so very placid. Like glass."

Christina looked up from her book to gaze at the

water. "It is usually calm like this, and cool in the summertime for boating and swimming. Though, of course, I am not *actually* supposed to swim. Mother would be quite angry if she knew."

Michael chuckled. "Very naughty of you, Tina."

"Shocking," said Kate, but she did not sound at all shocked. Her voice was heavy with laughter.

He wondered what it would be like if he could lure *her* to a moonlight swim one summer's night.

"But do you think there is a city under there somewhere?" Kate asked, to no one in particular. "A lost kingdom?"

"Semerwater isn't big enough for a whole kingdom," Christina said practically. "It is only about a hundred acres. But it *can* swell to twice that size during a storm. It isn't placid then."

"Indeed, most people around here would not care to be near Semerwater when it overflows its banks," said Michael. "The waves are whipped up, sweeping sheep and men into its depths."

"I have heard that sometimes after a storm, when the waters recede, there can be found strange artifacts," Christina added. "Amulets and cooking utensils. Perhaps the old legend came about because there is a prehistoric village under the waters. People *have* seen things there—even spirits at night."

Kate's brow creased, and her arms tightened around Amelia. Her dark eyes took on a strange, haunted light as they stared out over the concealing water. "I would not like to be here to see that storm," she whispered.

Michael laid his hand gently on her shoulder. She must be thinking of the storm that gave her that scar, and took her mother's life. She shivered under his touch, but did not move away. He wanted to do more, to fold her in his sheltering embrace and hold her close, to tell her that she would never have to fear rough waters again. Yet he sensed that she would not welcome his embrace—that she was very far away from him at that moment. She stared out over a vista he could scarcely even imagine, at a life that was past and that he could have no part of.

Who are you? his mind whispered urgently. *Who are you, Kate the curst?*

Chapter Fourteen

*T*he sunlight hurt his eyes, piercing like tiny pin-pricks. Julian Kirkwood slid on his new smoked-glass spectacles, and leaned his head back against the tufted velvet cushions of the carriage. The shades were drawn over the windows, yet the day was still too bright. He had been too long confined in the cool dimness of the convent hospital. Far too long.

Now he was going home. Home to London.

Home. Such a strange word, a foreign word. His family's estate was here in England, their grand London house. They were all his now, his birthright, his great fortune. His family was gone, all but his sister Charlotte, who had sent this carriage to fetch him at Dover and who waited to welcome him back from the dead.

But the paradise of his life in Venice, his true home, was gone forever, snatched away from him by a cruel fate.

A sharp pain pierced his head, and he groaned in pain and grief.

Katerina. His lost princess, the Renaissance Beatrice who was meant to be his own. She was dead, and he had to flee from Italy to try to be free of her memory, her alluring ghost. The memories of her dark eyes, filled with all the secrets of the many lives she had lived before, haunted him day and night. Even in that cold, bare convent, she danced through his dreams, beckoning to him. She was *his*! His. How could he live without her?

Perhaps here, in England, in a chilly land that held no memories of her, he could begin to forget.

He groaned as the carriage jolted over the ruts in the road, sending more shards of pain into his head. "Katerina," he whispered. "My princess."

Chapter Fifteen

"Michael, my dear, I had the most interesting letter from Charles today," Lady Darcy said. "I have it here in my workbox someplace. . . ." She dug about in said box, laying aside bits of embroidery and netting in search of the elusive letter.

Kate did not mean to eavesdrop. She was sitting at the pianoforte next to Amelia, listening to the child play a short piece by Haydn, and the rest of the drawing room was very quiet. The tea things were cleared away, and Christina and Michael were both absorbed in their own books. The picnic at Semerwater earlier in the day, the long, sweet hours in the sunlight and fresh air, had brought on a weary heaviness that grew greater as the time to retire approached.

Kate turned over the page of Amelia's music and watched the three people grouped around the fireplace. Michael glanced up from his book and smiled lazily at his mother. The dancing firelight cast a red gold glow over his hair, and she had the silliest wish that the smile was meant for *her*.

"Interesting news from Charles, eh?" he said. "London must be lively at this time of year, all his friends opening their townhouses for the Season. I trust his work in the House of Lords is going well?"

"Oh, yes, of course—when he can find time to sit in on sessions, of course," Lady Darcy said rather dismissively, as if politics had no bearing on "interesting" things. She still searched through her box. "But this news is even greater! And it concerns us all."

At that, even Christina blinked up from her book. "All of us?"

"Yes. Ah, here it is." Lady Darcy drew the paper up with a flourish. "Mary is enceinte at last!"

Christina sighed in a way that clearly stated her sister-in-law's pregnancy could have nothing to do with *her*. "I'm very happy for her, I'm sure."

Michael surreptitiously nudged his sister with his foot. "That is excellent news, Mother. I know Charles and Mary have been longing for such a blessed event for many months."

"Yes, indeed. A new future Earl of Darcy," Lady Darcy said happily. "Yet that is not all he writes. It appears Mary is not doing as well as could be hoped. She keeps to her bed much of the time, and things are becoming so very busy in Town right now. Charles says he cannot possibly manage on his own, and asks that we come to Lindley House to assist him."

Christina's book dropped to her lap. "London? Truly?"

"Yes. As soon as we can organize things here, he writes."

Michael watched his mother with narrowed eyes. "Surely only *you* need to go to London, Mother. To act as Charles's hostess and such. And Christina could go with you, but there is no need for my presence."

"Of course there is!" Lady Darcy cried. "Christina and I could not possibly travel such a distance on our own. We shall need your escort on the journey, and when we are in Town. Charles will be too busy to always squire us about. And you have not been to Town in ages, Michael. It cannot be good for a young man such as yourself to be always buried in the country. This will make a nice change."

"Spring is a very busy time for the farm, Mother," Michael answered. "Just as it is for Town Society."

Lady Darcy waved her hand in a dismissive gesture. "That is what bailiffs are for! We *need* you, Michael. It would not be for long. Charles writes that he intends

to take Mary to Darcy Hall in the summer, and they
will await the birth there."

"Oh, yes, Michael!" Christina suddenly urged. "Just
think of it—London. Museums and the Royal Botanic
Garden, lectures, bookshops. I could not go to them
on my own."

Kate stared very hard at Amelia's sheet music,
stared until the black notes blurred. Michael would
leave her soon. London was very far away, and he
would surely be there until the summer. Or even
longer—Town could be very enticing, with lovely ladies, ballrooms, gaming hells, delights of all sorts. Perhaps once he was there his old life would lure him,
and he would forget all about Thorn Hill and his
dowdily dressed governess.

She swallowed past the bitter lump in her throat
and blinked hard against the sudden itchiness behind
her eyes. She was being ridiculous! She had no claim
on Michael Lindley, none at all, and he had none on
her. She had been alone for a long time now. Why
did the thought of being deprived of his presence, of
not being able to see him every day, to hear his voice,
cause her such distress now?

It was that kiss. It had cast a spell over her, making
her feel such strange, dizzying emotions. If she didn't
know better, she would think it was Shakespeare
again—Puck and his fairies flitting about Thorn Hill,
sprinkling a love potion into unwary humans' eyes. She
knew only that she felt an aching loneliness at being
alone without Michael. A disconcerting displacement.

Amelia finished her piece, to the applause of everyone in the room. Kate pushed down all her fears and
qualms, and gave Amelia a sunny smile. "That was
lovely, my dear," she said. "You must have been practicing a great deal."

"I think London would be good for *Amelia,* too,
Michael," Lady Darcy said. "She is too young for the
opera, of course, but perhaps there are some afternoon concerts she could attend."

Amelia's attention swung toward them, her blue eyes wide. "Concerts in London?" she cried. "Really?"

Lady Darcy laughed happily, as if sensing an imminent victory. "Yes, darling girl! And museums, and carriage rides in the park, and ices at Gunter's. It could be quite delightful. If your papa will agree."

Before Kate could stop her, the child slid from the pianoforte bench and dashed across the room to throw her arms around her father. "Oh, please, Papa!" she beseeched.

Michael caught her up in a hug. His gaze met Kate's over Amelia's golden curls for a very long, suspended instant, and Kate had to turn away for fear he could read all her thoughts writ large across her face. But *his* was expressionless. She pretended to fuss with the pages of music, blinking hard to keep from crying. Silly, foolish tears—all at the thought of being left behind! It was ridiculous and childish. She was a woman grown.

A low, echoing rumble of thunder sounded outside the window, as if to mimic and mock her sadness. Even nature was in impending turmoil tonight. Holding the music in her hand, Kate turned her head to gaze out the window into the darkness. A fork of blue white lightning split the sky, closely followed by a louder clap of thunder. Yet there was yet no cool rain to follow, only the heavy, hot smell of sulfur seeping even into the drawing room. Amelia gave a muffled squeak at the thunder.

"Very well," Michael said at last, his words breaking the cloud of anticipation. "I am sure the bailiff can manage without me for a few weeks. We will all go to London. You, Mother, and Christina, Amelia, me—and Mrs. Brown."

Mrs. Brown? Kate's gaze swung away from the hovering storm, back to Michael's face. Had she heard him aright? Was she to go to London, too? He smiled at her and gave her a faint nod.

She *was* for London. With him. She gave him a small smile in return.

"Oh, splendid, Michael!" Christina cried, clapping her hands. "I can visit the Royal Botanic Garden at Kew. I read they have a new species of *Helleborus* I must examine."

"And I can hear concerts!" Amelia said brightly. She wriggled out of her father's arms and ran back to Kate, clambering up onto her lap. "And you will be with me, Mrs. Brown. We can see the Tower. . . ."

"Michael, dear," his mother murmured. "I am not certain Charles and Mary will have room for *everyone*."

Michael shrugged, completely unconcerned. Obviously, he had made his decision and that was that—an event Kate could only be grateful for. "Then we can take our own house, someplace near to Lindley House, Mother. It would be better if we had our own establishment, anyway. One you could order to your own liking, and not have Mary constantly underfoot."

Lady Darcy looked most uncertain. She flickered a glance at Kate and Amelia, and one at Michael, then finally nodded. "Our own house would be quite satisfactory. I will send out inquiries tomorrow."

Kate hugged Amelia closer, half listening to her bright prattle of all the things they could do in the city. Kate was happy to be invited along, of course—she could scarcely deny the quick, delighted leap her heart made when Michael said her name. Yet, underneath, there remained a strange, biting disquiet.

Here, in the haunted isolation of Thorn Hill and Yorkshire, she could almost pretend the outside world didn't exist. There was only this jumble of a house, and the presence of the people who inhabited it—Christina, Amelia, Michael. Michael above all, with his beautiful, scarred face, his tangled past and angel's laugh—his glorious kiss. Here she could pretend that she had been newborn from the moors. Venice never existed. Julian Kirkwood never was, with his hot gray eyes and possessive touch. Her lies were true. Here in Yorkshire.

In London, she would meet the wide world again, and see her true place in it. And Michael would see his. He might miss the luxuries and pleasures of his youth, and see that there were women in the world far more beautiful and less complicated than she. Women of his own station.

Perhaps she, too, would be captured in reminders of the past.

"Oh, Mrs. Brown," Amelia concluded breathlessly. "Does it not sound splendid?"

"Yes, *cara mia,* "Kate murmured, kissing the child's brow. "Splendid, indeed."

Chapter Sixteen

*I*t would seem she was doomed in this house, despite her happiness in it, to never sleep peacefully a night through.

Kate lay on her bed in her darkened chamber, watching the glow of lightning send swift, flashing sparks across the floor. Thunder growled somewhere in the distance, rumbling unhappily over the moors. There was no rain yet, but it still hung heavy in the clouds, threatening, menacing. She thought she could smell the deceptive sweetness.

The weather made her restless, made her legs and hands ache to move. Sleep, blessed, devouring sleep, was far beyond her reach, lost in storms both outside Thorn Hill's walls and in her heart.

The thought of going to Town, of being there with Michael, was an alluring one. Kate did love the peace of Thorn Hill, but a small part of her missed the movement and color of a city, the attraction of theaters and shops. She could just imagine the wonder that would light Amelia's little face at the sight of bareback riders at Astley's, or the taste of an ice at Gunter's. It would be *fun* to see the sights with them, to enjoy all the innocent little diversions of genteel Town life.

But here at Thorn Hill, she was safe—as safe as she could ever be. No one knew her as anything but Mrs. Brown the governess. She herself could even begin to imagine that that was exactly who she was, that she belonged in the house, with this family.

Kate rolled onto her side, pounding her fist into a

yielding feather pillow. She did not know why she was fretting over this so very much. In a few days, will she or nill she, they would all be making their way to London. She didn't want to be left behind, so she would just have to set aside her silly worries and trust that everything would turn out well. No one would recognize her, especially in her current guise. And she would always keep to the shadows. She would enjoy the city, and then they would come back here for a warm, lazy country summer.

But that did not help her *tonight*.

She couldn't lie in bed any longer, eyes wide open, waiting for the storm. She would just go out for a quick walk, before the rain fell in earnest.

Kate got out of bed, disentangling herself from the clinging bedclothes. Without bothering to light a candle, she dressed hastily in the dark, pulling on her chemise and a muslin day dress. Her stockings and half boots were tucked under a chair where she had left them, and her shawl was draped atop the dressing table.

The house was silent, the garden even quieter. Yet the atmosphere was tense somehow, as if the very flowers and trees waited for the storm, trembling in taut anticipation. Overhead, pale gray clouds, lighter than the purple black sky above them, scattered and skittered, blown about by the same wind that caught at Kate's skirt and hair. It was a witching night, ripe for all manner of mischief and mayhem.

Kate moved swiftly along the pathways, impatiently pushing her loose hair back from her face. She hardly knew where she was going; her feet took her where they would, the night luring her onward.

She came to the edge of the garden, and found a half-open gate that led out into who knew what. An enchanted wood, mayhap, where the fairies and imps and gnomes held sway. An otherworldly place, where a human could vanish into another life, another realm.

Kate laughed as she slipped out of the gate, out of the known world. A different realm would be *just* what she needed tonight. A wildness had seized her heart and would not let it go. She heard the soft whisper of distant water calling to her, the gurgle of a river somewhere nearby.

Without a glance behind, she followed its song.

Where was the foolish sorceress going?

Michael paused by his chamber window, his attention caught by the flash and flutter of pale cloth against the darkness of the garden. He peered past the window glass, and saw what he thought—feared—he would see there. Kate, hurrying down the path as if demons were snapping at her heels. Her hair streamed behind her, a loose banner caught by the wind, and she wore only a light shawl wrapped over her muslin dress.

In the blink of an eye, she vanished from the garden, slipping through the stout gate. Michael rubbed at his eyes—it was as if she had been only a vision, a spirit of the night. Yet he knew very well that she was all too real. Kate had truly been there in the garden, running away from the safety of the house even as a storm threatened. It was just the sort of thing that the changeable, curst woman would do.

And it was just like *him*, foolish errant knight, to go after her.

Michael caught up the coat he had just discarded and hurried out into the night.

Kate had no idea where she was going—she just followed the sound of the river's murmuring. The passage she found beyond the gate could not truly be called a road; it was too narrow—more a footpath, or a trail for horses. *Very thin horses,* she thought, as a vine snagged her hem. But it obviously led somewhere.

She traced its twists and turns, thunder clapping in the heavens above, closer and closer, until it became like cannon fire.

As she reached the edge of the beckoning, ribbonlike river, a new fork of lightning lit the air around her, nearly setting the tips of the trees alight. The sharp, sulfurous smoke bit at her nostrils, and she was suddenly deeply aware of how far she was from the house. How very alone she was.

She glanced back over her shoulder to the pathway. It would be so easy to turn around and retrace her steps, yet she could not. Not yet. Her feet were rooted to the mossy riverbank, and she had to stay, at least for a moment, and find out what the night was telling her.

There must be some reason why she was here. She would just stay for a few moments, and see if that reason came to her.

Kate sank down to sit back on her heels, watching the river as it rushed past her. It was placid enough now, if swift—not yet swelled by the coming rains. Yet it seemed there was something beneath its cool, silvery surface. A babbling tension, a roiling passion, just waiting to burst free and overflow its grassy banks.

Another bolt of brightness flashed, and for an instant Kate thought she glimpsed a woman on the opposite bank. A figure clad in flowing white, black hair streaming in the quickening breeze. The person or spirit beckoned to her, holding out its hand, calling to her on the wind. Kate blinked, cried out—and the vision was gone, leaving only a dark blank.

Then the clouds split, and released the heavy burden of their rain to the earth. It was cold and needle-like, pelting against her skin and hair, soaking through the cloth of her dress as if it were paper. Still she stayed, staring transfixed at the spot where the figure had been.

Kate slowly rose to her feet, swaying against the gale. "Mother?" she whispered.

"Kate! What are you doing, you curst woman?" she heard someone shout over the roar of the rain and wind.

Kate frowned, bewildered. That was not her mother's voice—not a woman's voice at all, but the deep, hoarse, angry tones of a man. She laughed hysterically, covering her wet face with her hands. Well, she had fancied this was a night for spirits and elves, hadn't she? It had to be a river god, sprung up to drag her into the cold, watery depths she had escaped once before.

But the hands that caught her shoulders in their grip were far too warm, strong, and *solid* to belong to any supernatural creature.

"Kate!" Michael shouted, pulling her back against him, away from the river. "What are you doing?"

Kate stared up at him, still stunned by the storm and the vision, not sure if this was all real or not. The thick waves of his hair were slicked back, darkened by the water, giving him a new, austere beauty. The raindrops beaded on the tips of his eyelashes, sparkling like tiny diamonds.

She caught at the collar of his coat, clinging for her sanity—her very life. "Did you see her?" she gasped.

His glance darted swiftly over her head. "See what?" he said skeptically. "Did you come out here following someone?"

"I—no, of course not," she answered, feeling suddenly exhausted and deeply foolish. She had come running all this way, leaving her warm chamber for the vagaries of a night on the moors, and for no good reason at all. She couldn't explain her bizarre compulsion even to herself. She felt the full coldness of the rain at last, and shivered. It was almost as if she jolted awake after a long spell of somnambulism. "I don't know."

Michael shook his head. "Oh, my dear Kate," he said, with an odd, humorless bark of laughter. "The only thing *I* know is that you must get inside this very moment, before you catch the ague."

He bent down and caught her under her knees, swinging her up into his arms. Kate was so surprised by the sudden movement, so overcome by the pounding of the rain, the chill, the glimpse of *something* by the river, that she made no protest at all. His body was warm and alive under the wet layers of his clothes, and she slid herself close, as close as she could possibly get. She wished she could just disappear inside of his heat, never to be seen again.

"Back to Thorn Hill?" she murmured, clinging to his shoulders.

"It's too far back now," he said, as he turned back onto the pathway she had abandoned to chase the river. She noticed that he was limping a bit, his footsteps uneven over the soaked ground. She nearly insisted on being set down, but one glimpse of his grimly determined face silenced her. She subsided wearily back against his shoulder.

"There is a cottage, or rather a hut of sorts, not far," he continued, still following his course. "It's used sometimes in sheep-shearing season. Not large, but there's a fireplace. You can warm yourself there."

"And you?"

He glanced down at her, a strange glowing light in his eyes, turning the sky blue a silvery color in the dark. Like the eyes of a lethal jungle cat. "I assure you, *I* am already *warm* enough, Kate the curst."

Kate lapsed back into silence, and very soon they came upon the tiny cottage. It was a square, stone dwelling set back among a grove of trees. There was only one window, but firewood was piled under a small shelter outside. Michael pushed open the stout, rough wood door with his shoulder and slipped inside.

For a moment, the sudden silence was deafening to her ears. The stone walls were obviously thick, muffling the thunder and the bullet sharpness of the rain.

"It's not much," Michael muttered, lowering her to her feet. "But it's home. For now, anyway." He held her arm for a moment longer, making sure she was steady on her feet before he went to kneel down by the hearth and take out a hidden tinder to start a fire.

The building was really far too small to be a *cottage,* Kate saw as she leaned back against the door, shivering in her soaked clothes. It was truly more of a hut, one room with the stone hearth at one end and an old, dusty table and chairs at the other. There was just the one window to let the outside in, but rows of shelves rose up along one wall, holding rough woolen blankets, pillows, a few jars of food, and pottery jugs that surely held cheap drink.

Kate wrapped her arms around herself, watching Michael as he knelt by the grate, coaxing the first, faint embers of the fire into stronger flames. They leaped high, casting his skin and wet hair in a gold light that made him appear an angel in truth.

An angel who had saved her from—who knew what? From herself, probably. She still was not sure what had driven her out alone into the night. A desperation to escape from herself, to escape the sticky web of lies she had woven, perhaps. All her life she was taught that to lie, to hide her true self away, was essential to self-preservation, was practically a requirement of life and nature. And she had done what she needed to do to obtain her new life here.

But at Thorn Hill, life was *not* mere existence, not an endless vista of snatching at what one could get without a thought to the rightness of it, or to the other people it might harm. Here, life had a texture, a purity, she could never have imagined before. People sometimes did what was best for others, despite the fact that it might not be the easy thing, the desirable thing. It was better than anything she could have envisioned. She wanted it for herself, this life, in a way she once might have wanted a jewel or a house. She lusted for it.

But it was not hers, and it never would be. *That* was what had driven her from the house tonight, she realized now, to stumble blindly away from the glittering lure of all she desired. That was probably what her mother was trying to tell her now. And Kate would have been lost when the heavens opened and the cold rain poured down on her. Lost—if Michael had not come to her rescue. Her knight. Her angel.

The fire was full of roaring life now, the orange flames leaping high, crackling like the snaps of demons' whips. Sweet-acrid smoke scented the cold, damp air of the hut, curling around her as if to entice her away from the door. Michael glanced back over his shoulder at her. There was no smile on his lips, no pirate grin to make her melt. He was frowning, his face shadowed with concern.

He ran his hands through his wet hair, pushing the strands straight back from his face. The firelight danced over the planes and angles of his face, the sharpness of his cheekbones and nose, the strong line of his jaw. He looked so austere in the flickering light, like an ascetic monk from centuries long past. Austere—and more beautiful than she had ever seen him.

"Kate," he said quietly, gently, as if he spoke to a madwoman. "I ask you again, why in blazes were you abroad on such a night?"

"I could not sleep," she answered weakly. "I needed some air."

He frowned skeptically. "With rain threatening?"

Kate shrugged. "I did not know if it would rain or not. I don't know this strange Yorkshire weather."

He smiled at last, but not his usual merry grin. It was a more rueful half smile, barely touching the edges of his lips. But it was enough—for now. "And I do not understand you strange Venetian women." He pushed to his feet, and grabbed one of the blankets from the shelves before crossing the room to her side. He swirled the rough gray wool over her shoulders, tucking it close about her throat. "Come closer to the fire before you catch a terrible chill."

She let him slip his arm around her shoulders and lead her to the warm, welcoming circle of the flames, and sat down without a protest on a cushion he laid there for her.

"You are still shivering," he said.

Yes, she was. But not merely from the rain. He was so near to her she was intoxicated by it, overcome by the longing to touch him, to feel his strong reality, his heat, and know that he was no dream. Without waiting

for an answer, he knelt beside her and reached for her
foot. He placed it against his thigh, his strong fingers
unfastening the buttons of her half boot from the stiffened leather. Then he reached for her other foot and
did the same.

"Your clothes are wet through," he muttered
roughly. "You should take them off, wrap up in more
of these blankets. Otherwise you will never get
warm."

Take off her clothes? How could she, in front of
him? She had never been naked in front of a man.
Once, she had been prepared to bare herself before
Julian Kirkwood, but his opinion had never mattered.
Michael's did. Her shivers increased, coming from a
core of emotion and need deep inside of her. She had
fantasized before, in her most secret dreams, of taking
her gown off for him, watching his body rouse to hers.
She had imagined what *he* would look like, stripped
for her gaze, her touch. Somehow, it had never been
like this. They had never been nude together in her
fantasies because they might catch a chill!

Still—she shivered. And not from cold.

"What of you?" she murmured. "You are also
wet through."

"I am used to it," he answered briefly. "I am a
hardy Yorkshireman now, you know."

"I don't care. I would hate it if you caught the ague
because you came out in the rain to rescue me," she
said. He opened his mouth as if to protest, but she
held her hand up in an imperious gesture that said
she would brook no arguments. "No. I insist. We will
both remove our wet garments. It seems foolish to sit
around in them when we are both widowed adults
who should have better sense. Here, I will turn my
back if you will turn yours. All very proper."

He laughed, but the sound was not humorous. It
was unreadable, full of mingled bitterness, disbelief,
self-scorn. "Oh, yes. Very proper."

Kate couldn't look at him any longer. If she did,
she would surely snap with the tension that had her

strung as taut as a violin string. She turned away, shaking with the cold and the uncertainty. She eased the sleeves of her dress down her arms, pulling at the gathered neckline until her torso was free of the wet, clinging muslin. The rest of the fabric slithered down her body until it lay in a sodden pool around her feet.

Kate stood there in only her chemise and stockings, her bare arms and throat exposed to the warming air, prickling with goose bumps. She again wrapped her arms around herself, as if that could offer her some protection. Behind her, she heard the slide and rustle of Michael's garments as he shed himself of them. She closed her eyes tightly, and in that darkness she envisioned it all—the thin, wet shirt sliding away from his body, leaving his muscled chest bare to the night. Visions of his strong, elegant hands loosening his dark breeches, easing them off his hips, shimmered temptingly in her mind. The black cloth slid lower and lower. . . .

Kate groaned, and covered her eyes with her hands, pressing hard, even though her back was turned. Even that would not eradicate the alluring picture of Michael undressing.

"Kate? What is wrong? Are you all right?" Michael said. She heard a whisper of sound, a rustle, then felt the warm embrace of a blanket easing over her shoulders.

His hands just barely brushed the skin of her throat as he wrapped the cloth snugly around her. Then the light caress dropped away, leaving her strangely bereft.

"You are shaking," he said quietly, deeply.

"The rain," she managed to whisper.

She felt him step back from her, moving away into the room. "Yes, of course. After you are—finished, come and sit by the fire. A good blaze has taken hold at last."

Kate nodded, and under the shelter of the blanket she wriggled out of her chemise and unfastened the ribbon garters to roll down her stockings. With those garments kicked away to join the coil of her gown, she stood there completely naked, with only the cover of the rough blanket.

It was such a bizarre situation she almost laughed aloud, a hysterical giggle bubbling up to her lips. She pressed one hand hard to her mouth, holding the sound in. The blanket started to slip, and she yanked it back up. What would it have been like to find herself in such a position in Venice, with Julian Kirkwood or one of the other men who flocked to her mother's house?

For a moment, she allowed herself to imagine it. Being isolated in the midst of a rainstorm with a man like Kirkwood, both of them naked, all alone. She almost shrank away physically at the thought, at the memory of how his black eyes would kindle and heat when he watched her. Of how he would often claim she was *meant* for him, when in reality he did not know her at all.

She would not be safe with someone like that. She would be as the hunted fox, unable to find a safe place to go to earth. Here, the only danger was that *she* might attack *Michael*, leaping on him to tear the covering cloth away from his flesh so she could devour it, lose all her ugliness in his angelic beauty.

"Kate," he called. "Come and sit by the fire. You are shaking like an autumn leaf in the wind. I promise you that despite my behavior in the library the other night, you have nothing to fear from me."

"I know that," she answered. "I have always known that you could not hurt me." And that was true—physically. Michael was a strongly muscled man from working on his estate, but she was quite certain his strength would never be used against someone weaker than he. Her heart, on the other hand . . .

She turned and padded toward the crackling, inviting lure of the flames. Michael had taken the remaining blankets and the pillows and fashioned a nest of sorts by the hearth, a low settee she could sit on. As she settled herself there, adjusting the heavy fabric so that no bare skin could be seen, Michael picked up her discarded gown and spread it out neatly on the hearthstones beside his shirt and breeches.

"Hopefully, they will be somewhat dry by the time we leave," he muttered, dropping down to sit beside her. Close, close enough for her to feel the heat of his body mingling with that of the fire. But not so close that she could touch him without stretching her arm, wriggling across the improvised sofa. His hair was beginning to dry, curling into damp waves against his brow and the nape of his neck. His own blanket slid a bit off of one sun-bronzed shoulder, revealing a delicate tracery of white scars that echoed the ones on his cheek.

Kate sucked in a sharp breath. She longed to lean over, to press her mouth to those scars and feel their roughness under her lips. Her heart ached at the pain he must have suffered, the terrible reminder every time he looked in the mirror. If only her kiss could erase those marks, erase every hurt for him, as it healed her own soul just to be near him.

But kissing him would be sheer folly, for she knew she could not stop with a mere kiss. She would have to touch, caress, *feel* every inch of him, until she was every bit the wanton her mother had been. The wanton Kate feared had always lurked in her own heart, just waiting for the right man to unlock it. Her body screamed out that Michael *was* the right man, but her mind—at least the corner of it that was still sane— told her that could not be.

She leaned back against the pillows, focusing her attention on the fire. "Do you think the Semerwater will rise tonight?"

"And bring up your drowned city? I don't doubt that it will overflow its banks, but I doubt the city," he answered. He also reclined in their cozy nest, still too far away for her to touch but still near. So very near. "I am glad all of Thorn Hill's sheep are safely gathered in their barns."

"It will not be as the lake we sat beside at our picnic."

"No."

They fell quiet for a long moment, listening to the crackle of the fire, the lash of the rain and wind against the window. Kate felt her body growing heavy, sinking into the luxury of being warm at last. Michael's scent, of clean soap mixed with sweet rain and the spiciness of his skin, wrapped around her like drugging smoke.

"Tell me a tale," she murmured. "Another Yorkshire tale."

Michael laughed quietly, a sound full of the same luxurious lassitude she was feeling herself. "I fear I don't know many. Peg o' the Well, the bridge trolls, the gytrash—but you already said you would never cross another bridge without fearing the little beasties. I hesitate to frighten a lady again."

Kate wrinkled her nose. "No. Trolls are not terribly interesting, nor are old crones who drag poor children down into wells."

"Then *you* tell a tale, Kate. A story of Italy."

She thought back to all of the romantic fables that had so occupied her mind in her youth, during the lonely hours in her well-appointed chamber with only books for companions. They were nearly all tragic, full of lust and love, death and redemption. Perfect for a stormy night. "There is Paolo and Francesca. But you must know that one, since you traveled in Italy. It is a sad tale, yet one worth repeating."

"Then tell it to me."

Kate gazed up at the ceiling, but she did not see the rough, dark wooden beams and peeling whitewash. She saw a summer garden in Rimini, lushly green, filled with sweet perfumes of flowers. She saw a woman, all loops of golden hair and swaths of blue brocade, sparkling with a jeweled kirtle and pearledged cap, sitting on a marble bench awaiting her true love.

"It is a true story," she began. "Or so they say. It happened in Rimini in the twelve hundreds. I know the tale from Dante. Francesca was a beautiful young noblewoman, who was married to Gianciotto Malatesta, a cruel man many years older than herself. But she was in love with Gianciotto's handsome, gallant younger brother, Paolo, and he with her. Their other brother, Malatestino dell'Occhio—the One-Eyed One—also loved Francesca."

"She must have been quite the beauty."

"Indeed she was, and you are interrupting. Where was I?"

"The One-Eyed One."

"Yes. Well, he was even uglier than Francesca's husband, and totally insane, too. One day, Gianciotto and Malatestino went off riding. Francesca was left in her chamber, reading aloud to her maids the tale of Guinevere and Lancelot. Just as Guinevere falls helplessly in love with Lancelot, Francesca loves Paolo. The girls made many remarks about the tale, but Francesca was in a strange, sad mood. Musicians were brought in to cheer her up, playing madrigals. But she is still sad, and dismisses them. Paolo then comes to her, and together they read about Guinevere and Lancelot. Soon Francesca comes to these lines: *Tra le braccia lo serra e lungamente, lo bacia in bocca.*"

"That is the song you were singing in the garden at Thorn Hill," Michael said. While she told her tale, he had moved closer to her—or she to him. She felt the soft touch of his breath against her bare neck. She could not move away. They were bound by invisible, silken cords woven of the night, the rain, the romantic tale.

She turned onto her side, facing him. He did not look at her; his gaze was on the fire. Yet she felt the tension in his body, the coiled power of his muscles and sinews. They were so acutely aware of each other they could *be* Paolo and Francesca, trapped in an undeniable, uncontrollable passion, but always awaiting the armored fist of Gianciotto.

"Yes," she whispered. "That is the song I was singing." She had forgotten about that, about how on her first night at Thorn Hill she had wandered alone in the garden, full of hope and apprehension and strange longings.

"Tell me what it means."

"It—it means 'Thereat she takes him by the chin, and slowly kisses him on the mouth.' And then Dante said, in his great poem, 'That day they read no more.' "

A silence descended on their small hut, heavier, more charged, like the violet blue lightning flashing outside the window. Kate did not turn away from staring at Michael's profile, as sharply etched as a Roman coin. Finally, he turned his face toward her, and their stares clashed and melded.

"What happened to them?" he said hoarsely. "To your lovers?"

What *had* happened? Kate found she could scarcely recall her own name in the power of his stare, let alone the fate of two people from six hundred years ago. But then she *did* remember, and it was chilling. "Oh, it is not happy. Francesca's husband leaves her one night, and Malatestino tells him that Francesca is unfaithful, that another lives in her heart. Francesca, thinking Gianciotto gone, invites Paolo into her chamber, where they embrace and kiss each other into forgetfulness."

"But the husband returns."

"Oh, yes, and runs the lovers through with his sword. Now, according to Dante, they are blown eternally around hell by whirlwinds for their sins."

"And does she still sing that song, in the winds and the brimstone?"

"If she is with her love, even in the winds, I imagine she would."

"Will you sing it to me now, Kate? Please?"

Kate feared her voice would strangle in her throat. She touched the tip of her tongue to her dry lips, and slowly began, wobbly and off-key, *"Tra le braccia, lo serra . . ."*

But she did not finish. Michael's lips swooped down on hers, swallowing the words into his mouth, catching her breath, her sense, her thoughts, everything. She was surrounded entirely by *him*, his heat and scent, the palpable force of his passion.

Her own passion, her desire, rose up to meet his, equal if not even greater. With a low moan, her arms came around him as she rolled to her back, drawing him down onto her. His weight was heavy and sweet. She had tried to force away her feelings for him, tried to push them down, stamp them into oblivion, yet they would not be gone. They burst free now, leaping up into glorious splashes of color under his kiss. She needed him—it was a force no mortal could contain— it was as free and elemental and undeniable as the storm that raged outdoors. He could not be hers forever, but he was now. Just as she was—and always would be—his.

Impatient, driven by long-denied love, Kate shoved the blanket off of his shoulders. It fell to his hips, leaving his skin bare for her seeking, caressing hands. It was everything she had dreamed it could be, hot, smooth, taut satin stretched over muscles and bone, shifting and bunching under her touch. She scored her fingernails lightly along the long groove of his spine, almost to the very cleft of his buttocks and then back up again, to plunge into the hair at his nape.

He groaned, his tongue seeking hers, tangling and clashing, full of heat and moisture and the quick rush of hot breath. It was not a calculated kiss, practiced and smooth and designed to seduce. It was quick, rough with need. Kate's fingers delved deeper into his damp hair, drawing him even closer, while her other hand palmed over his shoulder, feeling the slight roughness of the raised pattern of those scars.

The blanket she was wrapped in seemed to abrade her sensitive skin with its coarseness, and she was burning with a fever that boiled deep inside. She shoved the cloth away, and Michael's hands came up to help her, stripping the coverings away until she was completely bare beneath him. She raised up her leg, and with her foot pushed his own blanket all the way off. At last, they were skin to skin, their bodies pressed against each other. His hair-roughened chest rubbed over her breasts, raising her nipples to sharp, sensitive points. Her other leg wrapped over his tight buttocks, clasping him to her so he could never escape. She felt the faint crookedness of his thighbone, the pattern of more scars imprinted on his precious flesh.

In his imperfections, he was perfect to her. And tonight, she could show him that fully. Wrapped in the unreality of the storm, they were free. They were just a man and a woman overcome by passion for each other, and she could no more have turned away from that than she could cease to breathe.

Once, she had read ancient texts on the fine art of lovemaking, had listened to her mother's careful instructions on pleasing a man. All of that education was vanished now that she needed it, entirely lost in her sheer need for his touch. She wished she *could* remember, could make him scream out with pleasure from all the little tricks she had heard of, but her mind was in a hot, filmy whirl. She was lost. All she could think of was *him*.

Her head fell back against the pillows, his lips trailing a ribbon of fire down her arched throat, along her collarbone. She tightened her leg around him, and felt the heavy heat of his penis against her belly, impossibly tight and engorged.

"Michael," she sobbed. *"Dolce amore."*

"Kate. Kate of my consolation," he whispered against the soft underside of her breast. His fingers rolled her sensitive nipple, bringing fresh waves of delight. His breath was hot and sweet, and she had the sudden, irrational desire for bigger breasts. Hers were so small, and now she longed to entice him with womanly bounty rather than too-slender limbs and a high bosom. Even that vague wish vanished as his lips closed over her nipple, drawing it deep into his mouth. Kate's back arched beneath his hot suckling, and she murmured incoherent Italian love words. Slowly, his damp warmth drew away, and he blew lightly over her pebbled, coral flesh.

"Open to me, Kate," he whispered, and she felt his hand against her thigh, trailing fingertips inexorably closer to her cleft. A cleft that was damp and pulsing, flowering for him alone. "Please, open to me."

"Yes," she gasped. Her thighs fell open to his coaxing caress, like a lotus, and her breath caught in her throat. She couldn't breathe, couldn't move, with the marvelous suspense of waiting for his touch *just there*. She ached, but it was a pleasurable pain. His fingers delved ever so lightly into her opening, teasing her, enticing her. She felt the rush of her own moisture onto his hand, the twisting, urgent need. Yet it was not enough. Not nearly enough.

"Please!" she panted, begging. "Please."

"Do you want more?" he said roughly. His body slid away, down hers, until he knelt between her open thighs. "Like this?"

One finger slid very deeply inside of her. It was strangely rough, a burning stretching, yet it was so delicious. He pressed up, against her pubic bone, seeking—something.

And then he found it, pressing lightly on a tiny fold of skin that seemed to hold all the secrets of the universe. Kate's eyes pressed tightly shut, and behind them light and colors shattered and refracted like the wild whirl of a kaleidoscope. Every nerve ending in her body sang out.

"Like this, Kate?" he said again, his voice a low growl.

"*Sì*, like that."

"You're so wet," he muttered. "But very tight. It must have been a long time for you, my bonny Kate."

A long time! Kate's eyes flew open at those words, memory washing over her like a cold ocean wave. Some of the erotic haze built around her senses shattered, letting in the reality of all her lies. She was meant to be a widow, the respectable widow of a mythical English soldier. Yet, in truth, she was a virgin. A tight virgin.

It seemed a bit late to confess this, with both of them naked and sweaty, him kneeling between her open thighs. Also, she could not seem to put together a coherent thought, a plausible lie to add to her supply of deceptions.

But she *had* to say something. "I—my husband," she gasped. "He couldn't—I never . . ."

Michael rose over her, his body parallel to hers, his face hovering above her, wreathed in firelight and smoke like an angel's halo. The sheen of sweat glossed his skin, and his eyes, now a dark gray blue, were serious. "I don't understand."

A war wound. That sounded as good an excuse as any. "He had a—a war wound. He could not make love to me."

"You are a virgin?" he whispered. She could not read his tone, his expression. But she *could* still feel his manhood, engorged against her hip.

"Sì," she whispered back.

She sensed his shift away from her, the subtle withdrawal of his body from hers. "Then I should not—"

"No!" Kate did not realize she had shouted the word aloud until his gaze swung back to her, narrowed and startled. She could *not* lose him, not now. Her body was screaming for his; she needed him like she needed water and air. She needed him to be her first lover. "Please, Michael, *caro*. Do not leave. I want you. Do I have to beg, to plead?"

Instinctively, her hand smoothed along his shoulder and back, her fingers trailing a line to the jut of his hip, light, dancing. Until she closed her fingers around the hot satin of his erect penis. Agilely, she ran her fingertips over the tracery of veins, scoring her nails over the pulsing head. His breath sucked in sharply, and he seemed to lengthen even further in her hand.

"Do I have to beg, Michael?" she repeated, whispering roughly.

"No," he groaned. "I could never leave you now, Kate, even if I tried."

"Then make love to me. I need you."

" 'That day they read no more,' " he muttered. His lips covered hers in a new, ardent kiss. There was heat still, the force of unstoppable passion and sheer need, but also the bittersweet tenderness of destiny.

Kate had always secretly doubted, and even feared, Julian Kirkwood when he said they were *meant* to be together. She felt no such draw with him, no tug of memory or necessity or overwhelming love, and thus his words felt strange and unclean. Now she had an inkling of what he meant, for this moment felt like one she was fated for.

She opened her mouth to Michael's kiss, welcoming him joyfully even as her legs fell apart and she felt the force of him against her opening. He was so thick, so heavy, she feared for an instant that he might not fit, and she *needed* him to fit. Those ridiculous thoughts vanished as he slid inside her, slowly, carefully, one exquisite centimeter at a time. It was vaguely uncomfortable, like the burning stretching she felt when he put his fingers there, only greater. But Kate knew to expect that, and she knew she had to relax, to ease his entry.

It would hurt for only a moment, an instant, and then he would be hers entirely. As she would be his.

"It will be fine, my love," he whispered. "My sweet Kate."

She wrapped her arms around his back, her hands sliding against their mingled sweat. She closed her eyes as she felt him still against the thin membrane of her virginity—the membrane that had been meant to earn her mother a great deal of money. But Kate gave it now freely, happily, her heart suffused with a glow of joy.

"I'm sorry, Kate," she heard him mutter.

"Michael," she answered. "Just love me. It is all that matters."

"I do. God help me, but I do." He braced himself on his arms and drove forward with one quick, clean lunge.

"Ah!" Kate squealed. The pain was sharper than she had imagined. But Michael held still inside of her, letting her slowly become accustomed to his length, and soon all she could feel was the great heaviness of him joined with her. Joining *them*—making them as one.

She opened her eyes and stared up at him, watching his face as he slowly moved against her. The discomfort was fading, and tiny prickles of some delicious new sensation danced along her nerves. It felt like the lightning outside, quick flashes of a heated glow, delight that built and built until the passion was too great. It had to explode into thunder.

There was a hum inside her brain, and everything vanished but their skin touching and sliding, his movement inside her, barely brushing deep, against her womb, then pounding away. She heard him moan and answered it with her own cry, closing her eyes so she could fully absorb this new, amazing delight, could feel his lips on hers, his body inside her own.

Then—the thunder. Like an explosion of stars, blue, purple, red, silver, shooting up into the sky. She tightened her legs about his waist, sobbing at the glorious release, while above her he shouted out her name.

"Kate!" he shouted. Then, softer, as he collapsed against her shoulder, "Katerina."

"Michael, my angel," she whispered. She reached up to caress his damp hair, sifting the silken strands through her fingers. She reveled in the weight of his body against hers, the ragged sound of his breath. Their skin was wet and sticky, clinging and catching. All around her in the fire-warm air was the sweet scent of passion and release.

She felt an odd sensation of *triumph* as they lay tangled together. She had given herself to him, and in doing so had not only found physical delights, but

claimed a part of her life for her own. She was not
Katerina Bruni any longer—no part of her was. She
was Kate. Kate Brown, who loved Michael Lindley.

It could not last, of course. Daylight would come,
and with it reality. But right now she was his. They
were the only people in all the world.

He shifted his weight off of her and sank into the
pillows at her side. A rush of cooler air skipped down
her damp body, but she did not have time to feel
bereft for long. He drew her against his shoulder,
holding her close as their breathing slowed.

"Kate . . . ," he whispered. His breath exhaled on
a soft sigh, and she knew he was asleep.

Dark, exhausted oblivion encroached on the edges
of her own consciousness, and she slipped into sleep
with a joyful abandon, a trust and peace, she had
never known before.

Kate's eyes slowly blinked open, and for an instant
she did not know where she was. It wasn't her bedroom in Venice, or her cozy chamber at Thorn Hill.
She was covered in a pile of rough blankets, and the
space around her was dark and chilly.

Something hovered at the edges of her blurry memory, but she could not quite grasp it. Was it a dream?

Then she heard a soft noise beside her, a sigh, a
shuffle. A hand, large, rough, gentle, brushed her hip,
and flattened in a soft caress over her skin. And she
remembered. She remembered *everything*. The storm,
Michael's coming after her in the tempest and pulling
her to safety in this cottage. The force of their lovemaking, a wild squall to rival any the clouds and sky
could produce.

She smiled, and shivered at the memory of his caresses and kisses, the heavy, sweet feeling of his body
moving on hers. She had read of lovemaking, studied
it, listened to her mother's friends laughing about it,
but *nothing* could have prepared her for the reality.
The amazing delight and overwhelming intimacy.

Kate rolled onto her side against the pillows. The

driving storm had ceased. There were no more silvery flashes of lightning, and the lash of the rain against the window had slowed to a gentle patter. But there was enough light from the fading embers of the fire for her to study Michael's face as he slept beside her, his hand against her hip.

In his slumber, he looked so very young. So powerful. The lines on his brow and bracketing his beautiful mouth—lines that spoke of his daily labors and tensions—were eased, his skin smooth, burnished by the firelight. His hair was tousled, falling over his brow and ears in a wild tumble of waves. Along the sharp line of his jaw, early-morning whiskers roughened, casting new shadows over his face. He exhaled softly, and reached for her again in his sleep, drawing her into the curve of his body.

Kate went very willingly, fitting the contours of her flesh neatly into the hollows of his. Her head tucked beneath his chin, her cheek rested on the muscled plane of his chest, and she breathed in deeply the intoxicating scent of *him*. It was a dark, rich scent, his soap overlaid with the sheen of sweat and musk, the lingering perfume of their lovemaking. He also smelled of woodsmoke, and the sweetness of rain lingered in his hair. There was even a trace of her rosewater perfume, clinging just *there* to the hollow of his shoulder.

Kate leaned forward to kiss that spot, very softly and gently so she would not wake him. He tasted salty-sweet, delicious. "Mmm," she murmured, and rested against him, closing her eyes to let this one perfect moment envelop her completely.

It was not yet dawn. The sky she had glimpsed outside the window was still dark, but turning the faintest pale gray at the edges. Soon, the sun would begin its inexorable climb into the sky, casting its morning radiance of pinks and oranges and yellows into every hidden corner, dispelling last night's storm entirely. A new day would be laid out for the world.

And especially for Kate. The night when she possessed Michael was magical, beautiful beyond all belief. But soon she would have to let go of it, tuck it into the most secret recesses of her heart, and move on with the day-to-day deceptions of her existence.

But, oh! It *had* been lovely. She had always halfway imagined that sex was something to be calculated, managed, almost playacted. Every movement, every cry and murmur, thought out to best advantage. Yet with Michael there had been none of that. She had not cared one whit what she looked like, sounded like. She wanted only to give and receive pleasure, to be with him at every second, to know they were *together*. And that was the way it had been, because he was who he was. Michael. And she trusted him, loved him.

"Caro mio," she whispered, stroking the very tips of her fingers softly over his skin, the crisp, light brown curls covering his chest. She felt his heart beating, steadily, reassuringly. "Thank you."

Kate wanted to stay there for all eternity, curled up against him beneath the shelter of their peasant-rough blankets. Yet even now, as she reveled in remembered delights and present warm contentment, she could feel something shifting inside of her. The knowledge of the swiftly approaching dawn, perhaps, reminding her that she had to make her way back to Thorn Hill. Back to her own quiet chamber before the household stirred and a new day began. Her muscles were beginning to tense at the thought of the consummate actress she would have to be today, meeting Christina and Amelia in the schoolroom and pretending that nothing had changed. That her whole world hadn't shifted and reformed beneath her feet yet again.

Or maybe it was the heavy burden of the secrets she bore, like a sack full of stones across her back. She had just added another rock to that store.

But somehow, she could not be truly sorry. Michael was her very first lover, and that was something she would have with her all of her life. Even when she was an old lady, snoring in front of her solitary fire, she would remember this night and smile.

If only *he* would remember *her* as fondly and sweetly. That would be all she could ask from heaven.

"Caro mio," she whispered. "Forgive me."

Under her gentle caresses, Michael moved and shifted, easing out of slumber. She felt the coiled strength of his muscles, the flexibility of his supple flesh, like a desert lion tumbling out of sleep. His breath escaped in one long sigh, ruffling the heavy, tangled fall of her hair.

"Hello," he murmured, his arms closing around her as his lips moved gently over her temple.

Kate closed her eyes, clinging to him for just a moment as if she would never let go. "Hello," she whispered.

"I hope you slept well?" he said, his voice still rough with sleep, and full of a lazy, sensual pleasure.

"Need you ask?" She tilted her head back, leaving herself open for the movement of his lips across hers. They brushed once, twice, before deepening into a heady kiss, sweet with the memory of their wild passion, the promise of even more, even greater, to come.

Kate's body kindled at that kiss, at the caress of his lean hands over her back, skimming lightly across her buttocks, lifting her closer to his hardness. Oh, San Marco, but she wanted him! Again. Wanted his body, his breath, his very essence. Surely there was time—surely it could not be wrong. . . .

The sharp tap of a windblown branch against the window dragged at her consciousness, not letting her slip away beneath the drugging waves of passion. With an enormous effort of will, she pulled her mouth from his, disentangling her body from his embrace.

"It—grows late," she gasped, and eased herself up until she sat against the pillows. The cold air of the room, ill heated by the dying embers in the grate, rushed over her bare breasts and shoulders, raising prickly goose bumps and reminding her even more urgently of the coming day. "We should go back to the house."

Michael fell back into their tangle of blankets with

a deep groan. He covered his face with his hands, rubbing hard as if to awaken himself from his own sensual dream haze. "I suppose we should, my sensible Kate, though I would much prefer to stay here. 'It is not yet near day. / It was the nightingale, and not the lark, / That pierced the fearful hollow of thine ear.' "

" 'It was the lark, the herald of the morn.' " Kate searched the dusty floor for her clothes with an increasing urgency, but she had to stop and smile at him, running the tips of her fingers along the side of his whisker-roughened face. "Oh, my dear. We quote Shakespeare even now. How can we do that?" She turned away, reaching out for her discarded stockings. They were still damp, so she cast them aside and just took up her boots.

He rolled up onto his elbow, supporting his tousled head on his palm. "What better time for Shakespeare? The old Bard of Avon was quite preoccupied with romance. I'm sure he must have written a scene much like this one." Michael's voice sounded lighter than she had ever heard it, teasing, gentle, almost whimsical.

It made Kate's heart ache with longing until she feared it might burst in her chest. How could she ever bear to be apart from such a man, ever again? Clutching the blanket against her naked body, she half turned to him and smiled, reaching out to touch him again. She couldn't resist. He grinned up at her, and caught her fingers in the alluring snare of his own, pressing warm kisses to her palm, her knuckles and wrist. She felt the rough, hot embrace of his tongue against the soft underside of her pulse, and she shivered deeply, drawing away before she damned the day and threw herself on top of him.

"A scene like this one?" she murmured, slipping her hand gently away and plucking up her chemise. "I hope not at the end of *Romeo and Juliet*."

"Heaven forfend. But you need not fear, my bonny Kate—I will never kill your cousin and have to be vanished from Verona. Or if I am, I will surely take you with me. Romeo was a fool to leave without Juliet."

"Indeed he was." Or perhaps just a fool for falling in love in the first place.

Kate edged away from the lure of his body, pulling the chemise over her head and easing it across her hips. The movement unleashed a wave of sweet, unfamiliar soreness, between her legs and along her back and buttocks. She saw a red abrasion along the tender underside of her arm, a mark of his passion, and she rubbed at it as if that motion would imprint the reminder of his kiss on her flesh forever.

But it didn't, of course. The mark would fade, just like everything else.

She heard the shift and rustle of his movement behind her, and his arms came around her waist, drawing her into the curve of his body as he rested his chin against her shoulder. Kate leaned back into him, reveling in his warmth, the lingering scent of their passion.

"Mmm," she sighed. "This *is* nice."

He kissed her cheek, the side of her neck, before burying his face in her hair. "Marry me," he murmured.

His voice was muffled, rumbling against her flesh, so that at first she thought she misheard him. She *must* have misheard him. "What?"

He drew back, reaching out to turn her to him and tilt her chin up with his long fingers. Staring directly into her eyes, he said it again. Loudly, strongly. Unmistakably. "Marry me, Kate."

Kate gaped at him, robbed of all speech, all feeling, all—everything. For one shining instant, she imagined she *could* marry him. That he could belong to her, that these glorious feelings could be hers forever. The words echoed around her—*Marry me, marry me*. Such simple, easy words, so blithe to say.

Such frightening, impossible words.

A chill like ice crept over her, pushing the warm contentment before it until she thought she would freeze to death. She drew away from Michael's embrace, wrapping her arms tightly about her waist. She couldn't look at Michael, couldn't face him for fear he could see her deceit written on her face. Her unworthiness.

"Oh, Michael, *caro*, I cannot marry you," she whispered. Her throat was dry, scratchy, so she could hardly force any words through at all. Her head whirled in utter confusion.

He didn't touch her, didn't reach for her, as if he sensed how brittle she was. How she would shatter like true ice. "Why not?" he said calmly, as if he was being perfectly reasonable. He leaned back against their nest of blankets and pillows, his hands behind his head.

He just seemed far too sanguine. Too damned *reasonable*. "Because I am the governess, of course!"

"Oh, Kate. Surely you know me better than that? I would not care if you scrubbed pots in the kitchen."

Kate buried her face in her hands, letting her hair fall forward and conceal her in its black curtain. He would care if he knew what she *really* was. What lies she had brought into his home. At first, they had been for her own protection. Then because she cared too much for her new life at Thorn Hill, for the people she had come to love and need. And now—now she could not bear to see disgust in Michael's eyes when he looked at her. Not after the glories they shared, the heaven she found in his arms. She couldn't bear it!

But neither could she marry him, and deceive him for the rest of their lives. She was not yet as low, as dishonorable, as all that.

"You *should* care," she whispered. "You must think of your family. . . ."

"My family!" Michael gave a disbelieving snort. "Kate, my family adores you. Christina is always talking of how Mrs. Brown says this—Mrs. Brown does that. She's been so much more comfortable in company since you came to Thorn Hill. And Amelia cannot do without you. She's been so quiet, and now she has blossomed."

"And I love *them*," Kate said. She pressed her hands hard against her closed eyes, trying to hold back a new flood of tears. "But your mother would not be pleased. Neither, I daresay, would your grand brother and sister-in-law."

"It is true that my mother can be a bit high in the instep. She would come around, though—she is not an unreasonable person. She would be beyond happy to have more grandchildren. And I don't care two straws about Charles and Mary. I never see them, anyway."

Kate shook her head desperately. She *had* to convince him that they could not marry. Yet what was there she could say when he was a man who was not motivated by the things other men of his station would be? "We are too different. It would be a terrible mésalliance."

"Kate, you make no sense. After last night, we *should* marry. And it would hardly be a mésalliance. Everyone would envy me for having such a beautiful, genteel bride."

Genteel. "Just because we—made love, you shouldn't feel obligated to propose to me. Please, Michael. We cannot marry, and that is all there is to it."

Michael seized her shoulders, swinging her around to face him. He smoothed her hair back from her brow, holding her face between his hands as if she were made of the most precious porcelain. "There is more to it than my family, our stations in life, isn't there?"

Kate stared up at him, at his beautiful features, etched with puzzlement and concern and the seeds of anger. Oh, San Marco, how she longed to tell him! To lay her head against his chest and pour out all the poison of the past. She was so tired, so unutterably weary, and her shoulders ached with the lonely burden.

But there was still that grain of selfishness, that sure knowledge that if Michael hated her, then her heart would break entirely.

Those tears she fought so hard to hold back spilled

free, falling down her cheeks in salty rivulets. "Michael, please. Just believe me. I cannot marry you."

"All right," he said soothingly, wiping away her tears with the gentlest of caresses. "All right, Kate. We are both very tired. We don't need to talk of this anymore, not now. I never wanted to make you cry, my bonny Kate."

"I—I'm sorry," she gasped, sniffling back those tears. She *was* tired, and utterly confused, and so full of longing and pain and love that she wanted to howl with it all.

"Shh." Michael lay back against the blankets, gently drawing her down with him until she rested against his chest. His arms were secure around her, holding her safe from all the world. "We have a little time before dawn. Let's just sleep a while longer. Everything will be clear in the daylight. It always is."

"You won't leave me now?" Kate murmured. She would have thought all the turmoil in her heart would never let her sleep again this night, but exhaustion made her limbs heavy. Her mind felt drugged, and she could not find a coherent thought. All she knew was she wanted him to stay close.

"I won't leave," he answered. As her eyes drifted shut and the world turned blurry and vague, she felt his kiss against her hair. And she thought she heard him whisper, "Kate the curst. Who are you?"

Kate's slender body was relaxed and warm in his arms, her hair falling in a black satin river across his bare chest. Michael ran the flat of his palm gently over that hair, along her back in the soft chemise, and then up again. Her breath was a cool rush against his throat, and she trembled under his embrace like a wild, trapped bird.

They were as close as a man and woman could possibly be, their bodies entwined after the heat of lovemaking, and yet it seemed she was a million miles away from him. More elusive than ever. At some moments, her dark eyes held the sweetest tenderness, the most fiery passion, the flashing sparks of heaven. Then, in the next instant, there would be a torrent of unknowable pain, almost panic. And then—nothing. As if an opaque curtain dropped over her thoughts and emotions, concealing all of her joy and pain alike to his regard.

He would think that he was growing closer to her, that they were closer to *each other,* then—this. When he caught her in his arms, drawing her down against him to urge her to her rest, it felt so like capturing a wild bird in a net, holding it tightly despite its mad efforts to escape captivity.

Michael never meant to invite such panic, such flight, with his proposed marriage. It had been a spontaneous plea—he scarcely knew what he was saying until the words hung loud in the air between them. But he meant it with his whole heart. It seemed *right.* It seemed meant to be. Ever since he saw Kate standing alone on the moor, the loveliest and most distant woman he had ever beheld, he desired her. She intrigued him, drew him in with just one glance from her dark, bright eyes. As he came to know her, watched her settle into his home and family, that intrigue only grew. The more he talked with her, the more he wanted to know. The more he craved just to be in her presence, within the spell of her perfume and the touch of her hand.

And their lovemaking . . .

His heartbeat quickened to remember, and his body stirred to heated life beneath the rough blankets. He had loved his wife, and he had liked and enjoyed all the mistresses of his past. Ever since a comely milkmaid introduced him to the joys of physical passion when he was thirteen, he had craved the erotic company of women. Their laughter and light touch, their kisses and heady perfumes, gave him unimaginable pleasure, and he worked very hard to please them in return. The cries of a woman as she found ecstasy were more intoxicating than the finest French brandy.

Yet never—not once—had he felt as he did when

his body joined with Kate's, and he opened his eyes to see her there beneath him, her throat arched and lips parted. This was beyond pleasure, beyond satisfying the body's cravings. Beyond even the two of them, Michael and Kate, at that moment. He had thought his heart would burst with the exultation, that he would break down and sob into the waves of her hair at the utter perfection of it all.

Even now, when passion was spent for the time being and she slept against him, he felt that wonder. Kate had given herself to him, when she had never done that for another man—not even her husband. It had been a shock to feel her tightness, to hear her breathless, halting confession. Yet it had also sent a primitive bolt of satisfaction through him that she was *his*. His alone.

Now, in the cold air of approaching dawn, he knew that was not so. She was no more his than was the wind or the water, for she was as mysterious as ever. But *he* was *hers,* as surely as if he had torn out his heart and laid it at her feet. She brought something to life in his soul that he had feared long dead—a sparkle of joy, a sense that wrongs could be forgiven, atonement made, and life become new and bright again. The feel of her hand as it brushed against his skin wove a spell of delight. The sound of her voice as she called his name, the way her face glowed when she spoke with Amelia, leaning her dark head close to his daughter's golden one. All those things cast a jeweled net around his heart, imprisoning it so he never wanted to be free again.

She protested that she could *not* marry him. She struggled and pulled against him, and it drove him insane to not know why that was. To not know how he could help her, how he could rid her of that need for flight. There were things he *did* know, though. He knew he would make her smile again, make her see life as brightly as he now did. He knew that, together, they could vanquish any fear or sadness.

And he knew that one day she would be his wife.

Chapter Seventeen

*K*ate folded the last of her garments and placed it neatly in the battered old valise. The clasp did not close, as usual.

"If I am going to be gadding about all the time, I must use some of my wages on new baggage," she muttered, pinching the stubborn old clasp together.

She stepped back and surveyed her bedchamber. The bed was neatly made; the draperies were drawn back from the windows to let in the waning daylight. Everything was just as she had found it when she first arrived at Thorn Hill. The tall wardrobe was empty of her clothes, the dressing table cleared of her brush, combs, and rosewater scent bottle. Her precious sapphire brooch was hidden deep in her valise. It was almost as if she had never been here at all.

The day she had known, feared, would one day arrive was nearly upon her. She was leaving Thorn Hill. Yet not as her dark imagination would have told her. She was not leaving alone. She was traveling forth in the company of the Lindleys, still safely a part of their odd, beloved household.

Kate sat down in the chair by the window, propping her chin in her hand to stare out at the garden. The landscape had now had a week to recover from the rampages of the rainstorm; the flowers and untrimmed bushes had sprung to a new, green life. They overflowed the walkways even more than before, almost with a bursting enthusiasm for the revival of spring. A solitary gardener, stooped and gnarled in a stained smock, labored at trimming and weeding, assisted by Christina. The girl was bent over a clump of yellow pimpernel, carefully pruning at its delicate branches and examining the cuttings she made in the late afternoon light. Her bonnet dangled down her back by its ribbons, as usual. Kate was surprised that Lady Darcy was not out there to lecture her daughter about her carelessness over her complexion.

Indeed, it was probably Kate's own duty to go down there and make Christina come inside, or at the very least put her bonnet on properly. But Kate had no desire to rise from her chair and go to the garden. Right now, she was too overcome by the same strange, lazy daydreams that had affected her all this long week.

A week. An entire week since her night in the sheepherder's cottage with Michael. That sweet, wild night. No, it had been longer—eight days.

Eight days in which she threw herself as hard as she could into work, driving Christina and Amelia along with French verbs, dancing lessons, and geography tests until they both protested wearily. Days in which she took all her meals in the schoolroom, and went for solitary walks along the pathways and roadsides— but never by the river or the lake. Never as far as the tiny cottage. She was careful not to be alone with Michael, not to converse with him except on the most harmless of topics, such as the weather or Amelia's progress with her Italian vocabulary. When they spoke, she saw the spark in his blue gaze that told her very clearly that he longed to speak with her alone, to explain, rectify, make clear, or whatever it was he wanted to say. That spark also told her that he yearned to kiss her, touch her—perhaps almost as much as she yearned to *be* kissed and touched.

Her bed felt very large and cold at night as she lay there alone and sleepless. But she could not venture down to the library. She was still too unsure—too scared. His words always echoed back to her, like the tempting song of a luring demon. *Marry me. Marry me.*

Did he regret those words now? She was sure he must. How could he not? He was an honorable man; he had proposed in the midst of their very compromising situation. But if she had said yes, had given into her own deepest yearnings, he would have come to regret his decent impulse when he discovered the truth of what his wife was.

Yet Kate still loved those words. Still cherished them—and always would.

Soon, she *would* have to talk to Michael about that night. She could not avoid him forever, not if they were to live in the same house. And if he repeated his proposal, she would have to find deep wells of strength within herself and refuse him again.

At least she had one thing she no longer had to worry about. Her monthly courses had started last night. There would be no child of that night.

Kate pressed her palm over her belly, over the dull cramping there. It was a good thing, of course—she did not want to bring a baby into the world to raise as she had been, a fatherless child. But there was still a tiny part of her soul that yearned for that kind of love, for a sweet, fat, fair baby like Amelia that would be hers to love and care for.

She stared out over the garden, watching as Christina finished her work and gathered up a basket filled with colorful, neat rows of greenery samples. *If only she were as careful with her curtsies as she was with her plants,* Kate thought, laughing.

That was what she needed to concentrate on now. Doing her job, getting Christina ready for her debut. That was why she had come to Thorn Hill. And she would also have to consider her own future, make plans that would be viable for the years ahead, not an existence made up of air dreams. She could save her money, maybe open a small school one day. Perhaps look about for a husband, an obscure, respectable physician or attorney.

Somehow, those ideas, once so appealing, once all she wanted, held little charm now.

Kate pushed herself up from her chair. She had to examine the schoolroom, see if there was anything they would need in London that was still to be packed. Then she must—

Those sensible plans were interrupted by a knock at the door. Kate automatically smoothed back her hair, brushed at her eyes for any stray tears.

"Yes?" she called. It was probably a servant, come to fetch her luggage.

"Kate, may I come in?" the low, rough rumble of Michael's voice said. "Quickly, before a maid comes along!"

Michael! Kate froze, her fingers pressed to her cheeks. Of course her day of reckoning *would* come, but now?

Don't be a coward, she told herself sternly. She truly had no need to be afraid of Michael, of all people. And he was right—a maid could see him lurking outside her door, and the gossip would spread through the house like a plague.

"Yes, come in," she said, and straightened the plain folds of her blue muslin skirt. She stood up very straight, clasped her hands at her waist, and tried to make her face expressionless and cool.

Michael had no such qualms. As he slipped inside the door, closing it quietly behind him, a wide smile tugged at his beautiful lips. His eyes were a brighter blue than the sky today, more like the green blue of turquoise stones, warm and sweet. He leaned back against the door, his arms folded over his chest. Though he made no move to come closer to her, it was as if he reached out to fold her in his embrace.

"At last," he said lightly, still smiling. It made Kate almost want to smile, too, to forget anything unpleasant or harsh or real. "You have been very elusive these last few days, bonny Kate."

Kate turned away from him, going back to the window to stare blindly down at the garden. Christina and the gardener were gone now, the sun sinking fast. Soon it would be time for dinner.

"I have been—busy," she answered softly. "The girls' lessons, getting ready for the journey to London . . ."

"Avoiding me?" His voice seemed quite close, closer than it should be. Closer than she wanted.

Kate spun around to find that he stood on the other side of her abandoned chair, one sun-browned hand resting lightly on its upholstered back. He no longer smiled but watched her carefully, unwaveringly. *If only he were closer.*

"I did not mean to avoid you," she whispered, knowing it was a lie. "I just thought it would be best if we had some time apart. Time to concentrate on our work."

"Yes," he said. "It is true that I have had much to do on the farm before we leave for Town. But I hope you know that I will always have time for you."

"I know that you care about my progress with Amelia and Christina—"

"No, Kate. Now you are being deliberately obtuse," he said gently. "For *you*." He leaned against the chair a bit more, swaying, and she saw that he was favoring his bad leg today.

"Oh, Michael, please sit!" she cried in concern, reaching out to plump the cushions of the chair. "You have been working so very hard—you must be careful of your leg."

"I am fine, just a bit of a twinge," he said, but he sat down nonetheless. When she would have moved away, he caught her hand in his, holding her in place. "No, Kate, do not run away from me now."

"I'm not running away," she insisted. Of course she was, though. He had washed after his day outdoors, and smelled of clean soap, the starch of a fresh cravat. His hair was still damp, waving back onto his coat collar, tempting her fingers to smooth and caress its rough silkiness. Then, of course, she would have to touch the arch of his brows, the sharpness of his cheekbones, the lips whose fiery kiss she remembered all too well.

She took her hand back from his, folding her fingers into tight fists, and perched on the arm of the chair, within a breath's touch yet still a thousand miles away.

"That's better," he said.

Kate still could not quite look at him. She watched a cloud of dust motes dance in the bar of sunset light. "Was there something you wished to talk to me about, Mr. Lindley? Amelia's lessons?"

"Yes, there is something I want to talk to you about, and don't call me Mr. Lindley," he said, a note of irritation creeping into his voice for the first time. "Prissiness doesn't suit you, Kate."

His words and tone pricked at first, like the sudden stab of a tiny but very sharp sewing needle. But then she had to laugh, for he was undeniably correct. She *was* being prissy, and it went against every fiber of her personality and desires. She had not been brought up to be prissy, and though it seemed a requirement of governessing, it would never come naturally. She relaxed a bit against the back of the chair, and suddenly felt more like herself again, after being bound up in knots of doubt all week. It was just Michael and Kate.

"Very well, Michael," she said. "No more prissiness, I vow. What did you want to talk to me about?"

He nodded approvingly, the hint of a smile coming back. He took her hand again, and this time she let him, her fingers soft and relaxed in the shelter of his clasp. "That is more like the Kate I know. I was scarcely acquainted with the pale creature who crept around my house these last few days. I thought the elves had captured you, and left a changeling in your place."

Kate laughed again, her weighted heart lightening just a bit at his teasing. "Perhaps they did. I just wanted you to have time—"

"Time for my work. Yes. And you needed time for yours. It cannot be easy to get a six-year-old ready for a journey, or to persuade Christina that she needn't take all her seven hundred plant specimens with her."

"Indeed."

"Yet I also fear that you thought to give me time to forget my proposal to you." His hand tightened on hers, as if he thought she might fly away.

And she would have—if she was not so frozen in surprise. She had been lulled by his teasing, his hand-holding, lulled into being comfortable with him again. Then he put the very thing she feared facing directly in front of her.

She had to answer him. He was waiting, watching her closely. He would not let her go this time, not without an explanation.

"It was kind of you to make your offer, Michael," she began.

"Kind!" He snorted.

"Yes. Because you are a kind man, an honorable one, no matter your protests to the contrary. And you did an honorable thing in offering to marry me. I will never forget that. But I cannot accept. I care about you too much, and for Christina and Amelia. Your station is too high for you to wed a mere governess. A *foreign* governess. Your family and Society would never approve."

And that was it. That was all she could say, and it was the truth—as far as it went.

Michael still did not turn away. He watched her, his face expressionless. "If that was all there was to it, bonny Kate, I could demolish your resistance in a mere moment. I live here quietly in the country, with no desire to cut a dash any longer. What *Society* do I have to impress? I have money and lands, no need to wed an heiress. I am a grown man, able to choose my own wife."

"Still . . ."

"No, Kate." He pressed the tip of his finger to her lips, cutting off her sputtering arguments. It was rough and delicious against the softness of her lips. Kate reached up and gently removed it before she could draw it into her mouth, tasting the salt of his skin on her tongue.

He raised her hand to his lips, pressing a quick, tender kiss to her palm before continuing. "There is more to this refusal of yours than our stations in life. And there is more to my proposal than so-called honor. I didn't set out that night to make love to you, Kate, but I can never regret that it happened. And I proposed because I *want* to marry you. That is all."

Kate longed to cry, to sob, to throw herself onto the floor and howl at the sheer pain of his sweet words. But she did not. Her only movement was to close her eyes tightly, holding in all those tears. All the regret. "I just—cannot, Michael. I'm sorry."

"We may not have a choice, you know, Kate," he answered implacably. "There might be consequences."

Kate shook her head. "No. I knew this morning there would be no consequences of that sort."

"I see." Michael fell silent for a long moment, holding her hand in his. Then he let her go and stood up. "But I warn you, Kate the curst—I will not give up. I can be a stubborn man when I choose, every bit as stubborn as you. And I won't rest until I am your husband. Or until I know the true reason why."

And he was gone, crossing the room silently and slipping out of the door as if he had never been there at all. But there was his clean scent still lingering in the air, the warmth of his touch on her hand.

Kate held her fingers out before her, studying them as if his kiss might still be imprinted there. As stubborn as she was, eh? Little did he know. *No one* was as stubborn as Katerina Bruni. She had once driven her mother and nursemaids and tutors wild with her insistence on having her own way. And never before had having her own way seemed quite so important.

She loved Michael, and as she loved him she would save him from making a terrible mistake. Even if that mistake would mean her own happiness.

For once in her life, she was going to do the right thing. No matter what.

*　　　*　　　*

I won't rest until I am your husband. Or until I know the reason why.

Michael remembered those words the day after he spoke them, as he stood on the drive watching servants hurry about, loading the carriage and the baggage wagon with everything they would need in London. He had to laugh at his own hubris. It had been foolish of him to challenge her in that manner. Kate truly had a stubborn streak in her as wide as the Semerwater, and when she did not want to speak of something a curtain came down behind her eyes, and she withdrew to a place deep inside herself. She had avoided him so adroitly for a whole sennight that he scarcely knew she was doing it.

And she stubbornly hid her secrets still, even after the shattering intimacy of their lovemaking. Secrets such as her virginity, and the sapphire he saw by accident on the day they met.

Surely his challenge would make her only *more* stubborn, more determined to hold her secrets and refuse to marry him. Even when marriage could make them both happy. Maybe he didn't deserve such happiness, after all the cruel things he had done in the past. But he wanted it, with a sharp yearning he could practically taste. His night with Kate had been a paradise he could never have imagined before, and he wanted her in his arms again. Yet he also wanted more. So much more.

He wanted to watch her beauty change and mature over the years, gray appearing in Kate's ebony hair as Amelia grew up and married and they saw their grandchildren. He wanted to dance with her at assemblies, see her at the other end of the table at dinner parties, and sit quietly by the fire with her on evenings at home. He wanted to walk with her across his estate, talk with her about everything that happened in their days, to grow old with her and die in her arms.

Perhaps Kate's secret was that she did not want the same things; she was just too good-hearted to hurt anyone. If that was true, then he would never darken her threshold again, never press his suit. Yet he sensed that was not the case. When he kissed her, her body rose up to meet his with an eagerness, a yearning, that could not be feigned. She watched him with admiration in her eyes when she thought he did not notice, admiration mixed with a strange anxiety, almost a fear he could not fathom.

So he would indeed be stubborn. He would learn what was keeping her from him, and demolish it if he could. Surely there was nothing so terrible that they had to be apart because of it.

"Michael, are the trunks properly secured?" he heard his mother say, and he turned to see her emerging from the house, followed by her harried lady's maid.

"Yes, Mother. Everything appears to be in perfect readiness," he answered.

She stepped up to the side of the wagon and reached out with her elegantly gloved hand to test the binding ropes. Apparently, it met with her approval. "Very good. I must say, I *am* looking forward to our time in Town. It will be nice to see Charles and Mary again, and attend some of the festivities with my old friends. We are so fortunate that the Prices were able to lease their townhouse to us on such short notice!"

"Fortunate, indeed," Michael said. Or perhaps it was not fortune, but his mother. When she set out to find something, it usually appeared. Even houses in London, unused by their neighbors for the Season.

"Give me my reticule, Rose, and then find your seat in the wagon," she instructed her maid, turning toward the coach as the girl scurried away. "It is past the hour for us to depart if we are to make good time on our journey. Where are Mrs. Brown and the girls?"

"Here we are, Mother," Christina called as she emerged from the front door. Her bonnet ribbons were hastily, sloppily knotted, and her arms were filled with books.

Kate followed, holding Amelia by the hand. Kate,

unlike Christina, was as neat and tidy as a bandbox in her gray pelisse and dark blue bonnet. She seemed her usual serene self, the quiet, perfect governess.

But now Michael knew all too well the dark, swirling, passionate depths beneath her pale gray surface. The wealth of secrets she held behind her dark eyes. She took his hand as he helped her up into the carriage behind his mother and Christina, her gloved fingers curled tightly around his for the merest instant. She gave him a gentle, heartbreakingly sweet smile, and the swift glance she tossed him from beneath her lashes was utterly unreadable.

Michael grinned as he shut the carriage door and reached for his horse's reins. Their time in London would surely prove to be most interesting indeed.

Chapter Eighteen

A melia kicked in her sleep.

The child *looked* like the veriest angel, with her golden curls and blue eyes, but in truth she was a little imp sent to torment people in their sleep. Kate decided this the third time the child's foot connected with Kate's hip, jolting her out of a drowsing sleep.

Kate edged away from Amelia, up against the pillows. The inn they had stopped at for the night was quite decent, as far as inns went. The sheets were clean and aired; the food was of edible quality, and the clientele respectable. But it was also quite small, and Kate had to share a tiny room with Amelia and Christina. She and Amelia took the large bed, while Christina insisted on sleeping in the truckle bed. Kate had thought that a very generous gesture on Christina's part, but now she knew the truth—Christina must have known about her niece's propensity for tossing about in her sleep.

It didn't matter, really. Kate would not be able to sleep well anyway in these unfamiliar surroundings. The small noises in the corridor and from outside the window, the murmurs Christina made as she dreamed about plants, all kept Kate from finding deep, dreamless sleep. In truth, she had not slept well in a long time.

Also, nature called and she had no desire to utilize the already-used chamber pot.

Kate made sure Amelia was safely tucked in under the bedclothes, away from the high edges of the bed, before she got up to look for her gown and shoes. She wore only her chemise to bed tonight, so it was just a moment's work to dress and slip out of the room.

It was quiet in the inn's common rooms, all the guests having long since retired. Only a porter dozed by the front door, and he nodded off again after directing her to the outdoor privy.

Her business concluded, Kate lingered in the deserted innyard. It was a lovely night, clear and fresh, the black sky scattered with a glittering handful of stars and planets. The still air, aside from a faint *eau du cheval,* was clean and cool. It was far preferable to the stuffy bedchamber, and being kicked by Amelia every five minutes. She would vow her hip was still bruised.

Kate smiled ruefully and rubbed at her aching muscle. She glanced around for a place to sit for a moment—and that was when she caught the faint, sweet scent of smoke. She was not alone in the innyard after all. She spun around, and saw, with not much surprise, that Michael sat on a rough wooden bench under a gnarled pear tree, smoking one of his thin cheroots.

The red, glowing tip cast a faint light over the sharp angles of his face, and he was surrounded by a silvery cloud of smoke as he exhaled. It all gave him a very diabolical allure.

The sly smile he tossed her completed the illusion of wicked temptation. Or perhaps it was more reality than illusion.

"My dear," he said. "We really must cease to meet this way."

"Ha," was all Kate was able to say, an odd cross between a cough and a laugh. She should have known better than to leave her bed in the middle of the night, should have known they would find each other. They always did. "If I didn't know better, I would say you are following me."

"I could say the same about you. After all, I was just sitting here alone, innocently enjoying a smoke, when here you appear. I see that you are sharing a chamber with my daughter."

"What?" Kate asked, bewildered by the sudden volte-face in the conversation.

Michael gestured with the cheroot, the red tip like a firefly in the night. "You were rubbing at your hip, which tells me Amelia must have been having a restless sleep. Sometimes, when she has a bad dream, she could go two rounds with Gentleman Jackson himself and emerge the victor. She has a mean right hook."

"*And* a mean right foot," Kate said. "She kicks like a mule."

Michael laughed. "Her nursemaid said she would grow out of it, which I sincerely hope is the truth."

"Is there any chance she will grow out of it before we reach London?"

"Now, that I doubt. But come, Kate, sit down for a while. Keep me company while I finish my cheroot," he said. Kate hesitated, thoroughly mindful of the sort of things that happened when they sat together at night, and she glanced toward the inn door. He obviously saw her, because he added, "I promise you will be safe with me. I won't leap on you at all, tempted though I might be."

Kate thought about this, a strange tingle of excitement on her very skin at the thought that *he* might desire *her* as she did him. And she really didn't want to go back to her bed yet. "Very well," she said, and sat down at the very end of the bench, leaving a good two feet between them.

Not that it mattered. She might as well have sat on his lap, for his scent, his warmth, his essence, crept across the distance like stealthy phantom fingers, wrapping around her. She leaned her head back against the rough trunk of the tree and closed her eyes. But that made the scent, the sharpness of the smoke, only more acute. She shivered.

"I'm sorry, Kate. You must be cold," she heard him say. She opened her eyes to see him taking off his coat, the cheroot clamped between his white teeth. He draped the coat over her shoulders, gathering it close at her throat. He was close to her, so close she could see the faint lines fanning from the corners of his bright eyes, the raised pattern of his scars. "Is that better?" he muttered, his hands lingering on the soft skin beneath her jaw.

"Mmm," she sighed. As she stared up at him in the moonlight, a voice whispered insistently deep in her mind. *Tell him.*

And she knew, in that flash of a second, what she had to do. What was right. Her heart constricted in cold fear, in a rush of sour panic. But she had to tell him, even if he cast her off here and now, left her at this isolated inn somewhere on the road to London. At least then she would know. There would be no more wondering, no foolish hope.

She had been taught all her life that to lie, to deceive, was a necessity, an imperative to self-preservation. No one could care for her true self, a fanciful, changeable, selfish girl, so she had to hide all of that. Lie, and lie again. Deception became even more essential when she changed her name and fled to England. It became second nature.

Yet she could not lie any longer. Not when she sat here staring into Michael's beautiful angel's face, knowing what she had done to him. She had to try to erase what she had learned in the past, to let it go entirely. She wanted to be a better person.

She wanted to begin to be worthy of him. Even if that meant losing him.

Kate reached up and caught his hands in hers, holding them tightly. "Michael," she said, but her voice was so weak, like a frightened child's. She swallowed hard past the fear. "I must tell you something."

He pressed a quick kiss to her fingers. "So serious tonight, bonny Kate."

"I fear I am more Kate the curst." She couldn't look into his eyes as she spoke, so she stared at their joined hands, as if by doing so she could hold him fast to her forever. "When I told you I could not marry, it was not because I don't want you, don't—care about you. It was because there are things about me that you don't know, things that would make me an unfit wife for a man in your position."

He leaned back slightly away from her, though they still held hands. "Secrets, Kate?"

"Yes. So many of them."

"Then tell me. You know that you can say anything to me—it will not change my feelings. You know all my dark secrets, all the things in my past I am ashamed of, and you did not judge me. I won't do that to you. If you are a thief and Bow Street is after you, I could hide you in the old priest's hole at Thorn Hill. Or in the sheepherder's cottage."

Kate gave a choked laugh at the thought of crouching in a hidden cabinet while Runners tore the house apart searching for her. Truly, only Michael could make her laugh at such a moment. "No, *caro,* I am not a thief. But I *am* a liar, and . . ." She paused, gathering every ounce of her courage. "A whore."

His fingers tightened convulsively on hers. "I will not let you use such a word to describe yourself, Kate. It's ugly, and a lie—so I suppose you *are* a liar for calling yourself a whore. You were a virgin when we made love."

"Only because I did not have the time to sell that particular commodity before I left Venice." Kate couldn't bear to touch him any longer, now that her unclean self was appearing. She let him go, and turned away to face the silent innyard. "I told you my mother drowned, and I nearly went with her."

"Yes," he answered quietly, soothingly, almost as if she were a skittish colt he feared to spook and drive off. "In a boating accident."

"We had gone to a party, you see, aboard a yacht that my mother's lover—her protector—owned. My mother was a courtesan, the most beautiful and expensive in Venice. As my grandmother was before her, and as I was soon to be. My true name is Katerina

Bruni. There was never any English soldier named Brown. I have never been married."

Kate had often thought that she could glimpse paradise in Michael's face, in his smile and the light of his eyes. Now, now when it was so very important and she was quaking in her slippers with fright and uncertainty, he was utterly expressionless. His sweet mouth was a straight, flat line, his gaze shuttered. He truly could have been carved of the wood from the tree they leaned against.

Yet he reached for her hands again. Surely that was a hopeful sign.

"You were a virgin," he said again, quietly.

Kate flicked the end of her tongue against her parched lips and nodded shortly, staring at their joined hands. "There—there was a man. He was in negotiations with my mother to become my protector, but he also died on the yacht. My virginity was very valuable to him."

"And not to you?"

Had her virginity been valuable to her? She had never truly considered that. It was worth money to her mother, pride to Julian Kirkwood, but . . .

Yes. She had valued it, but not as they had. "It was," she said. "As a gift. One I chose to give to *you*, Michael."

He released her hands, and one finger gently lifted her chin, forcing her to meet his gaze in the moonlight. His stare was still quite unreadable, while she feared her feelings were writ too large. Fear, apprehension, hope, misery—love. Surely it was all in her eyes for him to see.

"Why, Kate?" he said, still quiet and gentle. Terribly gentle. "Why did you give such a gift to me? I have no great riches to give you, no palaces or crowns. Only my scarred self, and a most odd family and house."

Kate feared she would burst into tears. Her throat ached; her eyes itched. It was more important now than it had ever been before that she hold control of her emotions, that she convince him of the truth—that she had changed. And she *had* changed. She was no longer the uncertain girl she was before the accident. She was a woman, and she knew what she wanted— a home, a family. Love.

But she was no longer willing to gain and hold all that with deceit. Michael had to know the truth—they had to be together just as they were, two flawed people who tried to be better. Or they had to part.

"I gave that gift to you, Michael, because I knew that I could trust you with it," she answered. "You are a good man, and I care deeply about you." She was trying so very hard to be brave, yet she could not bring herself to say it—*love*. Courage could go only so far on this night.

"And you did not care about this other man?" he said.

Kate turned away from him, wrapping her arms over her hollow stomach. She remembered Julian Kirkwood—how handsome he was. Truly the most beautiful man she had ever seen, with his smooth olive skin, gray eyes, and glossy black hair waving back from a noble brow. He dressed with elegant perfection, beauty in every detail. Not like Michael's rough country attire, his limp, and scarred face. Julian had spoken five languages, been knowledgeable about literature, art, science, history. And he had made it very clear that he desired her, adored her.

But she had feared him, from a place inside herself so deep, so elemental. His gaze, his touch, were too grasping, too intense. His beautiful eyes did not see *her*, Katerina, but a creature of his own imagining, his own desires and dreams. If her life had gone on as it had begun, if she had become Julian's mistress, she would have had to *become* his dream woman. His Beatrice. Her own self would be forever buried.

With Michael, she never felt that way. Perhaps he had not known the truth of her past life, her external situation, but he had always known *her*, her heart.

Ever since the moment they met on the moor. And she sensed his goodness, his deep strength, his passion. He possessed something far finer than elegant clothes and Continental polish. And something in Kate's soul reached out to grasp that.

She knew that her silence had gone on too long. She wiped impatiently, roughly, at her eyes, and turned back to Michael. He still watched her in perfect silence.

"Did I care about him?" she repeated slowly. "He was handsome, rich, charming. He was friends with my mother's protector, so she adored him and advanced his cause. I did not care about him. I feared him."

At those stumbling words, Michael came to warm life. He caught her by the shoulders, his hands strong and safe against her. "Did he hurt you, Kate?" he said fiercely. "Did he—"

"No! No, nothing like that. It was just—when he looked at me he saw Dante's Beatrice, Petrarch's Laura. A dream, a fantasy. He watched me all the time, all the time. He followed me to the shops, to church, staring. Always watching." Her voice rose sharply, and she knew she was becoming hysterical. Yet this was the first time she had ever told *anyone* of what had happened with Julian Kirkwood. With her mother, Kate always feigned contentment with her lot. Lucrezia would not have understood her daughter's fanciful scruples. Now the creeping cold feelings of Julian's staring at her, kissing her, came flooding back. It was so very unlike the warm *rightness* she felt in Michael's arms, under Michael's kiss. "I detested him. He wanted only a possession, not a real woman."

A strangled groan echoed in Michael's throat. For an instant, his grasp tightened almost painfully on her shoulders. Then he turned away, jolting to his feet. He strode two steps away, his back to her.

Kate buried her face in her hands. He was disgusted with her, disgusted with what she had been, with her lies. She wanted to tell him, longed to tell him, how very sorry she was. When she opened her mouth, all that came out was a sob.

In an instant, Michael was back with her, kneeling before her in the dirt of the innyard, reaching out for her hands like a drowning man.

"Kate, Kate of my consolation," he said, his voice a hollow echo she had never heard before. He sounded like she felt—as if surfacing from a cold depth. "I am sorry."

Utterly bewildered, Kate stared down at him. He was all shadows and angles in the dark. "*You* are sorry, Michael? Whatever for? You have done nothing."

"I am as bad as the man who would have bought you."

Kate gaped at him, completely nonplussed. Whatever she had been expecting, whatever she had been dreading, it was not *this*. "What are you talking about? You are nothing like him. He was selfish, delusional in his love. You are . . ." She faltered at that, for truly she had no words for all the things Michael was.

Still kneeling before her, he stared up at her, stark and lovely. "I insisted that we must marry, even though you said no. You refused, and I still thought that I knew best, that I could overcome your resistance. I only wanted what *I* wished for, you as my wife, not what you might desire. I'm sorry, Kate."

Sorry? Kate's mother had always said men were right no matter what they said or did, that women just had to go along with them if they wanted life to be pleasant and comfortable. And men would never, ever apologize, even if they were lying scoundrels. Yet here was a man telling her he was sorry for offering her the one thing she wanted above all others.

To be Michael's wife, to have him and his family as her own for the rest of her days.

"Oh, *caro mio*," she whispered. "I promise you, Michael, you are not as other men. You have nothing at all to be sorry for. *I* am sorry. I lied to you from before we met—I brought such ugliness into your life, into Amelia's and Christina's lives. But I swear to you, I *vow,* I never meant to hurt any of you. I only wanted . . ." Once again, words and logic failed her. She had only emotion, like a great, choking tidal wave of pain and love and longing.

Michael sat beside her again, his arm coming around her shoulders, holding her submersion at bay. She was safe for the moment, always safe when he held her in the dark. But the morning always came eventually.

"Tell me what you wanted," he urged.

"A new life," she said. "A new way of being, where I could find out who I am. No masks, no falseness. The irony, of course, is that I had to lie to obtain truth."

"Why did you decide to come to England?"

"I told you the truth about my father. He was English, but I had never seen his homeland. Only read about it, heard tales of it from others. And it is very far from Venice. When my mother died, I was so lost, confused—I did not know what to do." Kate closed her eyes as she remembered those days at Maria and Paolo's cottage, when she was so sick and sad. "My mother owned her palazzo free and clear—I would have inherited it. I could have gone back, found a protector, taken her place in the demimonde. But I could not."

And her mother's spirit had told her she did not have to. But she could not say that to Michael. Surely he already thought her a bedlamite.

"I came here seeking goodness," she said simply. "And I found it."

"Kate," he said hoarsely. She turned her face up for his kiss, and his lips met hers in the most tender of caresses.

"Oh, Kate," he murmured, his lips trailing a ribbon of kisses to her cheek and throat, never letting her go. "You are so brave."

"Brave?" Kate tangled her fingers in the waves of

his hair, returning his kisses. His cheek was rough beneath her lips, sweeter than oranges or marzipan. "I was a coward to lie to you."

He caught her face between his hands, forcing her to meet his forthright gaze. "You told me the truth in the end. That is what matters."

"But—"

"Sh. I cannot say I'm happy about it—about the life you had to lead, all the terrible things you faced. About the fact that you thought you *had* to lie to me, to anyone. That is all over, Kate. You are safe now."

Safe. Kate stared up at him intently, longing to believe him, still afraid to. It was all too fine; surely it was a dream that would be snatched away like a drop of water.

"It is late," he said softly.

Kate closed her eyes. "Yes. I never meant to leave Christina and Amelia for so long."

"Go to bed." He pressed one last fleeting kiss to her brow, and let her go. "We can speak more of this later."

She nodded, unable to look at him again for fear she might start weeping. She had never before in her life been such a watering pot! Wordlessly, she took his coat from around her shoulders and handed it back to him. Wrapping her arms about herself against the sudden chill of the night, she fled into the silence of the inn.

Michael sat in the deserted innyard for a long time after Kate left. He smoked another cheroot, wrapped in the bittersweet silence and smoke.

He had known Kate Brown was hiding something, of course, from that first day. That sapphire brooch was the most obvious sign, but there was also her air of sophistication and secretiveness, her bright flashes of sorcery. The longing and pain in her eyes when she thought herself unobserved. In his more fanciful moments, he had imagined she might be a spy, or a runaway princess from some exotic Mediterranean kingdom. A jewel thief. A duchess. He *should* have included courtesan on that dream list—it only made sense, perfect sense, now that he knew. The way she moved, smiled, the *knowingness* of her, beyond her years. Yet he had never thought of it. Perhaps because of the poetic dreamy innocence that enclosed her like a white mantle, the palpable air of her being set apart from the mundane world.

His sorceress. His curst Kate.

Michael drew deeply on the cheroot until he felt the sharp bite of smoke at the bottom of his lungs. Kate was the most beautiful, alluring woman he had ever seen. Surely she could have made a vast fortune in Venice. Instead, she had surrendered all her innocence and passion in Michael's arms, in a rough sheepherder's cottage while a storm raged around them.

He didn't know *what* he felt at this moment. He had felt love before in his life, and guilt—oh, yes, there had been plenty of fruitless guilt. He recognized the sweetness and fear of love now, blooming tentatively like a first rose of summer after a very black winter. He recognized the sharp tang of guilt. But there was also a bitter brew of hurt that she had felt she could not trust him, even after their lovemaking, mixed with something else—anger.

White-hot anger at people who were dead. Kate's mother, for trying to usher her own child into the life of a whore. And the unnamed man who wanted to buy Kate, to possess her like a horse or sheep or painting.

With a muttered curse, Michael dropped the end of the cheroot and ground it beneath his boot heel. If that man were before him now, Michael would thrash him to within an inch of his life for ever frightening Kate, ever making her feel as if she had no choices. It was true that he himself had once thought to possess Kate, as his wife. All those thoughts were gone now, vanished like the smoke.

He loved Kate, and he could think of nothing sweeter than having her love him, too, than spending their lives together as a family with Amelia. But it would have to be Kate's choice, and he sensed that she was confused and frightened right now.

It would have to be Kate's decision. Yet Michael had learned patience since his wild youth. He could wait.

Chapter Nineteen

"*J*ulian, my dearest brother. Do come and have some tea. I am sure it will do you some good. I have never seen you look so very pale."

Julian stayed at the window, staring out at the rain-soaked square, his back to the sumptuous chinoiserie fantasy of his sister's drawing room. It always rained in blasted London. The people moved about in a haze of cold grayness, scurrying like mice under dark umbrellas and enveloping cloaks. If he closed his eyes, he could almost feel the hot sun of Italy on his face again, see the vibrant colors. . . .

"Charlotte, my darling," he said. "I am your dearest brother because I am your only brother."

She laughed softly, and he heard the rustle of her silk gown as she rose from her settee and crossed the dragon-laced expanse of the room to his side. He opened his eyes when he felt her gentle touch on his arm, and he smiled down at her. In all his time away, wandering the Continent in a never-ending search for perfection, his older sister had not aged a day. Through marriage to Viscount Stoke, the births of two sons, and a rise to a position of social prominence, she maintained her auburn hair and milk white skin, her lithe horsewoman's figure, and the gray eyes they shared as a legacy of their French grandmother.

Eyes that were now tinged with concern as she stared at him. "Even if I had a hundred brothers, Julian, you would be the dearest," she said. "When I heard you were lost at sea, I nearly went mad." Her words broke off on a choked sob, and she buried her face in his shoulder.

"Sh," he murmured, patting her back gently. That concern had been there ever since his arrival in London. Charlotte would follow him about, proffering tea and lap robes as if he were an elderly invalid in Bath. She covered her eyes with her handkerchief every time she thought of his near death, and was always reaching out to touch his sleeve or hand, as if to assure herself he was there before her, alive and whole.

Or nearly whole. Part of him was lost forever under those cold waves—the part that could have been the best. After all those years of searching, he had at last found perfection, only to lose it. But he could not tell that to his sister. She could never understand the wild, bitter rush of longing that overcame him when he first saw Katerina Bruni in the Piazza San Marco, laughing in the sunlight, as beautiful and distant as Dante's Beatrice. Or the terrible pain of losing her, and not being able to grieve for his loss. He loved his sister, loved seeing her again and meeting his nephews for the first time. He even loved rainy old London. It was part of his heritage. Yet he mourned so deeply for the beauty that was gone.

"It is all right now, Charlotte," he said, holding his sister in his arms. "I am home with you, and we will never be apart again."

She nodded against his shoulder, her tears and flakes of her rice powder leaving a faint trail of dampness against the bottle green superfine of his coat. Once, such a desecration would have driven him into anger. Now he felt only vague bemusement.

"I give thanks daily to God for bringing you back, Julian," she said, brushing at the stain with her manicured fingertips.

"You never struck me as a particularly religious lady, Charlotte."

"I wasn't, before. Our parents, rest their souls, never paid much attention to our spiritual lives, did they?"

"No." Nor much else. Sir Nigel Kirkwood and Marjorie, Lady Kirkwood, had not cared much for children. They had spent most of their time traveling from one watering spot to another, in search of the perfect horse race, the perfect gaming hell, the perfect mistress or lover. One or two times a year, they would pop back into Kirkwood Manor to criticize their offspring's progress, belittle their physical appearance, hold some long, brandy-soaked house parties for their wild friends. Then they would be off again. Julian's best escape had been into his beloved books: poetry and stories of Italy and the glorious Renaissance. School had almost been a relief, except that it parted him from Charlotte.

Now *he* was the baronet. It was all his—the title, the manor, the social position. The yearning to wander, the aching dissatisfaction.

"They have been gone a long time, Charlotte, dearest," he said. "And you have made a fine life here."

She gave him a rather watery smile, and nodded her pretty auburn head. "You are right, of course. I am said to be one of the finest hostesses in Town. I just wish . . ."

"Wish what?"

"That *you* could enjoy this life I have made. We are invited everywhere—balls, suppers, breakfasts, the theater, salons. But you are so solemn, brother. Can nothing amuse you now?"

Julian had to laugh at her pout, and he bent his head to kiss her creased brow. Only Charlotte could take his lack of a social calendar as a personal affront. "I have not been in Town very long, Charlotte. You must give me time."

She laughed, too, leaning her head on his shoulder. "Quite right, Julian. You have been so ill. I'm silly to expect you to be immediately chipper and cheerful. You need to rest, not go dancing and card playing every night. I just want you to be happy, and I see such sadness in your eyes."

"I will be better soon, I vow." He would hide his grief ever deeper, away from Charlotte's sharp gaze and hovering concern.

"Yes. But you know, Julian, darling, there is yet another reason you should go out in Society more."

Julian stifled a sigh. He knew what was coming now. He had been expecting it ever since he arrived in London. "And what might that be?"

"Finding a suitable bride, of course! The Season is half over, but there are still many young ladies on the marriage mart. Miss King, Lady Veronica Steel-Haddon. And I hear that the Earl of Darcy's sister is soon to arrive in Town. She is still quite young, but such a fine family."

"I have only just arrived myself, Charlotte. It is much too early for such a serious matter."

"It is never too early! You have been away from England for so long. It's important that you have an heir."

"And I will. Someday." When he could forget about the dark eyes of his Renaissance princess, and bear to take a pale English rose in her place.

Charlotte nodded, pouting again. "I suppose I will have to be content with that. In the meantime, I know just the thing to cheer you."

"What is that? Another tea party? A musicale?"

"Not at all. An old school friend of mine, Elizabeth Hollingsworth, is back from Italy, and is holding a salon in a few days. She is a great artist, you know, and many very interesting people flock to her house. I don't understand art myself, but it is quite the place to be seen. *You* like art and such, Julian. I'm sure you would enjoy it."

"I met the Hollingsworths in Venice," Julian answered quietly. He remembered a portrait Elizabeth Hollingsworth had painted, beauty draped in violet satin, sapphires, and amethysts. What had happened to that portrait of Lucrezia Bruni, to all the lovely things in her house?

"Wonderful!" Charlotte said. "Then I know you will enjoy seeing them again."

Julian shook his head, pulling himself back into the present. Into a rainy city far from an elegant Venetian palazzo. "Very well, Charlotte. I will go to this salon with you."

"You won't be sorry, Julian. It will be a very fine evening, I'm sure."

Chapter Twenty

"*O*h, Mrs. Brown! Isn't it the most beautiful place ever? I'm sure princesses must live here." Amelia clambered over Kate's lap in the carriage, staring openmouthed out the window as they drew near London.

Kate put her arm around the child to steady her, watching the city approach over her little golden head. The first time Kate came to London, she had been tired and scared, not sure what was waiting for her in the teeming streets. She had seen only the moderately respectable lanes where her room was located, the crowds of busy people hurrying about their business in their drab brown and gray clothes. Brown cloth against gray stones, wet, grimy streets, cramped shops.

The route the Lindleys' carriage took after the outskirts of town were behind them was completely different. The streets were wider, quieter, cleaner, lined with tall, cream-colored houses shuttered in glossy black or dark green, confined in black iron gates. A few maidservants scrubbed at front steps or washed windows. Carriages and handsome horses bearing handsome riders rattled past. There were a few pedestrians, beautifully dressed ladies trailed by maids bearing packages. The parks were manicured and shady, inviting spots for a stroll or a quiet conversation beneath the trees.

Even Lady Darcy, who had been watching Kate and Christina with a vaguely disapproving, pinched air for hours, was distracted by the scenery. The coral-colored feathers in her bonnet bobbed and wavered as she turned to watch the houses. Christina had at last put her book down to examine the squares.

"It is a great shame to cut trees into such artificial shapes," she said, her voice as stern as any elderly schoolmistress, as she examined a row of topiaries. "The leaves bruise so easily."

Amelia leaned against Kate's shoulder with a happy sigh. "There are children walking in that park, Mrs. Brown. Will *we* be able to walk there?"

"Of course," Kate answered. "Every day, if you like."

And all the while, Kate tried to forget that Michael sat across from her, watching her. He was very subtle, but she knew he was glancing at her whenever he thought no one was paying attention. For she glanced at him just the same.

They had had no moments alone since her revelations in the innyard, no chance to speak of them. No opportunity for her to gauge his feelings about her true past, her lies. His manner had not changed toward her in the least. He was unfailingly polite, always making light conversation and little jokes to make the long journey easier. He would take her hand to help her into and out of the carriage, and though she thought—hoped—his grasp lingered slightly longer than was strictly proper, she was not sure. His lips never brushed her hair as she passed; he never took her in his arms when they met in dim corridors.

But here, in London, things would be different. Their world would expand beyond the close confines of carriages and inns; there would be gardens and houses where they could speak quietly together. If that was what he wanted.

Or perhaps he was just waiting for them to reach their destination before he dismissed her.

The carriage turned a corner onto a quieter street and slowed to a halt before one of the houses. It was not one of the grandest homes, but it was impressive and attractive, a tall expanse of pale brick with narrow, draped windows. The Prices were obviously a very respectable, well-to-do family—their botanist son would be a fine match for Christina. If Christina could eventually be brought to see that.

"Is this *our* house, Mrs. Brown?" Amelia asked, wide-eyed with wonder. "It isn't much like Thorn Hill, is it?"

Kate had to laugh. "It is not as large, to be sure, Amelia. But we don't need as much space in Town, do we?"

Christina critically examined the blossoms in the window boxes. "Someone is overwatering the petunias."

"Christina, dear," Lady Darcy said, with a soft sigh. "It hardly matters about the flowers. We are in London! You will have shops to visit, new gowns to order. So much more interesting than plants, as I'm sure you'll find."

Christina just rolled her eyes, and tucked her book away in a travel valise as a footman came out of the house to open the carriage door.

In the neat, marble-floored foyer, it became clear that they were not the first to arrive at the house. The double doors leading to the drawing room were thrown open, and at the commotion of arrival a lady appeared there. Kate, staying at the back of the crowd of family and servants, holding Amelia firmly by the hand, had to stifle a gasp at the sight of her.

Mary, Countess of Darcy, had her father's eyes and slightly elfin, pointed chin. It was almost like looking at Edward again, as Kate had last seen him, dancing on his yacht with her mother.

Not that young Lady Darcy looked anything less than feminine. She was tall but willow slim, aside from the slight bulge of her belly. Pale golden curls peeped from beneath a stylish burgundy-and-gray bonnet. Garnets sparkled in her ears and at her throat, and her burgundy silk pelisse draped gracefully over that pregnant belly. She laid a graceful, gray-gloved hand over the bulge, and said brightly, "Mother Jane! Michael, Christina! Here you are at last. I just came by to be certain all is in readiness for your arrival, since you won't stay with us at Lindley House."

"How lovely to see you, Mary," the elder Lady Darcy replied, kissing her daughter-in-law's rosy cheek. "But are you certain you should be out and about? Should you not be resting?"

Mary laughed, a light but strangely brittle sound. She waved her hand in a dismissive gesture as she kissed Christina in turn. "I only feel unwell in the mornings. Afternoons are lovely. I've called for tea— I'll just ring for more, shall I? You all must be parched after your journey. Christina, don't you look pretty! Such a young lady you have become. I can't wait for your first Season! What fun we shall have. And Michael. Handsome as ever."

"How are you, Mary?" Michael said, bowing over his sister-in-law's hand. "Beautiful as always, I see. Charles is a very fortunate man."

She laughed again, that brittle, breakable sound more pronounced. "Oh, Michael! I wish you would tell that to your brother when my modiste sends her bills around. He had absolute fits when he last saw how much I ordered for the start of the Season, though his bills from Weston must be twice as large. But of course, soon he needn't worry. It will be much too difficult for me to cut a dash when I'm as big as a house!" Her gaze shifted past him, a new smile, free of the tinge of bitterness, blooming when she saw Amelia. One golden brow arched inquiringly as she spied Kate holding the child's hand. "And Amelia! How she has grown."

"She is six now," Michael said. "But come, Mary, there is someone new for you to meet."

Kate stood up very straight, her clasp tightening on Amelia's as she resisted the urge to reach up and nervously check her bonnet and travel-tousled hair. Next to Mary Lindley's perfect modishness, Kate felt like a veritable scullery maid.

"How do you do, Amelia?" Mary said. "Do you remember me, your aunt Mary?"

Amelia hung back, clinging to Kate, and Kate re-membered how shy the child had been when they first met. She bent down and whispered, "It's quite all right, Amelia. Make your pretty curtsy now, just as we practiced." She gently urged Amelia forward.

"How do you do, Aunt Mary?" Amelia said quietly, dropping into a dainty little curtsy. Kate feared she would start beaming proudly for all to see. Amelia really was a perfect little lady.

Mary obviously agreed. She smiled and reached down to pat Amelia's rosy little cheeks. This couldn't help but endear her a bit to Kate, despite the tales of her high-ton ways. "She is beautiful, Michael! I can only hope my own children are as charming."

"You won't hear me quarreling with you about that," Michael said. "And this, Mary, is Mrs. Brown. She has taken Christina and Amelia ably in hand these last few weeks."

"Indeed?" Mary's gaze flickered up to Kate, that blond brow arched. Her smile grew distant. "How do you do, Mrs. Brown? Perhaps you will be seeking a new position by the time this little sprout requires a governess! Provided it's a girl, of course."

A new position? Kate could scarcely think what might happen to her tomorrow, let alone far away in some vague future. But she just smiled, made a curtsy of her own, and said, "How do you do, Lady Darcy?"

Mary's eyes widened. "You are from Italy!"

"Mrs. Brown is from Venus, Aunt Mary," Amelia said helpfully.

"Venice, Amelia, dear," Kate murmured. "Yes, Lady Darcy, I am originally from Venice."

"How perfectly extraordinary," said Mary, some-thing odd flickering across her heart-shaped face. Hope, grief, uncertainty? "My father spent many years in Venice before his sudden death last year. He loved it there. His letters were always full of the great beau-ties of your country—art, music, wine. Perhaps you heard of him while you were in residence there, Mrs. Brown? The Duke of Salton?"

Kate gazed into Mary's eyes, and for a moment she thought she glimpsed Edward there. Smiling, as pleased and mischievous as a small boy as he handed her mother a jewel box and watched her open it. She blinked, and the image was gone. She was back in this London foyer, trunks being piled around her.

"I—believe I did hear the name," Kate answered. "An English duke is noticed wherever he goes, I'm sure, Lady Darcy."

"Very true," Mary said slowly. "Especially if the duke was my father. He did so love spreading coin about on lavish parties and suppers! Tell me, Mrs. Brown, did you ever—" She broke off on another of her trilling laughs. "Oh, but I am so rude, keeping all of you standing about when you must be so tired. Come into the drawing room—have some tea. We will speak more later, Mrs. Brown."

As Mary took Michael's arm and turned toward the drawing room, Amelia tugged at Kate's hand. "Mrs. Brown," she whispered. "I need to use the chamber pot."

"Of course, Amelia, dear," Kate said. She called after Michael, "Mr. Lindley, I will just settle Amelia in her chamber, if I may."

"It is the yellow room," Mary said. "And I will send tea up for you, Mrs. Brown. Your chamber is next to little Amelia's."

"Thank you, Lady Darcy."

"Don't forget! We must chat more later," Mary reminded her before disappearing into the drawing room. Michael threw Kate a rueful grin over his shoulder.

Kate couldn't help but smile in return—despite the distinct sense that the "chat" was more of a threat than a promise.

"Mrs. Brown is a most unusual governess, Michael," Mary said, tugging Michael down beside her onto a settee beside the fire. His mother and Christina sat by one of the tall windows, Christina nodding dutifully as their mother spoke to her quickly and earnestly. No doubt lecturing her on some aspect of proper London behavior.

Michael turned his gaze from them to his sister-in-law, who watched him very closely as she handed him a cup of tea. *Unusual?* Mary had no idea. "Yes. I suppose she is. She has been so good for Christina and Amelia."

"I did think that Christina's complexion was looking less freckled than the last time I saw her," Mary said, nibbling at a cake. But she was obviously not yet finished with the topic of Mrs. Brown. "Mrs. Brown is very pretty."

"Not as pretty as you," Michael teased.

Mary did not smile, as she usually did at his teasing sallies. Instead, something strange, bitter and hard, flickered across her pretty face, and for an instant she appeared ancient and unhappy. "My mother, God rest her saintly soul, always said a man had only one use for a pretty servant."

Michael's hand tightened on his teacup, the delicate china creaking under the pressure. No one, not even his sister-in-law, could speak so of Kate. "Mrs. Brown is not a servant. And I do not have to explain myself to you."

"Of course not," Mary said. A gentle smile flickered over her lips, but it did nothing to soften her eyes. She patted his cheek lightly. "Not you, darling. You are not my father. He was terribly indiscreet, but since he was a duke—and a charming duke at that—no one cared. They just pitied my dear mother. And then there is Charles. You aren't him, either."

So that was it. "Has Charles also been—indiscreet?"

Mary laughed lightly, but she would not look at him. She watched Christina and his mother across the room, and crumbled another cake under her fork. "Oh, darling, it is all too dull. Let's talk about you and your visit to Town! Does your Mrs. Brown like Shakespeare?"

His Mrs. Brown. Michael feared he was grinning

like an idiot at the thought. "As a matter of fact, she does. Very much."

"Wonderful! *Romeo and Juliet* is at Drury Lane. I will procure tickets for all of us tomorrow evening. Charles will just have to make the time to come with us, won't he? We *are* his family, after all. Let's see— you, me, Mother Jane, Christina, Mrs. Brown. We will need one of the best boxes."

Michael glanced at her in surprise. The Mary he knew—the *duke's daughter,* the grand lady who married his brother in the wedding of the Season years ago—would not have been seen in a theater box with a governess. Perhaps impending motherhood was softening her.

As if she sensed his amazement, she gave him a rueful smile and took a sip of her tea. "She needs to be there to watch Christina, yes? And I can tell you admire her, darling, and since you are my brother I want you to be happy. Someone in the family should be; otherwise it will be too gloomy for this poor baby to be born a Lindley. Your Mrs. Brown seems a genteel, pretty sort. I'm sure she and I will be friends." Before Michael could question her about her "happy" remarks, she changed the subject and went back to her usual fluttering, social self. "Did I tell you I saw the Hollingsworths at Lady Symington's ball last week? Such a surprise to see them back from Italy. Are they not great friends of yours? They are having a salon at their house next week—we absolutely must attend."

Kate was drifting in some twilight world of blue purple mist between sleep and wakefulness, dreams flickering on and off like stars. It was hard to sleep in a new bed, as luxurious as it was with its feather pillows and embroidered hangings, and the noises outside her window were not like those at Thorn Hill. There were no night birds, no branches clicking at the glass. Only the hollow echo of horses' hooves and carriage wheels, occasional humming voices or tipsy bursts of laughter.

And the squeal of a door opening. For a moment, Kate thought it was part of the dreams, but then there was the shuffle of footsteps across the carpet, too real to be any dream. Without opening her eyes, Kate rolled onto her side, thinking—hoping?—it was Michael. It had been far too long since their night in the sheepherder's cottage, too long since she felt the touch of his hand, the heat of his embrace. And his perfect politeness since she revealed her secrets had been almost worse than shouting would be—uncertainty was cold and harsh.

But the hand that lightly touched her arm was too small to be Michael's. Kate's eyes flew open to find Amelia standing by the bed, peeking over the high mattress with wide blue eyes. Her little face was pale in the moonlight.

"Amelia?" Kate said, pushing herself up on her elbow. "Are you ill, *cara*?"

Amelia shook her head, her loose curls bouncing. She didn't wear her dressing gown, but her doll was tucked under her arm. "I had a bad dream."

"Oh, poor Amelia. It must be from being in a new place. Here, lie beside me for a while." She helped the child climb up onto the bed, tucking the blankets around them both. Amelia cuddled close, and Kate inhaled deeply of her sweet, sleepy-little-girl scent.

"London is very big, isn't it, Mrs. Brown?" Amelia whispered.

"Yes, very big indeed."

"Will I get lost in it?"

Kate laughed softly. "No, *angelina*. I will always be there to watch over you, and be sure you aren't lost. London will be quite enjoyable, you'll see. We will walk in the park, and go to Astley's to see the acrobats, and Gunter's for ices. Perhaps there will even be a toy store or two, with rows and rows of dolls."

Amelia clutched at her little china-headed doll. "Then Clarissa will be jealous."

"You don't think she might like a friend? One from Paris, mayhap, with a pink dress and eyes that close?"

Amelia considered this. "Perhaps she would, if the doll had yellow hair."

"Just like you, *cara*," Kate said. She kissed the top of those bright curls, and Amelia yawned against her shoulder. As she shifted under the blankets, Kate heard the rustle of paper and looked down to see a folded note in Amelia's tiny fist. "What's this?"

"Oh, I almost forgot," Amelia answered, her eyes drifting shut. "This was under your door when I came in, Mrs. Brown. It must be *terribly* important."

"I'm sure it is," Kate murmured. She slid it out of Amelia's hand. In the bar of moonlight, she could just make out her name written there, in a bold, black slash of ink. "Thank you for bringing it to me."

Amelia nodded. "Tell me a story," she said, around another yawn.

Kate tucked the note under her pillow. "A story about what?"

"A princess. An *Italian* princess."

"Hm, let me see. An Italian princess. Well, once upon a time there was a beautiful, golden-haired princess named Lucia. . . ."

By the time the rambling, spur-of-the-moment tale of Princess Lucia was complete, Amelia was fast asleep. For once, she was not kicking or tossing about. Only then did Kate slip from the bed and take her note over to the window to read.

It was from Michael, of course, but there were no declarations of undying passion, no renewals of his offer of marriage. Kate did not know what she would have done if those *were* written there—she had never been in such a muddle in her life. But all that was there was an invitation to the theater tomorrow night, along with his family. *Romeo and Juliet.* It was not *The Taming of the Shrew,* he wrote, but he hoped she would accept all the same.

Kate laughed softly. Passion, murder, and mayhem in Verona. Just what she needed.

Chapter Twenty-one

If I profane with my unworthiest hand
This holy shrine, the gentle sin is this:
My lips, two blushing pilgrims, ready stand
To smooth that rough touch with a tender kiss.

*T*he play was really not so bad, Christina thought as she peered through her opera glasses at the stage below. The theater was not something she usually looked forward to; it was silly and dull, and took time away from her studies, much like tea parties, assemblies, and dress fittings. But this was far superior to the traveling troupes they usually had in Yorkshire. The stage set was quite elaborate, evoking stone, ivy-covered walls and towers, and a hot, blue Italian sky. Right now, the boards were crowded with velvet-clad courtiers at the Capulet ball, dancing while Romeo and Juliet whispered at stage left. Juliet's white satin gown, covered in pearl and crystal beads, shimmered in the footlights, set off dramatically against Romeo's dark blue velvet doublet.

That was the one aspect of the production Christina could not quite approve of. The Romeo. He was far too old for the part—why, he must be *thirty,* at least! And his blond hair was thinning. He was not at all like the man in the box across the way. Now, *he* would make a fine Romeo.

Christina slowly shifted her opera glasses from the aging Romeo and his Juliet to that box. Yes, he still sat there. She had noticed him almost as soon as she had taken her seat, and that in itself was unusual, for she rarely noticed if a man was handsome or not. It mattered only if they knew about plants, like her friend Andrew Price. But this gentleman *was* quite unusual. There was certainly no one like him in Yorkshire.

He was tall and slender, like the fashionable poets the Ross girls swooned over, with black hair that was as glossy as the leaves of the *Zantedeschia aethiopicia*. It was brushed back in neat waves from his face, revealing the sharp lines of his cheekbones and jaw, the fullness of his lips. He had a rather tragic mien, adding to the Romeo-ness of him. Indeed, tragedy seemed to hover over him like a violet mist, and it was underscored by the black band around the sleeve of his perfectly cut dark red velvet coat. His gaze never left the stage, so he did not notice Christina spying on him. Not that it would matter if he *did*, for she would surely never see him again. No one as unearthly handsome could be found someplace as prosaic as the British Museum or a botany lecture.

When they first took their seats and Christina noticed him there, she had half turned to point him out to Mrs. Brown, who sat in the gilded chair behind her. Somehow, it had become second nature to share things with Mrs. Brown; it was so easy to confide in her. She always understood, not like Christina's mother, who *never* did. But something held Christina back, and she said nothing. She didn't want to seem foolish, like those bacon-brained Ross girls who were always chasing after gentlemen.

She continued studying him as the Capulet ball went on, and Juliet discovered the truth of Romeo's identity. The lady who sat next to the handsome man touched his sleeve lightly, whispering in his ear. He inclined his head toward her, yet his gaze never left the stage. Was she his wife? She was certainly lovely, with rich auburn hair held back by a bandeau of cameos and a gown of amber-colored silk. That would be the one good thing about making her debut and get-

ting married. She could wear things like that, instead
of this insipid pale yellow muslin. Perhaps she would
choose dark green—it would hide the stains from her
experiments so well.

But even if she decked herself in green satin and
diamonds every day, she could not catch the eye of a
man like that. She was too freckled, with wild, curling
hair. Not beautiful and exotic, like Mrs. Brown. Christina sniffed disdainfully and turned away from the
man. She didn't care. Really.

Romeo was at Juliet's balcony now, holding his
hands up to her beseechingly.

> *With love's light wings did I o'erperch these walls;*
> *For stony limits cannot hold love out,*
> *And what love can do, that dares love attempt.*

Would a man ever say such things to her? Christina
doubted it. The most romantic thing she had ever
heard was when Andrew Price brought her a sample
of clematis from London and said, "The color of the
leaves is just like your eyes, Lady Christina." And
truly, that was finer than any silly chatter of roses and
names and "love's light wings."

Eventually, Romeo and Juliet parted with a kiss,
and the curtain closed for an interval. Christina lowered the glass to her lap, and the man became a distant blur. She could only just see his Grecian head
turn toward the lady at his side.

"Well, now!" her brother Charles said, rousing himself from the nodding drowse he had fallen into some-
time during the prologue. He had become rather stout
since she had last seen him, and a bit too red in the
face. He contrasted so unfavorably to tall, sun-
browned Michael, and, not for the first time, Christina
was grateful for their life in the country.

"That wasn't bad, eh, what?" Charles went on. He
stood up, his pale blue satin coat shining in the light
like a gaudy sky. There were tiny rosebuds and vines

embroidered on his waistcoat. "I'll just fetch us some refreshments, then."

Mary glanced up at him, a small frown marring her elfin prettiness. "Charles, really, I don't think we need—"

"No trouble at all, lambkins," Charles said. He chucked her under the chin, bent down to kiss her blond ringlets, and exited their box with more alacrity than Romeo leaving the Capulet ball. Mary made a tiny noise deep in her throat, and though Christina pretended to study her programme, she saw her sister-in-law stare stonily at another box across from theirs. Next to the one containing the mysterious gentleman.

Christina peeked at the box, which was occupied by a very pretty, red-haired lady in a bright pink gown. She was surrounded by admirers, but as Christina watched, one more joined their throng. Charles's blue coat was unmistakable.

Mary's fingers tightened on her opera glasses, and her other hand covered the tiny swell of her belly under the red-and-gold muslin of her gown. Christina felt a terrible, bitter wave of pity, and an even stronger resolve—no man would ever treat *her* that way. Better to remain unmarried and comfortable in her studies.

"The play is quite fine, Mary," she said cheerfully, drawing her sister-in-law's attention away from that box. "We can see nothing like it in Yorkshire. It was very kind of you to procure tickets for us."

Mary turned to her and smiled—but her eyes were overly bright, almost manic. "I am very glad you are enjoying it, Christina. I adore the theater myself, but can seldom coax your brother to attend with me."

"Then he is a fool, to miss out on so much."

"I agree. A very great fool."

Mary's voice was full of steel, but thankfully Christina was saved from answering when Michael rose from his seat and said, "Shall we walk a bit?"

"Oh, yes, thank you, darling," Mary said. "The doctor says I must take light exercise regularly or my ankles shall swell, which would be a terrible tragedy."

She also stood, and took Christina's mother by the arm before sweeping out of the box. "Now, Mother Jane, you must visit my modiste while you are in Town. She could do wonders for dear Christina. . . ."

Christina trailed after them slowly, followed by Michael and Mrs. Brown. Perhaps they would encounter the tragic gentleman on their stroll. *That* would certainly be more interesting than yet more prattle about modistes!

"Are you enjoying the performance?"

Kate smiled up at Michael. It was dim in the corridor, the flickering sconces casting dancing shadows over the silk-papered walls and over Michael's face and hair, gilding him in edges of light. She did not take his arm—they didn't touch in any way—but she *felt* close to him. His clean, sweet, soapy scent reached across the narrow space to caress her bare arm.

She swayed a bit toward him, and answered, "Yes, very much. The production is quite fine. It was very kind of your family to include me in the outing."

They paused for a moment at the turning of the passage, letting the others get ahead of them, mingling into the crowd. Michael's hand brushed lightly over her fingers, under the fringe of her shawl. The silk clung to the dark blue superfine of his coat. "You should be able to attend the theater every night!" he murmured. "And balls and suppers, concerts— anything you like. Anyplace where your beauty could be seen and appreciated, as it deserves."

Kate gave a quiet laugh. "Oh, Michael. If I wanted that, I would have stayed in Venice. I much prefer evenings by the fire at Thorn Hill, listening to Amelia at the pianoforte. That is the only place where I have ever felt truly beautiful."

Michael laughed, too, a rough, rueful sound. He lightly brushed back a wisp of hair that had drifted from her tight chignon, tucking it back into its pins. "I also have a yearning for my own hearth. These crowds don't suit me after the quiet of the moors! How my old friends would laugh if they saw me now."

"Will you see any of them while we are in Town?" And if he did, would he give in to the lure of a noisy, wild past, the gaudy pleasure of the city? For Kate knew all too well how the past could beckon, even when it had been soundly rejected. She would hate to see that happen to Michael, her angel. He was perfect just as he was.

He shook his head. "Perhaps I will see one or two of them—Society is so small, it would be inevitable, especially if I attend even a fraction of the events Mary has planned. It won't be in the same way, though. I'm not the same man any longer."

"No."

His pensive frown turned suddenly to that familiar grin, bright and charming. "Enough of this nostalgia! *Romeo and Juliet* has enough gloom and regret to fill one evening. You look lovely tonight, Kate. *That* is what I really wanted to say."

Kate smiled, too, to make him happy. She tugged her shawl closer about her shoulders. It was a new purchase, a far too extravagant creation of black Spanish lace trimmed in silk fringe. She had hoped it would dress up her old dark blue silk, her one evening gown. "Thank you, Michael. I nearly had to come out in my day dress, for my silk went missing from the wardrobe."

His gaze shifted away, his smile becoming secretive. "Missing?"

"Yes. But then it turned up just in time for me to dress. It seems Christina had sent it down to be pressed."

"Ah."

"Yes. It's quite suitable for a governess, of course, yet I must say I rather envy your sister-in-law that red-and-gold muslin she is wearing! So very stylish."

"Oh, I wouldn't worry about it, bonny Kate," Michael said, offering her his arm as they resumed their progress along the corridor. "You would outshine every lady here if you wore homespun and ashes."

"Like Cinderella?"

"Exactly so."

Kate laughed, and gestured toward a lady in the crowd some distance from them, her back half-turned to them. She had dark hair, like Kate herself, but where Kate had always feared she appeared too much like a Gypsy dancer, this lady was a Madonna on a sunny chapel wall in Tuscany. She was very small and slim, with shining, straight black hair caught up like wings in a jeweled comb. She wore an exquisite gown of gold lace over ivory satin, and antique gold earrings swung flirtatiously against her rose-tinted cheek. She was only half turned toward them, the crowd flowing around her, but even from this distance Kate sensed her great confidence and style—and the expensive cut of her gown.

"I doubt I could outshine *her*," Kate said with a laugh. "She is so very . . ."

Then the woman turned fully toward them, and Kate's words faded. She knew her! It was Elizabeth Hollingsworth, the artist. Instinctively, Kate shrank back behind Michael's shoulder, as if she could somehow hide that way.

But there was no hiding. Michael's smile widened as he saw Elizabeth Hollingsworth, and he called, "Elizabeth! By Jove, but it's good to see you."

He started in the direction of Elizabeth, drawing Kate with him. When she hesitated, he glanced down at her with a questioning frown.

"Michael Lindley!" Elizabeth answered, her serene Madonna face breaking into a grin of her own. A mischievous saint. She broke away from her admirers and hurried toward them, going up on the toes of her tiny gold slippers to give him a quick double peck on the cheeks. Kate took the chance to slide her hand away from Michael's arm and slip into the shadows along the wall. "If it isn't old Hellfire Lindley himself. We haven't seen you in an age, you wicked man. Not since you chose to bury yourself in the country.''

Michael laughed. "Not since *you* chose to stay in Italy half the year!''

"Ah, well, it's the climate, you know. One of our daughters has terrible trouble with her breathing in the winter. The Italian sun is so much better for her. And better for *my* disposition! I do hate the cold.''

"You have daughters now?''

"Oh, come now, I am sure I wrote to you about it. Twin girls—Georgina and Isobel. They are growing like little weeds and are absolute terrors.'' Her oval Madonna face glowed with enviable maternal pride. "Thank heaven they are visiting my brother and his wife this month, or I would fear for my sanity! But we must find Nick. He went off to fetch some champagne, but I'm sure he must be quite lost in this crush. He will be in alt to see you again!''

"Of course, Lizzie. First, though, there is someone I would like you to meet.''

"Meet?'' Elizabeth's smile turned teasing. "Michael! Never say you have wed again?''

"Ah, no. I fear I have not been able to persuade the lady yet.'' Michael turned, and his brow arched to find her hiding by the wall. But he merely held out his hand and drew her forward, giving her no choice but to step into the light. "Elizabeth Hollingsworth, may I present Mrs. Kate Brown?''

"Mrs. Brown, I am so very—'' Elizabeth's smile froze, and it was as if all the color was pulled from her face, leaving her as pale as a marble statue. "But you're dead!''

Kate tossed a frantic glance at Michael, who watched Elizabeth with a puzzled frown. She wanted so much to run away, to leave the past behind her, as she had thought she had. Yet she could not. She was frozen to the spot, unable to run ever again.

"I went to the sale,'' Elizabeth murmured, almost to herself. She stepped closer to Kate, her gaze darting over Kate's face.

"I—fear I do not know what you mean, Lady

Hollingsworth," Kate managed to murmur. "I am quite alive."

"Yes. I see. Yes." Elizabeth gave a nervous little laugh and pressed her gloved hand to her brow. "You are too young to be her, of course. I'm sorry, Mrs.— Brown, is it? You just look very much like someone I knew in Italy. Someone who died."

"I am very sorry," Kate answered. "I *am* from Italy, but—"

"Very much alive. Of course. Forgive me, Mrs. Brown. I am not usually so fanciful! Am I, Michael?" But she still looked shaken, puzzled.

Michael glanced from Elizabeth to Kate and back again, his blue eyes narrowed. "Not at all."

"Now, we must find Nick, before the interval is over! He will be so happy to see you. And you both must come to my salon. Your sister-in-law has already accepted her invitation, and I won't take no for an answer. It will be very informal, just friends, no high sticklers allowed. Except for your mother, of course, Michael!" Elizabeth was chattering merrily again, the color slowly reappearing in her cheeks. But there was still something uneasy in her eyes. "There will be many of my Italian landscape paintings on display, Mrs. Brown, and I would so like to hear your opinion of them. I'd also like to hear how you came to be in England, and to meet Michael. Ah, there is my husband now! Come, let us greet him."

Kate and Michael followed in her wake as she hurried through the crowd. "Did you know her in Venice?" Michael whispered in Kate's ear.

Kate shook her head. "She knew my mother. She once painted her portrait."

"Then Elizabeth obviously thought you were your mother."

"Yes. Quite." And Michael drew Kate protectively close to his side.

Christina glanced around the crowded refreshment area, clutching a glass of warm lemonade as her gaze searched the faces around her. The people were a blur of bright silks and muslins, flashing jewels, bobbing feathers, stark white cravats, and fanciful waistcoats. There were handsome men and plain men, short, tall, stout, muscular. Even one or two who gave *her* admiring glances.

But there were no black-haired gentlemen, or claret-colored coats. The man from the box had vanished.

She finally retreated behind a potted palm, to sip at her lemonade and ponder this odd new sense of— disappointment.

Chapter Twenty-two

*W*hat *a remarkably fine evening*, Kate thought, with a ridiculous smile, as she stood at her chamber window and watched the street below transform in the twilight. The violet blue light suited the city scene, making the neat, pale houses seem aquatic and mysterious. The great exodus of the houses' occupants to their nightly amusements had not yet begun, though carriages were beginning to draw up to front doors. They waited patiently to convey well-dressed ladies and gentlemen to the theater, to ballrooms, to card parties, even to a secret assignation or two. The street was quiet, but seemed to hum with a barely hushed anticipation.

Just as Kate did herself. She had not yet changed out of her muslin day dress into the blue silk, and had just let her hair down to re-dress it into something a bit more elaborate for the Hollingsworths' salon. As she brushed out the long waves, she hummed a soft Italian tune.

Her ebullient mood was really quite unexplainable. At the theater, when they first encountered Elizabeth Hollingsworth and Kate was paralyzed by fear, she would have said she would *not* feel this way in London. Not with a dark cloud of discovery and humiliation looming overhead. Surely she should be on a knife-edge of anxiety! Yet the last couple of days had dispelled much of that fear. For whatever reason, Elizabeth Hollingsworth allowed Kate to keep her secrets, and Kate was very grateful to her for that.

They had been marvelous days indeed. Yesterday, while Christina went to a lecture at the Royal Botanic Society with Michael, Kate and Amelia strolled in Hyde Park. They walked by the Serpentine, watching boys sail their tiny boats on the water and observing artists capturing the sunny scene in watercolors and oils. They ate warm gingerbread bought from a peddler's cart, and Kate even persuaded an uncertain Amelia to try playing with a hoop—which promptly crashed into a tree, narrowly missing an elderly gentleman, two children, and four pug dogs. Kate still glowed with a warm pride when she recalled how a lady had complimented her on her "exquisite child, obviously so well-bred."

For one glorious moment, she could pretend that she was Amelia's mother, that she would be taking her to the park for years to come, would watch her grow into the beautiful young lady she promised to be. Kate had fantasies of beaming proudly as Amelia danced the opening minuet at her come-out ball, partnered by her equally proud father.

And today had been even finer! She took Amelia and Christina to the British Museum, where they observed the Elgin Marbles in all their glory, and shivered with Gothic delight at the Egyptian mummies. Afterward, Michael met them at Gunter's for tea and ices. While Christina regaled them with the details of the lecture she had attended, Kate surreptitiously observed the people around them. She fancied they watched her with envy, and again she was taken with the fantasy that this was *her* family, her handsome husband and lovely daughters. They were hers, and she was safe forever.

Kate laughed now at her silly daydreams; they were so contrary to what was real and true. But still her fear was gone. She felt only contentment and a new excitement at the prospect of the coming evening. It had been a very long time since she had attended a real party. Not including the ill-fated yachting outing, almost two years. She and her friend Bianca Maroni, the daughter of a friend of her mother's, had crept out to attend a masked ball during carnival. It had not ended well—Kate insisted on going home when she glimpsed Julian Kirkwood in the crowd. Yet she loved the music and the colors, the laughter, the sheer *life* of it all. She did not expect an intimate salon to be like a raucous masked ball, but there would be people there, conversation, art.

There was still a tiny twinge at the back of her thoughts, a fear of being discovered. Elizabeth Hollingsworth could very well recall that Lucrezia Bruni had a daughter, could quiz her more closely about her origins and realize the truth. Elizabeth had said nothing else at the theater, had simply chatted lightly about her children and Italy. Kate thought perhaps the glances from those sharp artist's eyes were too searching, but that was all. She did not betray Kate.

Kate felt she had passed some sort of test, some rite of passage, and she was safe. For now. Until she discovered what Elizabeth Hollingsworth was about.

Tonight, she would simply stay as far from the Hollingsworths as possible, would avoid any hint of personal conversation. She would talk of art with the other guests, and then perhaps find a quiet corner where she could observe and enjoy.

If only she had something besides her dull blue silk to wear! Something more like Elizabeth's gold-and-cream creation. Something that would make Michael's eyes darken with desire when he saw her.

There was a knock at the door, leaving Kate no more time for fruitless clothes envy. She pushed her hair back over her shoulder and called, "Come in!"

It was Christina, already dressed for the evening in a new muslin gown, of white flowers embroidered on white muslin. The white could have been insipid on her, Kate thought, but it actually looked quite striking next to Christina's sun-golden skin and green eyes. Her hair was tamed into smooth ringlets, brushed back and confined in a white ribbon and pearl bandeau. She held a long, pale pink box in her arms.

Kate gave her a smile. "You look very pretty, Christina."

"And *you* aren't dressed yet, Mrs. Brown!" Christina answered pertly, putting the box down across the foot of the bed.

"I was just about to see to my toilette," Kate said, and gestured with her hairbrush toward the dark blue silk gown hanging on the wardrobe door. She eyed the pink box, contemplating whether it contained some strange plant sample Christina was "experimenting" with. "I was just caught up in the view. Even London is beautiful at this time of day. The twilight transforms everything."

Christina joined her at the window, gazing down at the street scene. It was busier now than it had been even moments before, with more carriages arriving at front doors, more lights appearing in windows. In only seconds it would be full dark, and the night would begin in earnest, full of merriment and heartache for the people preparing to leave their homes for all manner of amusements and assignations.

What could the night hold for *her*? Her earlier glow of optimism still remained, a tiny glow at the bottom of her heart, along with a flutter of anticipation and uncertainty.

"It *does* have its interests," Christina agreed. "Yet I prefer trees and fields to stone and pavement. Nature, though certainly changeable, can be studied and understood. People never can."

Kate gave the girl a puzzled glance. "Has something happened, Christina?"

"Happened?"

"Here in London. You sound rather—sad."

Christina laughed. "Oh, no, Mrs. Brown! I am just a bit homesick, perhaps, but not *sad*. How could I be, when Mother has another headache tonight and thus *you* will be my only chaperone? And you will not be melancholy, either, when you see what I have for you. A surprise!"

"A surprise?" Kate asked, pleased, rather like a

child on Christmas morning. She liked surprises—
some surprises, anyway.

"Yes, in that box over there." Christina took Kate
by the hand and tugged her toward the bed. "Now
close your eyes. And no peeking!"

Kate obeyed, squeezing her eyes shut. She listened
to the rattle of cardboard, the rustle of tissue. A faint
hint of roses drifted into the air around her.

"All right, you can look now!" Christina said, an
unmistakable note of glee in her voice.

Kate's eyes flew open—and she gasped in astonishment and disbelief. There, spread out across her bed,
was the most exquisite gown she had ever seen. It was
fashioned of the most lustrous dark rose satin, with
short sleeves puffed and slashed to reveal pearl-
embroidered white silk. More pearls edged the low
vee of the neckline and encrusted the hem, scattered
among tiny, twinkling pink crystals. In the box could
be glimpsed a matching reticule and slippers.

It was a fantasy gown, attire fit for a duchess to
wear to Court. It was perfect in every detail.

Kate pressed her hand to her mouth, unable to utter
even a word. Surely she was imagining that gown. It
could not be meant for her—she was all gray and dark
blue now. This pink was the color of sunsets and rain-
bows and dreams.

Christina nervously fingered the satin of the gown's
sleeve. "Do you not like it, Mrs. Brown? Is it the
color? The trim?"

"I—did you *buy* this gown, Christina?" Kate managed to whisper. She reached out to touch the fabric
herself, and found it light as a cloud, clinging to the
tips of her fingers. "It is beautiful beyond all
imagining."

Christina grinned in delight. "Oh, I *knew* you would
like it! Though I did not buy it myself, of course. My
pin money would never pay for such things! It was
Michael's idea. I just helped a bit. I took your blue
gown, and we showed it to the modiste so she could

take your measurements from it. He had to be ever so persuasive to get her to finish it so quickly."

Kate's hand stilled against the gown. "Your brother?"

"Yes. He wanted to—oh!" Christina broke off, her cheeks turning raspberry red under her tan. "It was improper, wasn't it? *A Lady's Rules for Proper Behavior* says an unmarried lady can only accept small gifts from a gentleman, like books or flowers. But I'm sure my brother meant nothing improper, Mrs. Brown. You just seemed rather sad not to have a new gown for the salon. No one will know he bought it, I'm sure."

Of course it was Michael who had chosen the gown. The gown was so perfect in every respect, the perfect color, the perfect fabric. Stylish and attractive, but not too low-cut or clinging. Something a *ton* lady would wear, not a high-priced courtesan. Something that was exactly her taste.

Her earlier hopes of a future life came flooding back, greater and brighter than ever. For some reason, she longed to cry, to bury her head in the fine fabric and sob for happiness. But tears would spot the satin, and that would never do. She wanted to look her loveliest tonight, for Michael. For her love.

"Mrs. Brown?" Christina asked worriedly. "Is it really so dreadful? I'm sure it could be sent back, if needed."

Kate laughed, and dropped the gown to catch Christina in a great hug. "Oh, Christina! It is beautiful. I adore it."

Christina laughed, too, in relief and obvious puzzlement. "Oh, I am glad! I helped pick the color, you see, and I even looked through some fashion plates to find a style you might like."

"Such a sacrifice! And the gown is perfect. Here, *cara*, help me dress. We haven't much time, have we?"

Christina reached up to unfasten the tapes of Kate's day dress, brushing Kate's fall of hair out of the way. It had become tangled and would have to be brushed again. "I fear I have no jewels, Mrs. Brown. Just my pearls, and I'm wearing those. But I did bring some pink roses. We can put them in your hair."

"Roses? Wherever did you get those at this time of year?" Kate glanced back over her shoulder at Christina, who gave an abashed laugh.

"Oh, I saw them in a garden somewhere."

"A garden?"

"All right, in the neighbors' hothouse when they weren't home! But they had ever so many—I'm sure they won't miss a few in a good cause."

"Oh, Christina." Kate smiled at her and gently pinched her cheek. "You are absolutely incorrigible. I can see my lessons have had no effect at all."

Christina grinned. "Perhaps not all of them. But we have plenty of time together for you to turn me into a perfect lady. Don't we, Mrs. Brown?"

"Oh, yes, my dear. Plenty of time."

Kate and Elizabeth Hollingsworth had quite different ideas of what an "intimate gathering" meant, Kate thought as the Lindleys' carriage drew up outside the Hollingsworths' townhouse. Kate considered it to be five or six friends for supper and cards. Elizabeth Hollingsworth considered it to be half of London.

Carriages were lined up along the street, waiting to deposit their passengers on the doorstep. Every one of the windows—and they were not inconsiderable in number—was ablaze with golden light. Laughter and music positively emanated from the walls.

An old, half-forgotten thrill hummed in Kate's veins, and she remembered all those evenings she had huddled on the stairs of her mother's house, secretly observing the parties below. She had wanted to dance, to laugh and flirt, to drink champagne and sample the delicacies of the buffet table. But then she had been always observing; now she wanted to dance.

But only with the man who sat across from her now. Michael was dressed in the finest of fashionable

Town clothes, a well-cut dark green velvet coat with buff breeches and a cream-colored waistcoat, his immaculate cravat tied in complicated swirls and anchored with an emerald-headed stickpin. His burnished hair was brushed back neatly, trimmed off his collar. Yet he wore the garments as casually and carelessly as if still clad in the clothes he used to walk the fields in Yorkshire. He teased and laughed with his sister as they waited to disembark, smiling and at ease.

Kate smiled at them, feeling at ease herself. She would have imagined she would be terribly nervous going into London Society for the first time, meeting new people in the guise of her still strange role. But Michael's presence erased all those qualms, every fear. She wanted him to be proud of her tonight, to think her poised and charming and lovely, worthy of all he had given her. Both the gifts he knew of, such as this new gown, and those that were secret in Kate's own heart. Michael and all his family had gifted her with the sure knowledge that there was true goodness and love in the world. She was never sure of that before—the world she grew up in was rank with selfishness and deceit. But no more.

Tonight was a new beginning—she felt that very certainly.

And it had a fine start when she came down the stairs in her rose-colored gown and saw Michael's face as he watched her. His blue eyes were dark gray with desire, his lips parted as if he would kiss her passionately right then and there, lifting her off her rose-slippered feet with his ardor. So he *did* think her beautiful. It was gratifying indeed, and had to be enough for the moment, for they had no time for private conversation.

They arrived at the Hollingsworths' door at last, and Christina took the footman's gloved hand to step down from the carriage. Before she had to follow, Kate reached out to touch her fingertips to Michael's velvet sleeve. The fabric was rich and rough against the buttery soft kid of her glove, and she could feel his heat even through the cloth.

"Thank you for my gown, Michael," she whispered. "It is exquisite."

Michael stared deeply into her eyes, as if he could see all the secrets of her heart and soul written there. He leaned forward and kissed her, hard, fleetingly, his breath and lips branding hers. Kate's hand just brushed his jaw when he drew back, grinning down at her in the darkness. "Not half as exquisite as you are, Kate. I wish I had diamonds and rubies to put in your hair and around your throat."

Kate thought of her mother's sapphire brooch, hidden deep in her valise, its blue fire muffled and tarnished. Its rich glory was nothing to this moment. She should throw it in the Semerwater, she thought, discarding the last vestige of the past. "I don't need jewels, my angel. I only need you." As her love—her husband.

He smiled at her, that white pirate's grin that never failed to make her melt. "That *is* good news. It will save me a fortune on Bond Street."

Then he was gone from her, leaping down from the carriage without a hint of a limp. But they were not apart for long, for he reached back to help her alight, waving aside the footman.

At the doorway, he offered an arm each to Kate and Christina, escorting them up the stairs to the waiting gathering. "Oh, Michael," Christina whispered, glancing around with eyes so wide she looked almost as young as Amelia. "Isn't it lovely? Just look at those *Oncidium flexuosum*. They must be a new hybrid, to have petals just that shape. I have never seen such an example before."

It *was* lovely, Kate thought, and not just the flowers, though they *were* unusual, great, tall stems of purple-and-cream blossoms massed in large Chinese vases. They filled the air with a rich, exotic scent, enticing the gathering into an equally exotic room, arranged almost like a stage set. The walls of the drawing room were papered in pale cream silk, a neutral backdrop for the furniture and the plethora of paintings. The delicate gilt settees, chairs, and hassocks were upholstered in myriad shades of purple, from almost black to palest lilac. The windows were draped in lilac-and-cream striped brocade, which fluttered in the evening breeze, for all the casements were opened to the night, revealing a long terrace outside. A string quartet played Mozart in the corner, and purple-liveried footmen bore trays of champagne.

It did not seem as crowded as all the carriages would have indicated, for the room was long, wide, and airy. Many people strolled on the terrace or meandered through the open doors of the dining room, where a lavish buffet could be glimpsed. Kate was very glad of her new gown, for the other guests were elegantly clad indeed. She recognized a few famous personages from their sketches in the newspapers—poets, duchesses, artists, members of Parliament, and a well-known Italian opera singer.

Even Christina was awed into silence, gazing around at the people, the furniture, the art.

By far the most fascinating aspect of the gathering was that art. The paintings hung in rows and stacks on the walls, the cream silk a perfect backdrop for their vibrant colors. They were propped on easels in the corners and next to the vast marble fireplace. One large easel was draped in purple silk, obviously meant to be unveiled later. Kate feared she was gawking at them, craning her neck like a country bumpkin, yet she could not help herself. They were beyond beautiful.

Christina drifted away to talk to a group of young people, no doubt to quiz them about their knowledge or lack thereof of plants. Michael, perhaps sensing Kate's fascination with the art, fetched them glasses of champagne and strolled with her along the walls. A few people stopped to speak to them, to comment on how very long it had been since they had seen

Michael, and to be introduced to Kate. They greeted Michael's sister-in-law, young Lady Darcy, who soon vanished back into the dining room with her own cronies. Yet obviously the evening had not yet begun in earnest, for everyone was very casual and friendly, viewing the art and drinking champagne just as Kate and Michael were.

"Are these all by Lady Hollingsworth?" Kate murmured, as she sipped at her champagne and examined a portrait of two bright-eyed, dark-haired little girls. They sat beneath a green-leafed tree, gamboling with some spaniel puppies, their mischief and spirit shining from them. These were obviously the Hollingsworth twins, and Kate pitied any governess who came into contact with the beautiful imps.

"I believe so," Michael answered. "Though I think that classical scene of Athena over there is by her friend, the Duchess of Wayland. And I see a work by Angelica Kauffman, as well."

Kate nodded, moving to the next work. Another portrait, of a man on horseback near the same tree the twins played beneath. Kate recognized the man she had met at the theater, Sir Nicholas Hollingsworth. There were more portraits of the twins; of a redheaded woman in emerald silk; of a couple unearthly in their beauty, a golden man and a dark woman in a Spanish lace mantilla.

Kate turned a corner onto another wall, and faced a row of Italian scenes. The Tuscan countryside in summer, pulsating with color and heat. A vineyard beneath the sun, so real Kate could taste the sweet muskiness of the grapes. A villa, chalk white with a dark red tiled roof, a woman leaning from the window to shake a rug in the breeze. And—Venice.

Kate stood completely still before one work, unable to move or breathe. For one instant, she was no longer in this fine London drawing room, surrounded by the murmur of laughter and the soft strains of music. She was by a Venetian canal, half in shade, the sweet-sick smell of the water in her nostrils. She was staring across at her mother's house, pastel pink against the hot blue sky, dark red geraniums in pots lining the balconies. A face—a girl—could just be glimpsed beyond the half-open doors of one of those balconies, peeking out at the life below.

Who was that face? Was it the girl Katerina, whom Kate left behind? Was it her mother, waiting to see Edward's gondola arrive at her dock? Kate was mesmerized by this tiny glimpse of her old home, of the place where she had once belonged. It was strange, like a house remembered in a dream, and yet so very familiar. She reached out her hand, as if she could feel, not the paint, but the roughness of the stucco. . . .

"Michael, Mrs. Brown! I am so very glad to see you here," a woman's light voice called, drawing Kate back down into the drawing room. She jerked her hand away from the canvas, and turned to find Elizabeth Hollingsworth standing there.

Elizabeth's smile was open and welcoming, as bright as the diamond combs in her sleek dark hair. She let Michael kiss her hand, and smiled at Kate, but her eyes were watchful.

"Your work is amazing, Lady Hollingsworth," Kate said. "So very true to life."

"Thank you, Mrs. Brown," Elizabeth replied. "I see you are admiring one of my Venetian scenes. Is it like the city, do you think?"

Kate glanced back at the painting. *Too much like.* "I lived along a similar canal once. I would think myself back there again."

"It is the view from the window of a house I rented one year. My own abode was quite humble compared to that grand palazzo, of course!" Elizabeth stepped closer to the canvas, watching it rather than Kate. Her voice was dreamy, as if she, too, was in some lost world. "There was this young girl who lived there. Sometimes I saw her peeking out of the windows, and I imagined her as some sort of Juliet. Sheltered, cosseted, eager to be set free into life."

Kate reached out unconsciously for Michael, swaying with the force of the sadness. He took her hand in his, sliding it into the crook of his elbow, holding her upright with his strength.

"What became of your Juliet, Lizzie?" he asked softly.

Elizabeth turned away from the painting and stared directly into Kate's eyes. "I fear she died. In a boating accident. It was a great tragedy."

"That is sad indeed," Michael said.

"Yes. Too sad for a soiree," Elizabeth answered, a new smile curving the edges of her Madonna mouth. Kate received her message, though; Elizabeth would *not* betray her, even if she suspected her husband's old friend was being deceived. The force of that last summer, when they watched each other across the canal, still bound them. "Come, now, your glasses are empty. And you have not sampled any of the food. I have eggplant tarts, so Italian, and lobster patties, white soup. . . ."

Elizabeth took Michael's other arm and led them off across the room. She procured fresh glasses of champagne, and introduced them to some of the other guests. They were a vivacious, eclectic lot, and Kate soon found herself deep in conversation about poetry and the theater. It was truly turning into a lovely evening. She could become used to society of this sort, people who cared about art and books. And fine champagne! Kate helped herself to another glass from a passing footman's tray, watching with a contented smile as Elizabeth Hollingsworth ushered Christina around, introducing her just as she had Kate. Michael stood with another small group near her, and she could hear snatches of his conversation on Yorkshire farming techniques.

She half turned away from him to answer a question someone posed about Byron's *Don Juan,* and from the corner of her eye she saw the drawing room door opening to admit new arrivals. The lady who appeared there, a tall woman with rich auburn hair dressed with a feathered bandeau, had such a stunning peacock blue gown that Kate had to look up and examine it more closely. The peacock lady smiled at their host, snapping open her blue-and-green-feathered fan as she stepped aside to reveal her escort.

He was a tall, slender man with glossy black hair, godlike in his beauty and in the melancholy of his mien. His dark gaze swept slowly over the assembly, as if he could not quite bear to be among such mortals. To be among the living at all.

As indeed he should not be. He was dead. Drowned. *Julian Kirkwood.*

A high-pitched buzzing rang in Kate's ears, and she felt numb, a cold creeping over her like a glacier. Like an ocean wave. Her skin tingled, and the edges of her vision grew suddenly hazy. Her glass slipped from her nerveless fingers and rolled across the carpet beneath her feet. Ladies shrieked and jerked their silken skirt hems away from the splash of the golden liquid, but Kate did not notice. As if from far away, from another planet, she heard Michael call, "Kate? What is wrong? Are you ill?"

She swayed, the cold overwhelming. She couldn't fight it off, couldn't escape it—she would never be warm again. She would die of it.

Even as Michael's arms came around her waist, she heard another voice. A voice from beyond death, wrapping its velvet grip about her soul, dragging her under.

"Katerina! Katerina. You are *alive!* Oh, my Beatrice, my love, you are alive!"

As Kate sank to the floor, the last thing she saw above her was Julian's eyes, wide with wonder and perfect, perfect joy.

Then she felt nothing at all. Only the abyss.

Michael caught Kate up in his arms as she fainted, her rose-pink skirts spilling over his hands, an elegant mockery of the happiness that had been his only an instant before. Happiness that had been *theirs* as he watched Kate smile at him over her champagne glass and he knew that they would be together. There was nothing that could keep them apart.

Now she lay limp in his arms, her face pale. As white as funeral lilies. Her breathing was shallow, her skin cold. He stared down at her, stunned, afraid—afraid with a fear he had not felt since the day Caroline died in his arms. He was vaguely aware of Christina's panicked cries, of Elizabeth calling for a settee and some water, of Nick ushering the other guests away. There was a babble of confused questions, shocked comments.

One voice rose above them all, a man's tenor tones laced with happiness and amazement. "Katerina! You are alive . . . my love."

Katerina. *No,* he wanted to shout. *She is Kate. Bonny Kate, Kate the curst. The prettiest Kate in Christendom . . .*

He glanced up sharply to see a man leaning toward Kate. He was tall, Michael noted absently, and handsome. No scars, no limp, no sun-roughened complexion. He was a man any woman would fall in love with—and he was reaching for Kate.

The man did not even seem to notice Michael holding her. He reached out with his long, elegant hands, cupping Kate's face as if it were the most delicate of rose petals. He traced her nose, her lips, her eyelids, which trembled beneath his fingertips. "Katerina, my love."

Michael had never felt such hatred, such anger, in all his life. Kate was ill, and this man, whoever he was, behaved as if he had discovered a long-lost Botticelli. His face, his entire body, radiated love and joy. Love for Kate. *Michael's* Kate, whom he had vowed to always protect.

Clutching her close to him, Michael stepped back from the man. "Unhand her."

The man's hands fell to his side and he straightened. Rage suffused his face, turning his pale cheeks a hectic red, and the hands that had caressed Kate's face so gently curled into talons. "How dare you? I am Sir Julian Kirkwood, and this woman is mine."

His, was she? Well, Michael had a few things to say about that—and a few blows to land about this man's perfect face. But right now there were far more important matters to attend to. Matters of life and death.

"I don't care if you are the king of Sweden, you damned knave," Michael ground out. "Kate is ill, and I am taking her to a doctor. I swear by all that's holy, if you touch her again—"

"Michael," Elizabeth Hollingsworth's voice interrupted. "Come with me now. We'll put Mrs. Brown in my own chamber, and Nick will send for the doctor immediately."

Michael gave her a brusque nod and, without even another glance at the man, followed her out of the drawing room and up the stairs.

Kate stirred against his shoulder, but did not open her eyes. Michael held her close, so close he could feel the soft, butterfly flutterings of her breath.

"Everything will be well, Kate," he whispered. "I am with you. I will *always* be with you, I promise."

Christina stared in utter astonishment at the scene before her. She had expected London to be different, of course—but not *this* different.

The salon had been going along well enough, not so grand as the Royal Botanic Society lecture or the British Museum, but tolerable. The people she met were nice enough, even though they had never even read the *Ars Botanica;* the paintings were interesting, and the food was very fine indeed. She had finally escaped Lady Hollingsworth and found a quiet corner where she could enjoy some of those refreshments in peace. Then, just as she took a bite of a scrumptious lobster patty, the drawing room door opened and *he* appeared.

The gentleman from the theater, right here in front of her! And even more handsome in the brighter lights of the party than he had been in the dimness of the theater. He was tall, slim, dark, and with a tragically sad air worthy of a prince in one of Mrs. Brown's volumes of poetry.

Christina almost choked on her bite of lobster and quickly raised her napkin to her mouth, studying the prince-poet over the white damask folds. That was when everything went to perdition.

"Katerina!" the man cried. His voice, his tone, was unlike anything Christina had ever heard before. So full of anguish and joy, it was like a soaring opera aria. "You are alive!" And then, strangely, he called for someone named Beatrice.

But he rushed toward Mrs. Brown—*Mrs. Brown!*—his arms outstretched, his beautiful face suffused with light.

As Christina watched, frozen, Mrs. Brown turned as white as Christina's napkin. Even her lips were pale, as if all the blood left her and she remained only a hollow stalk. She dropped her champagne glass and collapsed in a heap of rose satin, caught up in Michael's arms.

Michael glared at the beautiful man as if he would kill him then and there, yet the man took no notice whatsoever. All of his attention, dark and intense, was on Mrs. Brown. Mrs. Brown, Katerina.

It was all so very unreal, like watching a scene of high tragedy in the theater. Christina would never have thought such drama could happen in real life, especially not in a London drawing room! Not among a *ton* crowd, where a careful facade was always maintained. Scandals could take place in boudoirs and on dueling fields, and they could be whispered about behind fans and teacups, but they were never *publicly* enacted. Unless one was Caro Lamb, or one of her ilk. Even Christina, buried in the country, knew that.

But here was a scene of high scandal, involving her own Mrs. Brown and a strange man.

Christina gave a panicked cry and dropped her plate and napkin, lurching forward. At last her frozen legs let her move, but it was too late. Michael swept out of the room with Mrs. Brown in his arms, followed by the Hollingsworths. The strange man stood alone in the center of the floor, staring after them as if he saw all promise of heaven slipping beyond his grasp. A tall, auburn-haired lady tugged at his arm, but he seemed not to see her.

All around them, at the edges of the room, a shocked silence hung in the perfumed air, a thick, palpable, living thing. Slowly, whispers and murmurs broke out in slow ripples—ripples that quickly became a gushing tide.

". . . is Sir Julian Kirkwood, you know. Bad business. Everyone thought he died in Italy. . . ."

"But who is that woman? She came here with Michael Lindley. . . ."

". . . obviously something between her and Sir Julian. Did you see the way he touched her, spoke to her? One would have thought Mr. Lindley would have more sense after what happened with his poor wife."

Furious, Christina whirled toward that last voice, her hands curling into fists. How *dare* they speak about her brother and Mrs. Brown in such a manner? She was stopped from doing battle only by the thickness of the crowd. She had no idea who had spoken, and the whispers were blending and growing. A few feet away stood her sister-in-law, Mary. Mary was almost as pale as Mrs. Brown had been, except for two spots of bright red high on her cheekbones. Her fingers tightened on her fan, almost snapping the delicate ivory sticks.

"Mary," Christina said, taking a step toward her. She feared Mary might faint, too, and that would not be good for the baby.

Mary looked up at Christina, eyes blazing like twin bonfires. "How dare your brother?" she growled. "How dare he bring a woman of low morals into this family! I have had quite enough of that sort of thing. I won't stand for it anymore!"

"Mary!" Christina cried, shocked. "Mrs. Brown is *not* a woman of low morals. She is—is an *angel!*"

Mary was obviously not listening. She turned away from Christina and disappeared into the crowd.

Christina pushed her way past a knot of people, intent on getting out of that room and finding Michael and Mrs. Brown. She hated London, and these cackling harpies! Only moments before, this was a civilized gathering, and now it resembled nothing so much as a lower circle of Dante's hell in the poem Mrs. Brown made her read. *Beatrice, indeed.* She wanted Thorn Hill, and her studies and plants, and her friend Andrew Price to discuss those studies with her.

She wanted to see Mrs. Brown, to be sure she was well. Christina wanted to weep.

"Get out of my way!" she shouted to three particularly annoying people blocking the doorway. She shoved past them, and crashed into another man. A tall, dark man in a black velvet coat.

The man from the opera—the cause of all this trouble.

"You!" she gasped.

He took her arm in his clasp to steady her but did not even glance down at her. He still watched the door, as if his joy would suddenly reappear there.

Christina shook off his hand. She was so angry she shook with the fury of it. Whether it was from his disregard for the scandal he caused, or his disregard for Christina herself, she could not say, and this made her even more furious. She reached up with her gloved hand and grasped his jaw hard, forcing him to look down at her. He had dark eyes, eyes like a Yorkshire midnight, or the black depths of the Semerwater.

"She is not *your* Katerina," Christina said fiercely. "Not anymore. You should just go away. Whoever you are. Go away, and leave us alone."

His eyes widened slightly, as if he awakened from some long dream. He did not draw away from her.

"And who might you be, little Valkyrie, to tell *me* what to do?" he said softly.

Christina stared at him mutinously. She felt so strange—tingling and light-headed, almost like the time she stole a bottle of cooking brandy from the kitchen and drank some of it behind the stable because she was angry at her mother. She didn't like this feeling, this not-in-control sensation, at all. She dropped her hand and stepped away from him.

"Just call me Brunhilde," she murmured. A tiny ghost of a smile touched the edge of his lips. Then, just as that tingling sensation started again, she felt a hand close over her arm and she was jerked back. The crowd quickly closed around him, and he was lost to her sight.

It was Mary who held Christina by the arm, Mary who dragged her toward the door. For such a slender woman, Mary was uncommonly strong, and Christina couldn't stop her forward momentum. Not even when she tried to dig her slipper heels into the carpet.

"Mary!" she cried. "Let go! Whatever are you doing?"

"I am taking you with me to Lindley House," Mary answered sternly. "The carriage is waiting."

"I don't *want* to go to Lindley House! I have to find Mrs. Brown. . . ."

Mary wheeled around and caught Christina's other arm with her free hand. She shook Christina until her teeth rattled. "You will not see that harlot again! A young girl does not belong in that den of vice your brother has created. It's too late for me, but *you* can escape!" She whirled back around, dragging Christina behind her out the front door and into the waiting carriage. Christina was so stunned by Mary's outburst she couldn't bring herself to break away. "I've had enough of the men in this family, do you hear me? *Enough.*"

Christina could only huddle miserably in the corner of the carriage, watching as the Hollingsworths' house,

Michael and Mrs. Brown, and the dark man receded away from her.

She was *alive*!

Julian paced the length of the Hollingsworths' library, unable to sit or stand still for even a moment. His Katerina was alive, and he had never felt so alive himself as he did at that instant. He had felt numb, cold, ever since he awoke in that damnable convent hospital. Not even coming back to England, to his sister and the lost threads of his life, could warm him. Only the sight of Katerina, laughing and smiling, so vibrantly beautiful, made *him* feel alive, too. Warmth and joy flooded through his very veins.

It was a miracle, unheard of outside the pages of novels. Now all of his lost dreams could be resurrected once again. He had his love, his life, back.

If only these blasted people would let him go to her!

Julian spun around to fix an icy glare on Nicholas Hollingsworth. The man had placed his chair right before the library door, so Julian would have to literally toss him aside to get out. Two years ago, Julian would not have hesitated to give him the thrashing he deserved. But now, weakened by his long illness and faced with Hollingsworth's sun-browned good health, he knew he could not. A futile fight would only lengthen the time he was apart from his Beatrice.

Nicholas Hollingsworth just grinned, and lit up one of his foul cigars.

"You have no right to keep me in here," Julian growled. "I must go to her! We have been apart too long as it is."

"Keep you here?" Nicholas answered affably. "Nonsense, Sir Julian. I am merely trying to be a good host. The crush out there has become unbearable, wouldn't you say? Why, ladies were even fainting! Care for a cigar? Or perhaps a brandy?"

Julian's temper raged out of control at the man's light indifference. Nicholas Hollingsworth had no understanding of real love, of what Julian had found! He lunged toward the door, only to be brought up short when Nicholas swooped from his chair to catch him in an iron grip. He pushed Julian back onto a settee and leaned against the door, arms crossed.

"You don't understand, Hollingsworth," Julian said, his thoughts burning with a frantic need. "I love that lady. I've thought she was dead this year and more. We deserve to be together now."

Nicholas shook his head. "Oh, believe me, Sir Julian, I understand about love. And I'm sorry for your grief. But I would say that the lady was not quite so overjoyed at your reunion. In fact, I would say that the expression that crossed her face right before she fainted could best be described as horror."

Horror? Certainly not. His princess was as happy to find him again as he was to find her. Or she would be—once this barbarian allowed him to see her. "She was overcome by the shock. She, too, believed me dead."

Nicholas shrugged. "I daresay. But the doctor is with her now, and my wife left instructions Mrs. Brown was not to be disturbed. By anyone. You would not want to disobey, Sir Julian—you would find I am a tame kitten compared to my leopard of a wife."

Julian subsided back onto the settee, surveying Hollingsworth with narrowed eyes. *Mrs. Brown,* was it? For the first time since he had seen her that night, some of his joy gave way to new questions. Where had his Beatrice been all this time? How had she lived? How had she come to be in London?

"Tell me, Hollingsworth," he said softly. "Who was that man with—Mrs. Brown? The one who looked like a country squire."

Nicholas lit another of his cigars, sending the noxious blue smoke out into the room. "That is my friend Mr. Michael Lindley, younger brother of the Earl of Darcy. The young lady you were speaking to is his sister, Lady Christina Lindley. I have only met Mrs.

Brown—or whatever her name might be—a few days ago. She is governess to Lady Christina, and, I understand, is Mr. Lindley's prospective bride."

Bride? Julian's hands clenched into fists against the brocade of the settee. Well—that was all before tonight. Now everything was changed. For all of them.

A sharp, frantic knock sounded at the door. "Julian?" his sister Charlotte's voice called. "Julian, are you in there?"

Nicholas gave Julian a questioning glance. "That is my sister," Julian said irately. Really, the man was too much—like a bullyboy at Eton who had never grown out of it. "Lady Stoke. If you would be so kind as to let her in."

Nicholas stepped aside and opened the door. Charlotte practically fell into the room, in a flurry of blue and green silk and feathers. Her cheeks were flushed almost to the color of her auburn hair. She swept right past Nicholas and alighted on the settee next to Julian.

"Oh, my dear," she said breathlessly. "Such an *on-dit*! Talk is positively *racing* about the drawing room. By the morning, everyone in Town will know of it. Who is that woman with Mr. Lindley? Why did she faint when she saw you? Who would have thought *my* brother could be so Byronesque? Tell me everything, Julian, right now. Is she the reason you have been so blue-deviled since you came here?"

Julian glanced over her plumed headdress at Nicholas Hollingsworth. Hollingsworth, damn his eyes, gave them an ironic little bow and backed out of the room, shutting the door behind him.

But this was not over. Not nearly.

Chapter Twenty-three

*M*ichael stared at the closed bedroom door in front of him, as if by simply *willing* it to open, it would immediately vanish and he would be where he belonged—at Kate's side.

Yet it remained firmly shut. When the doctor arrived, Michael had a swift glimpse of Kate in the elaborately draped bed, pale and small against the silk counterpane. Then she disappeared, and he was alone in the darkened corridor where Elizabeth had pushed him, saying that the doctor needed room to work and Kate needed quiet.

Quiet—he scarcely remembered the meaning of the word. Not since Kate burst into his ordered life like a comet trailing sparks of vivid color. All culminating in the grand explosion tonight, an eruption of drama, Kate sinking into his arms—a strange man reaching out for her.

What claim could that gloque have on Kate? Who was he?

Michael groaned and leaned his head back against the silk-papered wall. There was only one person the man *could* be—the one Kate had spoken of, the man who had tried once to buy her. But Michael knew now that the man's feelings went beyond those of a rake for his plaything possession. Love and joy were written clear on his face as he stared at Kate.

Michael understood perfectly what it felt like to love Kate—and what hell it would be to lose her. But he remembered the way she shivered when she spoke of her erstwhile suitor, the old fear lurking in her eyes. Michael would kill the man if he came near Kate again.

There was the soft hum, the kinetic rise and fall, of voices coming from below as the company made its slow way out of the Hollingsworth house and into the night, seeking other amusements. Other venues in which to spread the tale of the scandalous sights they had seen this night. Gossip would be rife, of course, speculation high. The actually rather small incident would become larger and more lurid with every telling. His mother and Mary would be furious, though hopefully it would not keep Mary from taking care of Christina this evening. He had glimpsed them standing together as he carried Kate from the drawing room, and it was one less concern on a night crowded with them.

He did care about the gossip, of course. He had spent years trying to live down the antics of his own youth, to make his name respectable once again. But any tittle-tattle, any scandal, was not a spot against Kate's being harmed.

Damn that man, whoever he was! He would not hurt Kate—he would not come into their lives. Michael would not allow it.

The bedroom door opened quietly, and he leaped up from his seat as Elizabeth slipped into the corridor. The talk from below had ceased; all the salon goers were gone.

"She will wake soon," Elizabeth said softly. "The doctor says she will be fine. She's just had a shock, and will need rest and quiet."

"May I take her home?" he asked hoarsely. By *home*, he did not know if he meant the Prices' leased town house or Thorn Hill, or someplace very far away indeed. He would take her anywhere she could be at peace.

"Soon, when she has fully awakened. Now I must go back. The doctor will need my assistance. I just wanted to tell you she will be fine, Michael." She paused, peering up at him with her discerning brown eyes. "You must love her a great deal."

"I do. More than I can say."

Elizabeth nodded. "Then all will be well." She gave a little laugh. "What's a bit of scandal next to true love, after all? As Nick and I know well."

She started to turn away, but Michael caught her hand to stay her for just a moment. "Lizzie—who is that man?"

"Sir Julian Kirkwood," she answered. "It was quite the *on-dit* when he reappeared in London. Everyone had thought him drowned in a boating accident in Italy. Such a tragedy. The Duke of Salton died there, you know, along with his mistress and her young daughter. So very sad. But Sir Julian, it seems, was the only survivor."

She gave his hand a small squeeze before making her way back to the bedroom. And Michael was left alone with his own seething heart.

Kate slowly blinked her eyes open, to find herself staring up at the ceiling of an unfamiliar chamber. A painted ceiling arched overhead, a scene of cavorting cupids against a blue sky. It was probably charming in the daylight, but in the light of flickering candles it was sinister. She lay prone on a soft counterpane, her aching head pillowed on feather cushions. Where was she?

A hand, bony but gentle, reached for her trembling wrist, holding it as if to check her pulse. Kate carefully shifted her head on the pillow to see an elderly gentleman sitting next to the bed, his bald dome of a head shining in the candlelight.

He gave her a smile when he saw her watching him. "Ah, so you are awake, young lady? Good, very good. Your pulse is stronger, too. I would say the danger is past. But perhaps I should bleed you just to be sure."

"You are a doctor?" Kate whispered. She felt as though her mouth were full of straw.

"Yes, I am Dr. Fielding. Lady Hollingsworth sent

for me when you fainted." He released her wrist to gesture toward the foot of the bed.

Kate shifted her gaze to see a dark-haired lady sitting there, a shawl tossed over her white-and-silver evening gown. And then Kate remembered *everything*. The salon, which had started out so very promising. The paintings, the music. And the arrival of Sir Julian Kirkwood, whom she had long thought dead. The shock of seeing him was paralyzing, and any vague, fantastic hope that he would not recognize her or remember her was shattered when he called her name.

Katerina.

Kate moaned and sat straight up in bed, her panicked gaze darting into the darkened corners, as if *he* was lurking there. Waiting to grab her and snatch her back into the past.

There was no one. The chamber was silent and deserted except for the doctor and Elizabeth Hollingsworth. And the easel she had glimpsed in the drawing room, the one draped and concealed. It was set up by the fireplace.

"Sh, now," Elizabeth said soothingly. "He's not here, my dear. Rest easy."

"You must lie back down, young lady, until the dizziness is gone," said Dr. Fielding. "You wouldn't want to faint again, would you?"

Kate slowly slid back down against the pillows, closing her eyes. Yes—it was best to stay here for as long as she could. Who knew what Julian was telling the gathered assembly about her, what turmoil awaited her outside this room? She needed to think, to plan, to be prepared. Yet she felt so tired. Exhaustion and shock seemed to weigh her limbs down with lead bars. She opened her eyes and stared again at the cupids. Now they seemed to be laughing at her.

"I will go and send for some tea," the doctor said, gathering his leather bag and standing up. "Some sustenance will do her good. Then we will see about the bleeding."

"Thank you, Dr. Fielding," Elizabeth answered.

When the man was gone, she slid off the foot of the bed and came around to spread a soft cashmere blanket over Kate's legs. "How are you feeling, Mrs. Brown?"

"A bit better, thank you, Lady Hollingsworth," Kate murmured.

"Good. For I fear you are going to need all your strength." Elizabeth took the doctor's abandoned chair, leaning her elbows on the side of the mattress. "You *are* Katerina Bruni, aren't you?"

It was no use denying it now. It was even something of a relief to say it. "Yes. I am."

Elizabeth nodded. "What an extraordinary journey you must have been on! To be so daring as to run away, to make a new life for yourself. It is just like a novel."

A wild, fluttering hope was born in Kate's heart. She turned quickly toward Elizabeth, reaching for her hand. "If Julian is alive, could my mother—"

Elizabeth shook her head sadly. "I fear your mother's body was found, as was the Duke of Salton's. She was buried on Isola di San Michele. It was a grand funeral, Katerina. All the gondolas in Venice came out to see her off."

Kate nodded, and subsided back down into the pillows. "Of course. Where is everyone now? Michael, Christina, and—Julian."

"You needn't fear that he will come bursting in here with his passionate declarations. Nick is keeping an eye on him until he leaves the house. Lady Darcy took Lady Christina away, in rather high dudgeon, I fear. Something about rescuing her from 'the men in this family.' And Michael is waiting outside. He can come in and see you when you're feeling stronger—if you want him to."

Kate nodded in silence. She would have to see Michael soon. She longed to feel his arms around her, hear his brandy-dark voice telling her she had nothing to fear. Yet this was one mess, one scandal, even he could not erase.

Elizabeth leaned closer and said quietly, "Does he know of your old life?"

"Yes, thankfully. I told him on our journey to London." Kate thought of that little voice that had told her to *tell him* in the dark innyard, and she blessed it now. "I couldn't keep the secret any longer from him, not when—well, when he had been so kind to me."

"And when you love him."

Ah. Obviously nothing could be hidden from Elizabeth's observant artist's eye. "Yes. I fear we did not anticipate such a scandal, though. I suppose I naively thought the past was gone, and everything would somehow work out just as I wanted."

Kate closed her eyes. "Yes. A fine new life."

"I am sorry, Katerina. I had no idea about Julian Kirkwood and yourself! Everyone knew that he was on that yacht with you, but not of his feelings for you. Or even that you were alive, of course. He himself only arrived back in Town a few weeks ago, and his sister had some fantastical tale to tell about his recovery in a convent."

"Hm. I'm sure a scandal can't be avoided now. Even at this moment speculation on who you really are and what you are to Julian Kirkwood and Michael Lindley will be running rife through the London streets. Gossip cannot be avoided. But it is not so bad as all that. Michael was a very naughty man indeed in his youth. He and his friends, which included my husband, were absolutely wild. Having a very daring bride cannot do him much harm, I'm sure, despite the fact that he's such a pattern card of respectability now."

"What about his family?" Kate said. "Christina and Amelia, his mother? *They* don't deserve a scandal. Christina will be making her debut soon."

Even Elizabeth did not have an answer for that. Her gaze shifted away, and they sat in silence for a long moment. Finally, Elizabeth stood up and said, "I have a surprise for you. Perhaps it will cheer you up a bit!"

Kate stirred, sitting up against the pillows and giving Elizabeth a small smile. "A surprise for me?"

"Yes. I was going to unveil it at the salon, as the centerpiece of my work, but I think you should have it instead." She went to the veiled painting on the easel, and drew back the cloth with a flourish.

Kate's mother smiled down at her.

It was the portrait that had hung in the palazzo's drawing room in Venice, always smiling down at every gathering and intimate tête-à-tête. None of its beauty was dimmed by time or distance. Lucrezia's eyes still glowed with a violet fire; her smile still whispered of delightful secrets. The blue-and-purple satin draped around her ivory shoulders, the ropes of sapphires and amethysts, shimmered and sang. Kate's mother was alive again, and always would be as long as this painting existed.

"It is—beautiful," Kate whispered inadequately.

"I think it is my finest work," Elizabeth answered. "Perhaps one day I could paint a portrait of you, to be its mate?"

Kate nodded silently. But she knew that maybe that wouldn't be possible. Perhaps she wouldn't have time to sit for a portrait, when she was looking for work or on a ship back to Italy.

"I have this, too," Elizabeth said. She picked up an object from a nearby table and came to deposit it in Kate's lap. "There was a sale of the contents of your mother's house. I bought this along with the portrait."

Kate picked it up, turning it over in her hands. The wood was smooth and cool under her touch. "The Chinese puzzle box."

"Yes."

Kate pressed at the hidden latch, and the little drawer slid open. It was empty, of course—the little parchment scroll was gone. She remembered how she had likened the Lindley family to this box, full of mystery and shadow.

"You know how to open it!" Elizabeth exclaimed.

"My daughters have spent hours on the silly thing, and never figured it out. But it *has* kept them occupied and out of mischief."

"They must keep it, then," Kate said, handing the box back to Elizabeth.

"Are you certain? By rights it belongs to you."

"No, it is yours now. But I will gladly accept the portrait."

Elizabeth nodded and folded the box in her arms, its secrets once again closed and hidden. "Would you like to see Michael now? If you feel strong enough."

Kate glanced toward the window. It was nearly dawn; she could see the hints of grayish pink light peeking around the edges of the curtains. "Yes. I think what I would really like is for him to take me home."

Wherever, *whatever,* home was.

The carriage ride back through the streets of London was quiet. The city was almost deserted in the hazy light of predawn; only street sweepers, ragpickers, and coalmen were abroad, along with a few carriages of other latecomers to bed. Even serving maids were probably just emerging from their humble quarters to sweep the hearths.

Kate was tired, deeply tired, yet her nerves and veins hummed with tension. With awareness of the man who sat across from her in the carriage. Michael had seemed happy to see her when she emerged from Elizabeth's chamber, had folded her in his arms and pressed a soft kiss to her brow. He was all solicitude when he helped her into the carriage, tucking lap robes around her and making sure she was comfortable. But he did not say very much, beyond inquiries into her health. And for the moment, that suited Kate. She feared she could not form any coherent conversation at all. Indeed, if she tried to speak, she might burst into embarrassing tears. So she leaned against the window, watching the city stir to life outside.

The silence was broken as the carriage neared their own street.

Michael shifted on his seat and said quietly, "Sir Julian Kirkwood is the man you told me about? The one who tried to buy you?"

"Yes," Kate answered, equally quiet. "I thought he was dead. I never would have dreamed he would appear again like that, or I would not have come to London! Never gone out in public."

"It doesn't matter," Michael answered as softly and casually as if he discussed the weather. "You won't encounter him again, Kate, because I'm going to kill him. Nick will serve as my second, I'm sure." His tone was ironhard, implacable.

"No!" Kate cried. The most appalling image flashed through her mind, of Michael facing Julian across a dew-speckled field, pistols at the ready, blood set to flow. Amelia could be left without a father, and all because of *her*, Kate. Because of her selfishness.

She loved Michael with all her heart, with everything she was. She loved Amelia and Christina as if they were her own daughters. Somehow, some way, she would make sure nothing happened to them.

"No," she repeated. "You must not challenge Julian to a duel. He killed a man once in Venice."

"I'm not scared of him, Kate."

No—but I am, Kate thought. "I know, but it would kill me if something happened to you because of my own troubles. What Julian did to me, or wanted to do, was a very long time ago. He can do nothing now."

"Kate, he insulted you!"

"I don't care about that any longer! I only care about *you*, about Christina and Amelia. They need you, just as I do." Kate shifted to sit beside him, taking his hands in her tight clasp. She had forgotten her gloves, and her hands were freezing cold, but his were warm. She wanted to curl into that warmth, to never leave it.

Her head dropped onto his shoulder, and his arms came around her, holding her close. "Please," she whispered. "Don't fight him, Michael. He can't hurt us now." Because she would not let him.

"If he leaves us alone," Michael murmured against her hair, his tone grudging and reluctant. "Then we shall see."

Kate knew she would have to be content with that—for now. The carriage drew up outside the Prices' town house, and Michael helped her down, carefully holding on to her arm as he led her into the foyer.

All of London was *not* still asleep, after all. Michael's mother stood waiting for them on the stairs, still clad in her nightcap and dressing gown. She had never looked on Kate with affection or liking. Of late, though, Kate had fancied there might be acceptance, at least, in Lady Darcy's demeanor. Now there was none of that. There was only icy disdain.

Lady Darcy held out a crumpled letter. "What is the meaning of this missive I received from Mary, Michael? She says she is keeping Christina at Lindley House because . . ." She peered down at the paper. "Because there are corrupting influences here, in the guise of a seemingly respectable governess who is, in truth, a light-skirts. There is also some garbled nonsense about Charles, and her father and Italy. I cannot make it out." She raised her frozen gaze back to her son. "What happened tonight, Michael? I demand to know the truth."

Michael's clasp tightened on Kate's arm, drawing her even closer to his side. "Mother, it is very late, and we are all tired. Can we speak of this later, at breakfast? It is all a misunderstanding, one I'm sure will be cleared up in a trice. I will fetch Christina home later, and try to talk some sense into Mary. Women who are in the family way are sometimes quite emotional, you know."

Lady Darcy crumpled the note in her fist. "No, Michael! I want to know *now.*"

Kate covered Michael's hand with her own. "It is quite all right, Michael," she whispered. "You speak with your mother. I'll just go up to my room."

"Yes, yes," Lady Darcy muttered. "Go to your room and pack."

Michael ignored her. His glance flickered searchingly over Kate's face, and she tried to give him a reassuring smile. "Are you sure?" he asked.

"Yes. I just want to lie down for a while."

"Very well." He looked back to his mother, his shoulders stiffening. "Mother, if you will come with me into the drawing room, we can discuss the matter."

Lady Darcy gave a disdainful sniff. "Well, if *she* says it is all right . . ." She twitched the hem of her dressing gown aside as Kate passed her on the stairs.

Kate held her head high and kept her face coolly expressionless as she marched to her chamber. She would not give Lady Darcy, or anyone, the satisfaction of seeing her wounded, weary heart. Only now, when it was gone, did she see how much she had truly longed for respectability, for a normal life of family and friends. For people to look at her with respect for who she was, not speculation as to what her price might be.

But what she wanted more than respectability, more even than the sweet passion she found in Michael's arms—what she wanted more than anything in all the world was Michael's happiness. His, and Christina's, and Amelia's. He had worked so hard to overcome his own past, to build a new life for his family in Yorkshire. And now she had destroyed it in only one night.

Surely, though, it could be mended! She had only to think of a way.

Kate closed her chamber door behind her and slumped back against it, staring out at the space that had so briefly been hers. It was familiar, her slippers and shawls scattered about, her hairbrush and scent bottle on the dressing table, yet it was altered beyond comprehension.

Kate caught a glimpse of herself in the shadowed mirror and hardly recognized herself in the madwoman reflected there. Her skin was chalky pale, her hair in violent disarray, strands straggling to her shoulders with Christina's pink roses wilting and askew.

Poor Christina. Imprisoned at Lindley House to protect her from Kate's corrupting influence.

Kate dropped her shawl and pulled off her fine gown, the gown she had taken such delight in but which was now creased and rumpled. She dropped it across the foot of the bed and put on one of her gray muslin day dresses. The roses fell from her hair, and she raked her fingers through the strands until all the pins scattered across the floor. Kicking them out of the way with the toe of her rose satin slipper, she lurched toward the window and threw it open.

The morning breeze was cool and fresh, washing over her face and blowing her loose hair back from her shoulders. There wasn't yet a hint of the heavy mustiness city air always held once the sun rose in earnest. The day was new and clean, the street quiet below her.

And Kate was seized with the sudden desire, the *need,* to be out in that day, to be free from this house. To run away, even if only for an hour. She whirled around and caught up her discarded shawl.

As she crept down the stairs toward the front door, she heard Lady Darcy's shrill voice echoing from the library, hanging over the foyer like a lead-lined cloud.

"I will not stand for it, Michael! I won't have this family whispered about, our name bandied in the penny press as it was when Caroline died. You must—"

Kate choked on a sob and ran out the door. She didn't stop running until she had left the quiet, elegant, genteel street far behind.

"I'm sorry," she whispered on a gasp, knowing Michael would never hear her. "For everything."

The park was still quiet. No fashionable carriages had yet appeared, no nursemaids walking with their little charges, or footmen with lapdogs on leads. Even the more serious riders, who enjoyed a good gallop along Rotten Row before the stylish crowds arrived, weren't there yet. Kate stopped her heedless dash at the edge of the Serpentine. Her side ached with the unaccustomed exertion, and her slippers—meant for dancing, not running—pinched. She leaned over, her hands clasped to her heaving stomach, and laughed.

It was a bitter laugh, one born of the thought of what her mother's old friends would say if they could see her now. Katerina Bruni, the most pampered and carefully bred would-be courtesan in Venice, standing alone in a deserted park, dressed in an old gray frock, hair tangled. About to be sick because she had run too far, and because she had caused gossip.

Or rather, *she* hadn't caused the gossip. Julian Kirkwood had.

Kate straightened, taking deep, careful breaths as the stitch in her side subsided. There were no words to describe what she had felt when she saw Julian standing there, very much alive. Shock, of course; a flash of hope that because *he* was alive, the others would be, too; dismay; a sense of unreality and illusion. Any vague wish that he might not remember her was quickly broken when he called her name. Her true name.

Katerina. His Beatrice.

Kate glimpsed a small bench beneath a tree and limped over to drop down on its hard, narrow seat. She closed her eyes and leaned her head back against the rough tree trunk. Once, when she was very young and foolish, she had briefly found a silly pleasure in Julian's fantasies, in his calling her his Beatrice, his dark-eyed Renaissance princess. For a girl who read poetry, who dreamed of fantasylands, it was romantic and flattering. To have such a handsome, wealthy suitor was what every girl wanted.

What every girl *didn't* want—or at least a girl like Kate—was a man who watched her in intense silence. Who seemed to want to make her into something she wasn't, a Renaissance princess in truth, an object of distant perfection. Not a real woman of emotion and anger and talk. When he had touched her, she shivered. Not from joy, as when Michael caressed her, but fear. Fear she was losing herself in the unholy glow of his eyes.

It had been very difficult, because she had known that one day she would have to submit to him if she didn't want to be cast out of her mother's house to make her own way. He was far wealthier than any other available suitor, a friend of Edward's.

Then this new life began. A life she could never have dreamed of before. Was it lost to her? Forever?

Kate felt a strange prickling sensation on her skin, a tense, tingling awareness. She opened her eyes, and found Julian Kirkwood standing several feet away at the edge of the Serpentine. Watching her.

Some of his physical perfection was marred. In the ever brighter sunlight, his flesh was very pale, as if he had truly been ill for a long time. He was even more slender than he had been in Venice, and his eyes were covered by the smoked-glass lenses of a pair of spectacles. But she *knew* he watched her, even from behind that concealment. She felt it, just as she had that day on the Rialto.

And suddenly, Kate was tired of being scared. Scared of his ghost, scared of the past. She had lived with it all for too long, and she was weary. She didn't have just herself to think of any longer, either—she had her family.

Kate pushed herself up from the bench and marched toward him, wrapping her shawl tighter about her shoulders, as if the flimsy lace could give her some sort of armored protection. Julian stood very still, watching her approach until she stood before him.

"How did you find me?" she demanded. "No—you needn't say. You followed me here, didn't you? You were watching our house."

He did not deny it. He simply stood there, with that maddening dignity, that loose-limbed elegance. "I was very concerned when I saw you running away," he said softly. "Did that man hurt you, Katerina? He seemed very angry when I told him what we are to each other."

Hurt her? Michael? He never could; his kind heart was incapable of hurting anyone. Not with the kind of deliberate, casual pain that was commonplace in Venice. But someone like Julian could never understand that. "Of course he did not hurt me. He never would. I simply needed some fresh air. And as to what we are to each other, you and me—we are nothing, Julian. We never were."

He *did* react to that, his shoulders drawing back as if she had struck him with a whip. "Katerina, how can you say that? I knew from the first moment I saw you, in the Piazza San Marco, that we were meant for each other. That we had been together many times before, in other lives, and we had found each other again. I loved you with all my heart—I love you still, even more."

Kate watched him, a strange sadness washing over her. Once, she could so easily have turned and walked away from him, from his delusions, and never spoken to him again. Indeed, that was what she should do. But now she knew what love truly was. She knew the piercing joy of it in her heart, the ecstasy, the hope, the fear and pain. Julian's love was not like hers for Michael—it surely had none of the sweetness and rightness. It was selfish and twisted. But in his mind, it *was* love. And this, Kate could not just leave. Once, her life had been bizarrely entwined with this man's.

"Oh, Julian," she said gently. "Those feelings—they were not for *me*. You never even truly knew me, saw me. You saw only a fantasy figure, a young Venetian girl you could pin all your dreams to. I was never Beatrice. I can't blame you. I didn't even know myself then. But I do now, and that girl you knew is dead. She died that day in the storm, and only I, Kate, am left. We were both given a great gift, a new life, and you have to find your own way in it. Just as I have found mine."

They were weak words, she knew. They could never convey all she had found in this "new life." Yet they were all she had. She could only hope they would give Julian some hope, too, a way to see past the illusions and fantasies he had lived on for so long—that they had *both* lived on.

She turned away to leave, to walk away and go home, but he reached out and caught her arm, pulling her to a standstill. Kate glanced back at him, a small kernel of fear fluttering to life in her stomach. His jaw was set in a hard line, a muscle ticking along his high, sharp cheekbone.

"It is not you saying these things, Katerina," he said, his voice deadly soft. "You felt the same way I did when we met—that we were two souls who found each other at last. I thought I would die of the pain when I lost you. It was as if a part of me was ripped away! And now we have a miracle; we have found each other again. How can you turn away from me so coldly? The girl I knew would have seen the truth, seen the great gift we have been given in each other. She would welcome it, embrace it! What were the odds of us finding ourselves in the same house last night? It was meant to be. We cannot go against fate."

Fate—meant to be. The words echoed hollowly in Kate's head. Julian's hand tightened on her arm, holding her fast even as she tried to draw away. *Don't be scared,* she told herself. They were in a public place; even now people were appearing at the edges of the park. He could not hurt her here.

Still, she was frightened. She longed for him to let her go, to stop saying these bizarre things. She wanted home, Thorn Hill; she wanted Michael.

"Do you even hear yourself, Julian?" she cried. "It was never like that between us. It was never *love.* You wanted to possess me. To possess something that never even existed. I am not sorry that you are alive, but our previous acquaintance is at an end. Now let me go!"

She tugged harder on her arm, but he was stronger. He drew her even closer, his free hand clasping around her other arm. She could smell his expensive cologne, feel the fevered heat of his body.

"Katerina, you have lived too long among these people," he ground out. His eyes were concealed behind those glasses, yet still his stare burned into her, held her. She was frozen, captured like a rabbit in a snare. "They have made you forget who you truly are. They have tried to make a Renaissance princess into a staid English governess. But they cannot—*he* cannot—know your heart. That scarred English squire . . ."

"Don't you dare speak of him!" Kate said fiercely. "He is a fine, honorable man, one someone like you could never fathom."

Julian's clasp lightened for an instant, as if in surprise, but before she could tear away it tightened again, bruising. "So that is it. What has he promised you, Katerina? Marriage? Country respectability?"

Kate said nothing. Her throat was closed, her mouth dry.

"Yes," Julian whispered. "That is it. Well, *I* can marry you, too. I can give you everything your scarred squire can, and more. You will be Lady Kirkwood, and will go back to Italy. Is it jewels you want, Katerina? Houses, travel, love? I can give them all to you, if you will only agree to be mine. To open your heart to me."

His tone was pleading, desperate, but Kate's fear had driven out all her pity. "My heart is already given to another. We are lovers, and I will never leave him. Not for someone like you—not for all the jewels in the world."

She gave her shoulders a sharp, quick twist, breaking away from him at last. Without an instant's hesitation, she turned and fled back along the banks of the Serpentine, dodging the people who walked there. They gave her shocked glances, angry frowns; she did not even notice. She only heard Julian's shout of anger and despair floating behind her, the sound reaching out with piercing, predatory talons, trying to drag her back.

Kate ran even faster *back* to the house than she had run *away* from it. It was as if demons from hell chased her down the well-manicured streets of London town houses, nipping at her heels. She stopped at the corner of her own street, leaning against the wrought iron rails of a fence to catch her breath and try to calm her fears. They would be tamped down, pushed into tiny, compressed shapes, yet they would not be altogether banished.

Julian had lost none of his obsession with her, his delusions of romance and fate. In fact, those strange fantasies had only grown in the long months of their separation. How could she ever be free of him, of all he stood for, again?

Kate pushed her damp hair back from her brow and neck, letting the heavy length fall down her back as she tried not to give in to helpless sobs. Crying would get her nowhere. Then she saw a most strange sight halfway down the street. At first, she thought it was a ghost, ethereal and insubstantial in the morning light.

Kate blinked, and saw that it was *not* a ghost. It was Christina, trudging along the pavement in her white gown.

"Christina!" Kate called, dashing to catch up with her. "Christina, whatever are you doing?"

Christina whirled around, and Kate saw that she had been crying. Her green eyes were red-rimmed, and her freckled face was pale and drawn, stained by tracks of dried tears. "Mrs. Brown!" she cried, and ran forward to throw herself into Kate's arms. "Oh, Mrs. Brown, it was horrible. Mary has become some sort of bedlamite, ranting and raving all the time about the sinful men of her family and woman's lot in life. She locked me in a bedroom, and I had to climb out the window and down a tree to escape. I got lost trying to find our house, and now—oh, Mrs. Brown!"

"Sh, *cara*," Kate whispered, smoothing Christina's

wild curls and kissing her cheek. "It is all right now. I'm sorry you had such a dreadful night."

Christina sniffled. "It wasn't *dreadful,* really, not until I got lost and I thought I would never find you or Michael again. The party was really quite interesting, and getting locked in by Mary even had its moments. Of course, that wouldn't have been quite so exciting if there wasn't a window to escape from. I would hate to be trapped at Lindley House forever. Now I'm dying for a cup of tea and something to eat. The food at the Hollingsworths was good, but that was hours ago."

Kate laughed, grateful beyond words to see that Christina's indomitable spirit was not broken, or even bent. If Kate had anything to say about it, it never would be. "I could certainly do with a cup of tea myself. And you should change your gown, Christina. That one is rather the worse for wear."

Christina nodded, and let Kate take her arm to lead her into the house. "I wouldn't be sorry to never wear another evening gown again. I just want to go back to Thorn Hill and see how my experiments are faring."

Thorn Hill. Kate could see it so clearly in her mind: its delightful jumble of brick and stones, its overgrown gardens and winding pathways. Its aura of peace and welcome, which could enfold a woman in its safety and never let her go. "I'm sure you will see it again very soon, Christina."

"And you, Mrs. Brown! Thorn Hill would never be the same without you." Christina paused on their doorstep and said, without looking at Kate, "Mrs. Brown, is that man in love with you?"

Kate could not prevaricate, could not pretend she did not know what man. Not with Christina. "He thinks he is," she answered carefully. "We knew each other a long time ago, in Italy, and he—devised of feelings for me. Feelings which I could not return."

"And now you can't, because you love my brother."

Kate was too tired, too sad, to deny it. "Yes. And

because that other man is simply not someone I could love."

Christina frowned thoughtfully. "He is very handsome."

"He is."

"And very sad. I feel sorry for him. But I am very glad you love Michael instead." Christina turned and disappeared into the house. Through the open door, Kate saw her kick off her slippers and dash up the stairs in her stocking feet.

Kate followed slowly, pausing to pick up the shoes before she made her own way up the stairs. The house was silent. There were not even any servants dashing around, going about their daily chores. All the doors were closed, and the absence of human life was palpable.

Yet that was good. The quiet, the lack of turmoil and upheaval and talk, made it easier to do what she had to do.

Chapter Twenty-four

*K*ate's room was exactly as she had left it. Her rose satin gown draped at the foot of the unruffled bed. The window draperies open, letting in bars of light and shadow.

She felt oddly detached from the scene, from the whole situation. Cold. Distant. She carefully placed Christina's slippers on the floor beneath the dressing table and took her own valise from the bottom of the wardrobe. It was the same old valise she had used on her journey to Thorn Hill, with its clasp that didn't like to stay closed and shabby sides. Once, she had resented its age, its secondhand nature. Now she felt a strange affection for it. It had carried her to Thorn Hill, to a new life she could scarcely have dreamed of before. Now it would carry her into—she knew not what.

She removed her few garments from the wardrobe, her petticoats and chemises and stockings from the bureau drawers, her books from the bedside table. A part of her urged her to move faster, to stuff them into the valise, to move quickly past the pain. Much as one had to pull a bandage swiftly from a wound, so as not to prolong the agony. But she folded the clothes slowly, carefully, tucking them in neatly.

There *was* pain. Her decision to leave, made so swiftly there in the park, caused a pain that was almost physical in her chest. It made her want to cry, to rail against the fickleness of the Fates like some character in a Greek tragedy. She hated Julian Kirkwood as she ran away from him, hated him with a raging passion for bringing *reality* into her beautiful fantasy life. He reminded her, sharply and finally, of who she truly was. She was not Kate Brown of Thorn Hill, no matter how very much she longed to be her.

But now, as she packed her meager belongings and prepared to fly again into an unknown world, she felt another, quite unexpected emotion—peace.

When she was a girl, she would sometimes stand in the Piazza San Marco and watch as the nuns from the nearby Convent of St. Cecilia marched past in an orderly line, on their way to prayers. Always more prayers. They looked like nothing so much as a row of ravens in their heavy, flapping black wool habits, and they were unnaturally quiet. Even the soles of their sandals made barely a click on the stones. Yet, on every black-framed, pale face was etched a glorious calm, a serenity that Kate envied. She never wanted to take the veil—even as a girl, she was too steeped in the worldly things, clothes, poetry, romance. Yet she envied them that serenity, envied them the knowledge that they served a higher purpose. That they served *goodness*.

She had to turn to good now, too, to something higher than her own selfish desires. She would not let Julian hurt her family. She wouldn't let gossip ruin Christina's future. She *definitely* would not let Michael duel with Julian! Even the thought of Michael being hurt sent a shudder of pain coursing through her. He had given her unimaginable beauty. She couldn't pay him back with ugliness.

And there *was* still a little selfish part of her, a part that did not want people, especially people she cared about, to look on her with disgust. She did not particularly like Lady Darcy, either one of them, but their disapproval still stung. And they were a part of Michael's family.

As Kate put her old, plain shawl on top of the contents of the valise, a flash of sunlight spread down her rose-colored gown, still draped across the bed. The luxurious satin seemed to shimmer to life, reminding her of all the silly hopes she had last night, when she first donned its soft loveliness.

She ran one fingertip along the pearl trim of the bodice. Then she picked up the gown, cradling it in her arms, and went to hang it in the wardrobe. She closed the stout wooden panels, blocking its pink glow once and for all.

As the soft satin disappeared, there was a short, sharp knock at the chamber door.

"Come in," Kate called. It was probably a maid, bringing breakfast. Good—she could use some sustenance before she found her way back to her old employment agency.

But it was decidedly *not* the maid. It was Michael who stepped into the room and closed the door softly behind him. He, too, had changed from his evening attire into the more familiar garb of dark blue wool coat, buckskin breeches, and plainly tied white cravat. His hair was still damp from washing, and she could smell the clean, enticing fragrance of his soap.

He was so very beautiful. An angel, in truth. Kate longed to run to him, to throw her arms around him and never let go, but she curled her hand tightly around the wardrobe door, holding herself back.

His sharp blue gaze moved over her, standing there by the wardrobe, and over to the valise on the bed. "So," he said. "Christina was right."

Kate swallowed hard. "Right?"

"She said she thought you were planning to run away." His voice was clear, calm, uninflected. It was impossible to tell if he was unhappy, happy, or indifferent to her plans. Kate had a flashing remembrance of the two of them entwined in ecstasy, and she sincerely hoped he was *not* indifferent.

"Christina is too smart for her own good," she said.

"Indeed she is, at times." Michael stepped forward to the edge of the bed, and pinched the valise's clasp between his fingers. "It still does not close. You should have bought a new one."

Kate stared at the silly old valise. Anything not to
look at Michael. "It hardly signifies. That one will take
me where I want to go as well as another."

"And where *are* you going, Kate the curst?" He
shoved the valise out of the way and sat down on the
bed, his booted feet swinging above the floor, hands
clasped between his knees. She saw with a pang that
his leg was stiff this morning, braced against the side
of the mattress. "Are you going away with him?"

Her gaze flew up to his, to find him watching her
steadily. But at least he was not indifferent. She could
see that now, so clearly. "Him? Julian?"

"Is there another one? Lurking around the corner,
mayhap, or behind a tree." His tone was deceptively
carefree.

Kate choked on an hysterical bubble of laughter.
Run away with Julian? When she had gone to so much
trouble to get away from him and his sort in the first
place? To escape his intense stares, his possessive caresses? No. "Of course I am not going away with Julian. I loathe him."

A frown puckered the smooth, brown skin of his
brow, creasing a sharp line between his eyes. "Then
where are you going? Surely you at least owe me
that."

She owed him her life, her very heart. "I don't
know," she admitted, leaning back against the wardrobe door. "Back to the employment agency, for one
thing. There must be another family who needs a governess or lady's companion, somewhere far away, like
the Highlands of Scotland where no one has heard of
me. Then I will find lodging. I have some of my wages
saved." And she could always change her name again.

Michael slowly shook his head. "Kate, Kate. Why
are you running away?"

"I'm not running away. That was what I did when
I left Italy. I am merely—seeking another situation.
I've certainly proved unsatisfactory in this one."

"No," Michael said, still so damnably calm. "You

are running from us, from me. And I want to know why."

Kate gave an exasperated laugh. Oh, the stubborn, darling man! Couldn't he see what she meant to do? "I am leaving because I care about you, and about Christina and Amelia. There is sure to be much speculation after last night, a scandal. I cannot put you through that. Not when you have worked so long to carve a respectable place for yourself. The old Katerina might have thought only of herself, of her own happiness, but I cannot!"

Michael smiled at her, a wide, enticing grin. "Oh, bonny Kate. I believe you have been reading too much poetry."

Kate paused. "Too much poetry?"

"Yes. Or perhaps too many Minerva Press novels. For are they not full of saintly, self-sacrificing ladies?"

"I am *not* being . . ."

Michael held out his hand to halt her words, beckoning her closer to him with his fingers, his smile mellowing, gentling. "Kate, I do see what you are trying to do, and I admire and love you for it. Very much. You only want to save others pain."

"Yes, I do want that," Kate admitted. She did step closer to him, as if drawn by a magical spell, and slipped her fingers into his clasp. He drew her down beside him on the bed, holding tightly to her hand as if he feared she might fly away. "You are the finest person I have ever known, and I never want to hurt you, Michael. I can't erase the past, but I can keep it away from you and your family if I leave now."

"Don't you see? It would cause me far more pain to lose you than any silly gossip could ever cause. I was only half-alive until I found you, losing myself in work, trudging from day to day. But you—you made the sun come out. Because of you, I like waking up in the morning, I can't wait to see what every day holds. You make me laugh, you make me think. You drive me insane. And Amelia and Christina love you, they need you. I can't help them learn to be young ladies. Only you can do that. Please, Kate. Do you hear what I'm saying?"

Kate stared at him in wonder. She reached up with one fingertip to trace the sensual line of his lips, his jaw and nose. He was so warm, so sweet and alive under her caress. *Did* she hear what he was saying? As clearly as a line of music. Every woman dreamed of such words, so full of heart and truth. "You don't want me to leave."

"Never." He caught her hand, pressing kisses into her palm, against the frantic pulse of her wrist. "I never want you to leave. Whatever was in your past, I don't care. It can't be as bad, as ugly as what is in mine. And it made you who you are today. A wonderful, mercurial woman, romantic woman."

"I don't want to leave," she whispered. "I never wanted to leave you and the girls. But Julian will still be here." Following her. Watching.

Michael gave a snort. "I don't care about him. He can go to the devil, and so can all the gossip-mongers. He'll soon find a new lady to torment, and they'll find a new scandalbroth to stew in. We will just go back to Thorn Hill, and forget about all of it. We have our own lives to lead. I've been away from the farm too long. Amelia has to practice her French, and Christina has to check on her precious plants. And we have a wedding to plan."

Kate's fingers curled tightly around his, a stream of pure, bright joy flooding through her heart. "You still want to marry me?"

Michael laughed, a joyful, open sound, like bubbles in champagne, summer sunshine. "Of course, widgeon. Have I not asked you at least twice? I have been waiting patiently all this time for your answer. Come, Kate. By the time Christina makes her debut, you and I will be an old married couple, and no one will recall what happened last night."

It was so perfect. It was exactly what she wanted, a husband she loved who loved her, a family, a home.

She had to close her eyes against the force of the happiness. Surely such joy could not be real, could not last! She wanted only to hold tightly to it forever, to never let it get away. "Your mother won't be happy," she whispered, opening her eyes.

Michael gave another snort. "My mother will come 'round when we give her another grandchild. In the meantime, she has decided to stay in Town with Mary and Charles for a few months. But we can go back to Thorn Hill this very day, if you will only agree, Kate."

Kate felt as if she was about to step off a steep precipice into she knew not what. She hesitated, studying his beloved face. "Yes," she said slowly. "Yes, I agree. Let's go home."

Michael gave an exultant, primitive cry, and his mouth swooped down to cover hers in the most exuberant, joyful kiss Kate could ever have imagined. His lips played over hers lightly, like a soft minuet, stirring her senses to a tingling, exquisite life. She moaned, drunk on the taste and scent and feel of him—he surrounded her, enveloped her, until she could think of nothing else. Julian Kirkwood, marriage, London, gossip, it all vanished, and there was only this, this magic she always felt when she was with Michael.

She looped her arms around his neck, dragging him closer, closer. Michael groaned deep in his throat, a sound of primal longing, and his mouth slanted over harder over hers, his tongue seeking hers in a new, frantic dance.

Every nerve, every cell in Kate's body hummed with life, with longing. She needed to feel Michael's skin against hers, feel his body inside her and know that they were together always. That nothing could ever come between them.

Frenetic with need, she slid her hands down to catch at his coat and push it from his shoulders. Michael let go of her to shake the heavy fabric loose, but his caress returned to her immediately, skimming along her back to cup her bottom and drag her into his hardness. Everything was a damp blur, a whirl of hazy, dizzy emotions. She leaned into him, into their desperate kiss, yet it was not enough. She tugged off his cravat and reached for the opening of his soft linen shirt, ripping at it, the sharp tearing sound echoing around them.

Michael's lips slid from her mouth, along her cheekbone to the delicate, sensitive spot just below her ear. The tip of his tongue touched her lightly just there, his breath hot in her ear. She gasped, her knees weak. He caught her against him, and whispered, "Bonny Kate—no one has ever been so desperate for me they actually tore my clothes off. I'm flattered."

"And so you should be," Kate whispered back. "I wouldn't tear the clothes off of just any man, you know. But why are you talking, when we're sitting right here on a bed?"

Michael laughed, and lifted her higher in his arms. "Your wish is always my command, *signorina*."

Christina pressed her ear tightly to the glass she held against the chamber door, straining to hear what was being said. She could make out only snatches of words—plants, Christina, mother, wedding, last night, Thorn Hill. And then, at last, that magical "I agree."

Then there were the obvious silences of kisses and caresses, the whisper of radiantly happy sighs. Christina stepped quickly away, for that was far more than she wanted to know at this point in her young life. And far more than she wanted to know *ever* about her brother! It was enough that Mrs. Brown agreed to stay with them, that they were going home to Thorn Hill.

How much she missed it! The gray-green expanse of the moor, the meandering rivers and the glassy Semerwater, the tracery of the ancient black walls along the hills. The myriad of plants and flowers, just waiting for her to observe and collect them. London was nice—the museums were a delight. But she missed home. She even missed her friend Andrew Price. He would surely be very impressed by all the new botanical tracts and seeds she had collected.

But today not even Nuttall—or daydreams of home—could hold her interest for long. Her thoughts wandered, drifting back to last night. Had it been only hours ago? It felt like a lifetime. It had been like a scene in a book, though certainly not the scientific works Christina preferred. More like a horrid novel, or a poem by Byron. Fainting ladies, mysterious anti-heroes, valiant knights, the miasma of scandal. It was unlike anything Christina had ever encountered before, or would certainly ever encounter again! There were ghosts and strange legends aplenty in Yorkshire, but rarely such displays of pure human foible.

She thought again of that man—Sir Julian Kirkwood. Even his name was like a character in a book. He had appeared like a wraith out of nowhere, a mage to transform Christina's mundane world and snatch her out of her comfortable complacency. She did not like him at all. He had hurt her Mrs. Brown, and he had such an aura of pain, longing, and passion that anyone coming near could not help but be burned. But he was strangely and deeply fascinating.

What could have happened between him and Mrs. Brown in Italy, that could cause such a burning fount of unrequited love? Christina could not begin to fathom. She didn't *want* to fathom such impractical and unnecessary emotion.

Plants she understood. Plants could be studied, rationalized, known. People never could. Especially people like Julian Kirkwood, who seemed to come from another world entirely than ordinary creatures like herself.

With a sigh, she turned back to her book, to the botanical matters she was comfortable with. As she turned a page, a slight blur of darkness outside the window caught her attention. She squinted past the slightly wavy glass to the street beyond.

There was a man in a black greatcoat standing on

the pavement outside the house, staring fixedly up at the building.

Sir Julian Kirkwood. Of course. She might not know a great deal about human nature, but she did know that a flame with the intensity of his could not burn out on only one night. She knew that from the poems in Mrs. Brown's books. Julian was like one verse Christina remembered—"If I should meet thee, After long years, How should I greet thee? With silence and tears."

She unlocked the window and threw it open, rising up on her knees on the window seat to lean out into the morning air. She started to call out to him, to demand that he leave, go away. Yet something written on his thin, handsome face stopped her, stayed her voice in her throat.

She had never seen such profound sadness, such ineffable longing. Such implacable anger. It made her shiver with an emotion she could not even begin to identify.

When she tried to slip silently back into the room, away from his intensity, her book slid from her hand and fell with a clatter onto the wooden windowsill. Julian swung toward her, and she could feel his stare through those blasted tinted spectacles. It was biting and intense, holding her immobile.

Finally, he turned and strode away down the street, enveloped in his black coat like a creature of stars and moons. Christina collapsed back onto the window seat, burying her face in her hands. Thank God they were going home soon, and everything would be peaceful and normal and happy again.

She rubbed hard at her itching eyes, as if she could erase the sight of him, and glanced back out the window. Julian Kirkwood was gone—but she knew she would not soon forget him.

Chapter Twenty-five

*O*h, it *was* good to be home again.

Kate stood on the corner of the busiest street in Suddley village, holding Amelia by the hand, and watching the movement and music of a busy morning. After the crowded strangeness, the stifling sophistication, of Town, it was a dreamland. The people going in and out of the shops—bearing baskets of fresh produce and spools of ribbon, herbs and books—the carts clattering past on the cobblestones, even the sight of the Rosses' carriage parked outside the apothecary, awakened new feelings of profound gratitude in Kate's heart.

She almost laughed aloud. Who could have ever thought when she first arrived here that she would think of Suddley and its environs as *home*? A spot more removed from her birthplace could not be imagined. Yet she welcomed it now, adored its very rusticity, its profound *Englishness*. Next to Thorn Hill, she believed she loved this village best of anywhere in the world.

It was made all the sweeter by the memory of how very close she had come to losing it forever.

Now it was hers. This life, this—everything. She and Michael had gone to St. Anne's yesterday and announced their betrothal to the vicar, asking him to read the first banns on Sunday. They would plan a small dinner party for all the neighbors after, to celebrate the upcoming marriage. And to squelch any rumors or speculation spreading northward from London.

All the neighbors. Even Lady Ross and her daughters. Kate watched those ladies now as they emerged from the shop, and she almost laughed again at their imagined reactions to the news. Her laughter began to fade, though, when the Ross litter gave her a collective suspicious glare and climbed hastily into their carriage.

Amelia tugged at her hand. "Why are you smiling, Mrs. Brown?"

Kate glanced down at the child, her grin widening at the sight of Amelia's puzzled frown. Kate reached out to straighten Amelia's little soft velvet hat on her golden curls, and said, "Because it is such a beautiful day, *angelina*!"

Amelia glanced around doubtfully. "It's actually a bit gray."

"Yes, but it's not raining, and it's not too cold, and we're not in foggy old London."

"That is true," Amelia said, nodding. "I do like being home again, even though Grandmama stayed behind with Aunt Mary."

"And I know something you will like even more."

"What?"

"Lemon drops, of course! Come, *cara,* we will just stop and get Christina's book, and then pop into the sweet-shop."

Amelia giggled. "Oh, yes, indeed, Mrs. Brown! Lemon drops are the *best.*"

They linked fingers and dashed across the cobblestone street. As they stepped up onto the pavement in front of the bookshop, the door of the Tudor Arms Inn across and down the street opened, and Kate watched as a man stepped out. His back was to them, yet there was something familiar about his tall, slender figure.

As he put on his hat, he turned in Kate's direction, and she almost screamed aloud. She pressed her gloved hand to her mouth to hold the panicked sound inside. Her skin turned cold and clammy, as if an icy wind suddenly rushed down the street, and she yanked

Amelia closer to her side, wrapping her arms around the child.

It was Julian Kirkwood, and he was surely no illusion, despite the very bizarreness of seeing him on Suddley's prosaic streets. He was enveloped in a black greatcoat, his eyes covered by those glasses with smoked lenses, and his raven's-wing hair under his hat. Yet it was undoubtedly him. He, too, froze for an instant when he saw her there, staring at her from behind those concealing glasses. Then he touched his fingers to the brim of his hat in a seemingly mocking salute, and turned to make his way along the street, away from them. Every person he passed stopped to watch him, for strangers were rare in Suddley.

Kate stared after him warily until he was gone from her sight. *He had followed her here.* Into her very home, her sanctuary! If Michael saw him, there would surely be trouble. The thought made her shiver. The knowledge that Julian was *here,* in this place she loved, made her feel ill. She feared she might retch right there on the lane.

She had been so foolish to imagine that her rebuff of Julian in the park would be the end of it. She had so hoped, had even managed to convince herself, that she would be out of his way in Yorkshire. But he had been a most persistent and pervasive suitor in Venice. Time and illness had made him even more so.

But Kate was no longer the yielding girl she was in Italy. Julian Kirkwood would soon be brought to see that. He would be out of their lives—one way or another.

"Mrs. Brown!" Amelia said plaintively, wriggling under Kate's tight clasp. "You're squeezing too hard."

Kate took in a deep breath, trying to push away the anger and the cold fear. She smiled reassuringly down at Amelia and loosened her hold. "I'm sorry, *cara.* Come, now—let's get those books and sweets so we can go home."

Julian leaned against the rough, half-timber wall, around the corner from where he had glimpsed Katerina. The country air was cool, but his skin felt fevered, blistered with longing and need. He closed his eyes behind his smoked-glass spectacles, yet he could still see her, her face pale, shocked, her arms wrapped around the child. A child who surely belonged to the scarred squire.

He had not meant for her to see him. Not yet. Not until his plans were complete, until he knew exactly what he had to do to bind his princess to him and eliminate the obstacles that stood between them for all time. He had been told that the Lindleys rarely left their estate, and so he assumed he could move fairly freely about the village. Seeing her today—it awakened all the feelings he had tried to cool on the long journey here. She was so beautiful, lovelier even than the girl she had been in Venice. There was a ripeness to her now, a deepening of her bloom. She was made for passion. For *his* passion.

Now his time was grown short, driven by that passion, by the need to make her his completely. His plans would have to take effect soon. Very soon indeed.

Julian reached inside his coat and touched the cold, heavy metal of his pistol. It waited patiently. But it would not have to wait long.

Kate paced along the riverbank, the earth, spongy from recent rains, dragging at the soles of her half boots, reaching up to stain the hem of her cloak. She didn't see the water rushing past, murky and quicker than usual. She didn't feel the chilly wind that buffeted her skin and tore at her hair. She had only one thought in her mind.

He had to leave. Now. This moment.

Julian Kirkwood had no right to be here, to follow her. No right to invade her life at all, to put the people she loved in danger. Not that he could see that; he was obviously blinded by his own dreams, his own visions of who she was and what her place in life should be. She could scarcely blame him for *that*—she had once shared such notions. She had believed that the world she grew up in was the only world open to her. To belong to a man was how that world moved, for a woman. And she had been resigned, in a way, to being bought by Julian, even through the creeping chill of her disquiet. Even with the way his touch and stare made her feel. She had been resigned to fulfilling his fantasies, to being his Beatrice, his Renaissance princess who loved him through the ages. After all, it was a harmless fantasy, as such things go. One of her mother's friends had a protector who liked to pretend she was a donkey. Being a Renaissance dream lady didn't involve whips or ropes, at least.

But it was not harmless now. Kate was a different person from that naive girl who thought she had no choice. She had made a new choice; she had a family, a place to belong. She had found love with a man who saw her for what she was, silly flights of fancy and all, and loved her for it. Michael didn't need her to be anyone but Kate. He and the girls, their world at Thorn Hill—that was her life now. And Venice, her girlhood, the Katerina Julian thought he knew—they were only a faint memory.

Yet he could not let her, or rather his fantasy of her, go. He had lived with only ghosts and memories for so long that they had obviously become real to him. Real in a way that a prosaic English life could not be. Kate could almost have pitied him. Almost— if he had not followed her here, endangering all she held dear. *Why* had he come? Why?

That was why she sent that note to him at the inn, summoning him to her. She had to face her fears, face his menace. She had to make it end before it went any further. And knowing Julian, she feared that she could only begin to fathom exactly how far he would go.

Her footsteps quickened, her gloved hands twisting together beneath the shelter of her cloak. Whatever could he hope to accomplish? She had no idea. Bullying never won a lady's heart, and Kate had made it clear to him that hers was given to another. Perhaps the cold waters that nearly drowned them both had driven him stark mad.

Whatever it was, whatever he imagined, he had to leave. Kate would not let him hurt her family, no matter what she had to do.

No matter what.

She heard a soft rustle behind her, and whirled around to see Julian approaching along the riverbank. She froze in her pacing, staring at him, watching him warily as he came to a halt beneath a tall, spreading tree. He watched her in return as he leaned his arm against a low-hanging branch. He had left behind his spectacles on this gray day, and his dark, naked eyes were full of a burning longing.

Kate fell back a step, startled by a sudden realization—she had felt just such a longing when she first glimpsed Michael, and saw his home at Thorn Hill. Her dreams at that moment had seemed just as distant, just as futile.

"Why are you here, Julian?" she said, steeling herself against any hint of softening or understanding. She could see that he was determined to have his way. But no more determined than she. Did he think this was a game of some sort, that she was a prize to be won? If so, it was a deadly serious game, one Kate was determined to win herself.

The corner of his mouth twitched, as if he fought a smile or a scowl. "You sent for me, Katerina." He reached inside his black greatcoat and brought out her note, carefully folded. As he did so, Kate saw the quick, hastily concealed flash of the silver hilt of a pistol.

Kate swallowed hard at the sight, glancing away. *A pistol!* "I meant, why are you here in Yorkshire? Why have you followed me?"

His long, pale fingers closed around the paper, crushing it. "You would not listen to me in London when I tried to talk to you, to reason with you. You ran away in the park like some petulant child. So I was forced to come to this godforsaken place to try to make you see sense."

Sense? A petulant child? Kate drew in a deep breath of cold air, trying to drive out the haze of anger and confusion that always overcame her when she saw him. "I told you in the park that I have a new life now, a life with a man I love—a man I intend to marry. I told you not to come near me again, not to importune me with your declarations. Then, having said what I wanted to say, I left. How could you possibly have interpreted *that* as an invitation to follow me to Yorkshire?"

Julian made a light *tsk*ing noise and shook his head in a gesture of wry disappointment. "Oh, Katerina. Life in England does not suit you. It has made you coarse and shrill. The girl I knew, the princess, always moved and spoke with such grace and dignity, such quiet beauty. Come with me, back to Italy. Back to who you were always meant to be."

Kate took a step back, remembering that gun. "I am to be married. Even if I was not, I wouldn't go with you as far as Leeds. That part of my life is finished."

He did not move an inch from the tree he leaned against so casually, yet it felt as if he edged ever closer to her, capturing her, cornering her. "Katerina. How stubborn you are. Did I not say I would marry you? I was wrong, very wrong, when I tried to make you my mistress in Venice. A man should cherish a jewel such as you. You don't need the country squire, or his squalling little brat clinging to your skirts. As my wife, you could have everything you want. I would drape you in jewels—"

"No," Kate said. She wanted to shout the word, scream it to the heavens. *Then* maybe he would understand. But she said the word softly, with all her heart behind it. "I have no need for your jewels."

She reached into the pocket of her cloak and came up with the object she had brought. Why she brought it, she did not know—she could not bribe Julian to go away. He had more money than he could spend in ten lifetimes. Yet brought it she had. Perhaps as a token for him, a reminder of a life they had both once seen that was gone. Perhaps a symbol that she did not want his riches. Or perhaps, though she truly wanted him to be gone with all her heart, she could not bring herself to entirely hate him. She understood longing.

Kate held out her hand, her mother's sapphire brooch glittering on her gloved palm.

Julian stared at the brooch, his dark gaze narrowed. "I remember when you wore that brooch. The day we were on Edward's yacht. You wore a bright blue silk gown, and that was pinned to your bodice. Your hair was loose, with sapphire combs. . . ."

"Yes," Kate murmured. For an instant, she could see that day living again, the sun and the sea, the laughter, the champagne, and the sudden terror. "I don't need jewels any longer. This belongs to the past, as should any feelings you have for me. I love Michael Lindley, and I will soon be his wife. Please, Julian—you must go now. And take this with you."

She took a step toward him, then another and another, always remembering the pistol she had glimpsed inside his coat. As she moved closer, she felt strength flowing through her veins, warm and bracing as strong brandy. Julian Kirkwood had no power over her any longer. She pressed the jewel into his hand, curling his fingers around its cool contours. He simply stared down at it, his face expressionless and still as marble.

"You take it, Julian," she said. "I don't want it now."

She started to step away, but his hand snaked out in a flash, clasping her wrist and drawing her close until she was pressed against his hard, thin chest. She could feel the fevered heat of him through her cloak, and she shook with the sudden cold force of her fear. If he forced her to the ground, drew that hidden pistol, there would be nothing she could do, no way she could fight him off.

She twisted her wrist in his clasp until sharp pain

shot up her arm. She barely felt the ache in her panic. She wanted only to be free, to not feel his body, the cool force of his breath on her cheek. "Let me go!" she screamed.

"This isn't over, Katerina," he said quietly, calmly. That was even more fearsome than any shouts would be. "We will never be over."

Then he released her, so suddenly she fell back a step. He still watched her, gray eyes burning into her.

And Kate did the only thing she could do. She fled, as fast as her feet would take her. At the top of the slope, where she would turn out of sight of the river and be on the path back to Thorn Hill, she stopped for an instant and glanced back over her shoulder, rubbing at her bruised wrist. Julian still stood where she left him, gazing down at the sapphire. The jewel in his hand dazzled even in the palest sunlight.

Kate spun around and dashed toward home. She wanted Thorn Hill, wanted to hold Amelia against her, feel Michael's welcoming kiss on her cheek. But even as she longed for all that, even as she raced toward it, she remembered that flash of silver, that glimpse of pistol. She felt again his hard clasp on her wrist and heard his words.

We will never be over.

Julian closed his fist around the brooch. The damnable sapphire, that was all she intended to leave him with, here by this gray river. The edges cut into his flesh, but he did not even notice. The pain was as nothing to the agony in his heart.

Why would she not listen? Why could she not see? She was meant for far greater things than life as mistress of a country estate here in this gray place. She belonged as his princess, high on a pedestal where all could admire her beauty. He had known that from the moment he first saw her, and the certainty only grew stronger with the miracle of their survival and their reunion. The despair he had felt at her death was turned to incandescent joy at finding her again.

Yes, she was different now. Harder, more stubborn, seduced by her country squire and his oh-so-English life. But surely the girl he knew was still there under-neath the prickles and calluses. Still there, shimmering like this jewel. She had to be brought to see that.

The small pistol he had bought in London weighed heavy inside his coat. He had not known then what he purchased it for, why he carried it to this lonely land. Perhaps now he knew the answer to that.

Yes. He did know. It was time to set his plans in motion. Once and for all.

He spun around and followed in Kate's footsteps, up the heather-covered slope of a hill. When he reached the summit, she was nowhere to be found. As far as he could see, in every direction, there was only gray. A person could get lost in that gray, never to emerge again. *That* was what would happen to his princess. She would drown in the moors, if he did not save her.

In the distance, etched against the lead-streaked sky, he could see the roofline and turrets of her squire's house. Thorn Hill, the man at the inn had said it was called. So appropriate for Katerina's new persona. Thorny, unapproachable, proper—prickly. As he stared at it fixedly, studying its ungraceful contours, he slowly became aware of movement, a flutter, nearby.

It was the figure of a woman in a pale dress, bending to study something in the center of a meadow. It could not be Katerina—this woman was too tall, and wore no dark cloak. Yet he still felt strangely drawn to her, compelled to see what she was doing. This corner of the world was seemingly deserted, no living thing, not even a bird, anywhere to be seen. Only this lady, mov-ing about on some mysterious, efficient errand.

His steps turned toward her; he just wanted to find out what in blazes she was doing. Perhaps she could tell him the secret of this windblown place.

As he drew near to her, he saw, with a sense of

fated inevitability, that it was the Valkyrie from London. A narrow-brimmed straw bonnet shielded her face, but there was no mistaking that fall of hair, curling, sun-streaked brown hair, and the slim, lithe figure swathed in pale blue muslin, not even a shawl against the wind. She held a small trowel and dug about in the loamy earth, occasionally holding up some sprig of vegetation to examine it minutely. He saw that she wore no cloak because it was spread out on the ground, collecting yet more bits of stems and leaves.

For just a moment, he forgot about the jewel in his hand until its edges bit into his skin, and he tucked it into his greatcoat's pocket.

"Well, Brunhilde," he called. "We meet again."

She shot straight up, like a slender arrow, weeds dangling from her hand. Her mouth was agape, her bright green eyes blazing as she stared at him.

She was not elegant, as he preferred ladies to be. Dirt streaked her skirt; mud caked her boots. Her hair was tangled. There was even a stripe of dust across one cheekbone, marring already freckled skin. There was none of the mystery that was a lady's finest allure, no hint of flirtatious smiles, no silk or perfume. She glared at him with obvious dislike, not even an attempt at polite prevarication.

She was young, of course. Perhaps she would grow into delicious femininity, to half smiles and soft laughter, to the sheen of satin and flash of diamonds. But Julian doubted it. More likely she would end up on a battlefield somewhere, wielding spears and flaming arrows. Indeed, even now she clutched at her trowel in such a way that he feared for his extremities.

He should just turn and walk away, leave the child to her digging in the dirt. But she distracted him for a moment, made him forget Katérina and her damnable stubbornness.

"*You,*" she said, her voice thick with disgust. As if he were a mere worm she found under her trowel. Or less than a worm, for she seemed to be a person who would have a strange fondness for bugs. That should have made him furious, added new layers to his temper. Yet he found it only made him want to laugh.

And he had not wanted to laugh in a very, very long time.

She took a step toward him, edging around her plant-laden cloak. "Why have you come here?"

Julian shook his head. "Such ill manners, Brunhilde! Perhaps I came here for my health, to imbibe the fresh air."

Her full lips, a pretty pale pink shade, pursed like a disapproving spinster's. "Your health? In Yorkshire? Most invalids choose Bath or Margate. No. You came here following Mrs. Brown."

Julian did not answer. He merely watched her.

"It will do you no good," she continued. "She is marrying my brother. The first banns will be called Sunday."

So, the Valkyrie *was* the squire's sister, just as Nicholas Hollingsworth had said. How could Katerina choose such a wild country family over all he, Julian, offered? It must be some sort of Yorkshire witchcraft. Would Brunhilde turn him into a toad if he lingered here too long?

No. She would have already done it by now.

"Banns are not a wedding," he answered softly. And when he had his way, there would never be wedding bells ringing for Kate and her squire. Never.

Bright pink spread across her cheeks, staining the bronzed color of her skin and absorbing the freckles. "She does not love you! You only make her cry. My brother makes her happy. You should go away, find some London lady to torment. I am sure they would like it exceedingly, since they seem to think torment is *romantic*. The silly cows."

Julian felt again that bizarre urge to laugh. What would this girl possibly find "romantic"? A bouquet of weeds? A basket of dirt? Surely she would shun poetry, jewels, subtle flirtations. She would see through blatant flattery in a trice.

Ah, if only she were older. Or he were younger, the idealistic young man he had been when he first entered Oxford, intent on finding a new, beautiful life away from his parents' ugliness. Before he found his dream in Katerina—and lost it again. He had the oddest notion that if he had met this fierce, unladylike Valkyrie at another time, she could have been the making of him.

Yet it was too late now. He was already far beyond ruin.

He took another step in her direction, and another. The mud caught at his boots, ruining the high polish of the fine Hessians, but he did not notice. He was too interested in watching her expressive face. Her eyes widened, as if she longed to move away, to run. She stood her ground, like a true warrior.

"What is your name?" he asked gently.

Her lips twitched. "Lady Christina Lindley. And yours is Sir Julian Kirkwood."

"It is. What do *you* think romantic, Lady Christina? What would win *your* heart?"

She tilted her head back, staring directly into his eyes. She *was* scared of him—he could see it behind the clear sea green of her eyes. But she refused to show it, standing perfectly still. "If someone sent me a newly discovered specimen of plant, something never seen before. That would be romantic. Chasing me across the country would not be."

Julian clasped her trowelless hand in his, staring down at it balanced across his palm. It was as unfeminine as the rest of her, with long fingers marked by scrapes and calluses, dirt trapped beneath the nails. It trembled at his touch, but again she did not draw away. The weed she held between two fingers dropped to the ground.

"What if I sent you a new plant?" he murmured. "Something with amazing healing properties, from China perhaps, or India. Would you soften toward me then, Brunhilde? Would you look on me with kindness?"

He bent his head to kiss her wrist. She smelled faintly of lavender and the clean, rainy scent of the earth. Her pulse trembled beneath his lips. And Julian felt something warm and deep, unexpected, stir in his soul. Something magical.

The spell was quickly broken. Lady Christina snatched her hand away from his grasp and used it to soundly box his ears. "How dare you!" she shouted. "You are a dreadful man, a rake who will pursue anything in skirts. You claim to love Mrs. Brown, you say that you would follow her anywhere, yet here you are kissing a stranger in a field. If you sent me the most amazing plant ever discovered, even one with the elixir of eternal life in its leaves, I would not cross the street to spit on you. Now, for the last time, go away!"

She whirled around, caught up her cloak and all the gathered plants in her arms, and marched away from him. She did not even glance back, and soon was lost entirely to his sight, leaving only the faint hint of lavender hanging in the air.

Julian gently touched his fingertips to his stinging cheek. Brunhilde certainly had a wicked right hook. She would be perfectly at home at Gentleman Jackson's. For an instant, his thoughts were clouded by a black haze of fury. No woman had ever *hit* him before. Not even Katerina. He wanted to run after Lady Christina, catch her in his arms, and shake her until some of her ridiculous nettles fell away!

But then—then he laughed. For truly, no woman had ever hit him before. No woman had ever dared, yet this scrap of girlhood boxed his ears and berated him as if he were a naughty schoolboy sent down to the headmaster's office.

This Lady Christina obviously cared about her family, about Katerina—her "Mrs. Brown." And Katerina had warned him, in a flame of spitting fury, to leave her family alone. Obviously, that meant the squire, the squire's brat daughter—and the squire's sister?

Julian rubbed again at his aching cheek, staring

toward the direction Lady Christina ran off in, as an idea slowly took shape in his mind.

Desperate times, after all, called for desperate measures. This Lady Christina would fit perfectly into his plans. It was as if she were sent to him for just that purpose. She would bring his princess back to him, whether she will or nill.

Chapter Twenty-six

*K*ate stared out of the drawing room window into the black night beyond. The darkness was thicker than any she had ever seen, unbroken by any hint of starlight or moonglow. The clouds had descended in earnest before dinner, lowering in thick banks to enclose their world.

Never had she been so grateful for the coziness of her family's own hearth. She turned away from the blackness, back toward the cheerful blaze laid in the marble grate. Michael and Christina sat beside it with the tea tray set before them, talking together quietly while Amelia played her new piece of music, Handel's Air in B-flat, at the pianoforte. It was a beautiful scene, one that could not help but make Kate smile, despite the weariness and strain of the long day behind her. Despite Julian and his hidden weapons. *This* was what was important, what mattered. This was what she had to protect.

Christina glanced up and saw her smiling. She smiled in return, rising from her chair and coming to join Kate beside the window. Christina wore one of her newer gowns tonight, a pale green sprigged muslin, and her hair was neatly brushed and confined in a green ribbon. The green suited her, yet her eyes seemed shadowed by the same weariness that lay heavy on Kate's own heart, and Christina appeared uncommonly serious this evening. Perhaps it was merely the haste of their removal from London, their mad dash across the country to reach home.

Or perhaps it was something more.

"It's going to rain again tonight," Christina said quietly, staring out the window. "I'm glad I collected the specimens I needed this afternoon. Surely it will be too wet tomorrow."

Kate smiled at her, smoothing back an errant curl into her green ribbon. "Too wet for *you*, Christina? Perhaps we should build an ark, then."

Christina laughed at the weak jest, but her eyes were still serious. "Mrs. Brown," she said, "I saw someone when I was out collecting my plants."

Kate froze. "Someone?"

"Yes. I had met him in London, too. Sir Julian Kirkwood. I never would have expected to see him *here*!"

"Oh, Christina." Kate closed her eyes against the fresh rush of pain. She had warned him to leave her family alone! Julian was a fearsome foe, but she would not have thought him the sort to torment young girls. She had underestimated him yet again. She thought of that hidden pistol, and of Julian encountering Christina alone in a meadow, and she shivered. "I am sorry he bothered you. It won't happen again, I promise."

Christina still stared out the window, a small frown puckering her brow. "He didn't—bother me. Not exactly."

"What do you mean, Christina? What did he do?" Kate asked frantically. By God, if he had *hurt* her . . .

Christina shrugged, but she would not look directly at Kate. "He just talked to me, really. He is a very strange man."

Strange, indeed. It was far more than that. "Listen, *cara*. Perhaps it would be better if you didn't go out alone for a while. Just until after he is gone from here."

Kate expected arguments, protests. Much to her surprise, Christina just nodded. "You are right. I have a lot to work on here, anyway. I am very behind on my experiments."

"Yes. And don't forget—the Prices are coming to tea tomorrow. Perhaps young Mr. Price would be interested in hearing about all you learned at the Royal Botanic Society lecture and the British Museum?"

A ghost of a smile touched Christina's lips.

"What are you whispering of so secretly, my dears?" Michael said lightly, breaking into their tense, quiet exchange. He laid aside the agricultural report he was reading and came to join them by the window. He put his arms around both of them, and Kate leaned her head against his shoulder. She wanted to melt there, to sigh aloud with happiness. "Perhaps you are talking of wedding plans."

Christina laughed. It was not her usual loud, free chuckle, but it was light enough. "Oh, Michael. You know I am absolutely hopeless at such things. If it was up to me, Mrs. Brown would wear her new pink satin, I would pick a bouquet from the garden, and we would all walk to church for quick vows before a wedding breakfast at the Tudor Arms. Fast and painless."

Kate smiled. Somehow, hearing Christina speak of wedding plans made that happy day seem all the closer, all the more real. And it made Julian Kirkwood recede into the pale background, where he belonged. "It won't be very different from that, I think. I doubt I will wear the pink gown—it is too grand. A new white muslin might be in order, and a bonnet with a veil. We can have the wedding breakfast here. But it *will* be very quiet, nothing fancy at all. A bouquet from the garden sounds just the thing."

"Can I have a bouquet, too, Mrs. Brown?" Amelia called, not missing a note of her music.

Kate and Michael laughed. "Of course, dearest," Kate answered. "And a new dress. Christina will have something new, as well."

"I don't need a new gown," Christina protested. "I can wear this one."

"No, no," Kate said. "It won't be a splashy London affair, but we *can* all have new clothes. Yes, Michael?"

He kissed her cheek. "You, darling, can have anything you want. Even—"

His words were interrupted by a sudden forking flash of lightning, spreading blue violet light across the infinite blackness of the sky. It was closely trailed by a clap of thunder, echoing loudly through the drawing room. Amelia's song faltered, and she stared toward the window with wide, frightened eyes.

"Another storm," Christina said softly.

"I don't like storms such as this!" Amelia whimpered. She slid down from the piano bench and ran over to throw her arms around Kate's waist, hiding her little face in Kate's blue silk skirt.

Kate did not like storms, either. Not one jot. They reminded her painfully of the day she lost her mother—the thunder and lightning, the driving fall of rain, the creak of timbers and glass. The first drops of water hit the window glass, leaden and cold, as she drew Amelia close. "It is all right, *cara*. Thorn Hill has withstood hundreds of such storms during its lifetime, and we are safe in its walls."

"Come over to the fire, Amelia," Christina said, holding out her hand to her niece. "I will tell you a story that will make you forget about the rain."

Amelia glanced up with a sniffle. "A story about plants?"

"Of course," Christina answered. "I don't know any other kind."

Amelia nodded and allowed herself to be led away to the warmth of the fireside. Their voices rose and fell in gentle unison as Christina began a tale of some intrepid plant hunter in India, and the sound was sweeter to Kate's ears than any music in a London theater could ever be. Kate stayed by the window, Michael's arm about her shoulders, watching the rain lash futilely at the glass.

Yes, they were safe here. Safe together. But for how long?

Somehow the heavy atmosphere in the night sky

echoed the heaviness in her heart. Wedding plans and Amelia's music had lightened it for a moment, but still it was there. Waiting. *Knowing*. Would she ever be free of it again?

Another flash of lightning lit the black sky, and for an instant Kate saw something in the tangled underbrush of the garden. A face, a form, lurking there, just outside their refuge.

She gasped, but when the lightning cleared and she peered outside once more, there was nothing. Just the trees and the flowers.

"Kate?" Michael asked in concern, his arm tightening around her shoulders and drawing her closer. "Is something amiss?"

"No," she whispered. "No. I just hate storms."

It was very late, the household all tucked up in silent sleep as the night's storm raged around them. It was a fierce one; the world outside the windows was turned to all hazy edges and blurry shapes. Thunder cracked and howled overhead.

Only Christina was awake in the midst of it. She huddled over the desk in her chamber, trying to organize her scribbled notes by the light of the candles. She was used to Yorkshire storms, even reveled in the passion and anger of them. The rains sometimes washed free interesting plant specimens that would ordinarily be hard to find. She was also used to being the only person awake so late at night. The quiet of the house was perfect for concentrating on her experiments and specimens without fear of interruption.

Yet tonight she could not concentrate on the fresh valerium she had gathered that afternoon. She could not even read one of the volumes she brought back from London. She could think only of Julian Kirkwood, and the way he bent his handsome head and kissed her wrist.

Christina had been kissed on the hand before, of course. She had even once been kissed on the cheek, by Andrew Price as they studied an example of yellow pimpernel along a pathway. That kiss had been quick, fleeting, and Mr. Price had immediately dashed away, his face all red. Julian Kirkwood had not run away, and Christina doubted he had ever blushed in all his wicked life. No, this had been like a kiss in one of Mrs. Brown's volumes of poetry. His lips caressed her skin, moving softly, gently, enticingly over her racing pulse.

For an instant, she felt a rush of shame at her roughened skin, the dirt around her nails. Then, anger at that shame, and—and something she could not define. Something warm and quick, something she had never felt before.

And *she* was the one who ran away.

Christina tossed down her pencil and pushed herself back from the desk in a fit of irritation. This was a man who caused Mrs. Brown great pain, who followed her across England, across the Continent, from Italy for all Christina knew, to torment her. Christina hated him for disrupting her family, her comfortable world at Thorn Hill. He had *no right* to be here! So how could she respond to his kiss with anything other than disgust?

But it had not been disgust she felt at his touch.

Christina sighed. If she was a Valkyrie in truth, she would find a spear and a chariot and chase him out of Yorkshire altogether. As it was, she had no idea what to do. Human nature was so very unpredictable, and annoying. Plants—that was where true happiness lay.

She stood up and moved out of the circle of candle-light to go to the window. The storm had not abated, and rain poured down, blown sideways by the force of the wind. Christina drew her shawl closer around her shoulders, and shivered as she peered down at the battered garden.

A quick flash of purple lightning illuminated the pathways and flower beds, and that was when she saw it. A quick, furtive movement behind one of the marble statues. It could almost have been a shadow of the statue, but then it slid away, along the path toward the house.

Christina shielded the glare of the window glass with her hands, leaning forward to peer closer. What could it be? A tree, bending in the wind? One of the Yorkshire haunts, wandering free in the storm? She had grown up hearing such tales of phantoms and water sprites. Yet she had never really been able to credit them. Only on nights like this one, eerie, otherworldly, surrounded by the shriek of wind and rain, could she almost believe them.

Goose bumps prickled her skin as she stared down at the garden, half fearing she would find a wild, hairy elemental spirit there. What she *did* see was even worse.

"The bloody bastard," she whispered, in a fit of deepest profanity that would have horrified her mother. She could think of no other words to describe what she was feeling. Describe *that man*.

It was Julian Kirkwood, skulking around Thorn Hill, creeping about like a vampire in that black coat of his. As another split-second flash of lightning lit the air, she saw him clearly if fleetingly. His black hair was plastered to his head by the rain, the collar of his coat drawn up over his neck and jaw. Yes, it was him.

Christina could not even begin to fathom what had driven him here on such an ungodly night. Not even love seemed sufficient excuse for such lunatic behavior. But then, she thought, she had never been a *romantic* creature at all. Perhaps if she were, if she had read more poetry instead of botanical tracts, she could understand such ridiculously Byronic behavior.

As it was, she understood only one thing. Julian Kirkwood upset Mrs. Brown, made her cry, and made Michael threaten duels. He upset their precious peace at Thorn Hill, and interrupted Christina's work. Now it looked as if he was about to break into her house, while her family slept peacefully just down the corridor, and cause who knew what kind of havoc. That, Christina would not allow.

She had not yet undressed for the night, and it took only a moment for her to put on her boots and find a cloak to cover her muslin gown. The house was still silent as she slipped from her room, the slumbering quiet broken only by the crashes of thunder, the creaks and wheezes of the old walls and floors. Christina needed no light except the lightning flickering across the windows; she knew these stairs, these doors, like her own hand—she had slipped out of them at night so many times. The house was a part of her, and she would let no one invade it. If she had her way, Julian Kirkwood would leave with no one the wiser that he had ever been here at all.

In the library, displayed with Michael's other Italian treasures, was a dagger from Renaissance Florence. Gorgeous, with its jeweled handle and the etched steel along its blade; lethal in its sharpness. Christina snatched it from its case, tucking it in the pocket of her cloak before pushing open one of the tall windows leading to the garden. She felt the dagger's weight there, hefty and comforting as it settled among the dried herbs and dirt.

For a second, the force of the rain blinded her, drove her back a step. She had been out in the Yorkshire rain many times, of course—the wet soil so often yielded up hidden treasures. Yet never had she braved a rain quite like this. It was almost a living being, coldly malevolent, driving like a primeval force. Its sharp droplets stung as they hit her skin.

Christina drew her hood closer about her face, struggling forward against the storm and against her own fear. She *had* to go on—her only other choice was to turn back, to run to Michael and tell him what she saw. Then Michael would duel with Julian Kirkwood, might even be killed. The thought of that was far worse than any rain could be.

She ducked her head and lurched on, leaning into the wind as she made her way around the side of the house where she had last glimpsed Kirkwood. Her gown and boots were quickly soaked to the core, and her cloak billowed behind her, caught by the mischievous hands of the wind.

"I am a Valkyrie," she muttered. "I control nature, I am—" Something hard and cold, freezing, deathly cold, caught her arm, and Christina screamed. It was the ghost of Robert de Botteby, come to drag her away! Just as her nursemaid had always said it would!

Her hood fell back with the force of her screams, even as the cries themselves melted away in the thunder. Christina yanked back on her arm, but it was held fast, and her vision was beaded with rain and nightmares.

A face swam into her view, peering closely down at her. It did not have the hideously deformed visage of de Botteby, or the canine fangs of the gytrash. It was the diabolically handsome face of Julian Kirkwood, lean and determined, death-pale in the lightning.

Christina's screams strangled in her throat. She scrambled for her pocket, for the dagger, but his other hand closed on her arm like an iron manacle. He dragged her close to him, so close she could feel the fever heat of him despite the chill that froze her very bones.

"Lady Christina," he said, his deep voice one with the storm. "So kind of you to meet me halfway like this. You are the final piece of my plan."

Chapter Twenty-seven

"*N*o!" Kate sat straight up in bed, disoriented and frightened. What woke her? Something in her chamber? The storm, still raging outside the window?

She rubbed at her aching eyes, taking deep, cleansing breaths. It must have been a dream, a bad dream brought on by the thunder and rain. She hated storms so very much, it was a wonder she had fallen asleep at all. This was not like *that* storm, she told herself. She was not adrift at sea, but safe in a warm, solid house.

She tried to remember her dream, yet it was gone. Only a vague, hazy sense of colors and emotions remained, floating like airy wisps at the edges of her mind. Even that was vanishing quickly as she became more awake. "It was only a dream," she whispered. "Brought on by the thunder."

Her heartbeat slowed in her breast, and she was finally able to open her eyes and see that the room around her was unchanged. Her trunk sat by the wardrobe, half unpacked from the London journey. Her books were stacked on the bedside table, her cloak draped over a chair like some lurking beast. But the fire had died down to mere embers, and there was a damp chill in the air.

Kate rubbed at her arms through the thin batiste of her night rail. The wind sounded like screams outside, human, female screams. It made Kate want to cry out again, to howl at the storm clouds until they vanished.

Perhaps that was what had awakened her, the cries of the spirits.

And if *she* was awake, surely Amelia was, too, and twice as scared. Kate slid out of bed and reached for her dressing gown. She would go look in on the child, and perhaps they could huddle together under the blankets until the rain ceased! Or at least Kate could forget her own haunts in comforting Amelia.

But Amelia still slept, her pink-and-white chamber softly illuminated by the glow of one candle in a night-light. She had kicked away the bedclothes, though, and held her poor doll by a long strand of silk hair. Kate tucked the blankets around her again, and gently kissed her down-soft brow. Amelia murmured and turned her head on her pillow, slumbering on.

As Kate straightened from the bed, she glimpsed the portrait of Caroline Lindley that now hung over Amelia's fireplace. Caroline's blue eyes were as clear and lovely as ever, yet Kate almost fancied, on this haunted night, that she wore a concerned air.

"You are always watching over her, aren't you?" Kate whispered.

Christina, a voice said in her mind, softly but insistently. *Where is Christina?*

Kate frowned. Yes—she *should* check on Christina before she went back to bed. Christina liked to think, to act, as if she were strong, untouchable, and unafraid of anything. Especially something as prosaic as a rainstorm. Yet Kate knew very well that the facade of solitary indifference was just that—a facade. Christina saw things most young girls missed, and she was affected by them far more deeply than she wanted to admit. Things like hypocrisy and truth and anger—and the insanity that could hide behind a beautiful face.

No. It wouldn't hurt to look in on her now.

Kate softly closed Amelia's door behind her and padded down the corridor to Christina's room. She raised her hand to knock, but the thick wood gave way under her light touch, easing open to reveal an empty space. A candle burned at the writing desk; its surface was still littered with open books, sketches of plants, and sheets of paper covered with Christina's neat handwriting. The bed was turned down, a night-dress laid out in snowy folds on the counterpane.

Christina herself was nowhere to be seen. Kate moved slowly into the center of the room, and time seemed to slow to a horrible crawl. The hair at the back of her neck prickled, and she reached up to touch it. Her own fingers were icy cold.

"Don't be silly," she told herself. "Christina could be in the library, fetching another book. That's all. You have simply been reading far too much poetry lately."

And this night would be enough to give anyone the chills, to make him imagine he saw haunts where there was only moonlight and shadows. Somehow, though, Kate knew that was not the case.

She sped around the room, searching for any sort of clue as to where Christina might have gone. Obviously, she had not been to bed, and her cloak was missing. Would the girl really have been foolish enough to go out in such weather, perhaps to seek out some botanical specimen? Christina was a sensible girl, yet where her plants were concerned anything was possible.

Kate paused by the window and bent down to pick up a green satin hair ribbon that had fallen to the floor. As she stood up, a fork of lightning split the sky and she gleaned a flash of movement at the edge of the garden. It was too large to be a shadow, too far away for one of the garden's manicured trees. She snatched the candle from the desk and held it up, casting some illumination through the thick, wavy glass.

Another spark of lightning gave her a glimpse of a pale dress, a banner of long hair in the wind—and a black figure bearing the girl away. The wind—or was it a true scream?—rose outside.

"Christina!" Kate cried. It had to be Christina and Julian. He was a demon indeed, an evil creature that

no storm could touch, and he would haunt her forever.
Now, somehow, he had spirited Christina away from
her home into the storm. For what? Revenge? Hatred? To entice Kate to follow him?

If it was *that*, then his despicable action worked. For
Kate would follow him into the mouth of hell itself to
get the girl back. But she would not do it alone. She
had not the strength to stop Julian and his pistol.

Kate slammed the candle back down on the desk
and ran from the room, pausing only to find her own
cloak and boots before dashing to Michael's chamber.

He had obviously slept as fitfully as she this night.
The bedclothes were tossed to the floor, and he
sprawled across the mattress in only his trousers. His
bare chest rose and fell with the slow rhythms of slumber, and his hair fell over his brow in tousled, sun-
kissed commas. For the moment, his dreams were
quiet ones, and in sleep he looked young and carefree
and serene.

I am sorry, Michael, amore, Kate thought remorsefully. Sorry she had to pull him from his peaceful unconsciousness, sorry she had brought this trouble to
his house.

"Michael!" she said loudly, throwing herself down
on the edge of the bed and shaking his shoulder until
his eyes blinked open. "Michael, wake up, please!
Something has happened."

He reached up with a deep groan, catching her hand
in his. "Kate. Why do I get the feeling this is not an
amorous visit?"

Kate choked on a hysterical laugh. "Christina is
gone."

"Gone?" His half smile vanished, and he sat up to
reach for his discarded shirt. "Gone to where?"

"I could not sleep, so I went to look in on Christina
and Amelia. Amelia is sleeping soundly, but Christina
was not in her room. Her bed was not slept in, and—
" Kate broke off, swallowing hard against the rush of
cold, nauseating fear as she remembered again the

glimpse of Christina being dragged away by Julian Kirkwood.

"Sh," Michael said soothingly. He rubbed at her back in gentle circles, as if she were as young as Amelia. For an instant, Kate longed to curl into his embrace, into the safety and care and love, but she could not. There was not even that instant to waste. "She is probably just in the library, Kate."

Kate shook her head. "No, no! I fear I saw her outside, being carried away by . . ." Her English deserted her, fear leaving her only with her old Italian, the language of her past. *"Quando sono arrivata era ormai troppo tardi. . . ."*

Michael's clasp tightened on her shoulders, holding her steady. "By what, Kate? I fear my Italian is rusty." His voice held a sharp edge, but none of her own hysteria.

She *couldn't* become hysterical! Not now. She took in a breath, and said, "By Julian Kirkwood. They were outside in the rain, and he was taking her away from the house. He is in the village—Amelia and I saw him when we were there yesterday."

Kate half expected questions, doubts, statements that it must have been all a dream, recriminations that she had not told him about Julian's being in the neighborhood. That she was a wild, poetry-poisoned female. She should have known better, from Michael.

"Blast!" he cursed, the one word a low, swift explosion. He reached for his coat, pulling it on over his half-open shirt. Kate silently took up his boots and handed them to him.

"Where could they have gone?" she said. Her earlier panic was vanished, pushed away by necessity and adrenaline, replaced with a cold calm. There would be time for tears and apologies later, when Christina was safely at home.

"I have no idea, but we *will* find them. They could not have gone far in this storm—and not with my heathen sister kicking and screaming, as she is sure to do." Michael gave her a grim smile. Kate watched as he drew a long, inlaid box from the bottom of the wardrobe and opened it to reveal a pair of perfectly polished dueling pistols. He removed one and secured it, along with a bag of shot, inside his coat.

Kate did not say a word.

"Come, my love," he said. "We have to wake the servants, so they can form a search party and ride out after me. You must stay here and alert—"

"No!" Kate cried, remembering the gun Julian was carrying about. He could already have used it on Christina. "I can't wait here. I'm going with you."

He turned to her with a frown. "Kate, it is dangerous out there, and this Kirkwood is a madman."

"I *am* going. I'm the one who brought this lunacy to Thorn Hill—it's my fault Christina is in danger. I can help you find her, Michael. If you make me stay behind, I will just follow on my own."

He gave her a quick, wry smile, and took up her hand in his to press a kiss to her palm. It was swift, fleeting as a raindrop, but it quieted her heart. Truly, she was not alone in this nightmare. She would never be alone again.

If only Christina was not hurt.

"I know better than to argue with Kate the curst," he said. "We will go together. Stay close to me."

She nodded. "We will find her, Michael. Julian is a strange man, one who lives in his own dreamworld, but surely he would not harm a young girl. Surely."

Michael just turned and left the room, their hands entwined, a pistol in his coat. And Kate found she could not even truly reassure herself.

It was a hellish night.

Michael could not see five feet in front of him for the impenetrable curtain of rain, which drove like tiny needles into his skin. They had managed to ride for a short while, until the uneven ground forced them to leave the horses behind and go forward on foot. Now they walked, the mud and slimy vegetation sucking at their shoes. The wind howled like a living creature around their heads, tearing at their hair and clothes.

The lamp he held aloft on one hand did them less than no good, casting a light over only their own faces. His other hand held tight to Kate's, her fingers as stiff and cold as frozen rose petals in his clasp. He glanced back at her. Her pale face, framed by her sodden hood and beaded with raindrops, stared ahead in fierce determination. Her dark eyes constantly flickered, glancing into the trees and shadows and hillsides around them in a frantic search for any sign of Kirkwood and Christina. Once in a while, she would stop, her posture as tense and alert as a doe, but then she would shake her head and they would move on.

They could not speak—the wind and thunder were too loud. He could only press her hand, trying to send her warmth and courage. And she would squeeze back.

Christina, Christina, he thought. His foolishly brave, brilliant, awkward sister. Where was she in this wild night? Was she afraid—did she call out for help? How had she fallen into Kirkwood's clutches in the first place?

For a second, he saw not the dark night around them, but a sunny, long-ago day at Darcy Hall. Christina was learning to walk on the green summer grass, her tiny face fixed in lines of a vast determination beyond her years. Her light brown curls, soft and downy, glistened in the light, and she held out her chubby arms to keep her balance. She fell, not once but many times, always popping back up immediately to try again. At last, she stumbled five, ten, fifteen steps in a row, collapsing into Michael's arms with a crow of triumph.

"Tina!" he had cried happily, twirling her around. "You are the most brilliant baby ever."

She rested her little head on his shoulder with a happy sigh. Michael had been fifteen when his surprise sister was born, a young man with no time for infants. But from that moment on, she held his heart in her tiny hand, and he was helplessly in love with her baby self.

He had caught her safely on that day when she was learning to walk. He would keep her safe now.

"Are we near the sheepherder's hut?" Kate shouted.

He glanced back at her. "Not far," he shouted back.

"Perhaps we should stop there for a moment and get our bearings. Maybe they have even been there!"

Michael nodded. Kate's face was drawn and miserable in the rain, and they were having no success in their wanderings. Perhaps once they were warmer and reasonably dry, a flash of inspiration would come to them and they would know where to find his sister.

For they had to find her soon. Before it was too late.

"Whatever you are trying to do, it won't work." The girl's voice rang out in the cold, damp air, as clear as condemning church bells.

Julian glanced away from the one window in the miserable hut, back to where Christina Lindley sat in the corner. She did not huddle into herself, or weep pitiably as any ordinary, mortal female would. She perched on a pile of moth-eaten cushions she had found somewhere, legs crossed, back straight as a board, and head held high. She looked like a haughty Persian queen, despite the wild hair that hung dripping over her shoulders in seaweedlike clumps and the sodden cloak covering what appeared to be an evening dress of pale green muslin. Green eyes, as clear and piercing as sea glass, stared at him with unwavering coldness.

If she had in truth been a queen, Julian very much feared his head would be rolling into a basket right about now. And he would deserve it.

What was he trying to do? Prove his deep love for Katerina by kidnapping this child? Lure his Beatrice to his side with violence? Now, as he stared across the bare, dusty room at this fierce Valkyrie, he saw how foolish that was, how cruel. It was as if the clear green of Christina Lindley's eyes formed a mirror, held up to his soul to show it in all its twisted blackness.

But he could do nothing but move forward. Fulfill his plans. He and his Katerina were fated to be together, and this wild night was when that fate would be met. Once and for all. He could not care for this girl. She was merely an instrument.

Christina gave a deep, long-suffering sigh and rolled her gaze up to the low ceiling. "You needn't stare so. It's rude. And you didn't answer me."

Rude? Julian laughed—he couldn't help it, despite the storm-soaked desperation of their circumstances. He had snatched this girl away from her home, dragged her roughly into the cold rain like some hunchbacked, leering villain in fiction. Yet she lectured him about *rudeness*.

It was absurd. A ridiculous denouncement of the dark quagmire his life had become in the last year or more. Or perhaps it had always been like this. And always would be.

Christina's lips pursed in that hard, disapproving spinster's moue she was so good at. "And now you laugh. You must have grown up in a barn somewhere, Sir Julian, raised by pigs and horses, since your manners are so atrocious. Far worse than mine ever were, and *I* had to have a governess to make me fit for polite Society."

"And I now have you, Lady Christina. I vow you are far more a trial than any governess could hope to be." A trial she might be—but the girl was his key to luring Katerina to his side. For that, he could endure any scolding. And then be rid of her. Any way he could.

One of Christina's golden-brown brows arched, and for an instant Julian saw the great beauty this awkward colt would one day be. Her face was a perfect oval, with soaring cheekbones and full, inviting pink lips, not to mention those luminous green eyes. But there was intelligence etched deep in her every glance, a knowingness far beyond her years, and assurance that *she* knew what was best for the world. A bossiness his sister, Charlotte, would envy. One day, she would lead some poor besotted man on a merry dance to hell. Julian would pay his last farthing to see a spectacle like that.

But he couldn't, because by the time she married he would have been long since transported for kidnapping. And it would serve him right, too. He had a vision of himself chained to the deck of a Botany Bay–bound ship, Christina on shore, laughing at him as her slender figure receded farther and farther away.

That would not happen, though. Soon, his Katerina would come to him, and he would have everything he had ever dreamed of. Ever worked for.

"*I* did not choose to come here with you, as you may or may not recall, Sir Julian," she said tartly. "So if I am a trial to you, you have only yourself to blame. The least you can do is answer me when I talk to you."

Julian ran his hands through his wet hair, pushing the strands back from his face. "Do you always chatter on so much?"

"Chatter? I wasn't aware I was doing so. But no, I don't *talk* a great deal. I don't have time for it, with my work and studies."

Thunder crashed again outside the window, one clap piling on top of another until all the world seemed to collapse in a great cacophony around them. "What are your studies, Lady Christina? Needlework? The harp?"

She gave a most unladylike snort. "Needlework! I study botany. Plants. The natural world."

Julian had to suppress a snort of his own. He should have guessed—a budding bluestocking. That would explain the weeds she had been gathering.

Her eyes narrowed, fixing on him like the tip of a sword. "You need not scoff. Perhaps if *you* had an interest outside of yourself, an area of study that could be of benefit to the world, you wouldn't have to go around kidnapping people. You would be able to see when someone doesn't love you."

A flash of temper moved through Julian, as hot and quick as the lightning outside. This ridiculous child was right. Katerina did not love him—she never had, and all the force of his passion could not make her. The dreams he had built so elaborately around her in Venice, the life he planned for the two of them, even his great joy at finding her alive, none of it mattered. It had been just that—a dream, constructed only of his own desires. And everyone could see it, even this girl. Everyone except him, and that was more infuriating than anything he had ever known.

They laughed at him for his folly, surely. Even worse, they pitied him, as Christina did now. Her face softened as she watched him, her lips turning down at the corners.

But it did not matter. He was set on his course now—they all were. Fate had brought them here, and he could not fight against it. He could only fulfill it. Even to the last drop of blood—his, or this girl's. Or his Beatrice's.

"I am sorry," Christina said quietly. "I don't know what happened between you and Mrs. Brown in Italy, but she is marrying my brother now. They love each other very much. I can see why you would care so much for her. She is like no one else I have ever met. Yet surely you can see—"

"What do you know about it?" Julian burst out. He crossed the cramped space of their shelter in only a few long strides and grabbed her arm, pulling her to her feet. Her eyes widened, but she still maintained her perfect dignity, her disapproving-governess expression. Somehow, her very stillness inflamed his temper even more, and he dragged her close to him, drawing her up, flesh to flesh, until only the toes of her boots were still on the dirt floor. She stiffened and tried to twist away, but he held her fast.

"What can you know about love, about passion?" he growled. "You are just a foolish child!"

"Foolish I may be, but I am *not* a child," she answered. She gave up her writhing struggles and leaned against him, her long, callused hands pressed to his shoulders. And he felt the truth of her statement in her body. She was *not* a child, but a woman, a woman with ripe, soft breasts and a slim waist, supple under his hands. "It is true that I have not met a man I could love, but I *do* know what love is."

"Oh, do you now, Brunhilde?" Julian murmured. He held Christina against him, clinging to her warm body as if it were the only lifeline in a drowning world. "Perhaps you could enlighten us ignorant mortals."

"It isn't selfish, or cruel," she insisted. "It doesn't obsess. It wants only the happiness of the loved one—even if that means another person. That is true love."

"I love Katerina," he said. He must. He had dreamed of her for so long. The memory of her was all that kept him alive in that cold, white convent hospital. She was all he had ever wanted, and the loss of her grieved and infuriated him. Made him want to hurt her, as he had been hurt; to make her hear him, as he had never been heard. No matter what it took, life or death.

So he had snatched away something she cared about, a girl she obviously looked on as a sister or daughter; he had thought it would make her listen to him at last. Instead, he had destroyed the last tiny corner of his soul that was pure. He was lost forever.

Christina stared up at him steadily, and reached out to touch his cheek with the gentlest, softest caress. Her fingers were rough from digging in the dirt, not manicured and smooth like those of all his mistresses, but it felt like an angel's wings touched his skin.

"Do you love her, Julian? Truly love her?" she whispered. "Then take me back to Thorn Hill now, and leave Yorkshire forever. Let her marry my brother in peace. She doesn't belong to you—she never did."

Julian drew Christina even closer to him until there was nothing between them. Nothing but the un-crossable chasm of the past. He stared down at her, his fierce Valkyrie, his seaweed-haired mermaid. "I can't," he groaned. "She's all I have. We are meant to be together."

Christina nodded sadly, her fingers trailing down his cheek and jaw. "Then you are lost."

"As you are with me." Still in that haze of storm and white-hot temper, Julian covered Christina's mouth with a bruising, wild kiss. Her lips were wide and mobile, chapped from her long hours outdoors, and he could taste the intoxicating rain and innocence. She stood in his arms, stiff and still, her hands pressing against his chest, but he could not let her go. When had he ever been so innocent as her, so certain in beliefs about the world around them? Never—not even in farthest childhood.

She parted her lips on a low moan, and he took the split-second advantage, touching the tip of his tongue to hers. Even there she tasted of the rain, of green, fresh things and a belief in unselfish love.

For a moment, she melted against him, returning the kiss with a sudden sweet fervor. Julian groaned, and slid his hands beneath her cloak, over her strong, supple back, seeking the soft weight of her breast. . . .

He found instead a sharp, stinging pain in his shoulder. His arms fell away from her and he stumbled back a step. She stared at him, wide-eyed, her face white. She looked deeply shocked. In her hand, she clasped the jeweled handle of an antique dagger, scarlet at its very tip.

Scarlet with his blood.

Julian glanced down to see that she had nicked him in the fleshy part of his shoulder, blood only just beginning to seep through his coat. It was hardly a life-threatening wound, but it stung like the very devil, and his arm was quickly growing numb. He leaned back against the wall, pressing his hand hard to the scratch.

"Touché, Brunhilde," he gasped. "Usually when a lady objects to a man's attentions she simply calls him a cad and walks away."

"I hardly had that option," she whispered hoarsely.

"Considering I'm your prisoner. You're fortunate I didn't knee you in a sensitive area instead. I've heard *that* is very painful indeed."

"Fortunate that you stabbed me instead?"

"It's a mere scrape. Bind it up with feverfew and clean linens, and you'll be well in a trice."

Despite her brave words, her brave Valkyriesque wielding of weapons, her voice was faint, her face growing whiter by the second. She swayed and shook as if she were still out in the storm. Julian feared she would be sick, but instead she dropped her dagger and fled into the night, leaving the door open to the blowing wind and rain. He saw that she veered not toward her home, but in the opposite direction into the night.

"Blast," he muttered. His arm ached like hellfire. He should collapse where he stood, waiting for Michael Lindley's retribution to fall onto him—and letting the little heathen run where she would. After all, she had *stabbed* him! This little kidnapping caper was not going as well as he had hoped. Now it was over, ending where it had always been destined to—in blood and pain.

Yes, he should just let the Valkyrie do what she would. She was obviously quite capable of taking care of herself. But he could still taste the sweetness of her on his lips, feel her lithe, delicate strength against his body. It was his fault she was out in the storm now, her face white and confused. He had to make sure she was all right, that she made it safely back to her home.

From being her kidnapper, her tormentor, he now had to be her guardian. *Blast* was right. This was a role he was completely unsuited to.

Julian swiftly removed his coat and shirt, biting back curses at the new wave of painful protests from his shoulder. He ripped up the linen of the shirt into bandages, using them to bind up his shoulder before easing back into his coat. The tight pressure would stop the trickle of blood and hold his arm still until it could be properly seen to.

Before he dashed out into the night after Christina,

he took out the sapphire brooch and placed it carefully on the cushion where she had sat like a Persian queen. It twinkled there in all its sky-blue glory, mocking him for the folly that had brought him here. His own fated folly.

He scooped up the discarded dagger and staggered out into the storm. He had to finish this. To complete the circle of his fate.

Christina ran blindly through the rain, not knowing where she was going or where she could possibly be. She knew only that she had to run, to get away from the sheepherder's hut—and from Julian Kirkwood.

He had kissed her. Her first real kiss, born not of tenderness and affection but of anger and madness. And she had stabbed him.

She had not consciously decided to commit violence in that moment. All of her emotions were bound up in a swirl of fury and confusion, in the first flickerings of a crazy passion, and the dagger was in her hand before she realized what its heft and strength meant. She had to be away from him, away from the emotions and fears and needs that were ripping her comfortable world to shreds.

Now she *was* away from him, but her emotions still blazed away, hotter and more furious than ever, threatening to consume her. She couldn't outrun them; the rain, cold and driving, couldn't even drown them. Her lungs felt as if they would burst, and she could not cease shaking.

Christina stumbled over a stone and fell, landing hard in the viscous mud. It was chilly and thick, but it was *real*. The earth was something she knew and understood, and she lay there, sobbing out all her heartache in its indifferent welcome.

Slowly, her tears ceased to drum in her ears, and she heard the rain, the thunder, the very faint sound of someone calling her name. And something else. The rush and roar of another familiar friend.

Semerwater. Rising and roiling against its banks,

straining to break free—just as Christina herself was. It was very near, just over the rise of that hill. Calling to her.

She drew herself to her feet, stumbling toward the cursed waves.

The sheepherder's cottage was deserted.

Kate had truly expected nothing else; it was a wild hope that Julian might have brought Christina here. But her heart sank anyway to find the room deserted, to find no trace of them. She stood just inside the doorway, staring around the desolate, dusty space in silence. For a moment, her ears rang to not have the wind shrieking in them, to not have rain pounding on her head.

Her memory had transformed this place into a bower, a warm haven. It was, after all, the room where she had given herself to Michael, had found love and joy beyond all imagining. Tonight, she had dared to hope she would find answers and solace here.

Yet, in reality, it was a flimsy, dirty place. The floor was made of earth, a musty smell in the air that spoke of how long it had been since a fire was lit in the small grate. The only sign of life was a pile of cushions and blankets in the corner.

Behind her, Michael shook his head, sending droplets of rain into the darkness. "You should take off your cloak, Kate," he said gently. "Wrap up in one of those blankets in the corner."

Kate nodded numbly and tried to answer, but her voice was gone. As she turned toward the dim corner, Michael went to the window and stared out at the night they had just left. "Where could she be?" he muttered, his tone thick with anger and anxiety. Kate's heart ached, for she knew those emotions all too well. She wanted to shout them out into the thunder, to rail against the madness that had brought them to this moment.

But she could not, not until they found Christina. All she could do right now was keep moving, come what may. That was the only way she could help Christina.

She would scream afterward.

Kate reached down to take up one of the old blankets in the pile. As she dislodged the cushion on top, a heavy object fell off, landing against her boot. She bent down to search for it with her fingertips.

"I found a candle here on the windowsill, but there's no way to light it," Michael muttered. Their lamp had gone out long ago, leaving them to stumble around by the glow of lightning.

Like the flash that lit up the room now. Kate saw a sparkle on the floor, an enticing glitter. *Her brooch.* The sapphire she had given Julian Kirkwood in a vain attempt to convince him to leave.

She snatched it up, balancing the jewel on her palm. "Michael. They were here."

He swung toward her. "What?"

That was when they heard it. A scream of utter despair.

Chapter Twenty-eight

Christina stared out over the Semerwater. The scene was as different from their picnic there as London was from the moon. Its usually placid, glassy surface roiled and pitched in white-tipped waves, a wild mélange of green and brown that threatened to engulf all in its path. The tree they had sat beneath on that sunny day was half submerged, and the waters had become a wild, living monster.

She could well believe there was a drowned city under there, its ghosts screaming for revenge, for retribution for their sad fates.

Christina balanced on a fallen log several feet from the reach of the swelling waves, below a sharp slope. She was unable to turn away from the scene. The wind seemed slower than before, merely tugging at her cloak rather than tearing at it. Her feet were numb in her ruined boots, keeping her rooted to the wet, rotten wood of the log.

Her tears had ceased, her racing heart slowed to a thud. She could see clearly now, see the water and sky as a black inevitability. A reflection of the darkness and selfishness of her own heart. She could not run anymore.

"Christina!" Julian shouted behind her. "Come down from there. You need to go home, to get out of this storm."

She climbed down from the log and walked a few more steps toward the water before turning to gaze at him. How beautiful he was, like no other man she had ever seen, or even dreamed of. Deceptively beautiful, like the brilliant, alluring petals of the *Amorphophallus titanum*, which drew its prey close with its fragrant loveliness and then devoured it.

"Why did you come here?" she shouted. "Everything was perfect before! We were happy. Why did you ruin it?"

He moved closer to her, his uninjured arm stretched out. She saw that he wore no shirt, that his shoulder was bound up in the white linen beneath his black coat. *He will catch a cold,* she thought, in a flash of complete irrelevance.

"I'm sorry, Christina," he called. He was obviously feeling weak, his strength swiftly waning. Only the need to get her inside, out of the rain, kept him upright. "Truly. Please, come with me now. Come home."

"How can I trust you?" she argued. She would sooner break off her own arm than take that hand. It would only snatch her away again, and she would be lost forever.

"I don't know," he answered hoarsely. "But you must. We only have each other now."

Christina stared at him, tempted—so very tempted—to take that hand. She swayed toward him, fingers outstretched. Then she heard her name, shouted above the storm.

"Christina!" Michael called.

She quickly half turned, glimpsing her brother through the rain, his horrified face. But it was too late. The momentum of her sudden movement overcame her, knocking her off-balance, shifting the center of her body to her feet. Her fingertips barely clasped Julian's hand, and she fell backward in a tumble of pain and screams, her body falling, rolling down the sharp slope inexorably toward the waiting water.

Rather than let her go, even to save his own life, Julian's hand tightened like an iron band on hers, and they fell together in a tangle of limbs.

Christina struck a stone on her left side, and she

heard a sickening snap from her forearm. Pain engulfed her, enfolding her like a white-hot blanket, and she screamed, struggling against the tugging darkness. It was all over—she knew it—she was going to die at fifteen years old, never to see her brother, her niece, her mother, Mrs. Brown again. The pain and terror were horrible, yet underneath there was a strange, cool calm. A peace.

She clung to Julian's hand as they tumbled into the freezing water, and the nothingness closed over them both.

Someone screamed out, a wild cacophony that went on and on with no end, no blessed fall of silence. Only slowly did Kate realize it was *her* scream.

She smothered her mouth with her hand, pressing tightly to her lips as she stared at the spot where Christina and Julian had stood only seconds before. Their fall seemed to happen in a bizarre, slowed-down time, a blur of white and black against the night sky as they tumbled out of sight, into the water. The waves washed over Christina's head as the Semerwater rose to claim her.

Grief and wild pain stabbed into Kate's heart, and she became an incoherent, barbaric thing, howling and scrambling down the slope after Christina. When she fell, she crawled on. The water would not claim someone else she loved! Not this time. Not unless it took her, too.

"Christina!" she cried, the wind ripping her words away. For one flashing instant, she saw Christina's head bob above the surface of the lake.

Michael overtook Kate on the downward slope, reaching down to clasp her hand and pull her up out of the mud but not pausing in his dash toward the water. None of her own panic was reflected in his face. He was grimly determined, his jaw set, eyes cold as the rain beaded on his lashes.

"Stay here, Kate!" he shouted, clasping her shoulders to make sure she was steady on her feet. "No matter what happens, stay here."

"Why? What are you doing?"

He didn't answer, just pulled off his boots and coat, pushing them into her arms. Then he whirled about, and, in a split second, dived into the water, swimming hard toward his sister.

Kate sank slowly to her knees, cradling his clothes against her. She stared after him as his sleek head appeared and disappeared in the waves. Christina had vanished.

It was obvious that Michael was an expert swimmer, but how long would his leg hold out? How long would it be until their limbs froze in the water and they sank to the lost city below? Kate longed to turn away, to pray—to go after them, join them in whatever befell them. But all she could do was kneel there in the mud, watching, waiting, getting colder and colder.

This was what she had feared since the day she realized she loved Michael. Her past had come into the present to drag them all down. For a few golden days, she dared to think she could be happy, that she could make Michael happy, too. That she could live as an ordinary woman, with a home and family.

That had been nothing but deadly folly.

"I'm sorry," she whispered. "Don't punish them for sins that were entirely my own. Save them—and I'll go away from here. I'll do anything."

A fork of lightning struck nearby, singeing branches and sending a sizzling frisson all the way into the ground. The air was hot with the sharp scent of sulfur, and Kate was blinded by the glow. She squeezed her eyes shut.

When she opened them, it was to a miraculous sight. Michael stumbled out of the water, Christina limp in his arms. Her head lolled against her brother's shoulder, her hair trailing like mud-streaked serpents, her left arm bent at an alarming angle. Her cloak was gone, and she wore only a soaked muslin gown, but her chest moved erratically with the effort to breathe.

Michael limped toward Kate as she scrambled to her feet and raced over to throw her arms around them both. "She's alive!"

"Barely," Michael answered roughly. "Her arm is broken. We have to get her back to Thorn Hill, and you, too. You will catch the ague."

Kate could not bring herself to care. She draped Michael's coat over his shoulders, and hastily ripped off the hem of her wet night rail to bind up Christina's arm. "Come on. The search party can't be far behind us."

Michael hurried up the slope. Kate made a move to follow, but paused to glance over her shoulder at the lake. It had burst beyond all boundaries and was rising fast now—and there was no sign of anyone else in the unforgiving water. She stared out, peering through the sheets of cold rain, the blackness of the night.

She half turned, reaching for Michael and Christina—and froze when a shout washed over them, colder and thicker than the rain could ever be. She spun back around, her wet hair clinging to her face, and saw a sight straight from her most haunted nightmares.

Julian Kirkwood stood on the banks of the lake, lit by the glow of lightning like a pagan god of the sea and sky and vengeance. He shouted after them, one arm raised, the other dark with a scarlet stain along a wet white sleeve. "Katerina!" he called. "This isn't finished. I came here for *you*."

This had to be a dream, part of this terrible nightmare. But still he seemed so real, sounded so . . . Kate fell back a step, stumbling in the mud. "Michael!" she gasped. Then, louder, "Michael!"

"Kate, we must—" Michael said hoarsely, but then he turned and saw what she did, the figure on the overflowing bank. The flash of silver on a raised pistol. Michael went very still, then slowly, so slowly, lowered

Christina to her feet, balancing her against his shoulder. "Kate. Come and hold Christina."

A terror unlike any Kate had ever known engulfed her, colder than any floodwaters. Never had she seen such steely resolve in her love's eyes, never felt such—she did not even know what she felt. A hot confusion swept over her wet skin.

"Michael, no! We must not go near him," she pleaded, even as she took Christina's limp weight against her own shoulder. "We need to go home. He can't hurt us now—he bleeds!"

"Kate, my curst Kate," Michael said gently. He reached out and softly touched her cheek, for only an instant. "He says it is not finished. Well, I will finish it for him. If you can, take Tina and head for the path. I will follow."

He drew his own gun from inside the coat he had discarded before he'd dived into the lake, and turned away from her, walking away into the storm as calmly as if he strolled the gardens on a summer's day. As if he did intend to finish this, all of this that had begun on a long-ago day in Venice, one way or the other.

Kate longed to run after him, to stop him, hold him to her, but she could not. She could only stand there, frozen, her arms around Christina. The girl moaned softly, and Kate held her, murmuring gentle words.

Finish it, she thought. *Finish it.* As she could not.

"Katerina," Julian shouted, even as Michael came nearer to him, even as their guns leveled at each other in the lightning. "I loved you truly. I would have done anything for you! We were meant to be together, to love each other forever. How could you have let that go? How could you have driven me to this?" He swayed in the wind like a leaf, the arm that held the pistol aloft shaking. "I never wanted to hurt that girl, but I would have for you."

"Shut up, you bloody bastard!" Michael shouted, still with that strange calm in his voice. Kate felt tears trickle down her cheeks, mingling with the cold rain until she did not know where one ended and the other began. She clung to Christina, her gaze fastened to the two men, unable to look away. "You have hurt my family for the last time."

Julian turned to Michael, as if in a blur of slow movement, his own gun extended. For a moment, it wavered there. Then it fell away, into the water. "Yes, squire," he said. "I have."

Then Julian turned and followed the trajectory of his pistol, down, down, into the embracing waves, and he was gone. Michael stood there for a long moment, his gun poised as if to fire after the vanished body, before he lowered it, still staring into the Semerwater. The Semerwater, which swallowed all in the end.

Kate leaned her cheek against Christina's sodden hair and wept. It was finished.

Chapter Twenty-nine

"Mr. Lindley?"

"Yes?" Michael leaped up from his chair by the library fire to face the doctor, who stood in the doorway. It was seven in the morning, past time for the sun to appear, but it was still dark and dreary outside the windows of Thorn Hill. The storm had slowed to a mere rainfall, yet its effects still haunted his home and would for a long time to come.

Michael had scarcely known his own name by the time they'd stumbled into the foyer, his sister borne on a makeshift litter and Kate, who had fainted on the road, carried in Michael's arms. He was crazed by the cold and the grief, the wild fear, the bloodlust that had overtaken him when he saw Julian Kirkwood poised on the banks of the Semerwater, gun in hand. It took the combined efforts of the butler, the housekeeper Mrs. Jenkins, all the footmen, and most of the maids to persuade him to let go of Kate's cold hand, to let them carry the women upstairs and tuck them into their warm beds.

It had taken even longer for them to convince him to change his wet, filthy clothes and take a glass of bracing warm brandy by the fire. Safely out of the way as they scurried hither and yon, bearing blankets and pitchers of hot water up the stairs, escorting the doctor immediately to the chambers when he arrived.

Michael knew very well he could be only a nuisance to the doctor and the servants if he insisted on helping them, on being there in the middle of the nursing chaos. He had no medical training beyond bandaging superficial cuts in the fields, and he felt so wildly frantic with fear he could only clutch at his love and his sister and shout at the heavens for their recovery.

No—it was better for everyone if he stayed in the library. But his heart ached for any scrap of news.

He stared into the red gold, shifting flames leaping in the grate, yet all he could see was Christina when he grabbed her body in the water. White and stiff as a naiad, she floated in his arms like someone already lost. Her green eyes opened as they surfaced, but she did not see him. She just gazed up into the night, and whispered, "Julian."

And then Kate fainted at his feet on the long trek home, her lush mouth a thin grimace of pain. She had been beyond brave all night, through all the long nightmare, until the weight of it crushed her.

He was thankful that Amelia still slept tonight, watched over by her nursemaid. It was their only blessing.

Julian, he heard Christina whisper again. Julian Kirkwood—the man who had brought them all to this dark nadir. There was no sign of the man's body in the lake or along the shore; surely he was dead. No one could survive such a deluge. The force of his own evil actions killed him, saving Michael the trouble, and the pleasure, in the end.

He still itched to pull that trigger, to be the one who sent the man to hell. It was never to be.

But if Kate or Christina died, Michael would follow the man into hell itself to take his revenge.

If they died—they could not. They were young, vibrant, their lives full of promise ahead of them. He and Kate had a future together, a family to raise, nights of glorious passion to share. Christina had her studies to pursue, important work waiting for her.

They could not die. He would not let them.

When the doctor appeared at last in the library doorway, it was like a longed-for visitation, a tiny glimpse of hope. Michael jumped up from his chair, his gaze searching the man's face carefully for any hint in his expression of the women's fate. Dr. Burnside did not look grim, yet he did not seem overjoyed, either. Rather, he looked much as Michael himself felt—drawn, exhausted, worried, hopeful.

"How are they, Dr. Burnside?" Michael asked roughly.

"It is too soon to tell. I have set Lady Christina's arm and tended to her cuts and bruises. If the break heals correctly, she should be fine, given time and rest. She is a fortunate young lady indeed."

"And Kate—Mrs. Brown?"

A flicker of uncertainty crossed the doctor's face, and he turned away to fuss with his case. "I'm afraid Mrs. Brown has developed a fever. I have bled her, and left a tincture of arnica, which may serve to cool her temperature. She is sleeping quietly enough for the moment. If she awakens, give her some laudanum, and I will be back later this morning to look in on her." Dr. Burnside put on his greatcoat, turning up the collar in anticipation of going back out into the weather. "Now I have other patients I must attend to, if there is nothing else, Mr. Lindley? It is truly a nasty evening for our neighborhood."

"Indeed. Thank you, Doctor." As the man departed, Michael dropped back down into his chair. He was very grateful the doctor hadn't asked awkward questions about what they had been doing out in the storm. Michael feared his wits were scattered and he could never answer coherently.

Kate was ill—very ill. He felt numb, that one thought swirling around and around in his mind. His bonny Kate, brave Kate, who had overcome so much to begin her life anew, could be snatched away from him. Never had he felt so helpless, so *angry*!

He buried his face in his hands. "Kate," he muttered. "You can't leave."

The library door clicked open, and his hands fell away as he turned toward the sound, half anticipating that Kate herself would be standing there, laughing at him for his despair. But it was his daughter, staring at him with wide, frightened blue eyes. She pulled at a long lock of her hair, a habit she had quite abandoned when Kate came into their lives.

"Rosebud," he said hoarsely, trying to give her a reassuring smile, though he feared it was more of a grimace. "You should be in bed."

Amelia stared at him steadily. "Someone is ill."

"Yes. Mrs. Brown and Aunt Christina, I fear." He held his hand out and she scurried forward to clasp it in her small fingers. He drew her up beside him on the chair, and she cuddled close.

"Will they die?" she said gently. "Like my mama?"

"No," he answered. "They just need some time to rest and recover."

Amelia considered this in silence for a long moment before nodding slowly. "We should pray for them."

"Yes, rosebud. We should pray for them." *And for ourselves.*

Pray—if only he could, Michael thought hours later as he sat by Kate's bedside, watching vigilantly for every breath, every flicker of an eyelash. He wanted to pray, but he could not remember how to, not properly. He could only whisper, "Please. Please." Over and over.

He held Kate's hot, dry hand in both of his, trying to force all of his strength into her soul. If only he could make her see his plea, his fear—make her stay with him. But she was so very pale, except for a hectic flush of crimson slashed across her cheekbones. Her hair was pushed back from her fevered, damp brow, falling over the white pillows in a river of black. She shivered, despite the thick blankets and the warm bricks at her feet, and occasionally she murmured something incoherent, tossing in agitated fever dreams.

She *was* living, but in some twilight world only she could see. A world where he could not follow, no matter how hard he tried. No matter how he struggled to keep her with him.

He reached for the basin of cold water on the bedside table and wrung a cloth out in the liquid, smoothing it over her brow and neck. Once, long ago, he had thought he had found contentment. A settled life, a family, a place where the past was finished, or at least where he could make amends for it. Could raise his daughter in peace. He liked his new world, his home and work. Yet there had been one thing missing from his life, and that was *life*. The color and dash leached from the planet when Caroline died, the sudden, dizzying joy of love and laughter.

He found that again only when Kate came to Thorn Hill. Kate, who was unlike anyone else he had ever met or dreamed of. As changeable as the wind, beautiful as the night, she made him laugh again. Made him feel. He loved her more than his own life. He needed her, and so did his family. She completed them, made them whole, and they couldn't lose her.

"Kate," he said, raising her hand to his lips. Her fingers, hot and bone-dry, trembled in his. "You can't leave. We have too many things still to do—watch Christina make her grand debut, see Amelia grow up. Grow old here at Thorn Hill together, playing with our grandchildren in the garden. This life is no good without you. I promise, if you come back, I will take better care of you in the future. No one will ever hurt you again."

Her fingers jerked against his clasp, and her head turned on the pillow. A soft rush of Italian words spilled from her lips, garbled sentences in which the only word he recognized was *mother*.

"She wants her mother," a quiet voice said behind him.

Michael's gaze swung around to find Christina standing in the shadows. His sister wore a dark blue dressing gown, the bright white of the splint on her arm stark against the brocade. Her hair had been so matted with mud and muck that Mrs. Jenkins was forced to cut the long locks. It curled around her face in short, glossy ringlets, giving her an air of vulnerable youth.

She smiled at him gently, and moved to the side of the bed next to him. He saw that the impression of youth was very wrong. His sister might still be very young in years, but her eyes, deep grass green, were full of a wary, ancient wisdom. She looked so solemn, like an ancient Greek woman watching her men march to war against the Trojans. Stoic and serious. His baby sister had grown up in only one night.

"You know what she is saying?" he said quietly.

"A bit. She has been teaching me Italian, though I haven't learned very much yet." Christina reached out to smooth Kate's hair back with a gentle touch. "I believe she thinks she is a girl again. She wants her mother. She's talking about a party, or some such. A carnival celebration."

Michael thought of the portrait downstairs, still in its crate, sent to him by Elizabeth Hollingsworth. He would have it hung here, where Kate could see it as soon as she awoke. And she *would* wake soon. She had to.

"And what of you, Tina?" he asked. "Would you like to see *your* mother, too?"

Christina paused, her lips parted in sudden uncertainty. "I—of course. If she can tear herself away from the joys of Town."

"I will write to her later this morning, and send the letter by special messenger. I'm sure she will want nothing but to be here when she hears of all that has happened."

The uncertainty twisted into a humorless smile. "Must she know *all* of what happened?"

"What do you mean?"

"I don't want anyone else to know of my foolishness. I never should have gone after Julian alone, without calling for you. It was stupid of me to think

I could manage him myself, could save you and Mrs. Brown the nuisance of it all. Now look. The pain is so much greater because of my arrogance."

There was a quiet sorrow, a depth of grief, in his sister's voice that Michael had never heard before. He studied her closely in the dim light from the bedside candle, the flame casting dancing shadows over the sharp angles of her exposed face. "Tina. Did that man hurt you? In any way?

She shook her head, not meeting his gaze with her own. She smoothed the edge of the bedclothes, tucking them closer around Kate. "No, Michael. Not as you mean. *I* was the one who hurt *him*. I stabbed him in the shoulder and ran away into the storm. I surely did not know what I was doing! But he tried to save me when I fell into the water. He wouldn't let go even when we were both dragged down and he could never pull me up. And now he—" She faltered, her hand crushing the smooth linen. "Are you very sure you saw no sign of him when you came after me in the water, Michael?"

He shook his head. He could not tell Christina of that last scene, of how he pursued Kirkwood with his pistol until the man dived back into the consuming waters. She had not seen it. She would never need to know. "I did not. I'm sorry, Tina. The currents were very strong, and the water murky. I was fortunate to find *you*. Your pale gown was bright in the darkness, or I wouldn't have seen you." Michael shuddered at the memory of how close he had come to losing her, how easily she could have eluded his search in that freezing water.

She nodded sadly. "Perhaps he has found some peace, then. I can only hope so." She leaned against his shoulder, her face suddenly grimacing into a mask of pain.

"You should be in bed!" he exclaimed, wrapping his arm around her to hold her upright. "Come, I'll take you back to your room, Tina."

"No," she whispered. "You stay here with Mrs. Brown—Kate. She needs you more than I do. I can rest a bit easier now that I see she is still here."

Michael nodded, and pressed a kiss to Christina's shorn curls. "Still, take some of that laudanum the doctor left. It will help you sleep." And perhaps chase away some of the nightmares from her damnable ordeal. Julian Kirkwood *had* hurt her, no matter what she said. He had brought that pained age, that sorrow, to her eyes. But now he would never hurt anyone again.

"Of course. I will come back in a few hours, so *you* can get some sleep, too. You will be of no use to her if you become ill yourself, Michael."

"I will stay here until her fever breaks."

Christina nodded, and made her slow, unsteady way to the door, leaving Michael alone with Kate again.

He reached for the bottle of tincture of arnica that Dr. Burnside had left, and poured out a dose for Kate. She was sleeping quietly again, no murmurs or agitated movements. Her skin was still hot and dry, her breathing shallow.

"Kate," he said, placing the cool cloth on her brow, trying to sponge away the fever that was sapping the very essence of her. "Don't leave me. I can't do without you. I love you."

Chapter Thirty

"*K*aterina."

Someone was calling her name. Kate could hear it, soft and coaxing, but it came from so far away, echoing as if down a long, hollow tunnel. A hazy light glowed around her, suffused with palest pink and shimmering gold. She felt so light, buoyant even, borne up by that glow, floating free.

Where was she? The last thing she remembered was being on the road back to Thorn Hill, the sharp, cold rain endlessly pelting her head, the chill seeping into her very bones until she could bear it no longer. She remembered falling, a wave of sick dizziness breaking over her. Now she was *here*.

It must be a dream, and she was still lying in the mud. But there was no time for dreaming, no time for sleep! Christina was ill—she had to get her back to Thorn Hill. . . .

"Katerina!" The voice was louder now, more insistent. Kate spun around to find her mother emerging from the haze of pink-and-gold light.

Kate was strangely unsurprised. Ever since that night in Maria's cottage—a night that seemed a lifetime ago now—Kate had known she would see her mother again. She had even looked for her in vain on the rainy night she and Michael first made love. Now Lucrezia Bruni was here, as beautiful as she ever was in life. Her hair, as black as Kate's own, fell down her back in a loose jumble, over the shoulders of her white gown. Her violet eyes glowed as she smiled.

"Oh, Katerina," she said. "How I have missed you, my daughter, my *bambina*."

Kate stared at her. "Am I dead, then?" she whispered.

"Not yet. Come, walk with me awhile."

She held out her slender hand, unadorned by the jewels she had so loved in life. It was white and cool, gentle, as Kate slipped her own fingers into her mother's clasp. They moved slowly along the corridor, through that soft air that bore the scent of summer roses. It was warm here, welcoming like a fire and a cashmere blanket on a winter's day.

"I am so proud of you, Katerina," her mother said. "I always knew you were a clever girl, but you are so brave, as well! You took my words to you in Italy much to heart and have made a grand new life for yourself. Of course, it is not the life I envisioned for you when you were a girl. You could have been the most celebrated courtesan in Venice. But no. A country house, a little girl hanging on your skirts—and she isn't even yours! I must say, though, that your young man *is* a handsome devil. He could have tempted even me to lead a life of virtue, I think."

Kate had to smile. Obviously, being a dream had not altered her mother's attention to a good-looking man one jot. "Yes. Michael is very handsome indeed."

"And you are happy with him. Happier than perhaps a grand palazzo in Venice could have ever made you. You will have a fine life with him."

Kate turned to gaze at her mother, at Lucrezia's serene and certain smile. "No."

Not even a whisper of a frown marred Lucrezia's brow, but her soft voice became puzzled. "No, *bambina*? You don't think you will have a fine life at this English house?"

Fine? Life at Thorn Hill would be a paradise. "I can't be selfish any longer, Mother. I've learned all too well the danger of that. Look what has become of us all, just because I grasped what I wanted without a thought to anyone else! Christina could have died.

Michael's family is embroiled in a scandal because of
my past. I love them. I can't hurt them again."

"So—what? You will just run away? Keep running
all your life?" Lucrezia turned to Kate, reaching out
to touch her cheek in an unimaginably tender caress.
"*Cara*, you have too noble a heart. Just like your father. You are so determined to make a sacrifice of
yourself, when it is so clear to see that the only thing
that could hurt that family now would be to lose you."

"But if I love them, how can I let my past hurt
them?" Kate said stubbornly. Something like hope,
small and bright and sweet, blossomed deep in her
heart, yet how could she trust it? How could she let
go of fear and truly be free?

"*Cara*. What happened was not your fault. It was
poor, deluded Julian Kirkwood's. I must say, I mis-
judged that man terribly, and so did Edward. Who
would have guessed that beneath all that charm was
something so dark? Ah, well—live and learn, yes? He
is gone from your life now, and you, and your dear
Christina, learned a valuable lesson."

"How do I know such a thing won't happen again?"

"You cannot, of course. Surely, Katerina, you know
that by now. Life is never certain. And sometimes we
have to let the people we love—especially intelligent
young girls—make their own mistakes, even though
we would sell our own souls to save them from it.
Your life with your Michael will seldom be easy or
simple, and you will always have to face gossip and
whispers. But that is surely nothing new! People
talked about us every day in Venice. You are strong,
cara. Stronger than you give yourself credit for. And
so is your Michael, and even your girls. Christina has
had a bad experience, but you are here to help her
make sense of it. They love you, as you love them,
and that is a rare gift. Don't throw it away."

Kate inhaled deeply of the sweet, warm air. She—
strong? She had always felt like the veriest coward,
scared of everything. Sheep, water, gossip. Her own
heart. She had overcome the sheep, and even the

water on this terrible night. Surely she *could* overcome anything! If she had Michael, her angel, beside her.

"You see now, do you not?" her mother said gently.

Kate smiled at her, that tiny flower of hope growing larger and more radiant in her heart. Soon, its petals would grow to such glorious dimensions that there would surely be no room for doubt or fear. "I see—because you were here to tell me."

Lucrezia shook her head. "Oh, no, *bambina*. You knew the truth all along. You will see it even more clearly when you wake up. Now our time together grows short. But I will always be with you, Katerina. And I will expect to see grandchildren very soon."

Her mother drifted one cloud-soft kiss over Kate's brow, and then she was gone. The pink-and-gold haze around Kate grew fainter, diffusing into darkness. There was a great rushing noise, a falling sensation. All the grand weightlessness was gone, and Kate was keenly aware of the aches and pains of her body. It was dreadful, like she had survived a terrible beating. Every muscle and nerve throbbed, and she was unbearably hot.

It was wonderful! If she could have managed it, she would have shouted and laughed with the delirium of simply being alive, of having her aching body to inhabit again. But her throat was so sore, her skin so tender, that it was all she could do to pry open her gritty eyes and croak out a soft, incoherent whisper.

She was in her own bedchamber, nestled under thick piles of blankets on her own comfortable bed. It was obviously near sunset; the light from the window had a soft, milky quality, and there was no more rain. A bright fire burned and crackled in the grate.

No wonder she was so hot! The fire and the bedclothes were stifling. Slowly, groaning a bit at the painful effort, Kate eased back the blankets and inched her way up to lean against the mound of pillows.

Then she saw it—her mother's portrait, hanging on the wall directly opposite the bed, where she would be sure to glimpse it as soon as she woke. Lucrezia smiled at the world in all her sapphire and amethyst glory. For an instant, Kate thought she saw a bright, mischievous gleam in those violet eyes, but then it vanished as if it had never been.

"*Grazie,* Mother," she whispered. "I'll see what I can do about those grandchildren."

A soft moan sounded from beside the bed, and Kate turned to see Michael fast asleep in a chair. He was a rumpled, unshaved mess, his shirt wrinkled, hair in desperate need of a wash, no shoes on his feet. The scars on his cheek stood out starkly against the exhausted pallor of his skin.

He was the most beautiful thing she had ever seen.

"Michael," she whispered, trying to reach out to him with one aching hand. "Michael, *amore.*"

"What . . .?" He started awake. For a second, his gaze was unfocused, as if he, too, awoke from a delirious dream. He stared down at her for a moment, and gave an exuberant shout. "Kate! My darling Kate, you're awake. At last."

He caught up her hand and pressed it between both of his, holding it as if he would never let it go.

"At last?" she said. Her voice sounded as if it were made of sand and rocks. "How long have I been— sleeping?"

"Two days now." He released her hand only long enough to pour out a glass of water from a pitcher on the bedside table. He slid one arm beneath her shoulders to help her sit up straight, holding the glass to her parched lips.

It was the sweetest liquid she had ever tasted, truly an ambrosia. And his strong touch was heavenly.

"Two days? Really?" she asked, her throat cooler from the water. He lowered her back to the pillows, but she would not let him go. "It can't have been that long."

"I fear it has been. We have been waiting for your fever to break."

"A fever?"

"From the chill. Kate, I never should have let you

go out into the storm with me! I should have locked you up here."

The storm! Yes—now she remembered it all. Julian Kirkwood stole Christina from Thorn Hill; she and Michael had to chase them to the Semerwater, swollen and wild from the rain. Christina and Julian fell into the water. . . .

"Christina!" she gasped. "Where is she?"

"Sh," Michael said gently, smoothing the tangled hair back from her face in a tender caress. "Christina is fine. She has a broken arm, but it was a clean break that should heal, given time. And her hair had to be cut off, though I don't think she minds that very much! She is sleeping now—you can see her soon. Amelia, too, is eager to see you. I think she is sitting out in the corridor, even though her nursemaid has ordered her to bed at least four times."

Kate laughed weakly. "Dear Amelia! How I long to see them both. And thank God Christina is well. Will her arm affect her work?"

"I think not. Christina would not let it. But you must be sure you are strong enough before you let them besiege you. You've been so ill, and I've been out of my mind with worry that I would lose you!"

"Oh, Michael, *amore*. I won't leave you—I can't. I'm afraid you are trapped with me for years to come, fanciful poetic notions and all."

Michael leaned his head close to hers, his lips pressing a gentle kiss to hers. "Praise be," he muttered. "I will hold you to that promise, Katerina Bruni—or whoever you may be."

"Kate Lindley?"

"I like the sound of that. *Mrs.* Kate Lindley."

Kate smiled up at him. "Then, *Mr.* Lindley, perhaps you would do something for your future bride?"

"Anything."

"Could you open the window before I suffocate?"

He chuckled, a low, rumbling, sweet sound. "Of course. The doctor said you should be kept warm, but

I don't think one small breath of fresh air would hurt."

"You succeeded in following the doctor's orders most admirably." Kate relaxed back onto the bed, watching Michael as he crossed the room to throw open the window. She was so very tired, bone-deep weary, and she needed more water. But even more than that, she needed to know. . . . "Michael. Are you sure Christina was not—hurt?" I've never seen anyone behave like Julian before. He was like a madman."

Michael braced his arms against the window frame and glanced back at her, his blue eyes a dark gray. "She says she was not hurt. She said she stabbed Kirkwood in the shoulder and ran away. But there is something. . . ."

"Something?" Kate said, alarmed.

He shook his head. "I cannot explain it. She has changed somehow, Kate. She seems—older."

"Perhaps after she rests and her arm heals, she will seem more herself? Or we can take her away somewhere for a change of scene. France? Vienna?"

"Kate, my dear, you shouldn't worry about these things until you are stronger." Michael came back to her bedside, reaching out to smooth the hopelessly rumpled bedclothes, taking her hand again.

Kate clutched at his hand. "Just one more thing—has Julian's body been found?"

Michael shook his head, his jaw taut. "There will be a more extensive search once the weather clears. Now, Kate, you must sleep. You have to get your strength back."

"Indeed. For the wedding."

He smiled gently. "For the wedding. If you are still sure you want to marry me, and my unruly family."

"Oh, yes," Kate answered softly. "I want it more than anything in all the world. I learned a great deal in the last few days, you see. Much is still confused and unclear, frightening, too. Yet there is one thing I know for certain now."

"Oh, yes, my love? What is that?"

"That love is the greatest gift, and only a fool squanders it for any reason. I'm not a fool, not anymore. I love you, Michael Lindley, and I want to be your wife."

"Oh, my bonny Kate." He gathered her softly in his arms, holding her as if she was the greatest treasure in the world. "How long I've waited for you to say that! I love you, too. You mean all of life to me. Promise you won't ever go away."

"No," she vowed. "I'll never go away. Not ever again. Truly, this Kate is curst no longer!"

Epilogue

*I*t was a bright, beautiful day when the wedding of the decade (for Suddley village, anyway) was held in St. Anne's Church. The glorious old stained-glass windows shimmered in jewel tones of red, blue, emerald green, and gold, casting their wealth of color on the worn stone floors. The even more gloriously uncomfortable narrow wooden pews were decked in wreaths and swags of white lilies, white roses, and dark green ivy. Cushions of white silk were laid down especially for the posteriors of all the guests, which included local families such as the Rosses (Miss Emmeline's face was noted as being unusually red and puffy from all the tears she cried over this engagement), as well as London notables. The Hollingsworths attended, Elizabeth clad in a very stylish gown and spencer of raspberry-colored silk, as did the bridegroom's older brother, the Earl of Darcy, sans his enceinte wife but wearing a coat of grass green satin that excited much comment. The church was so very crowded that many congregants were forced to stand at the back.

Kate saw none of this—the people, the flowers, the low hum of excitement hanging palpably in the flower-scented air—as she stood outside the open church doors, waiting to make her grand entrance. Butterflies fluttered hither and yon in her stomach, and her breath felt short and gasping. She had never experienced such excitement before, such a glow of wild anticipation! It didn't seem real.

Michael was waiting for her at the altar. Waiting to become her husband.

She unpeeled one gloved hand from the ribbon-wrapped stems of her white rose bouquet and pressed it to her stomach.

"Be careful!" Amelia said sternly. "You'll crush your gown."

Kate smiled down at her tiny bridesmaid—soon to be her new daughter. Amelia looked exquisite this morning in her pink muslin dress, her golden curls brushed to a sheen to rival the sun and bound with pink ribbons. She held her basket of rose petals very carefully. "Of course, *cara mia*. I don't want to crush my gown before we even walk down the aisle."

Kate straightened the skirt of her wedding gown, a lovely creation of palest blue silk trimmed with pearl beading and white gauze roses, brought by Elizabeth Hollingsworth from the most sought-after of London modistes. It was all she could have dreamed of for such a perfect day, a princess's gown.

She heard a swell of organ music from inside the church, signaling her cue to enter. "Marching slowly, with great dignity," as the curate had instructed when she first arrived. It would be all she could do to keep from dashing down the aisle into Michael's arms!

Kate turned to smooth back her lace veil, held to her hair by a wreath of roses and ivy. As she swept away the hazy cobwebs of lace, she thought she glimpsed a movement in the churchyard, behind one of the ancient stone sarcophagi. A flash of black and white in the sunshine.

But no. There was nothing there. Only the shadows of the gravestones.

Kate shivered, and sent forth another prayer of thanksgiving for this day. For her own life, and the lives of all her family. They had been preserved in that dreadful storm, and gathered now at this church for a wedding rather than a funeral. A wedding she had been waiting for all her life.

"It's time, Mama!" Amelia exclaimed. "We have to go in now."

"So we do." With one last glance back to the churchyard, Kate faced forward to the long aisle. To the man who waited for her there.

Amelia took the curate's instructions very much to heart, and moved into the church with a grace and dignity beyond her six years. She carefully scattered her petals to the left and the right. Kate smiled at her proudly—Amelia had called her *Mama*. No mother could ever have been prouder of her child than Kate was of Amelia at that moment.

And of Christina. The girl stood at the edge of the family pew, peering eagerly down the aisle. She, too, looked older than her years today, in another London creation of butter yellow muslin with a matching silk pelisse trimmed in antique lace. A yellow silk sling held her splinted arm in place, and her shorn curls were covered with a white-and-yellow bonnet. Her smile was full of happiness as she watched her niece, yet there was still something sad at the edges of it. Something serious in her eyes that even a wedding, and the solicitous presence of young Mr. Price at her side, could not quite ease.

As Kate followed in Amelia's flower-strewn wake, she grinned at Christina and gave her a little wave. She nodded to the Hollingsworths, and to Michael's still vaguely disapproving but undeniably elegant mother. She tried to move slowly, prettily, in time to the stately Handel march issuing from the organ, but when she saw Michael all the curate's careful admonitions flew away.

Never had she imagined anyone could be so unearthly handsome. He stood before the old altar, sunlight falling from the windows to gild his hair and skin in a wash of purest gold. He, too, wore London finery, a Weston-cut coat of Prussian blue and a waistcoat of ivory brocade. But he could have been clad in mud-splashed buckskin for all she cared. All that mattered—all that ever mattered—was that they had somehow found a way to come together on this perfect day. All the past, all the drama, all her fears, they were gone like the mists of a dream. *This* was real life. This was what was important, today and all the days to come.

Michael smiled at her, his white pirate's grin, and he completely defied convention by leaving his place at the altar, striding down the aisle to meet her halfway. He clasped her hand in his, and together they took the final steps into their greatest adventure.

"Dearly beloved, we are gathered here today, in the sight of God, and in the face of this congregation, to join together this man and this woman in holy matrimony. . . ."

All your favorite romance writers are coming together.

SIGNET ECLIPSE

COMING JUNE 2005:
Beyond the Pale by Savannah Russe
My Hero by Marianna Jameson
The Chase by Cheryl Sawyer

COMING JULY 2005:
Much Ado About Magic
by Patricia Rice
Love Underground: Persephone's Tale
by Alicia Fields
Private Pleasures by Bertice Small
Lost in Temptation by Lauren Royal

The steamy novels of
Sasha Lord

Under a Wild Sky
0-451-21028-X

Ronin, a battered warrior, seeks refuge from his
enemies in a secluded wood, only to be attacked by
forest men. But when Ronin takes the men's leader
captive, he soon learns that this young man he's
holding prisoner is actually a beautiful woman whose
passion for life and love matches his own.

In a Wild Wood
0-451-21029-8

When Matalia seizes Brogan trespassing in her
family's forest, they begin an adventure that will
endanger their lives—and they discover a passion
that will challenge their hearts.

Across a Wild Sea
0-451-21387-4

When a violent storm casts Xanthier ashore, Alannah
gives in to an untamed desire. And a promise made in
the heat of passion transforms their lives forever.

Available wherever books are sold or at
www.penguin.com

New York Times bestselling author

Lisa Jackson

Impostress

Owing her sister a favor, Kiera of Lawenydd
promises to pose as Elyn on her wedding day.
The ruse is to last just one night, but the
following morning, Elyn is nowhere to be
found! Surely Kiera won't have to spend the
rest of her life wedded to a man to whom she
could never admit the depths of her
deception—even as her desire for him
grows impossible to resist.

0-451-20829-3

**Available wherever books are sold or at
www.penguin.com**

S006

Three romance classics in one volume from
New York Times bestselling author
JO BEVERLEY

The Demon's Mistress
A wealthy widow hires a war-torn hero to pretend to
be her fiancé, but what will happen when he learns
the truth about the woman he has come to love?

The Dragon's Bride
The new Earl of Wyvern arrives at his fortress on the
cliffs of Devon to find a woman from his past
waiting for him—with a pistol in her hand.

The Devil's Heiress
No one needs Clarissa Graystone's fortune more than
Major George Hawkinville. Now he must ignore
the hunger in his heart as Clarissa boldly
steps into his trap.

0-451-21200-2

Available wherever books are sold or at
www.penguin.com

N598

051C17-1